GREG RUCKA PRESENTS

COMPASS™

VOLUME 1: THE CAULDRON OF ETERNAL LIFE

WRITTEN BY **ROBERT MACKENZIE & DAVE WALKER**

ART BY **JUSTIN GREENWOOD**

COLORS BY **DANIELA MIWA**

LETTERS BY **SIMON BOWLAND**

COVER BY **JUSTIN GREENWOOD (WITH BRAD SIMPSON)**

LOGO AND DESIGN BY **ERIC TRAUTMANN**

EDITED BY **ALEJANDRO ARBONA**

COMPASS™ CREATED BY **MACKENZIE, WALKER & GREENWOOD**

COMPASS, VOL. 1: THE CAULDRON OF ETERNAL LIFE. First printing. January 2022.

Published by Image Comics, Inc. Office of publication: PO BOX 14457, Portland, OR 97293.

ISBN: 978-1-5343-2053-6.

INTRODUCTION BY GREG RUCKA

I AM FOND OF SAYING THAT social media has no redeeming factors whatsoever, or at least that its redeeming factors are so few and far between they do not outweigh the incredible amount of harm it is doing to civilization, society, and interpersonal relationships. I stand by this position, even if Dave and Robert are the exception that proves my point.

I met them via Twitter. This may be the only truly positive thing Twitter has done for my life. That they lived in Australia and I lived in the U.S. made actually *meeting* them a challenge, but in 2015 or thereabouts I found myself in Brisbane for a comic convention, and they took me to dinner and they took me to a pub and then they took me to a whisky bar and by the time I was back home it was a done deal, and a friendship had formed.

Now, despite what you may or may not believe, I do not, as a matter of course, turn to my friends and ask them if they have an idea for a comic. It is, in fact, something I actively avoid doing, for all of the reasons you might imagine and a host of others you probably can't.

Thing was, these guys had good ideas. And not only that, they dropped them the way leaves come off trees in autumn. We'd be in a conversation and I'd watch the two of them race off on a tangent and ten minutes later they'd have the plot for an 18-issue maxi-series or four seasons of a television show or how to fix this or that continuity in this or that comic/show/pop culture franchise. Not everything was a gem. Sometimes, I swear to God, I just wanted them to shut up.

Sometimes, they dropped gold.

COMPASS was gold to me, for a number of reasons. I loved the historical setting, and the historical inspiration. I loved the details of the research, and that it picked a truth that was unknown to the vast majority of people and extrapolated it into an action-adventure-pulp mashup that was pretty much exactly my kind of jam. I loved Shahidah and Ling as protagonists. I loved the fact that it flipped so many tropes on their head, yet kept the heart of those tropes.

I wanted to read the story they were telling me. More, I wanted other people to read it. I wanted it, as they say, *out there*.

The moment I realized these things, I knew Justin Greenwood was the artist to tell it with them. I'd just finished working with Justin on *Stumptown* and it had been a terrific experience, one of the most effortless and rewarding collaborations I'd had in years. If he brought that energy and creativity to Dave and Robert's work, I figured we'd have one hell of a book to show people. And if we got Simon Bowland to letter it, and if we could get Daniela Miwa to color it, and if we could convince Eric Trautmann to come in on the design work...

...well, you'd have the book you're holding in your hands. Or are reading on your iPad, or your Kindle, or you whatever. You know what I mean.

I am pleased to have my name on *COMPASS*, and I am honored to have been part of the team that has brought it into the world. I am especially grateful to Alejandro Arbona, as well, for bringing his wealth of editorial experience to this process.

Most of all, I'm grateful to all of you willing to give us a try. There's familiar in these pages, absolutely, but there's something more, too—something that I find engaging and exciting and that has been missing on the stands. Speaking for all of us, I hope you will come with us on this adventure, back in time, dancing between history and myth, with all the wonder and excitement that is in store. ⌖

GREG RUCKA

May 2021
Portland, Oregon

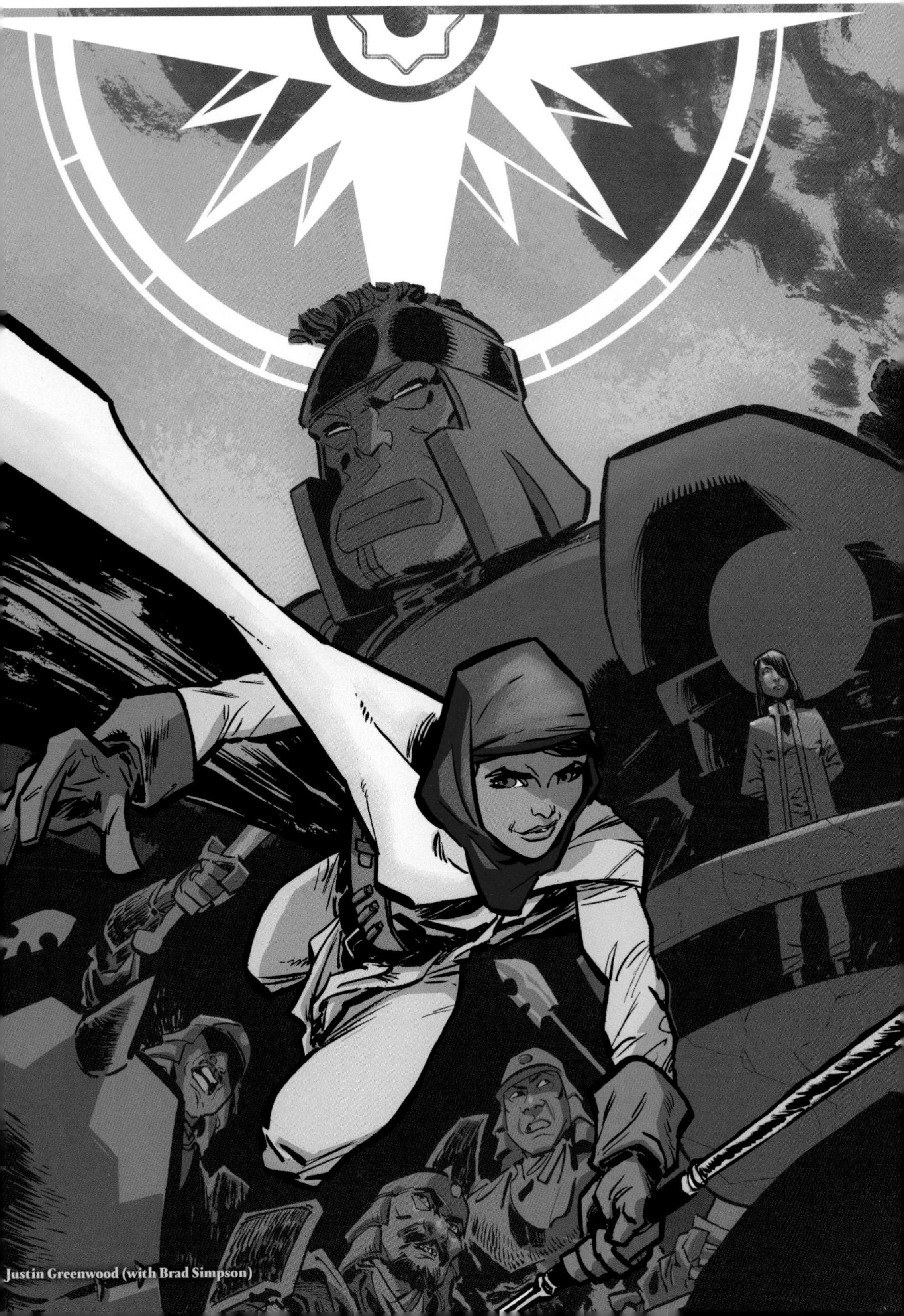

Justin Greenwood (with Brad Simpson)

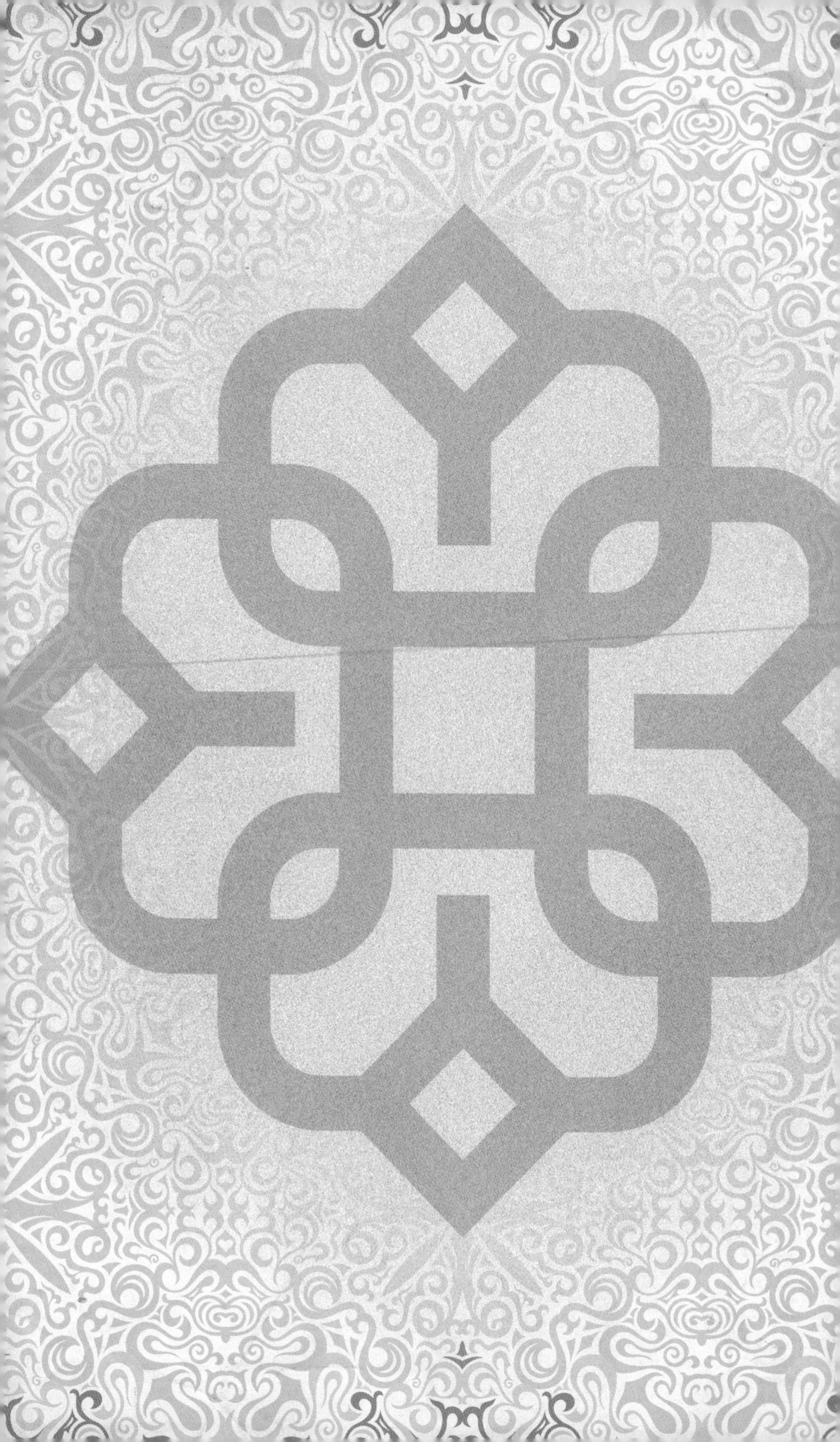

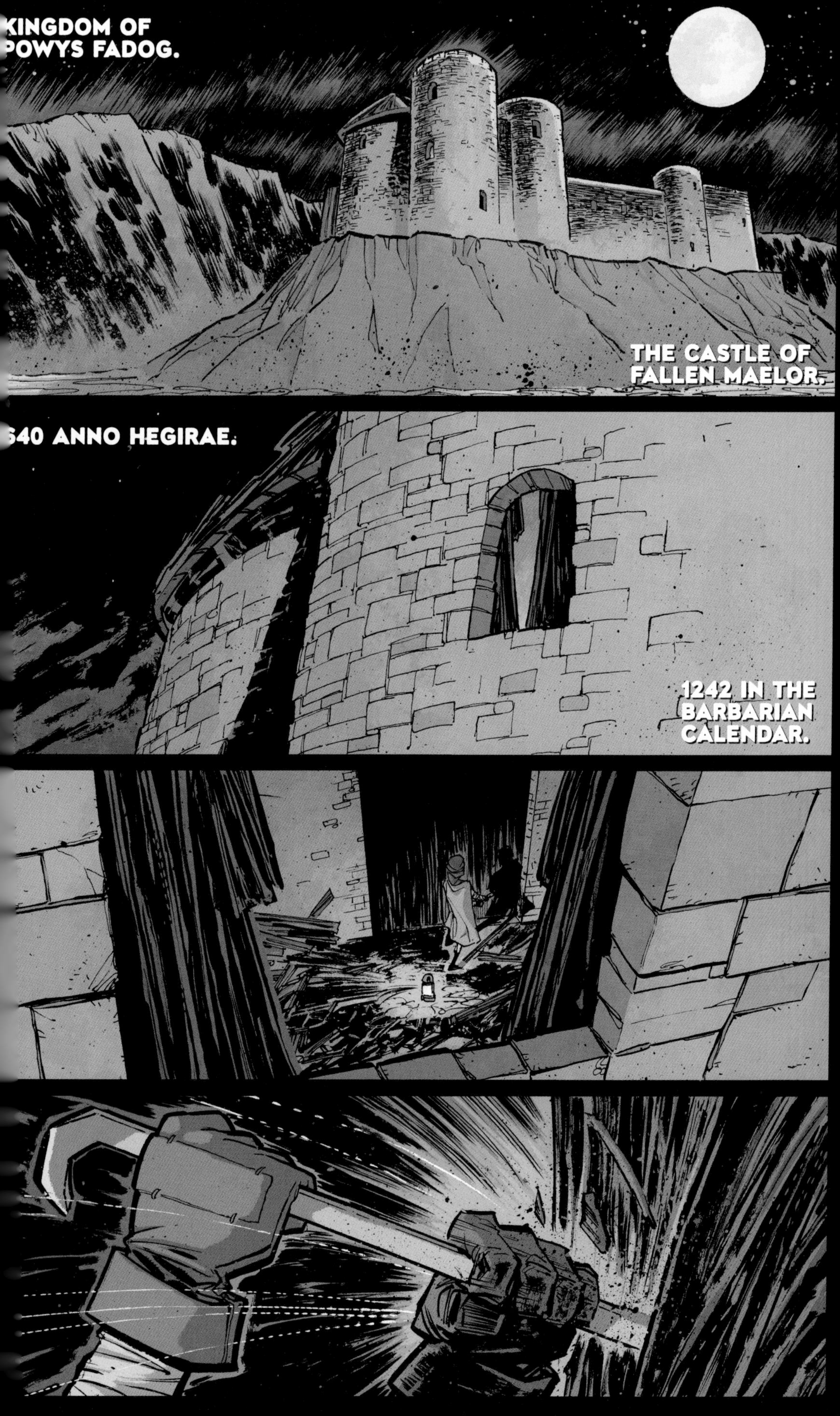
KINGDOM OF
POWYS FADOG.
THE CASTLE OF
FALLEN MAELOR.
640 ANNO HEGIRAE.
1242 IN THE
BARBARIAN
CALENDAR.

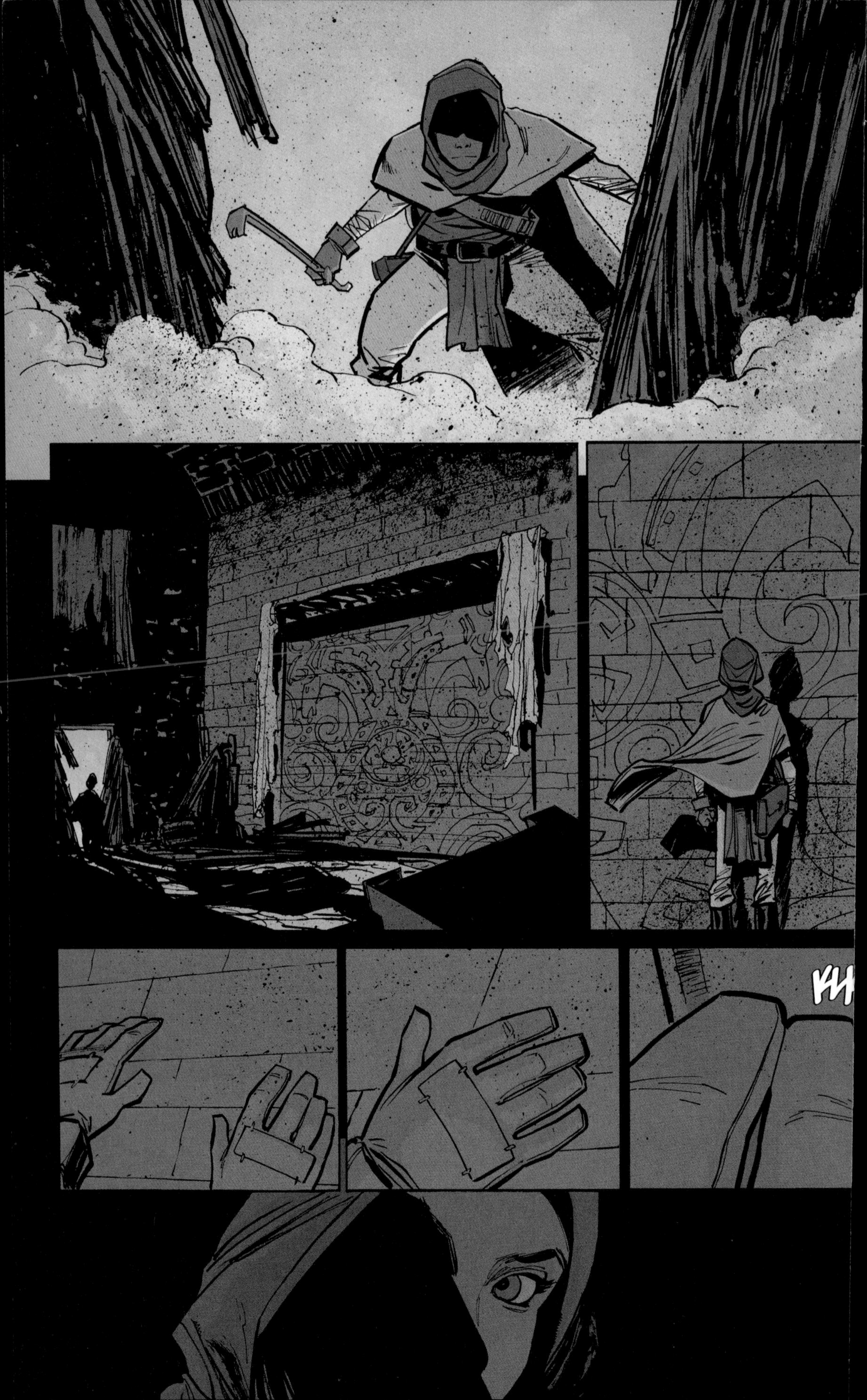

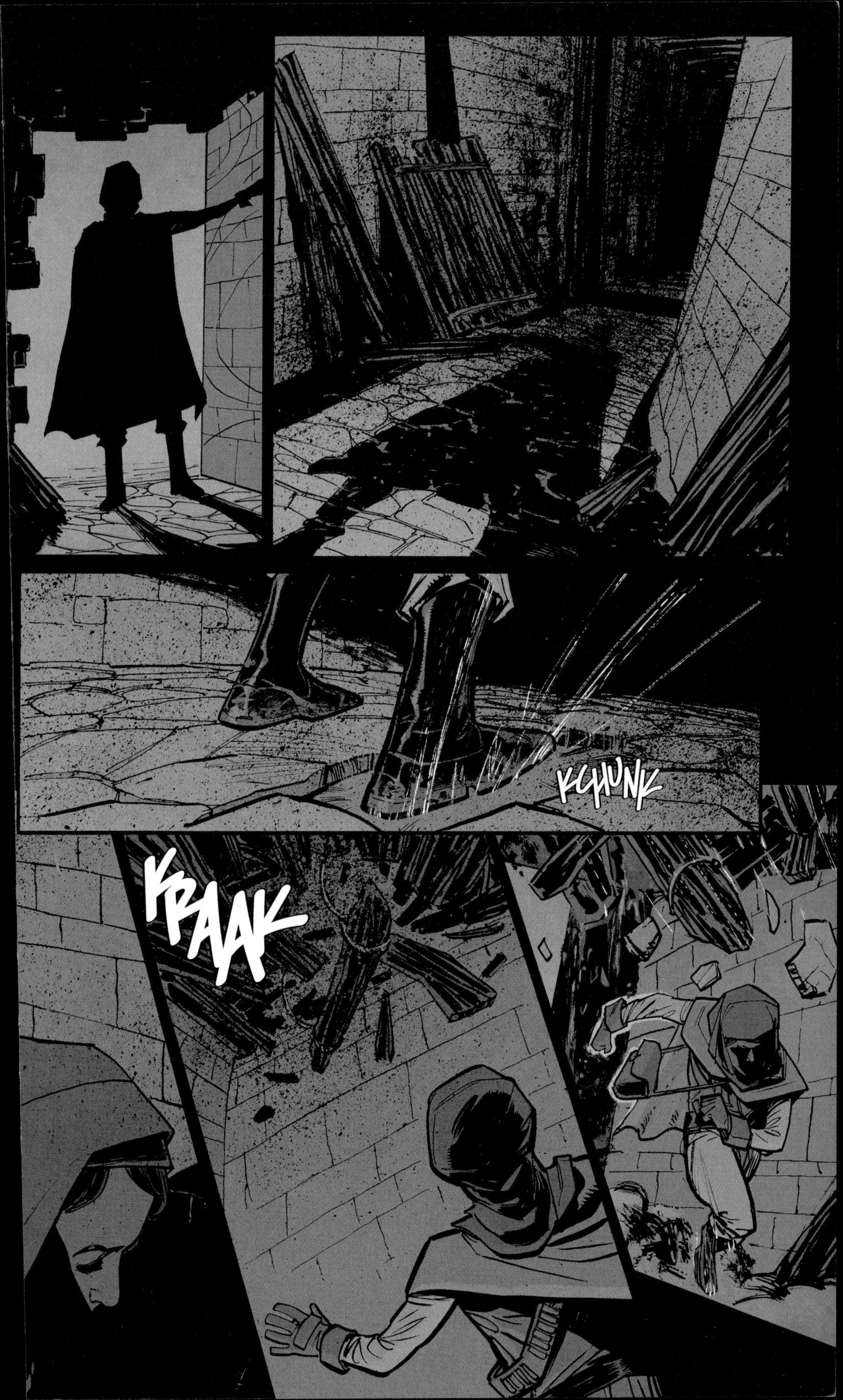
KCHUNK
KRAAK

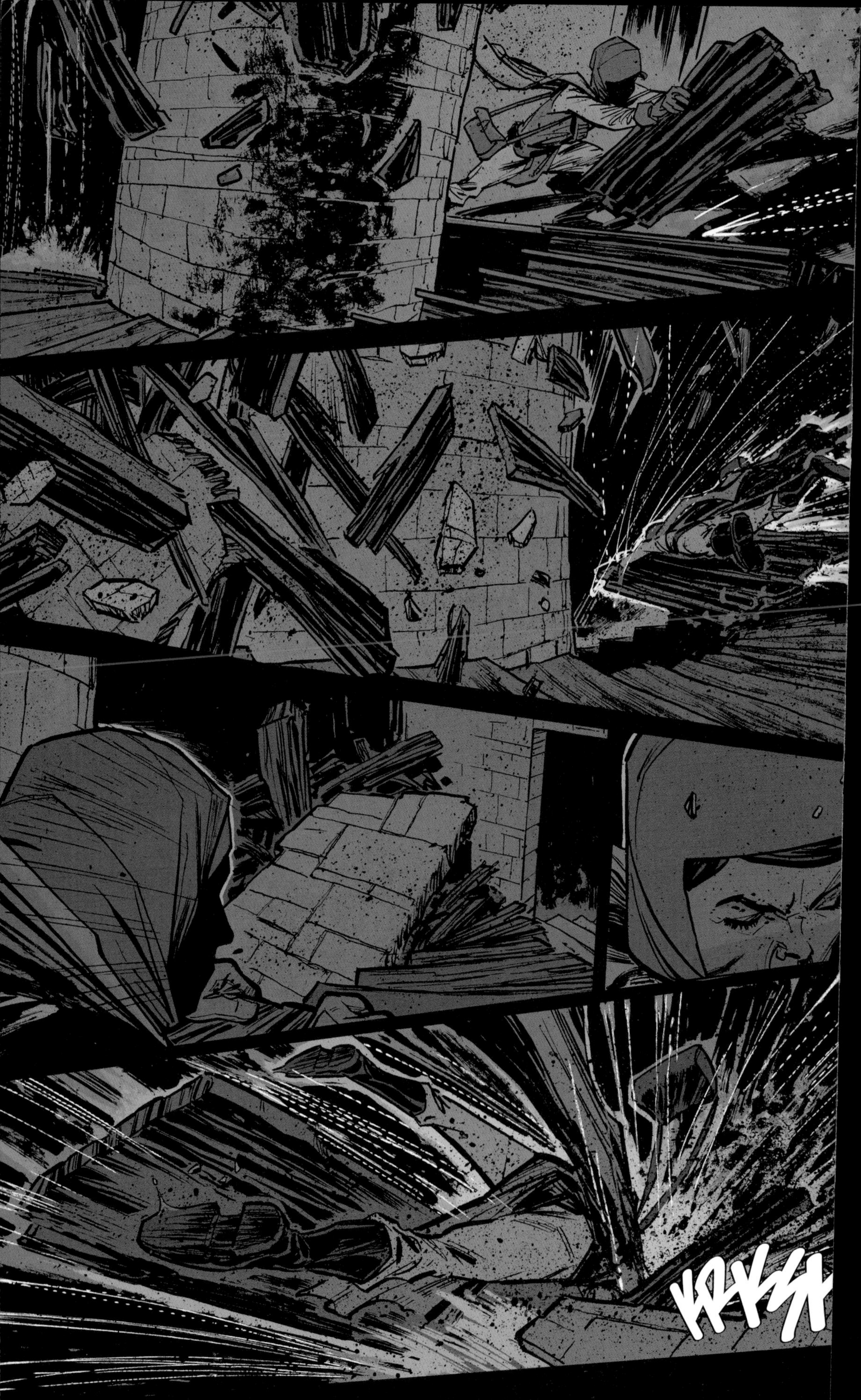
KRKSH

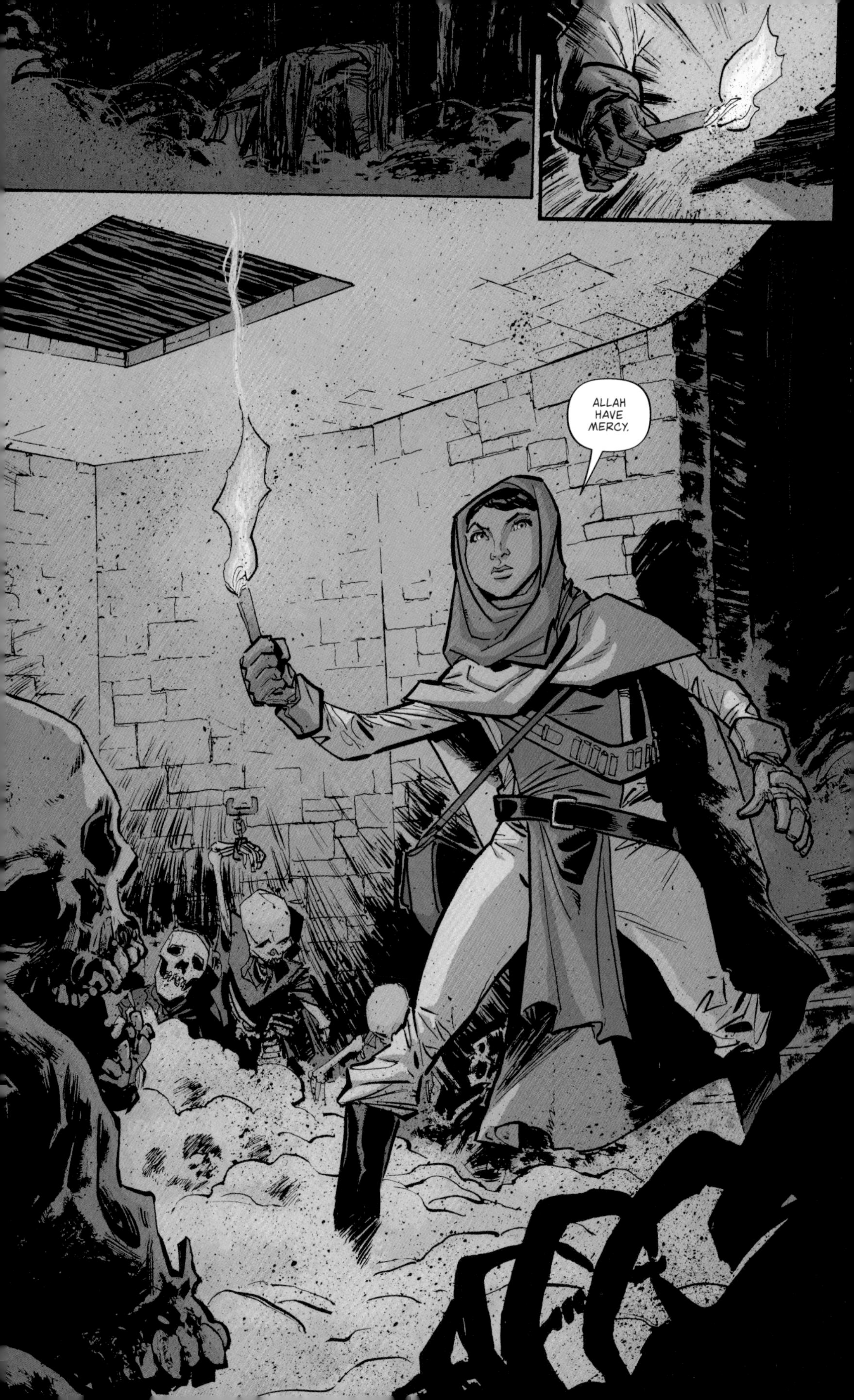
ALLAH HAVE MERCY.

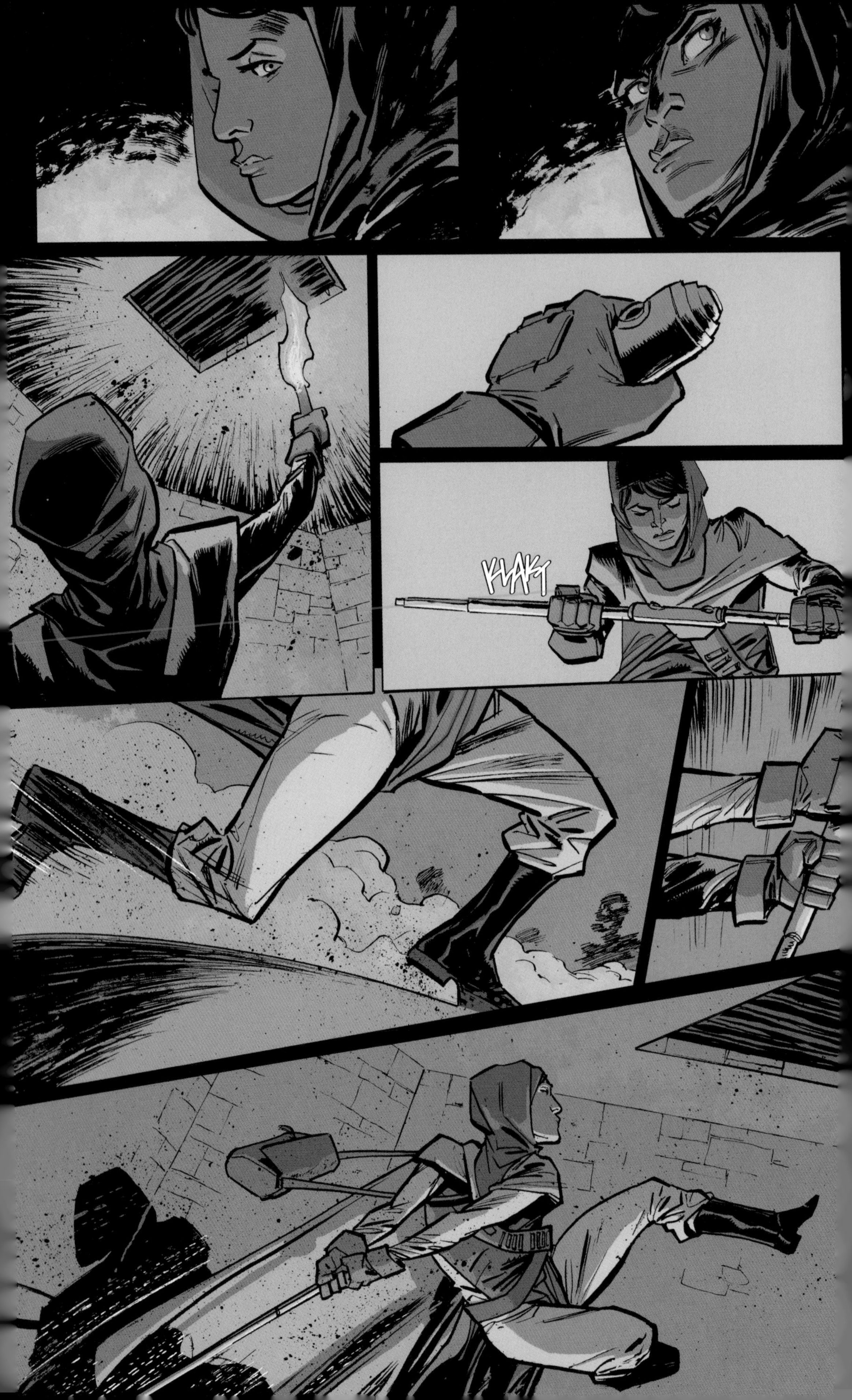
KLAKT

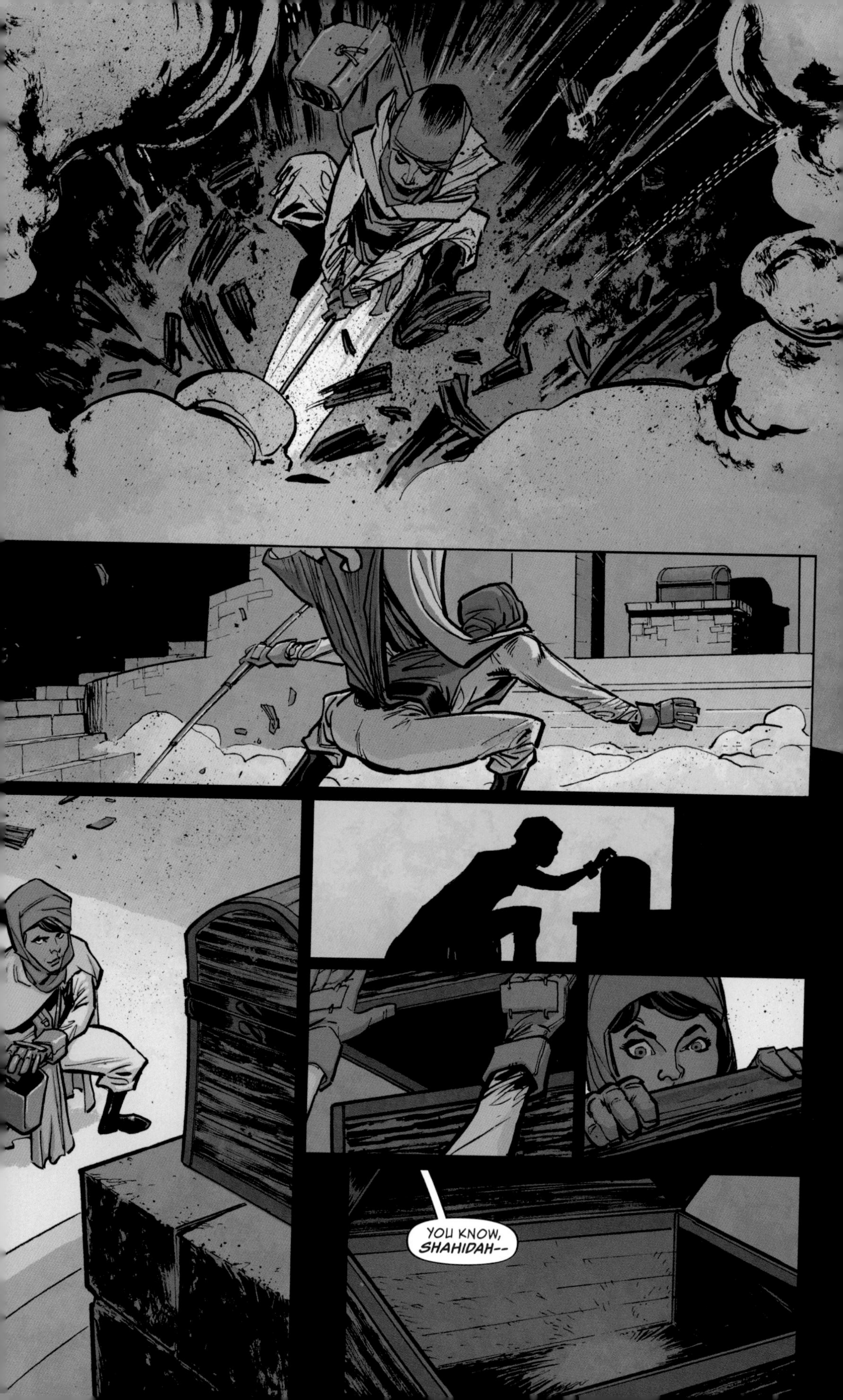
YOU KNOW, SHAHIDAH--

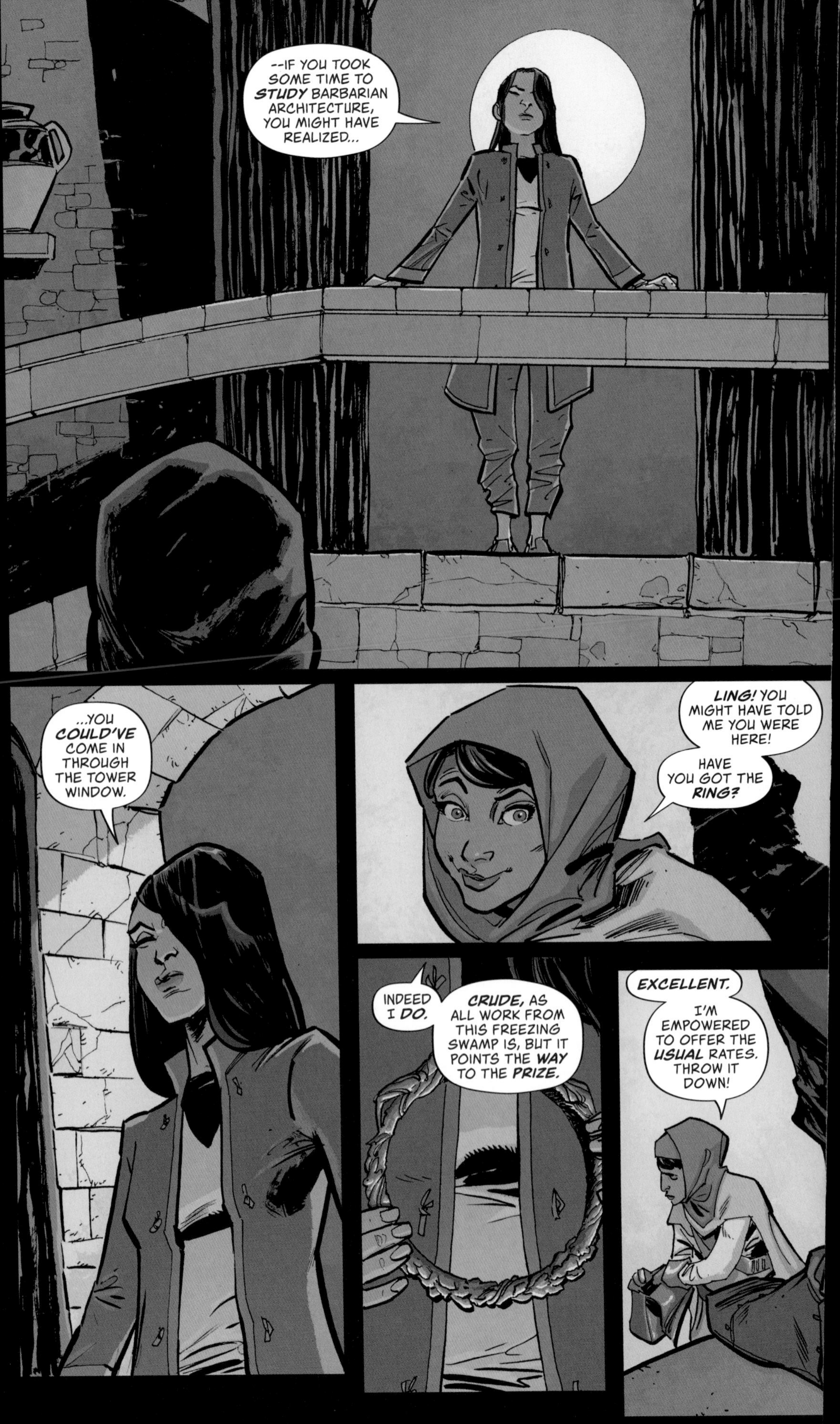
--IF YOU TOOK SOME TIME TO STUDY BARBARIAN ARCHITECTURE, YOU MIGHT HAVE REALIZED...
...YOU COULD'VE COME IN THROUGH THE TOWER WINDOW.
LING! YOU MIGHT HAVE TOLD ME YOU WERE HERE!
HAVE YOU GOT THE RING?
INDEED I DO.
CRUDE, AS ALL WORK FROM THIS FREEZING SWAMP IS, BUT IT POINTS THE WAY TO THE PRIZE.
EXCELLENT.
I'M EMPOWERED TO OFFER THE USUAL RATES. THROW IT DOWN!

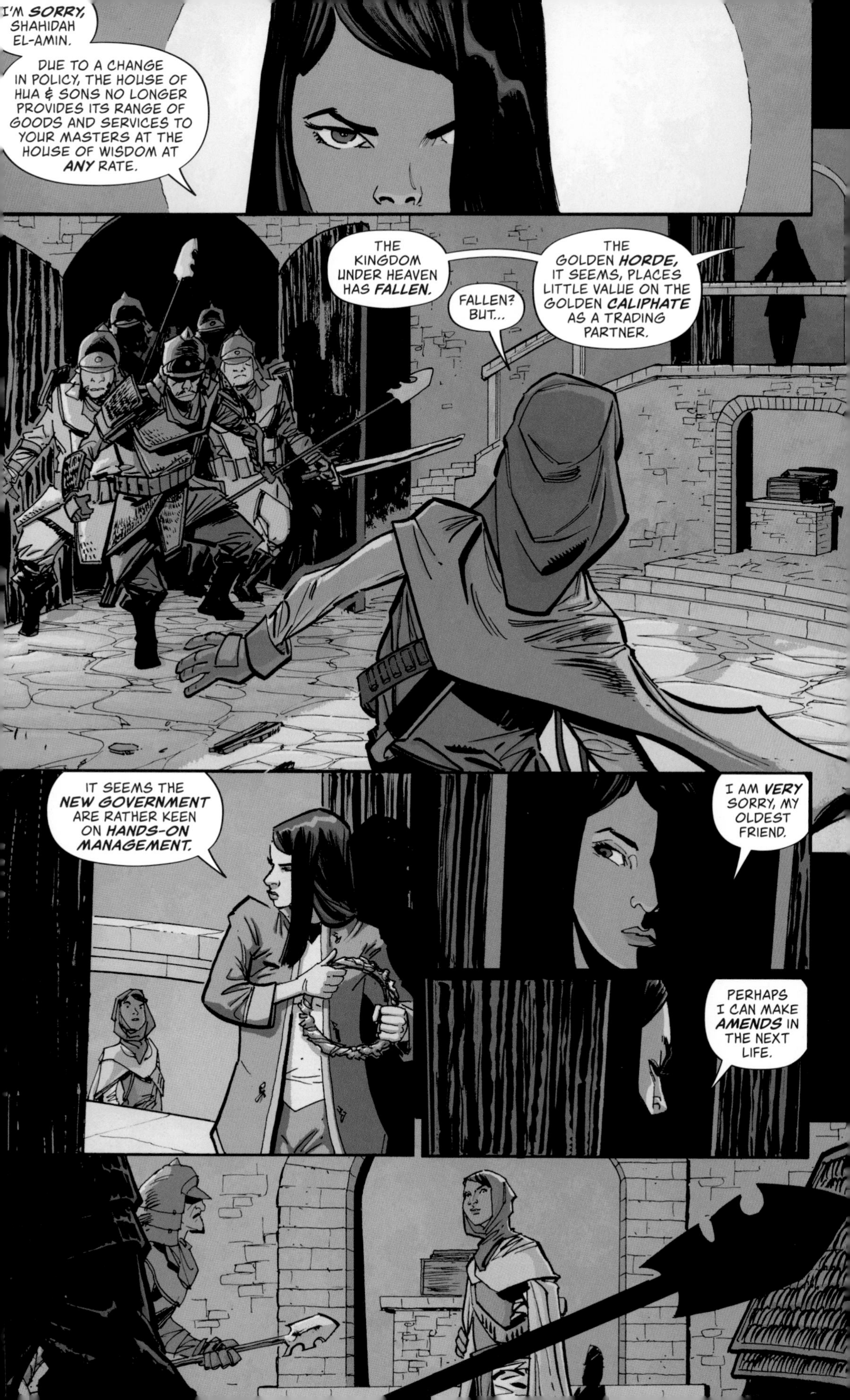
I'M SORRY, SHAHIDAH EL-AMIN.
DUE TO A CHANGE IN POLICY, THE HOUSE OF HUA & SONS NO LONGER PROVIDES ITS RANGE OF GOODS AND SERVICES TO YOUR MASTERS AT THE HOUSE OF WISDOM AT ANY RATE.
THE KINGDOM UNDER HEAVEN HAS FALLEN.
THE GOLDEN HORDE, IT SEEMS, PLACES LITTLE VALUE ON THE GOLDEN CALIPHATE AS A TRADING PARTNER.
FALLEN? BUT...
IT SEEMS THE NEW GOVERNMENT ARE RATHER KEEN ON HANDS-ON MANAGEMENT.
I AM VERY SORRY, MY OLDEST FRIEND.
PERHAPS I CAN MAKE AMENDS IN THE NEXT LIFE.

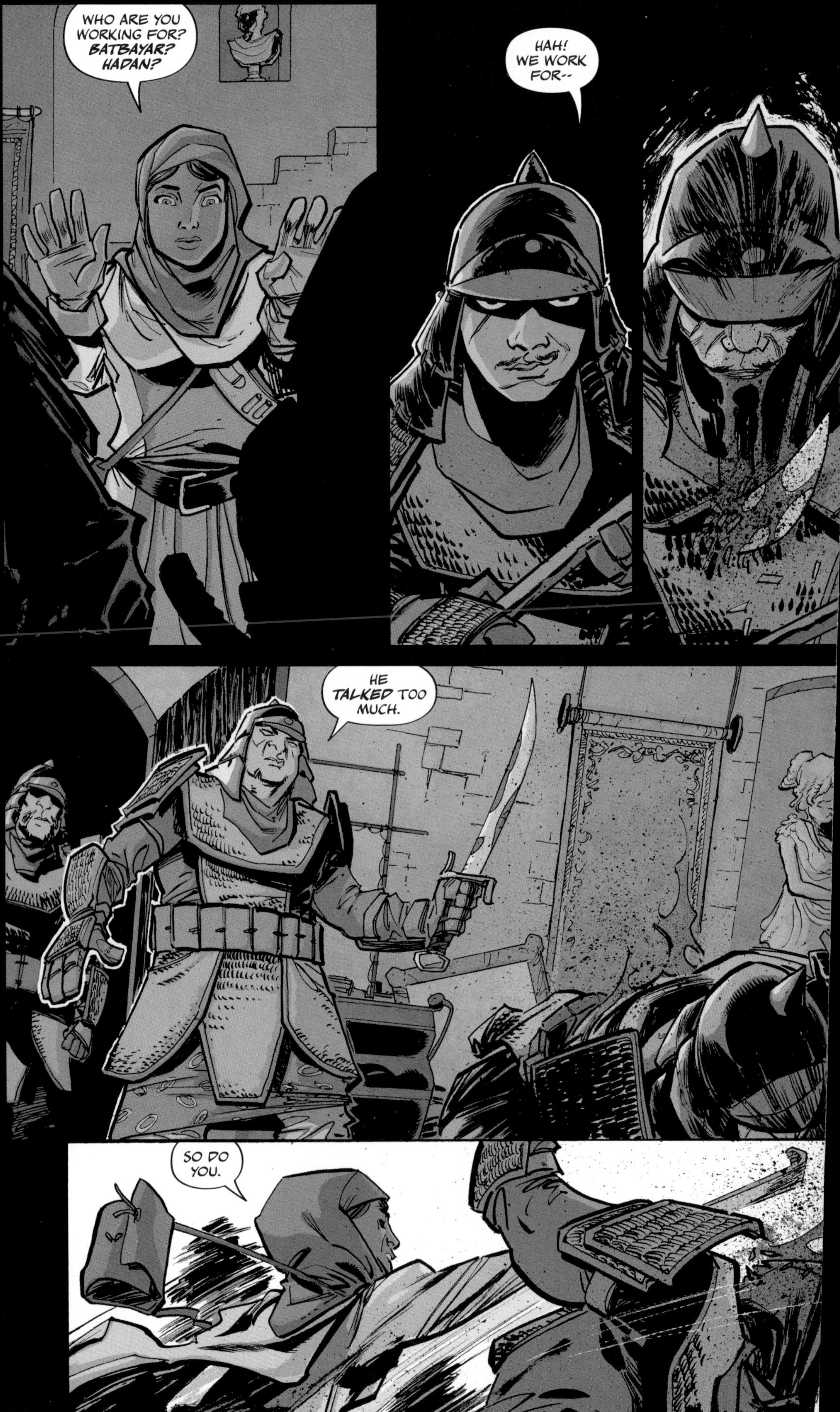
WHO ARE YOU WORKING FOR? BATBAYAR? HADAN?
HAH! WE WORK FOR--
HE TALKED TOO MUCH.
SO DO YOU.

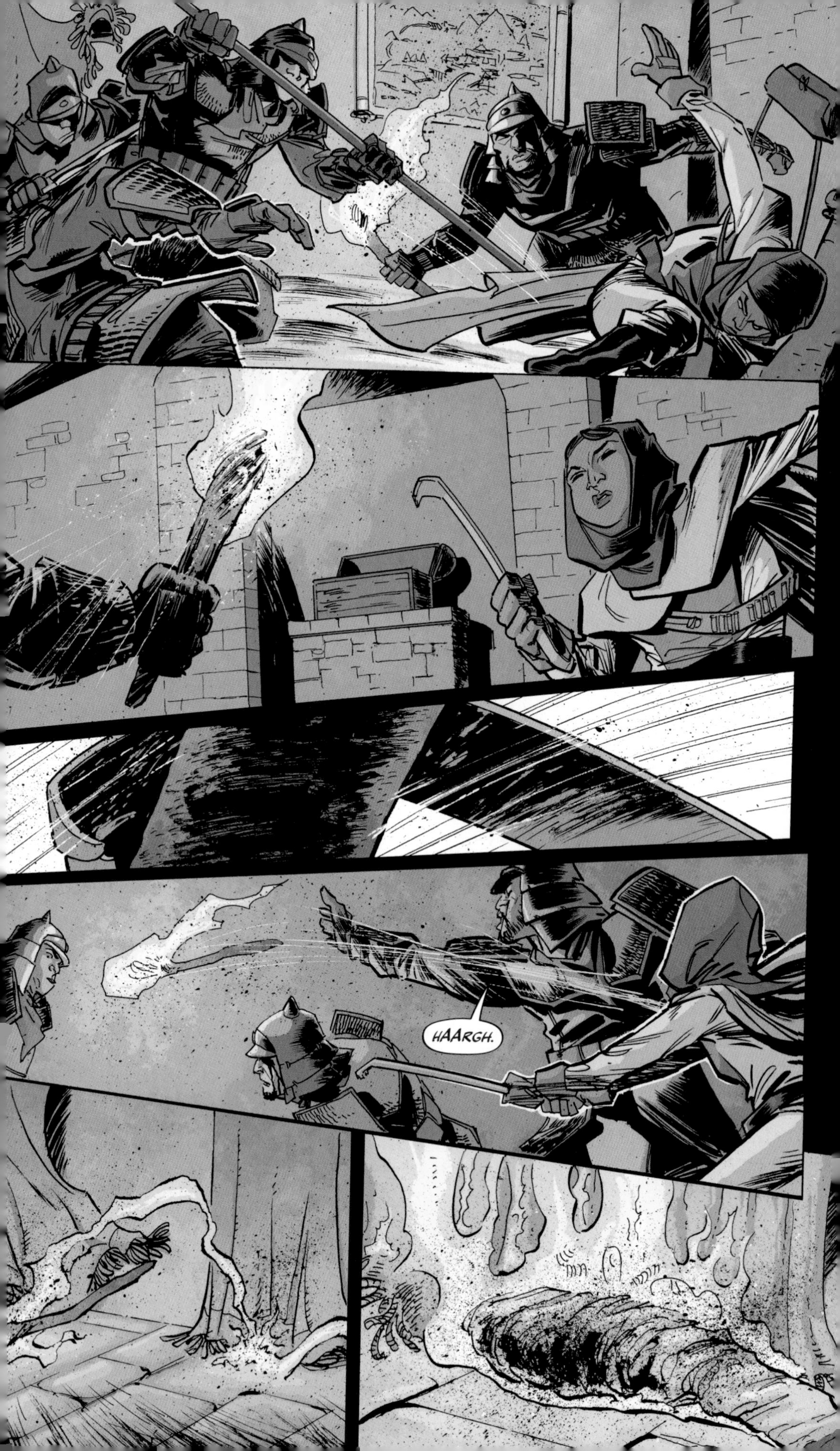
HAARGH.

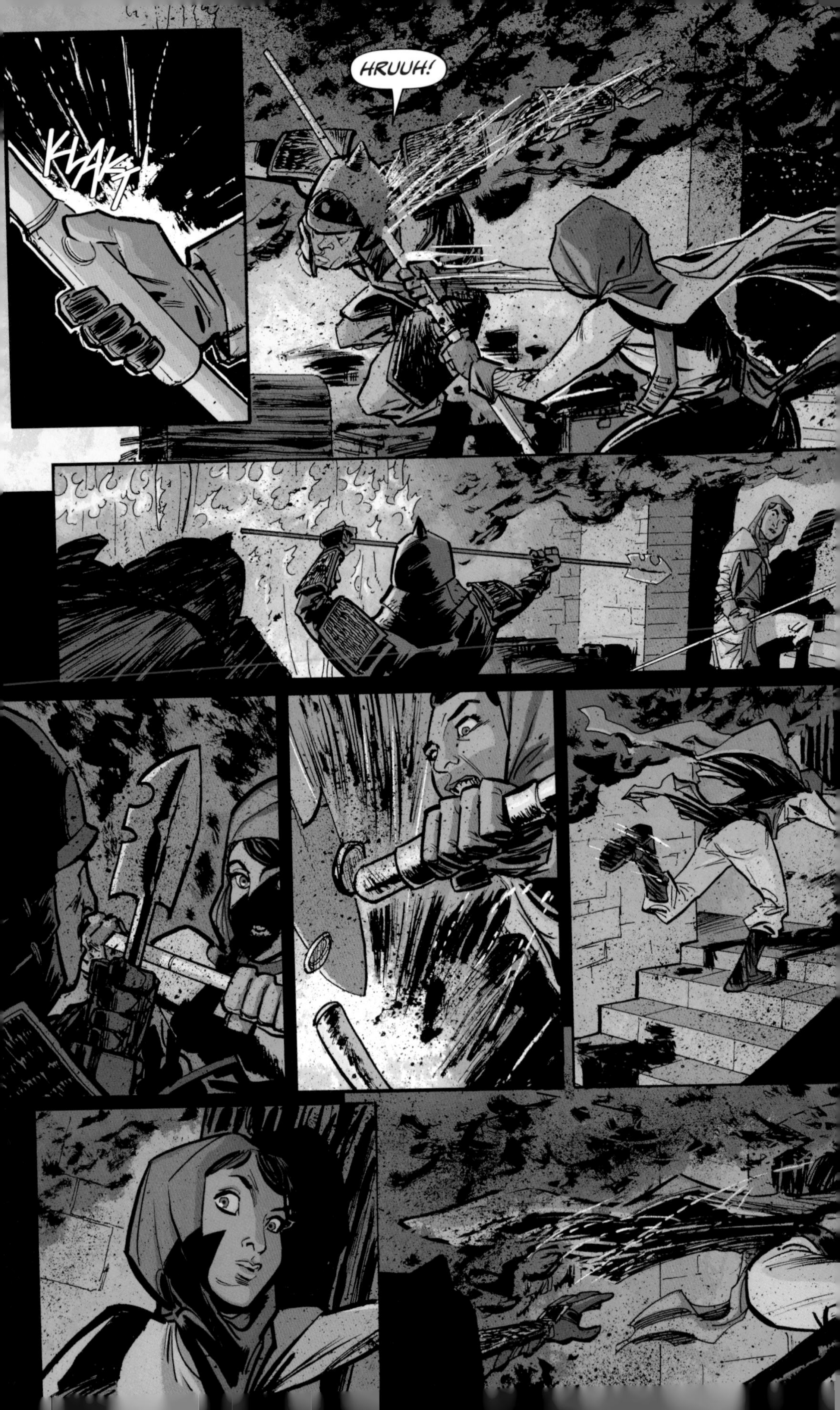
KLAKT
HRUUH!

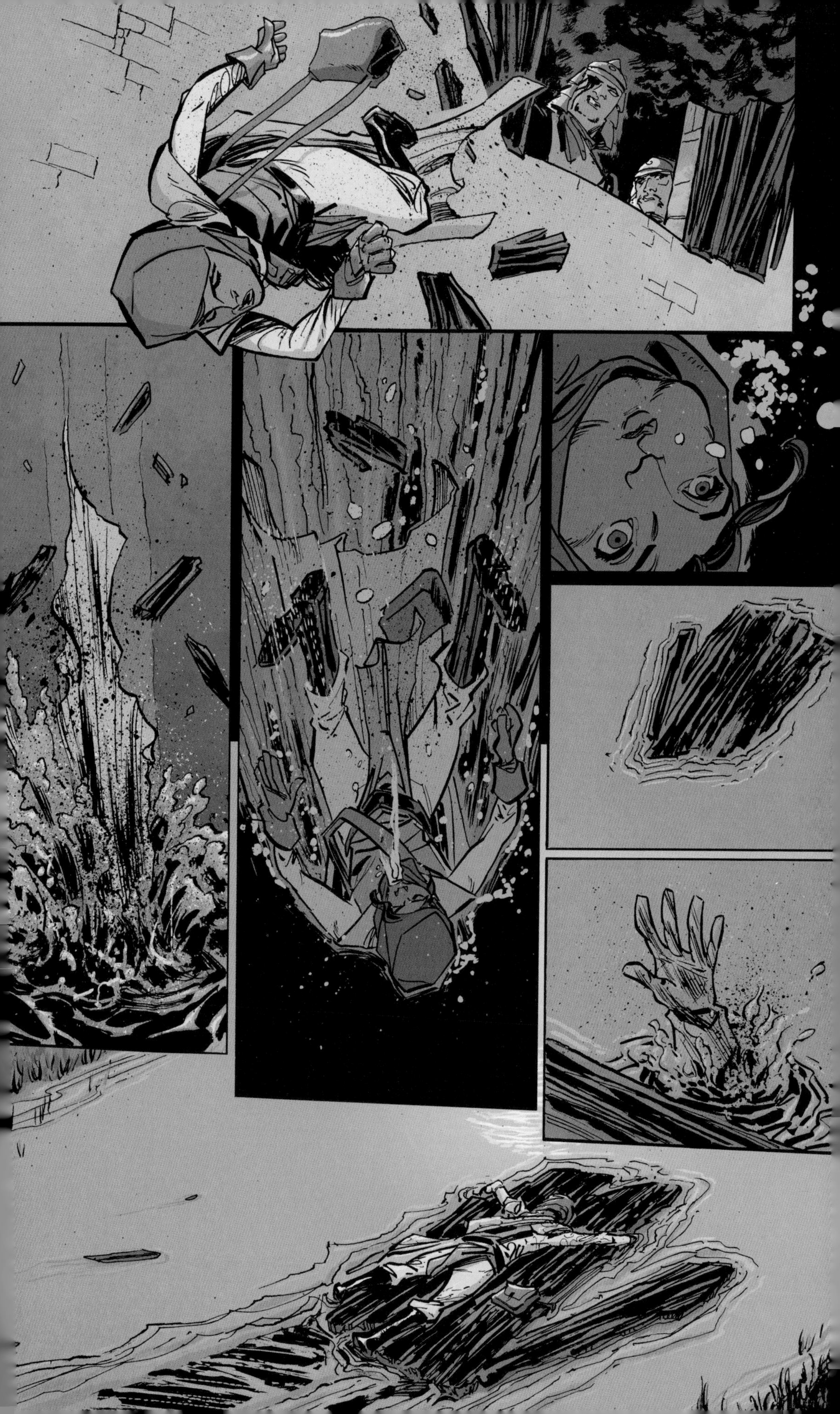

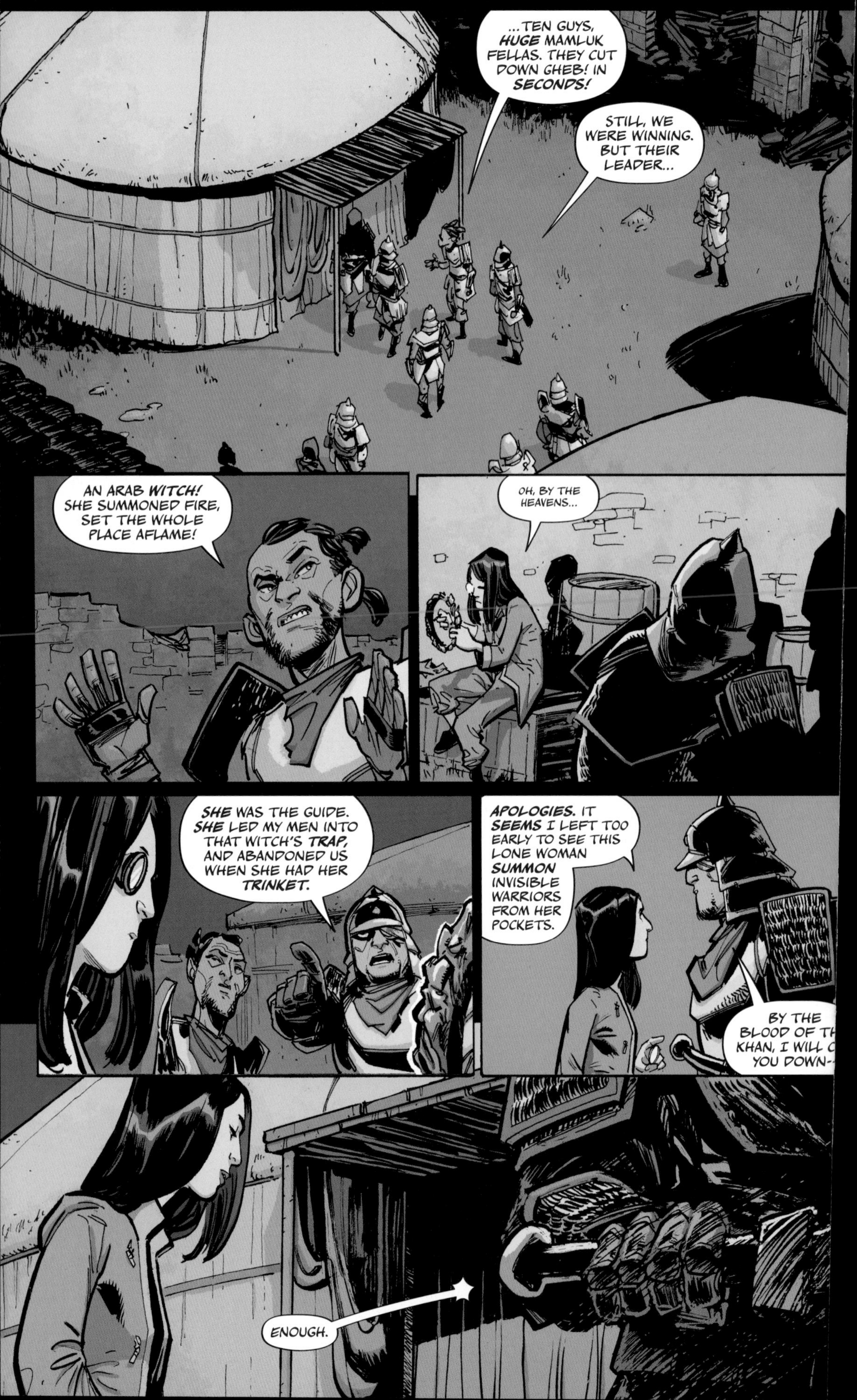
...TEN GUYS, HUGE MAMLUK FELLAS. THEY CUT DOWN GHEB! IN SECONDS!
STILL, WE WERE WINNING. BUT THEIR LEADER...
AN ARAB WITCH! SHE SUMMONED FIRE, SET THE WHOLE PLACE AFLAME!
OH, BY THE HEAVENS...
SHE WAS THE GUIDE. SHE LED MY MEN INTO THAT WITCH'S TRAP, AND ABANDONED US WHEN SHE HAD HER TRINKET.
APOLOGIES. IT SEEMS I LEFT TOO EARLY TO SEE THIS LONE WOMAN SUMMON INVISIBLE WARRIORS FROM HER POCKETS.
ENOUGH.

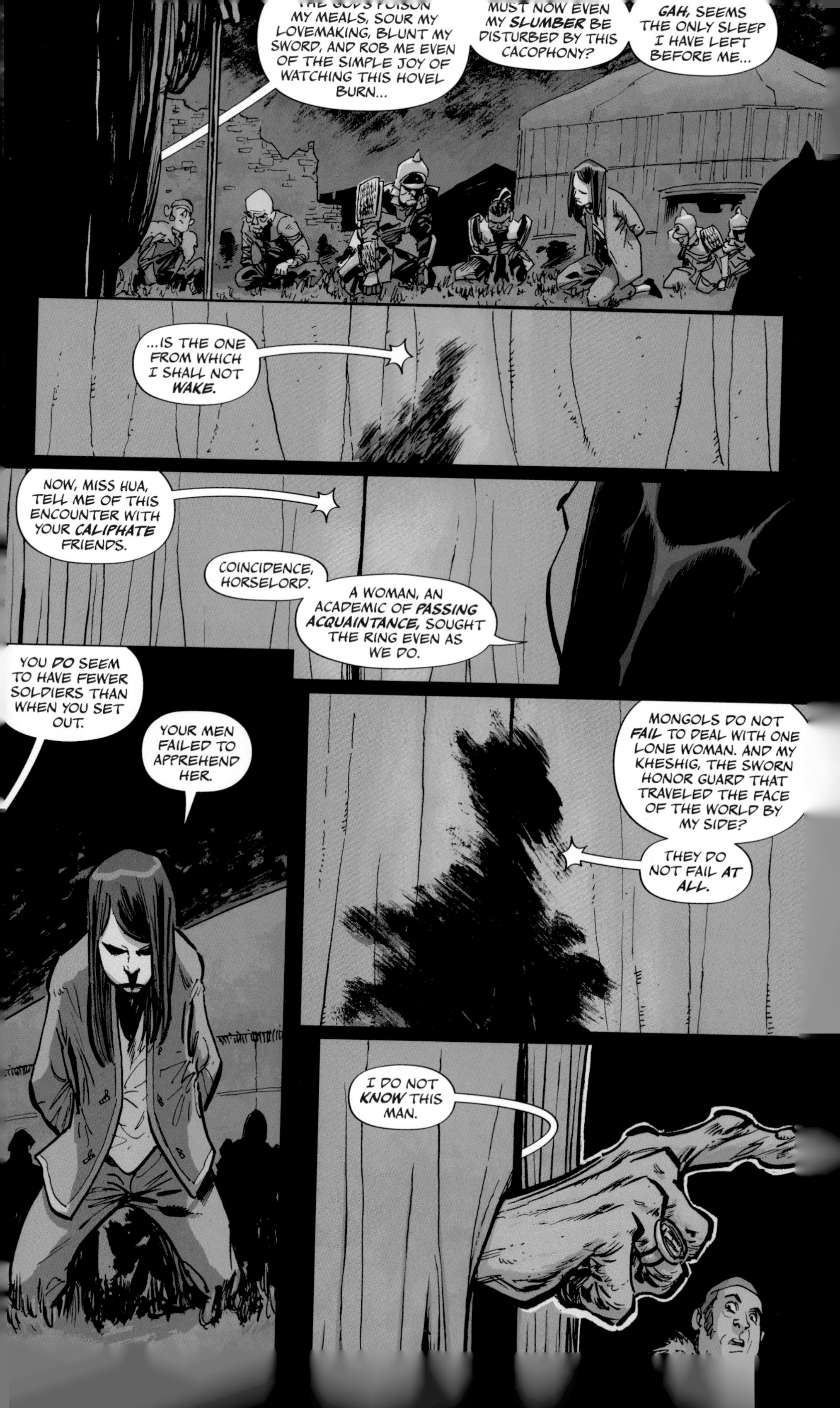
THE GODS POISON MY MEALS, SOUR MY LOVEMAKING, BLUNT MY SWORD, AND ROB ME EVEN OF THE SIMPLE JOY OF WATCHING THIS HOVEL BURN...
MUST NOW EVEN MY SLUMBER BE DISTURBED BY THIS CACOPHONY?
GAH, SEEMS THE ONLY SLEEP I HAVE LEFT BEFORE ME...
...IS THE ONE FROM WHICH I SHALL NOT WAKE.
NOW, MISS HUA, TELL ME OF THIS ENCOUNTER WITH YOUR CALIPHATE FRIENDS.
COINCIDENCE, HORSELORD.
A WOMAN, AN ACADEMIC OF PASSING ACQUAINTANCE, SOUGHT THE RING EVEN AS WE DO.
YOU DO SEEM TO HAVE FEWER SOLDIERS THAN WHEN YOU SET OUT.
YOUR MEN FAILED TO APPREHEND HER.
MONGOLS DO NOT FAIL TO DEAL WITH ONE LONE WOMAN. AND MY KHESHIG, THE SWORN HONOR GUARD THAT TRAVELED THE FACE OF THE WORLD BY MY SIDE?
THEY DO NOT FAIL AT ALL.
I DO NOT KNOW THIS MAN.

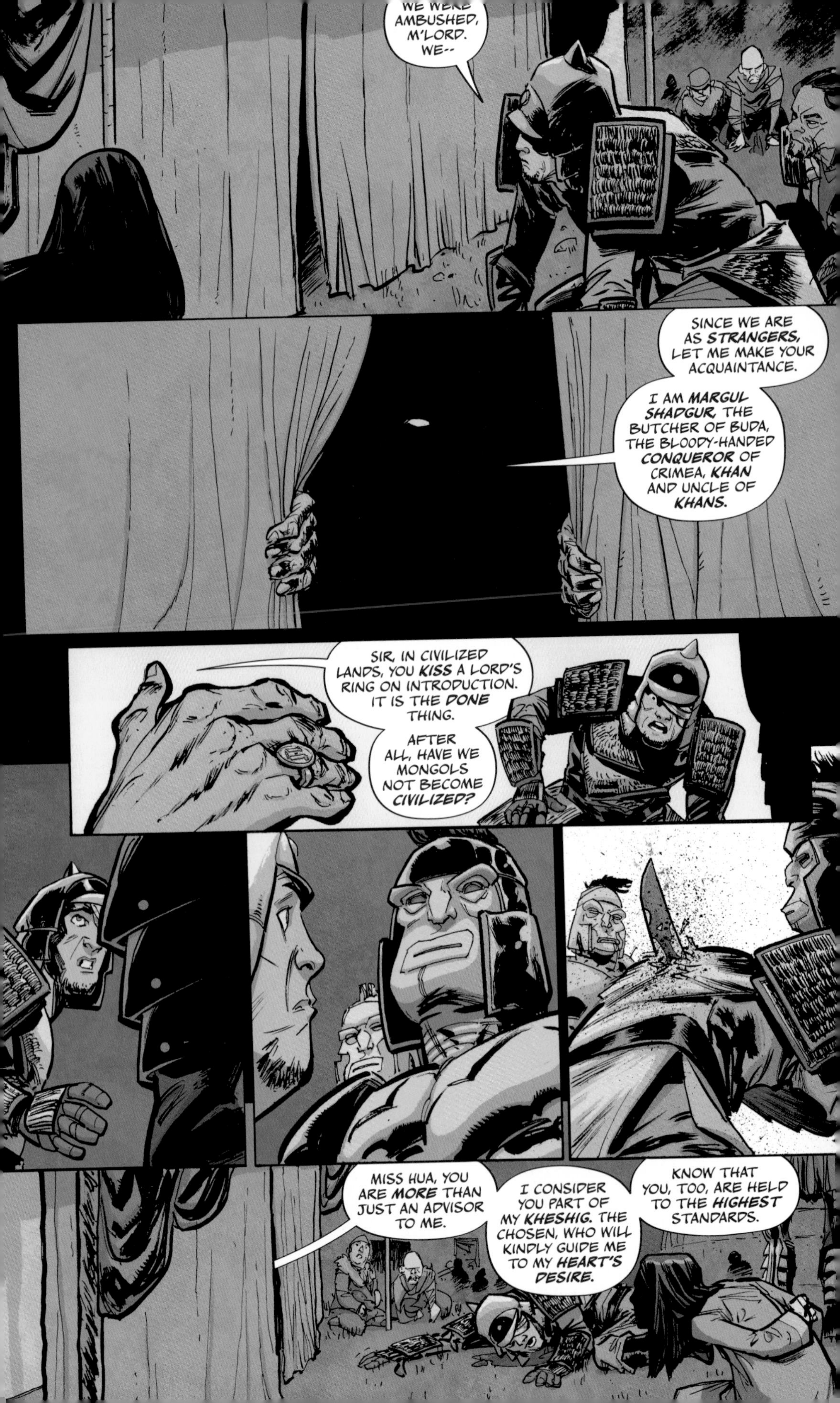
WE WERE AMBUSHED, M'LORD. WE--
SINCE WE ARE AS STRANGERS, LET ME MAKE YOUR ACQUAINTANCE.
I AM MARGUL SHADGUR, THE BUTCHER OF BUDA, THE BLOODY-HANDED CONQUEROR OF CRIMEA, KHAN AND UNCLE OF KHANS.
SIR, IN CIVILIZED LANDS, YOU KISS A LORD'S RING ON INTRODUCTION. IT IS THE DONE THING.
AFTER ALL, HAVE WE MONGOLS NOT BECOME CIVILIZED?
MISS HUA, YOU ARE MORE THAN JUST AN ADVISOR TO ME.
I CONSIDER YOU PART OF MY KHESHIG. THE CHOSEN, WHO WILL KINDLY GUIDE ME TO MY HEART'S DESIRE.
KNOW THAT YOU, TOO, ARE HELD TO THE HIGHEST STANDARDS.

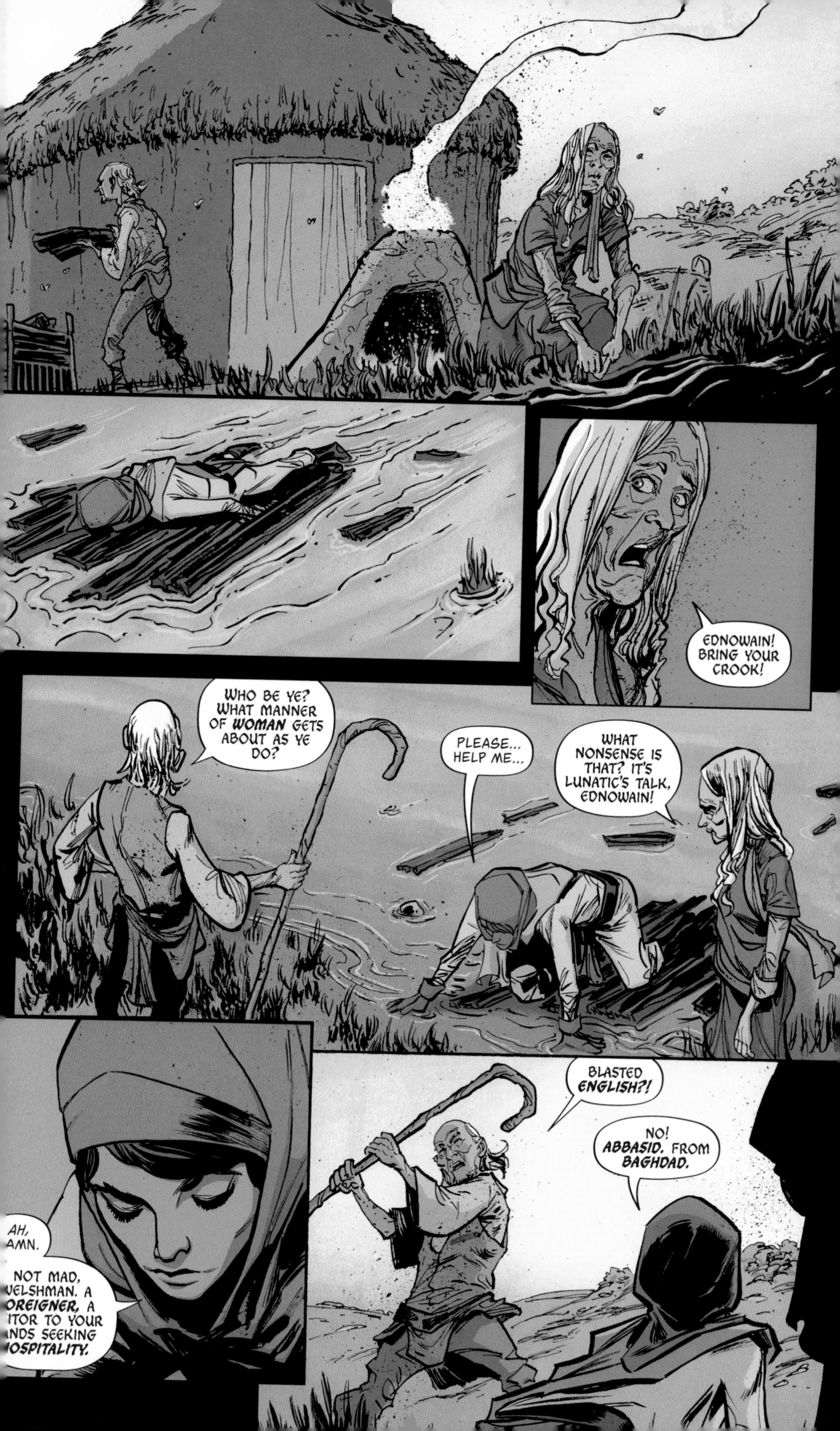
EDNOWAIN! BRING YOUR CROOK!
WHO BE YE? WHAT MANNER OF WOMAN GETS ABOUT AS YE DO?
PLEASE... HELP ME...
WHAT NONSENSE IS THAT? IT'S LUNATIC'S TALK, EDNOWAIN!
AH, AMN.
NOT MAD, VELSHMAN. A OREIGNER, A ITOR TO YOUR NDS SEEKING OSPITALITY.
BLASTED ENGLISH?!
NO! ABBASID. FROM BAGHDAD.

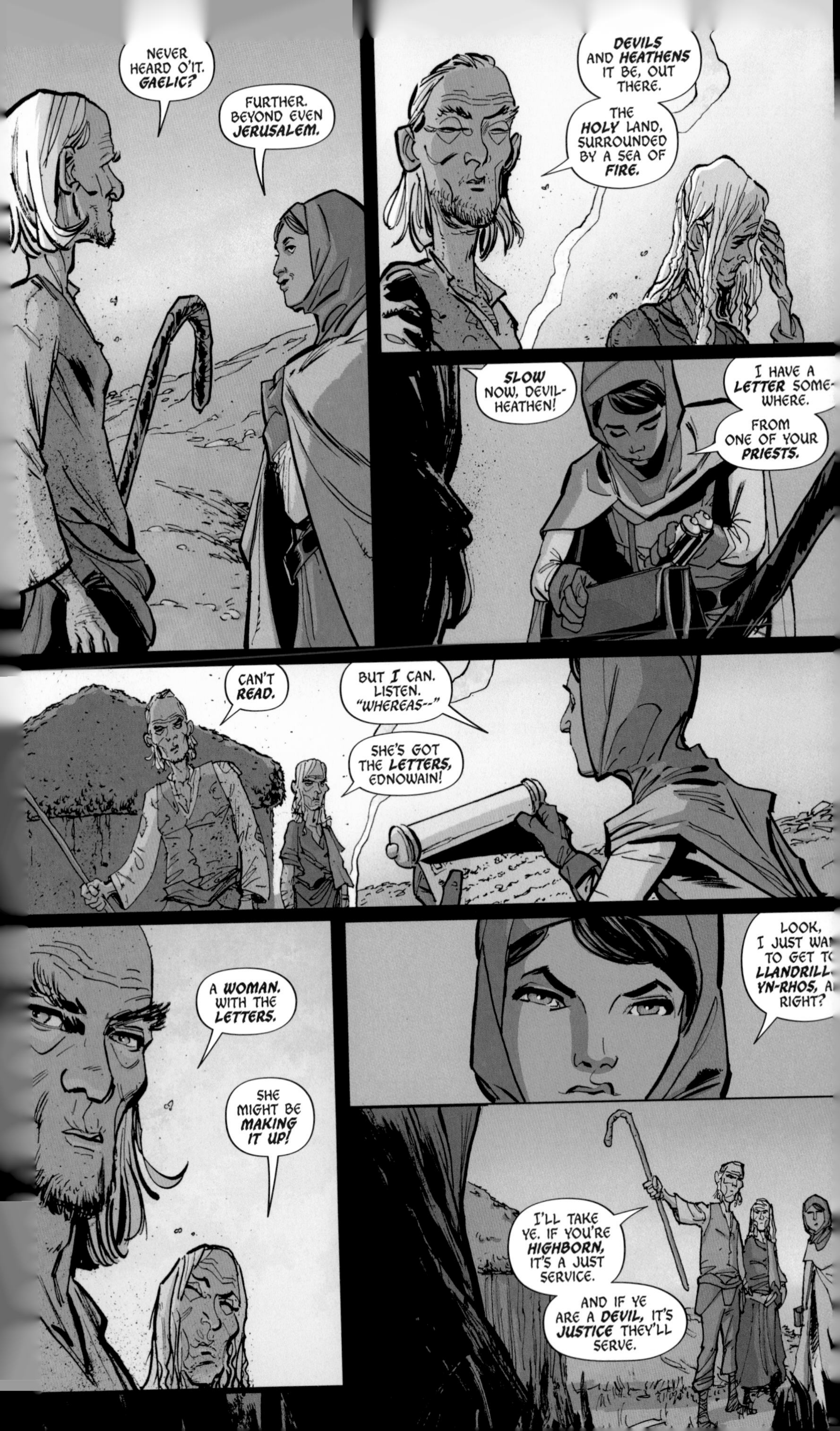
NEVER HEARD O'IT. GAELIC?
FURTHER. BEYOND EVEN JERUSALEM.
DEVILS AND HEATHENS IT BE, OUT THERE.
THE HOLY LAND, SURROUNDED BY A SEA OF FIRE.
SLOW NOW, DEVIL-HEATHEN!
I HAVE A LETTER SOME-WHERE.
FROM ONE OF YOUR PRIESTS.
CAN'T READ.
BUT I CAN. LISTEN. "WHEREAS--"
SHE'S GOT THE LETTERS, EDNOWAIN!
A WOMAN. WITH THE LETTERS.
SHE MIGHT BE MAKING IT UP!
I'LL TAKE YE. IF YOU'RE HIGHBORN, IT'S A JUST SERVICE.
AND IF YE ARE A DEVIL, IT'S JUSTICE THEY'LL SERVE.

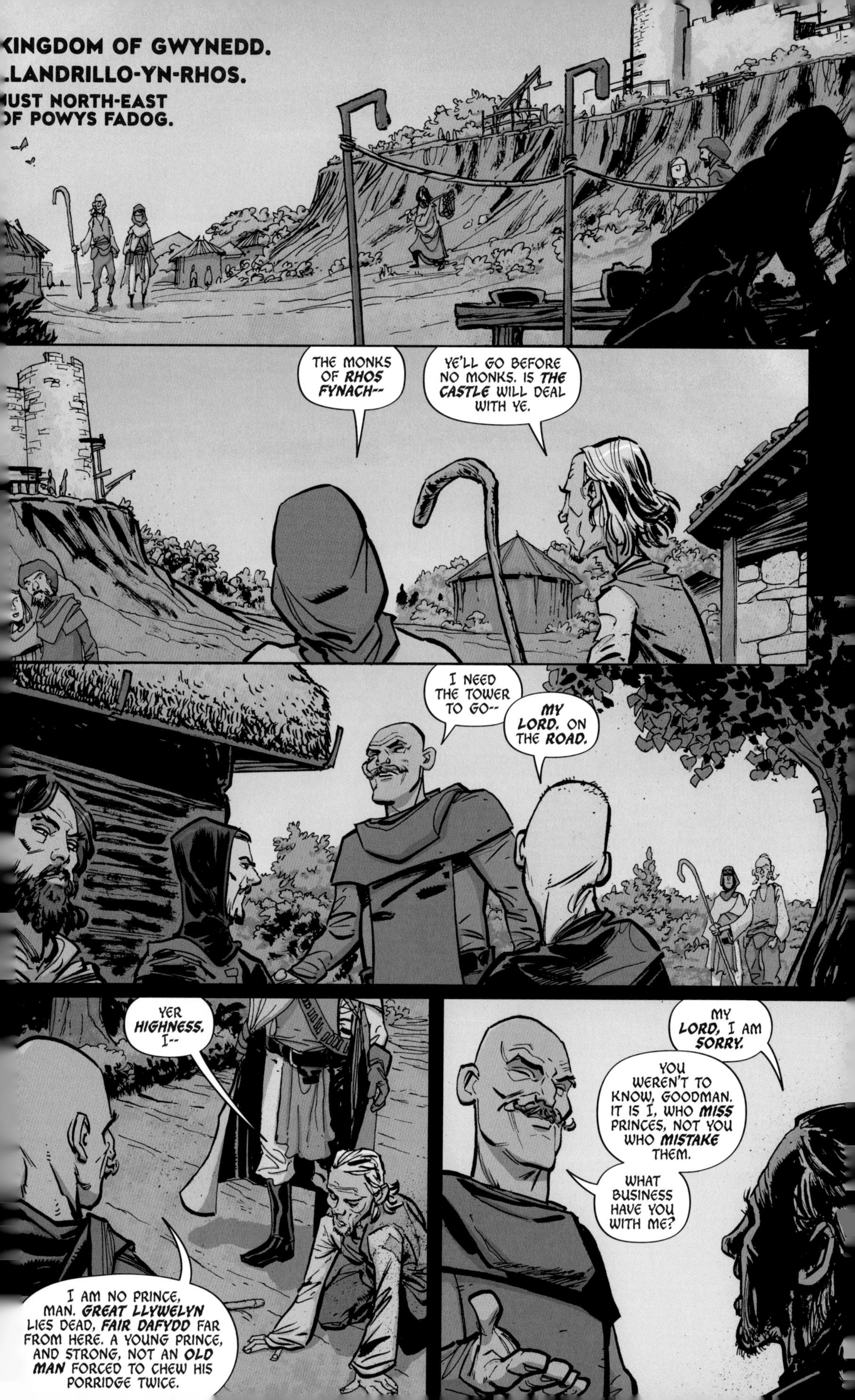
KINGDOM OF GWYNEDD.
LLANDRILLO-YN-RHOS.
JUST NORTH-EAST OF POWYS FADOG.
THE MONKS OF RHOS FYNACH--
YE'LL GO BEFORE NO MONKS. IS THE CASTLE WILL DEAL WITH YE.
I NEED THE TOWER TO GO--
MY LORD, ON THE ROAD.
YER HIGHNESS. I--
I AM NO PRINCE, MAN. GREAT LLYWELYN LIES DEAD, FAIR DAFYDD FAR FROM HERE. A YOUNG PRINCE, AND STRONG, NOT AN OLD MAN FORCED TO CHEW HIS PORRIDGE TWICE.
MY LORD, I AM SORRY.
YOU WEREN'T TO KNOW, GOODMAN. IT IS I, WHO MISS PRINCES, NOT YOU WHO MISTAKE THEM.
WHAT BUSINESS HAVE YOU WITH ME?

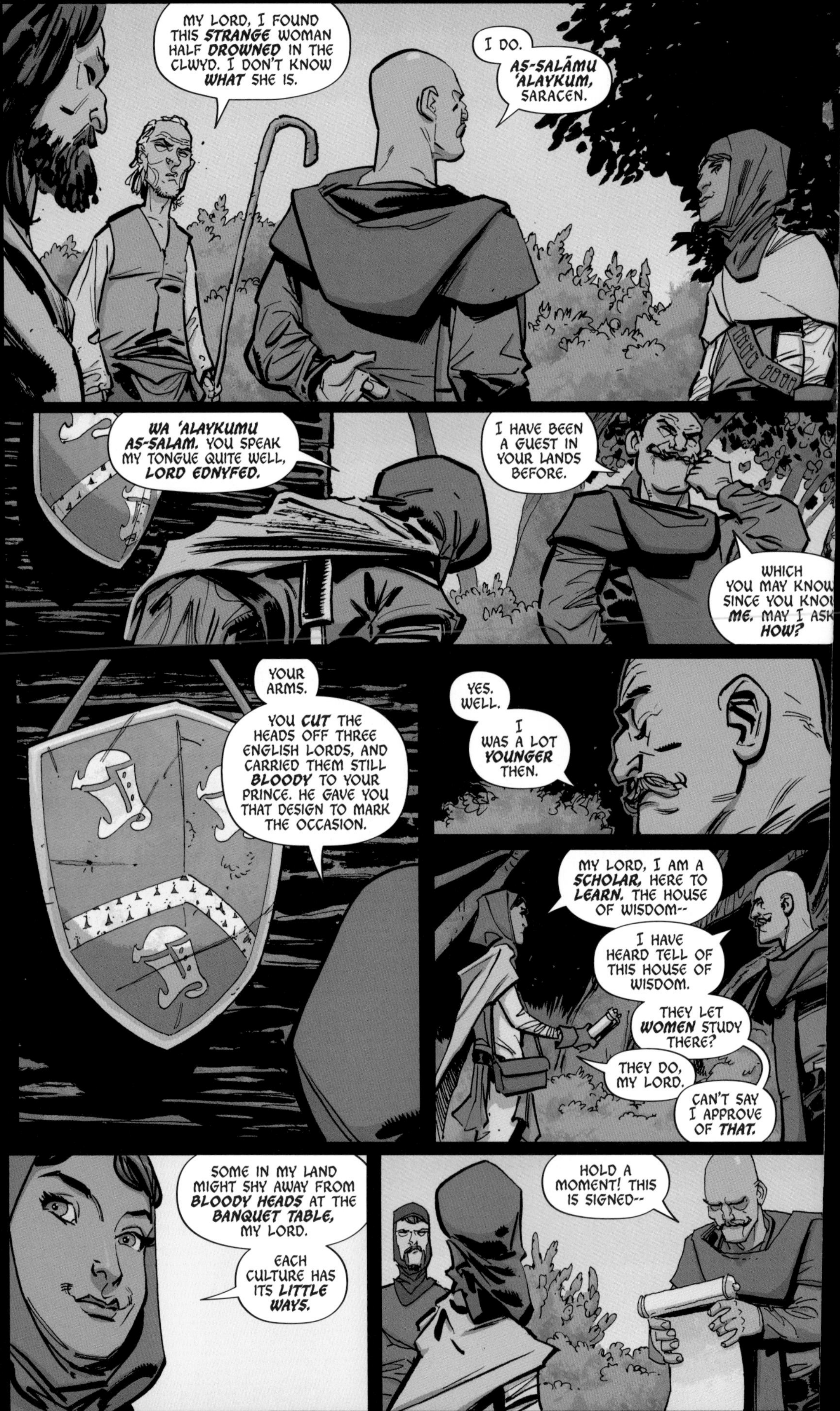
MY LORD, I FOUND THIS STRANGE WOMAN HALF DROWNED IN THE CLWYD. I DON'T KNOW WHAT SHE IS.
I DO.
AS-SALĀMU 'ALAYKUM, SARACEN.
WA 'ALAYKUMU AS-SALAM. YOU SPEAK MY TONGUE QUITE WELL, LORD EDNYFED.
I HAVE BEEN A GUEST IN YOUR LANDS BEFORE.
WHICH YOU MAY KNOW SINCE YOU KNOW ME. MAY I ASK HOW?
YOUR ARMS.
YOU CUT THE HEADS OFF THREE ENGLISH LORDS, AND CARRIED THEM STILL BLOODY TO YOUR PRINCE. HE GAVE YOU THAT DESIGN TO MARK THE OCCASION.
YES. WELL.
I WAS A LOT YOUNGER THEN.
MY LORD, I AM A SCHOLAR, HERE TO LEARN. THE HOUSE OF WISDOM--
I HAVE HEARD TELL OF THIS HOUSE OF WISDOM.
THEY LET WOMEN STUDY THERE?
THEY DO, MY LORD.
CAN'T SAY I APPROVE OF THAT.
SOME IN MY LAND MIGHT SHY AWAY FROM BLOODY HEADS AT THE BANQUET TABLE, MY LORD.
EACH CULTURE HAS ITS LITTLE WAYS.
HOLD A MOMENT! THIS IS SIGNED--

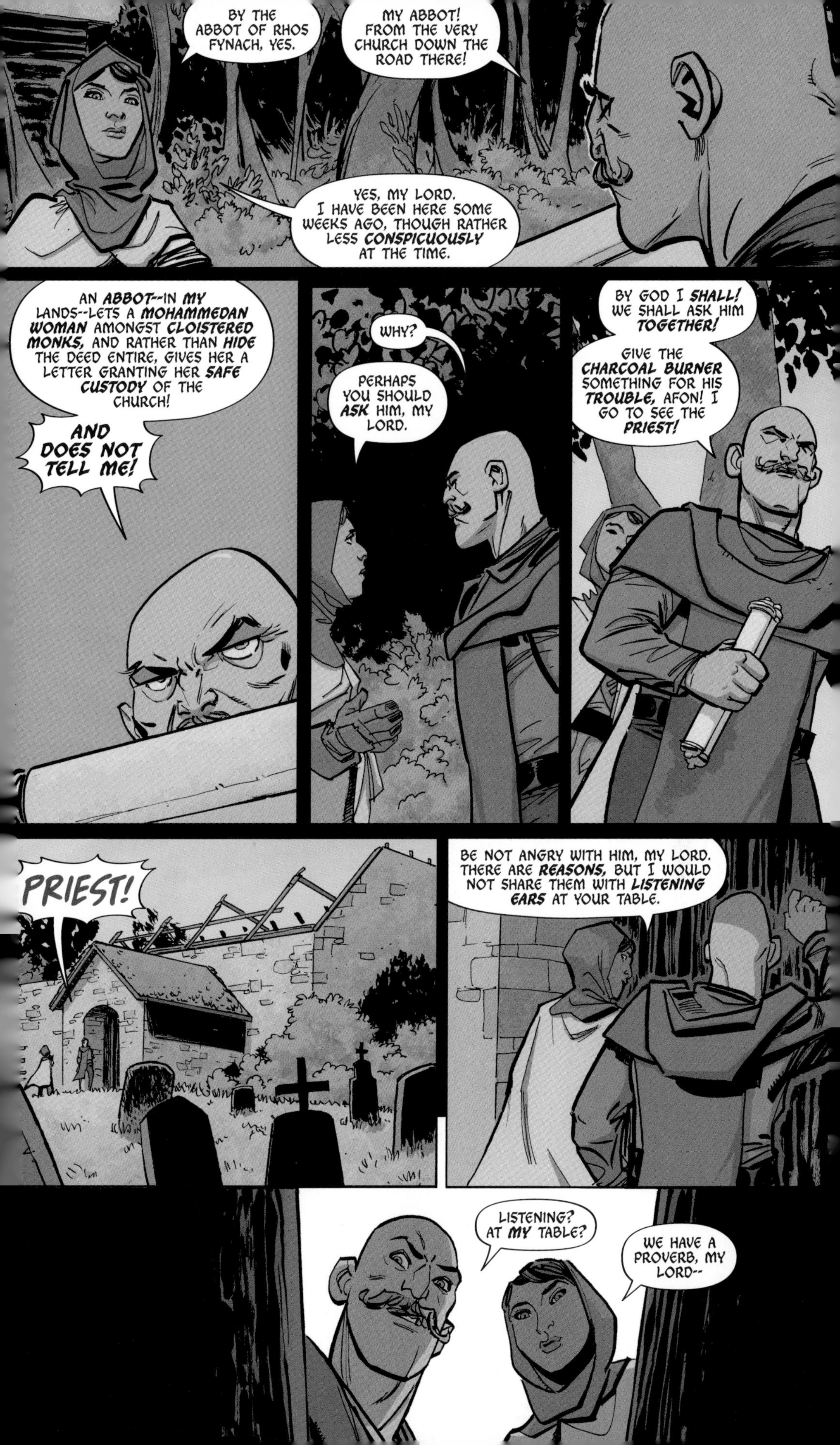
BY THE ABBOT OF RHOS FYNACH, YES.
MY ABBOT! FROM THE VERY CHURCH DOWN THE ROAD THERE!
YES, MY LORD. I HAVE BEEN HERE SOME WEEKS AGO, THOUGH RATHER LESS CONSPICUOUSLY AT THE TIME.
AN ABBOT--IN MY LANDS--LETS A MOHAMMEDAN WOMAN AMONGST CLOISTERED MONKS, AND RATHER THAN HIDE THE DEED ENTIRE, GIVES HER A LETTER GRANTING HER SAFE CUSTODY OF THE CHURCH!
AND DOES NOT TELL ME!
WHY?
PERHAPS YOU SHOULD ASK HIM, MY LORD.
BY GOD I SHALL! WE SHALL ASK HIM TOGETHER!
GIVE THE CHARCOAL BURNER SOMETHING FOR HIS TROUBLE, AFON! I GO TO SEE THE PRIEST!
PRIEST!
BE NOT ANGRY WITH HIM, MY LORD. THERE ARE REASONS, BUT I WOULD NOT SHARE THEM WITH LISTENING EARS AT YOUR TABLE.
LISTENING? AT MY TABLE?
WE HAVE A PROVERB, MY LORD--

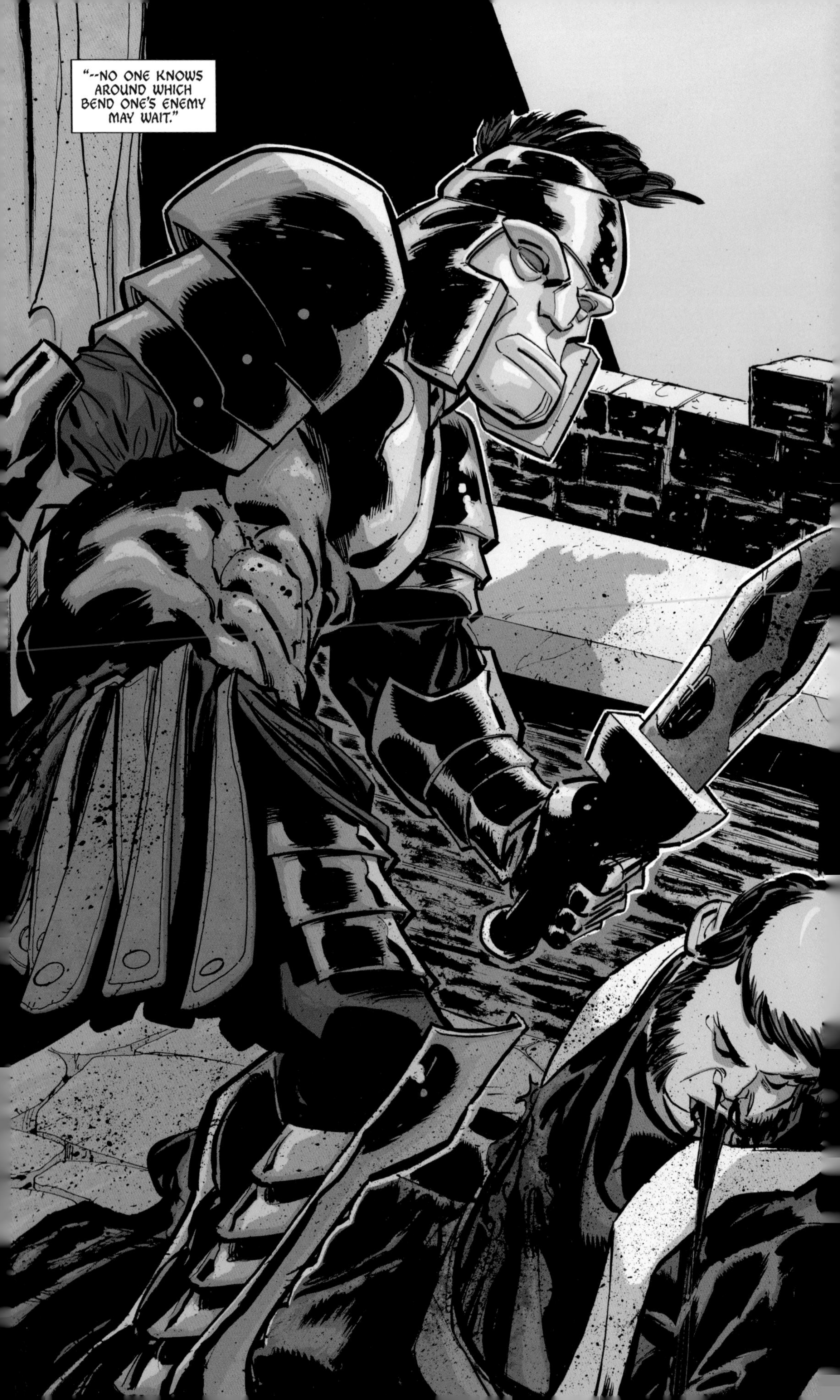
"--NO ONE KNOWS AROUND WHICH BEND ONE'S ENEMY MAY WAIT."

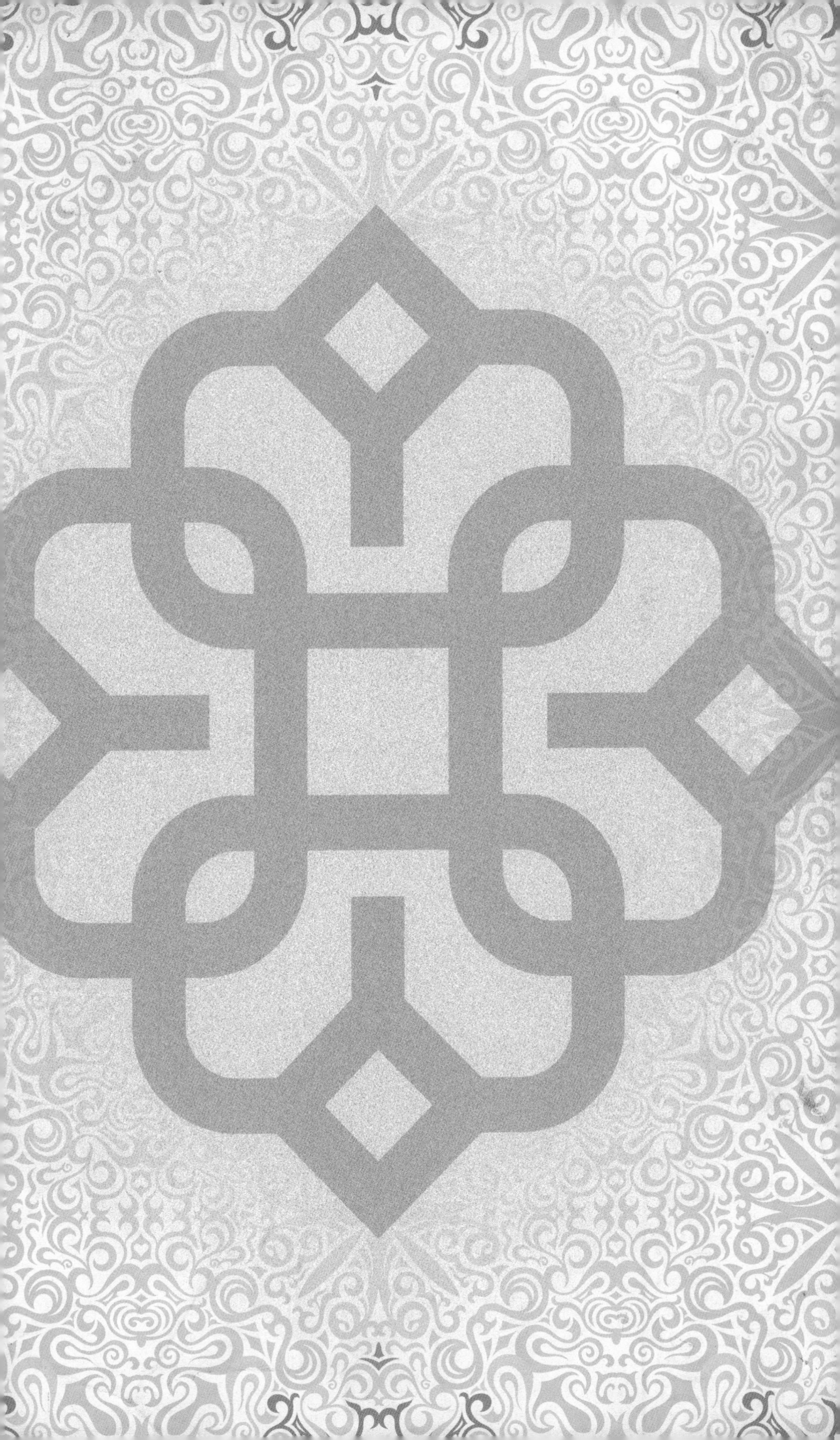

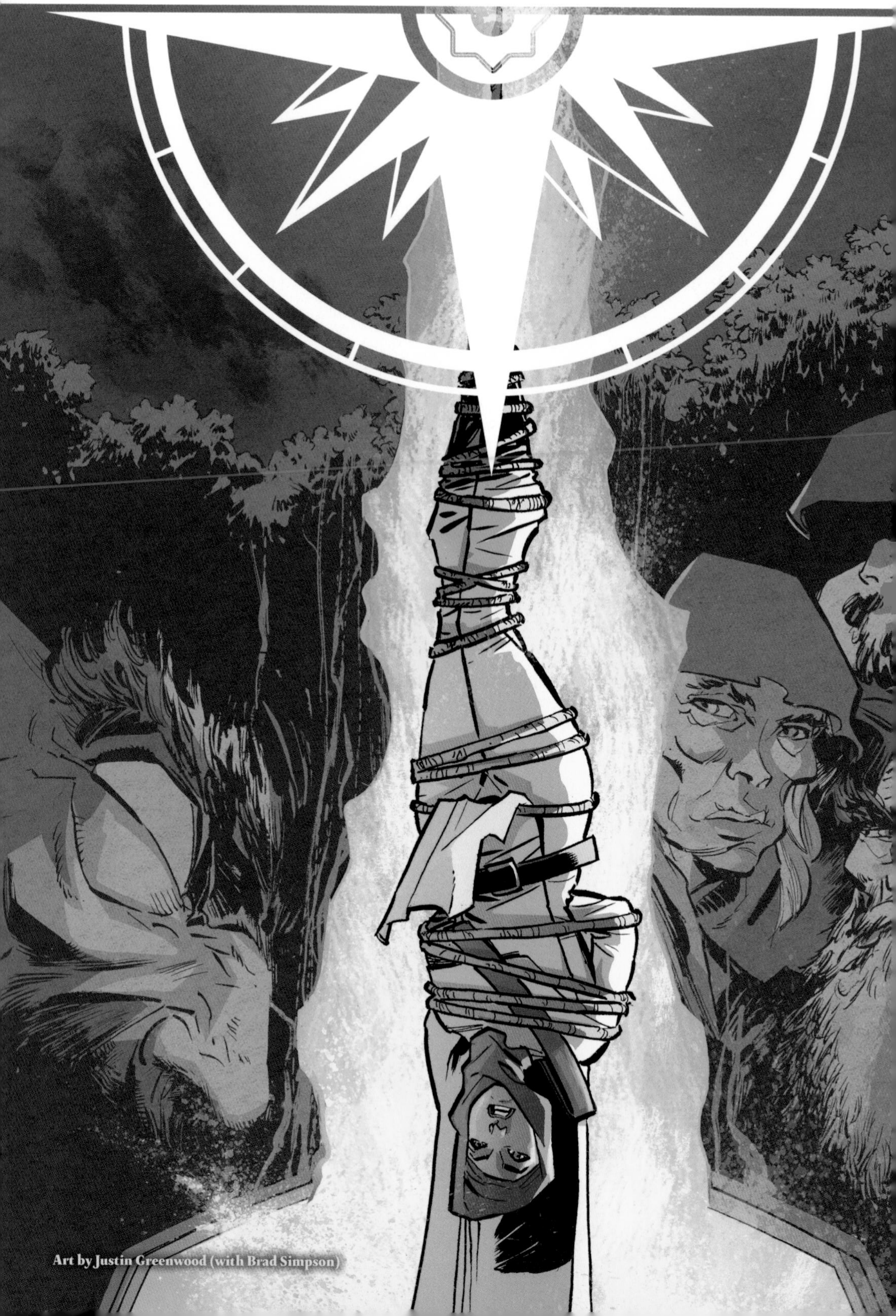

Art by Justin Greenwood (with Brad Simpson)

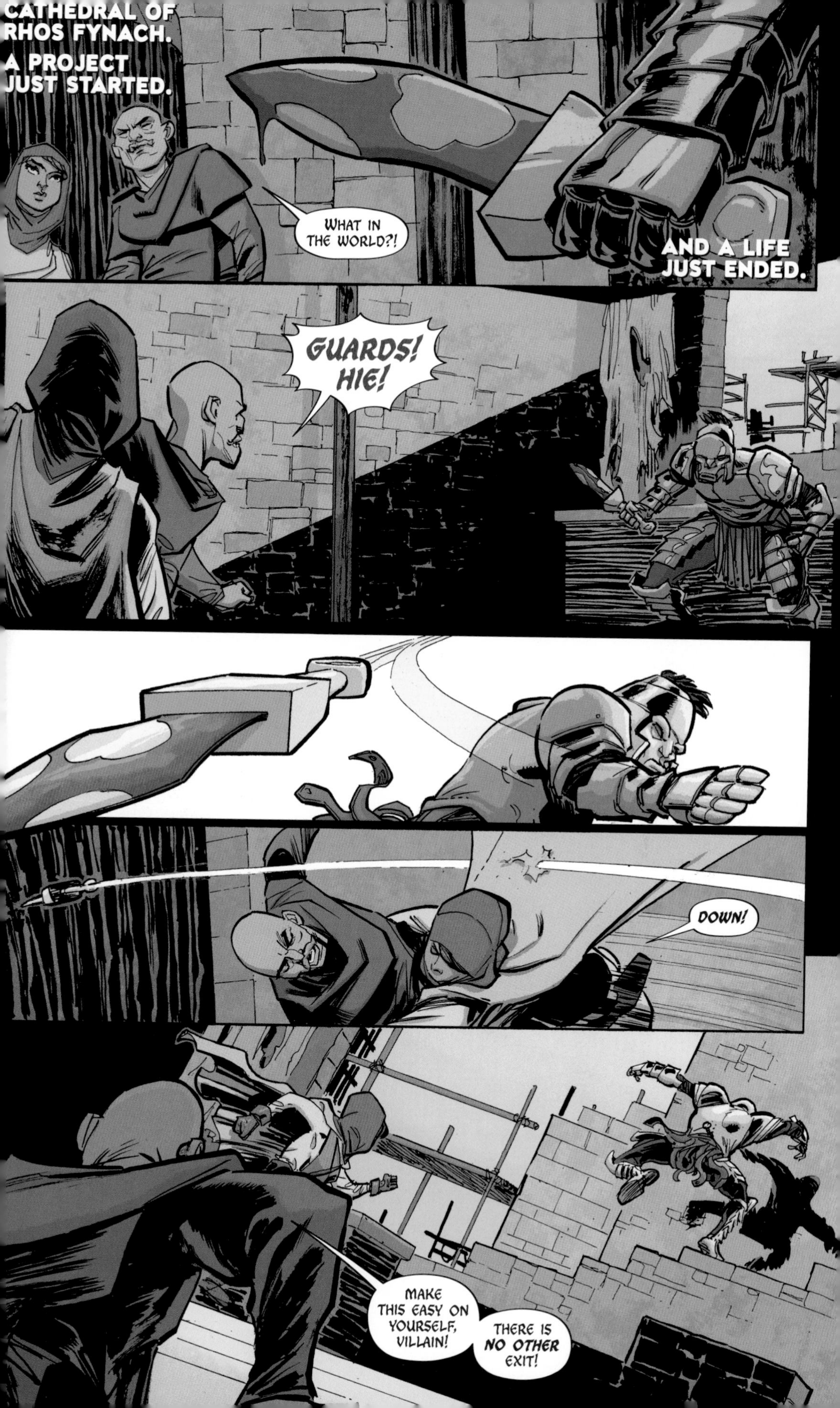
CATHEDRAL OF RHOS FYNACH.
A PROJECT JUST STARTED.
WHAT IN THE WORLD?!
AND A LIFE JUST ENDED.
GUARDS! HIE!
DOWN!
MAKE THIS EASY ON YOURSELF, VILLAIN!
THERE IS NO OTHER EXIT!

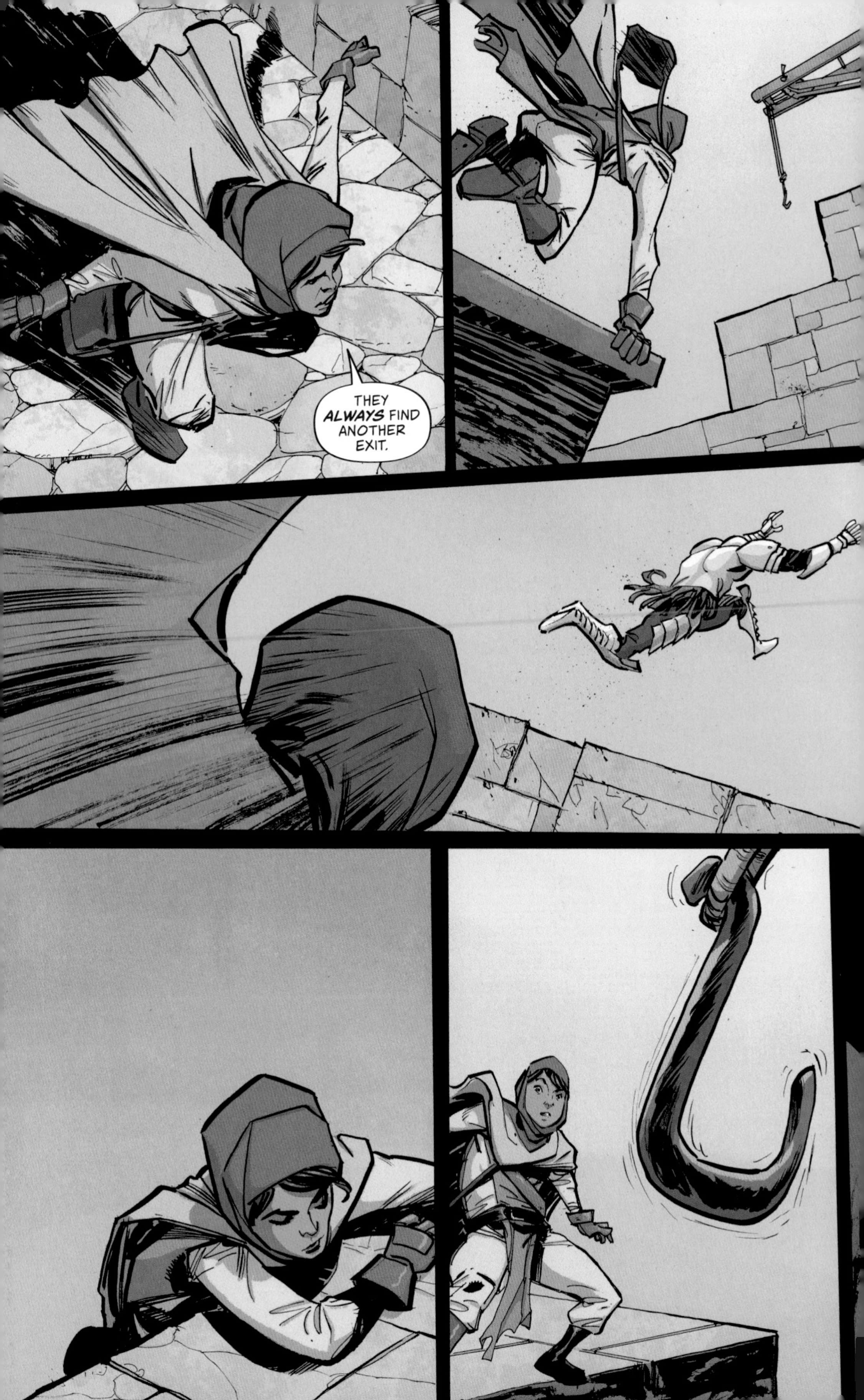
THEY ALWAYS FIND ANOTHER EXIT.

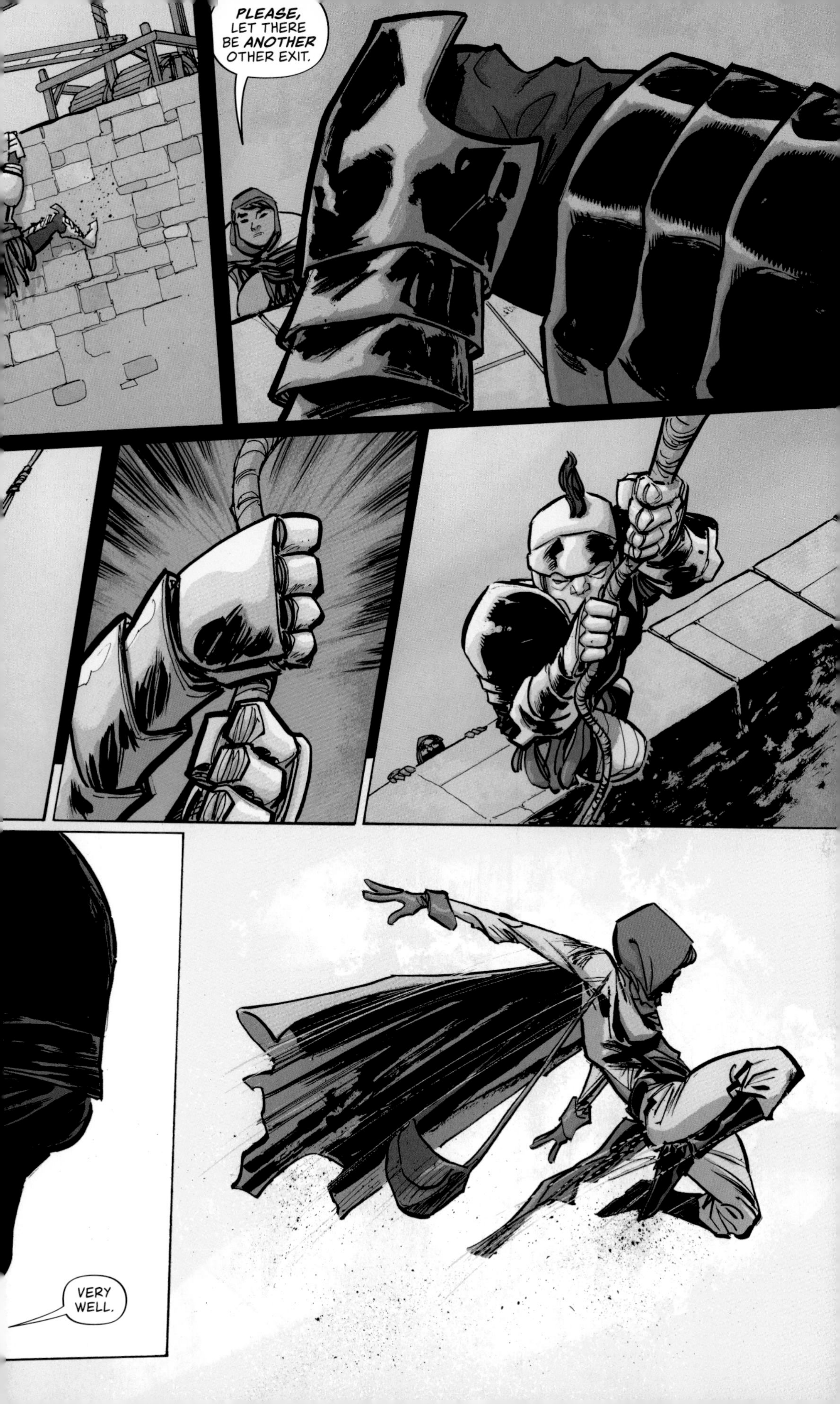
PLEASE, LET THERE BE ANOTHER OTHER EXIT.
VERY WELL.

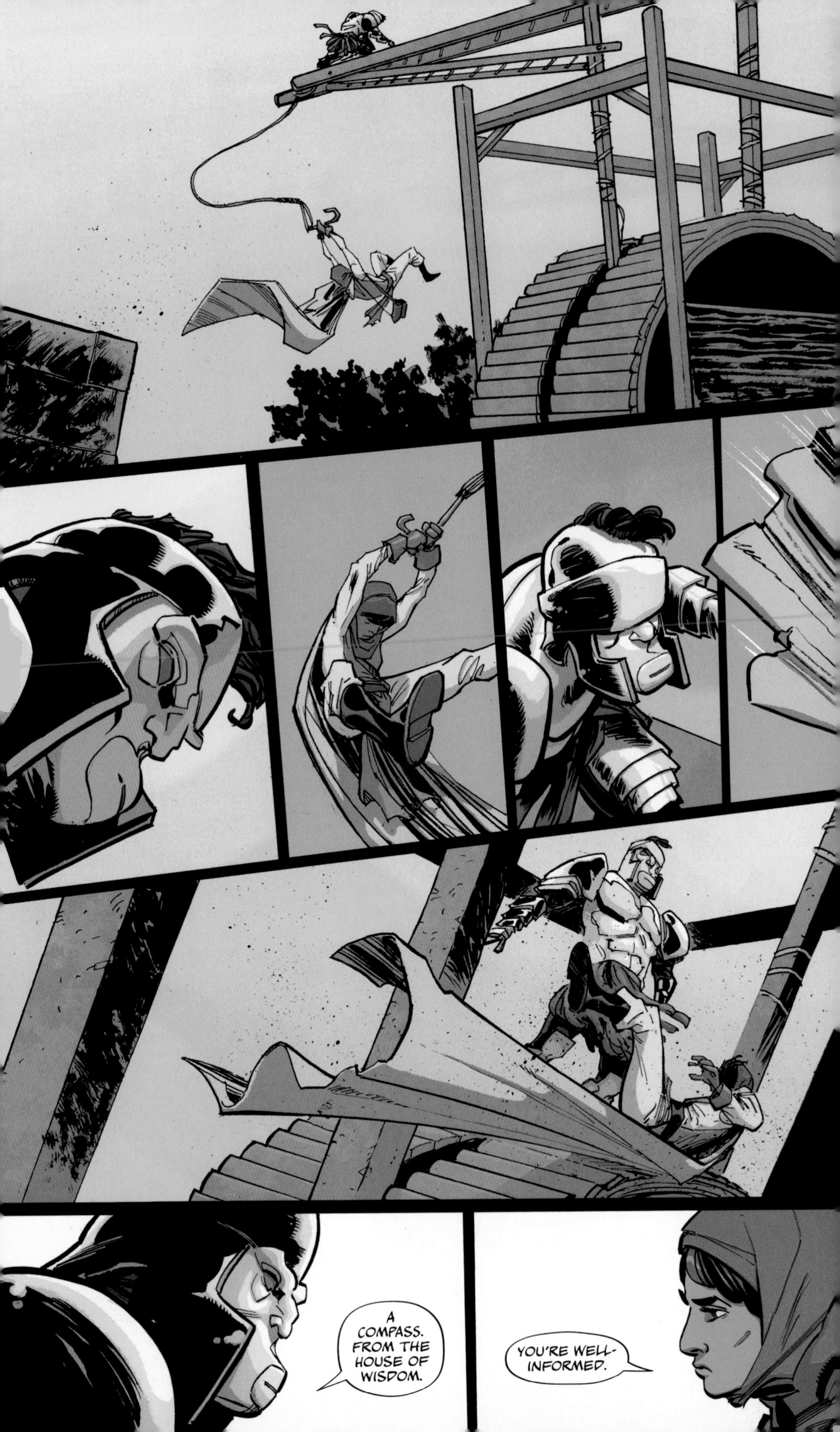
A COMPASS. FROM THE HOUSE OF WISDOM.
YOU'RE WELL-INFORMED.

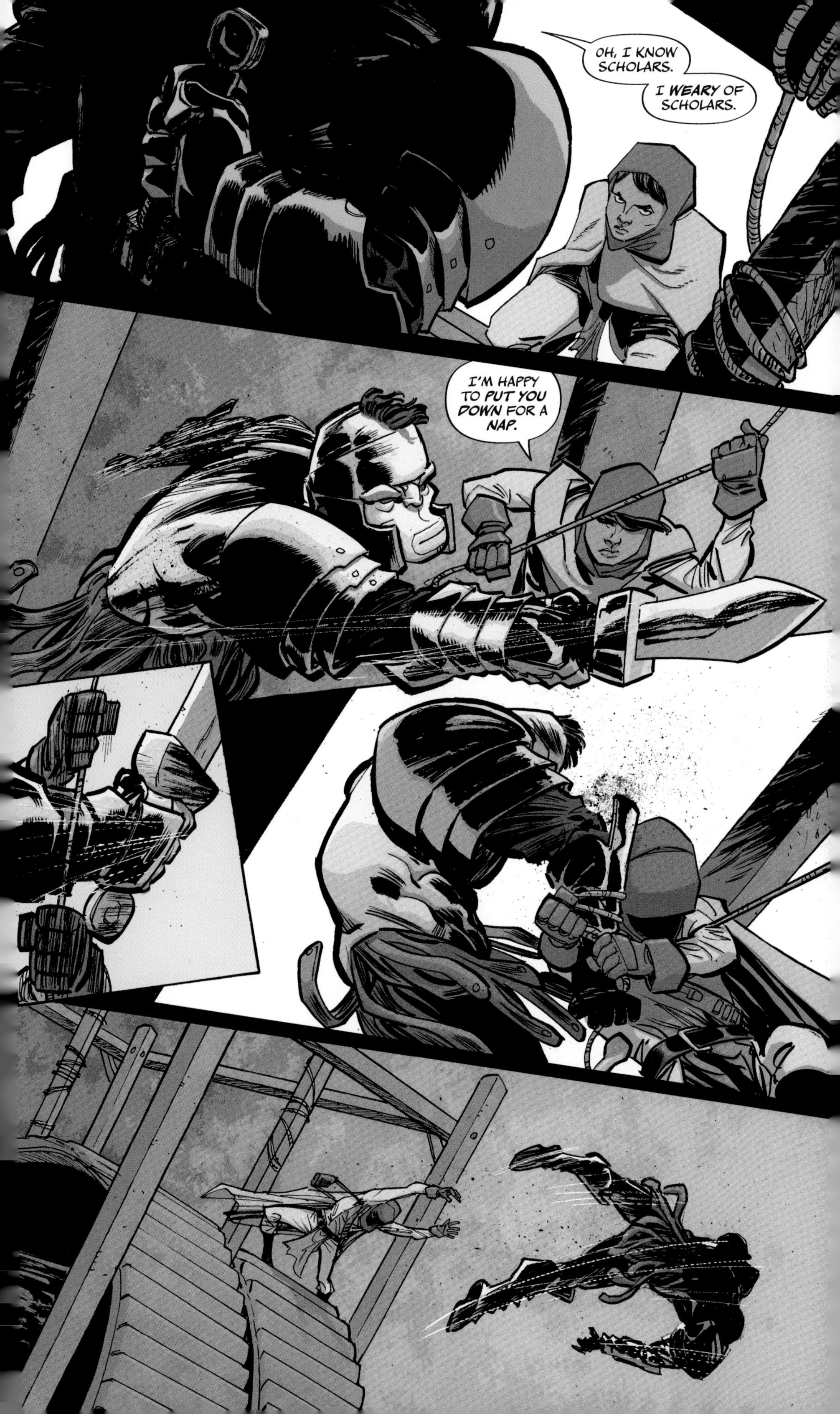
OH, I KNOW SCHOLARS.
I WEARY OF SCHOLARS.
I'M HAPPY TO PUT YOU DOWN FOR A NAP.

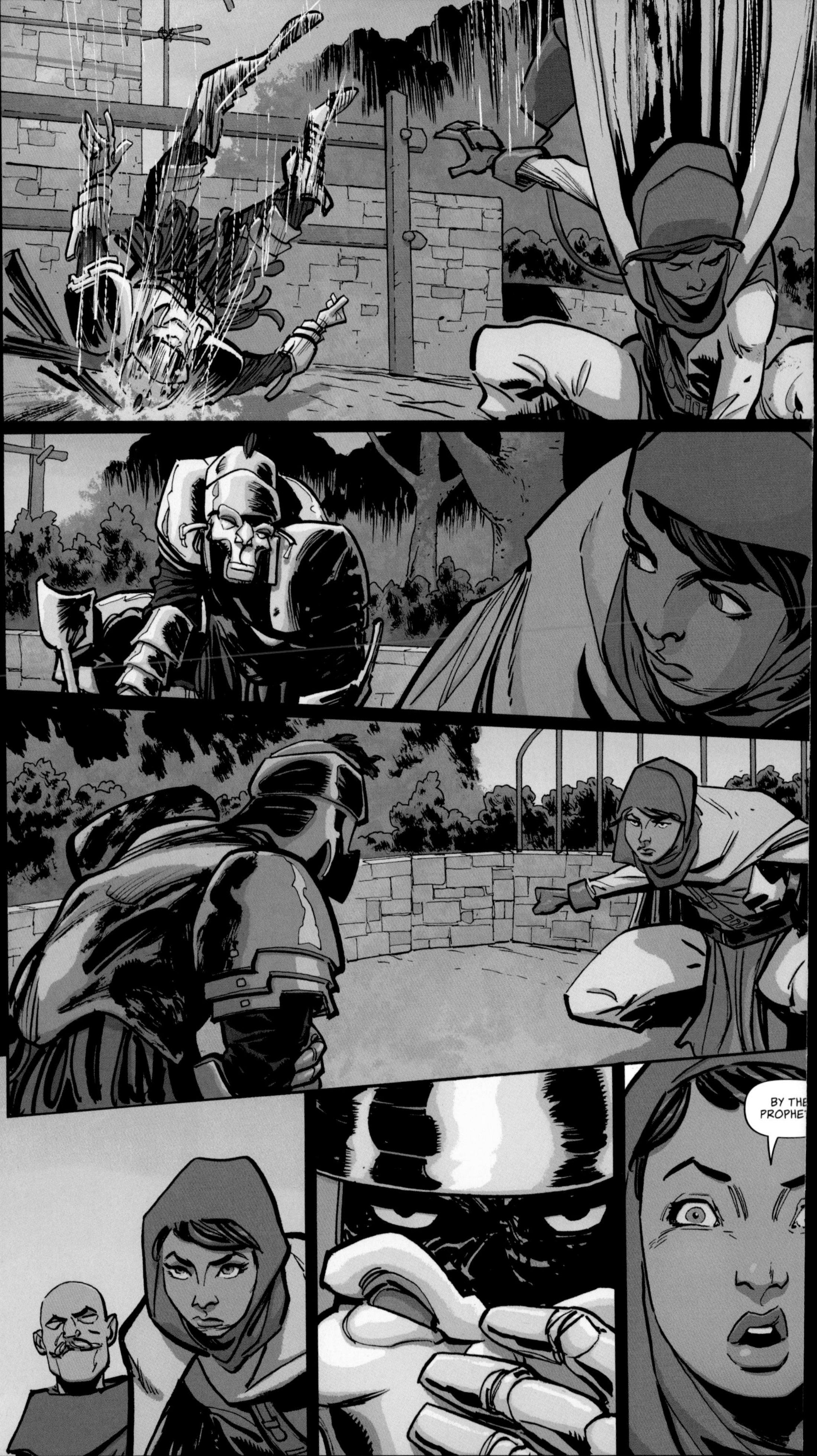
BY THE
PROPHET

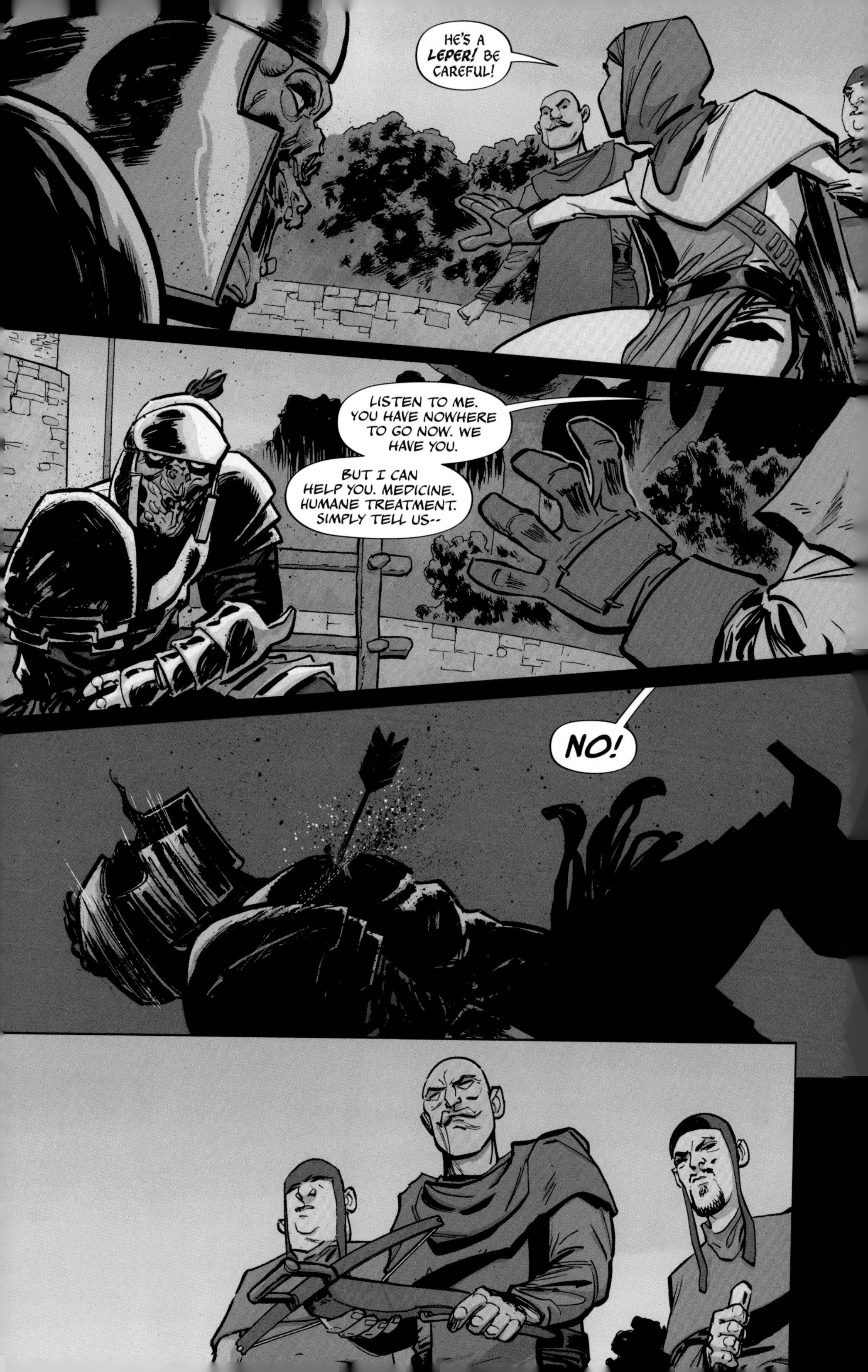
HE'S A LEPER! BE CAREFUL!
LISTEN TO ME. YOU HAVE NOWHERE TO GO NOW. WE HAVE YOU.
BUT I CAN HELP YOU. MEDICINE. HUMANE TREATMENT. SIMPLY TELL US--
NO!

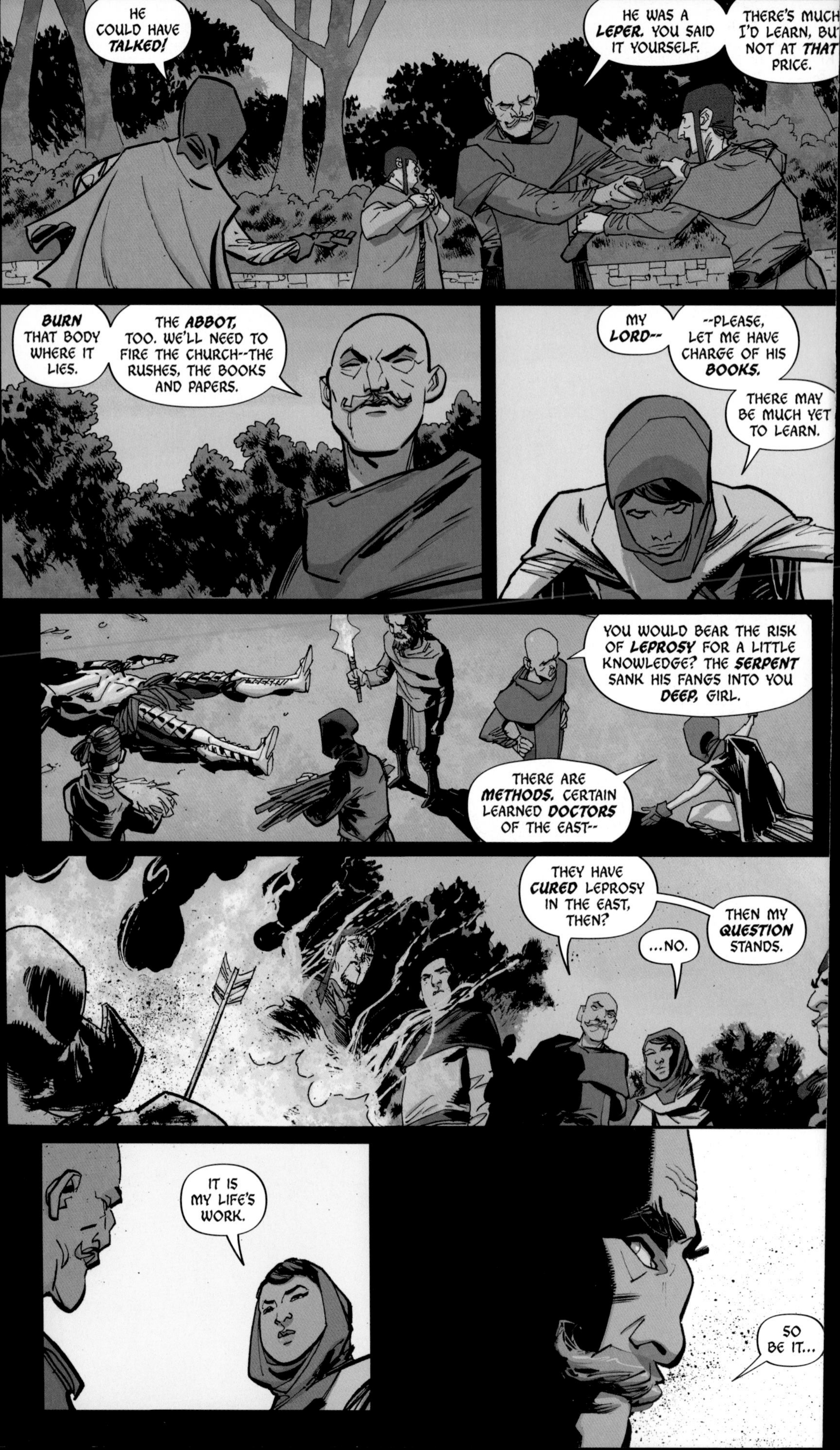
HE COULD HAVE TALKED!
HE WAS A LEPER. YOU SAID IT YOURSELF.
THERE'S MUCH I'D LEARN, BUT NOT AT THAT PRICE.
BURN THAT BODY WHERE IT LIES.
THE ABBOT, TOO. WE'LL NEED TO FIRE THE CHURCH--THE RUSHES, THE BOOKS AND PAPERS.
MY LORD--
--PLEASE, LET ME HAVE CHARGE OF HIS BOOKS.
THERE MAY BE MUCH YET TO LEARN.
YOU WOULD BEAR THE RISK OF LEPROSY FOR A LITTLE KNOWLEDGE? THE SERPENT SANK HIS FANGS INTO YOU DEEP, GIRL.
THERE ARE METHODS. CERTAIN LEARNED DOCTORS OF THE EAST--
THEY HAVE CURED LEPROSY IN THE EAST, THEN?
...NO.
THEN MY QUESTION STANDS.
IT IS MY LIFE'S WORK.
SO BE IT...

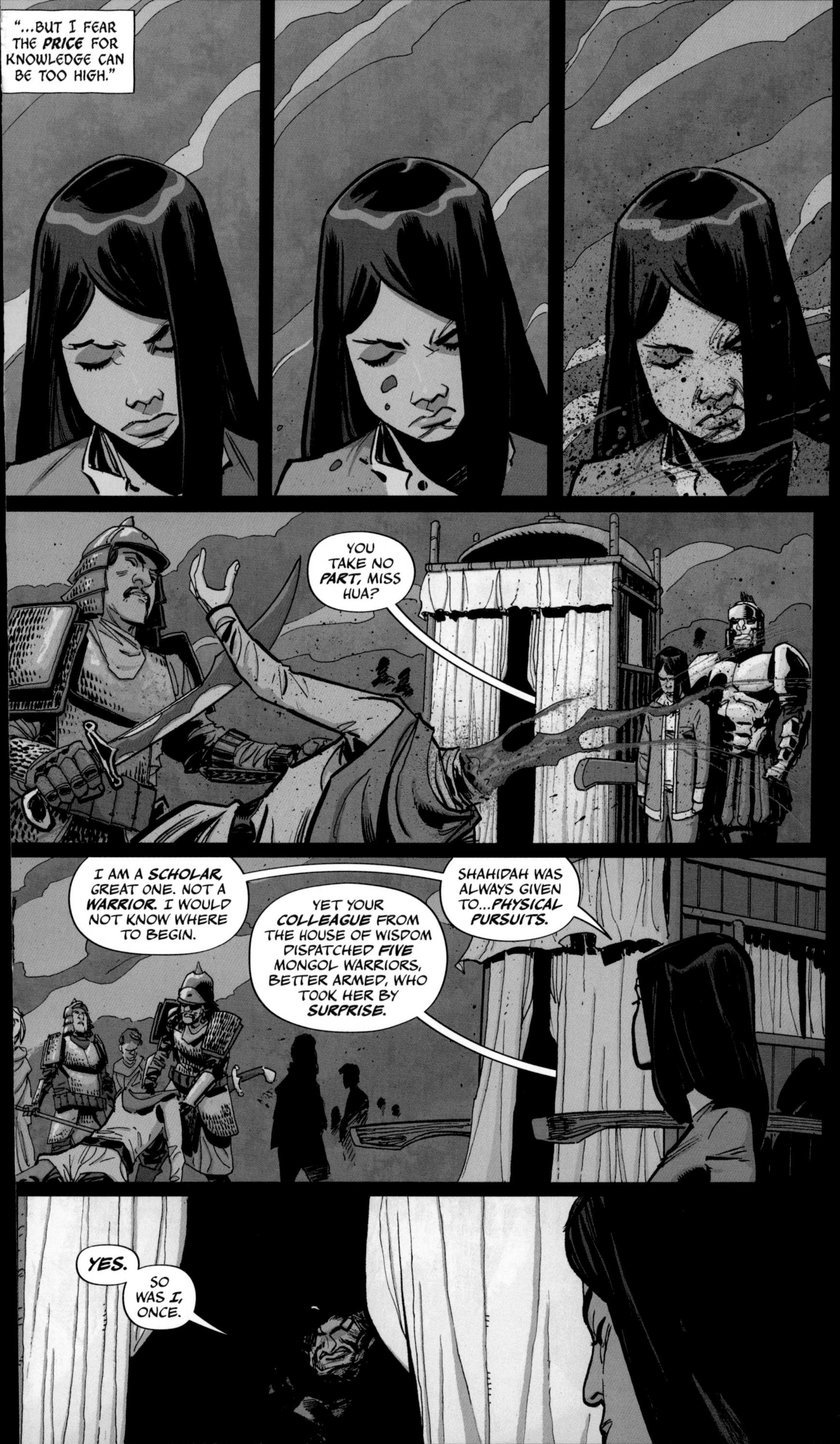
"...BUT I FEAR THE PRICE FOR KNOWLEDGE CAN BE TOO HIGH."
YOU TAKE NO PART, MISS HUA?
I AM A SCHOLAR, GREAT ONE. NOT A WARRIOR. I WOULD NOT KNOW WHERE TO BEGIN.
YET YOUR COLLEAGUE FROM THE HOUSE OF WISDOM DISPATCHED FIVE MONGOL WARRIORS, BETTER ARMED, WHO TOOK HER BY SURPRISE.
SHAHIDAH WAS ALWAYS GIVEN TO...PHYSICAL PURSUITS.
YES.
SO WAS I, ONCE.

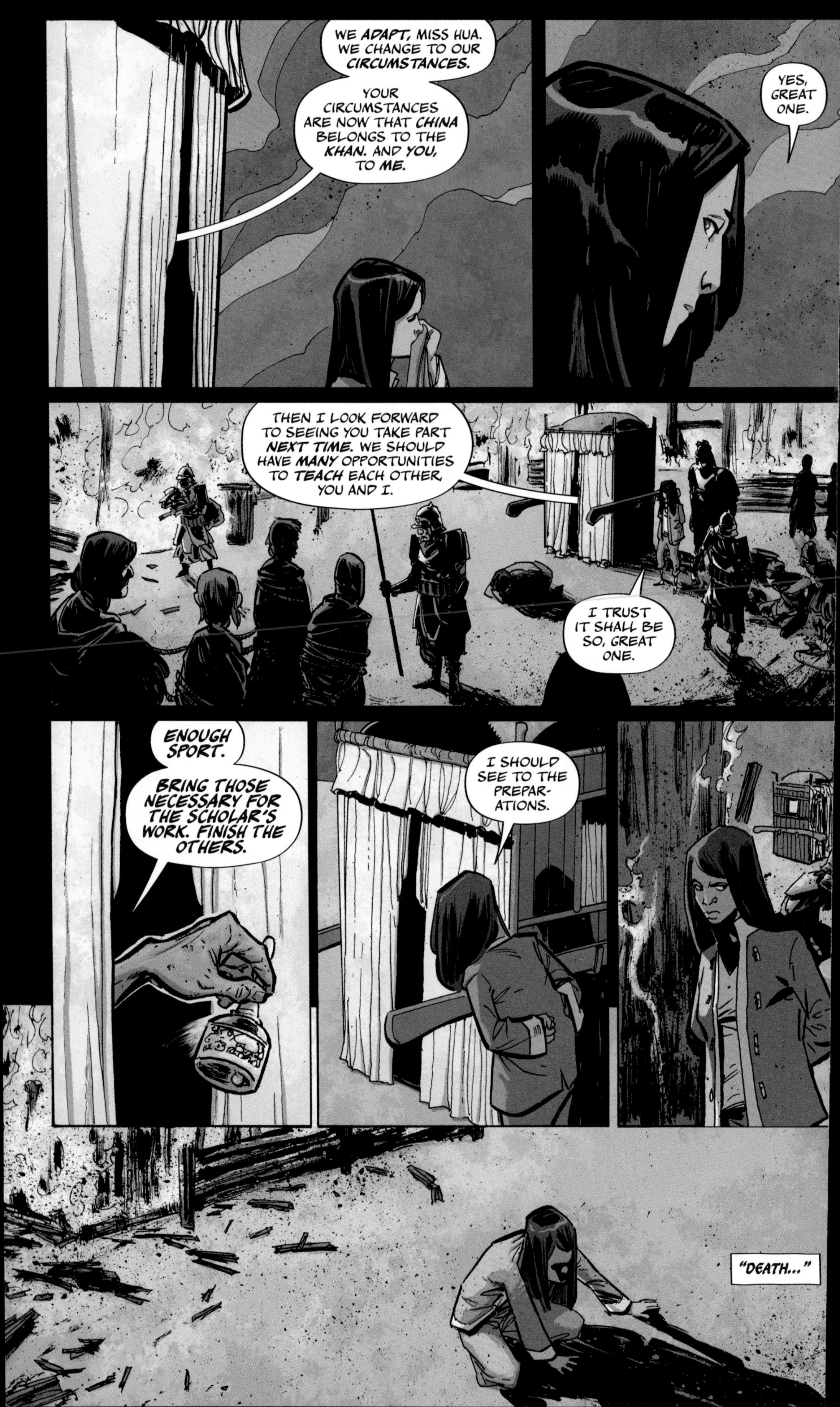
WE ADAPT, MISS HUA. WE CHANGE TO OUR CIRCUMSTANCES.
YOUR CIRCUMSTANCES ARE NOW THAT CHINA BELONGS TO THE KHAN. AND YOU, TO ME.
YES, GREAT ONE.
THEN I LOOK FORWARD TO SEEING YOU TAKE PART NEXT TIME. WE SHOULD HAVE MANY OPPORTUNITIES TO TEACH EACH OTHER, YOU AND I.
I TRUST IT SHALL BE SO, GREAT ONE.
ENOUGH SPORT.
BRING THOSE NECESSARY FOR THE SCHOLAR'S WORK. FINISH THE OTHERS.
I SHOULD SEE TO THE PREPAR- ATIONS.
"DEATH..."

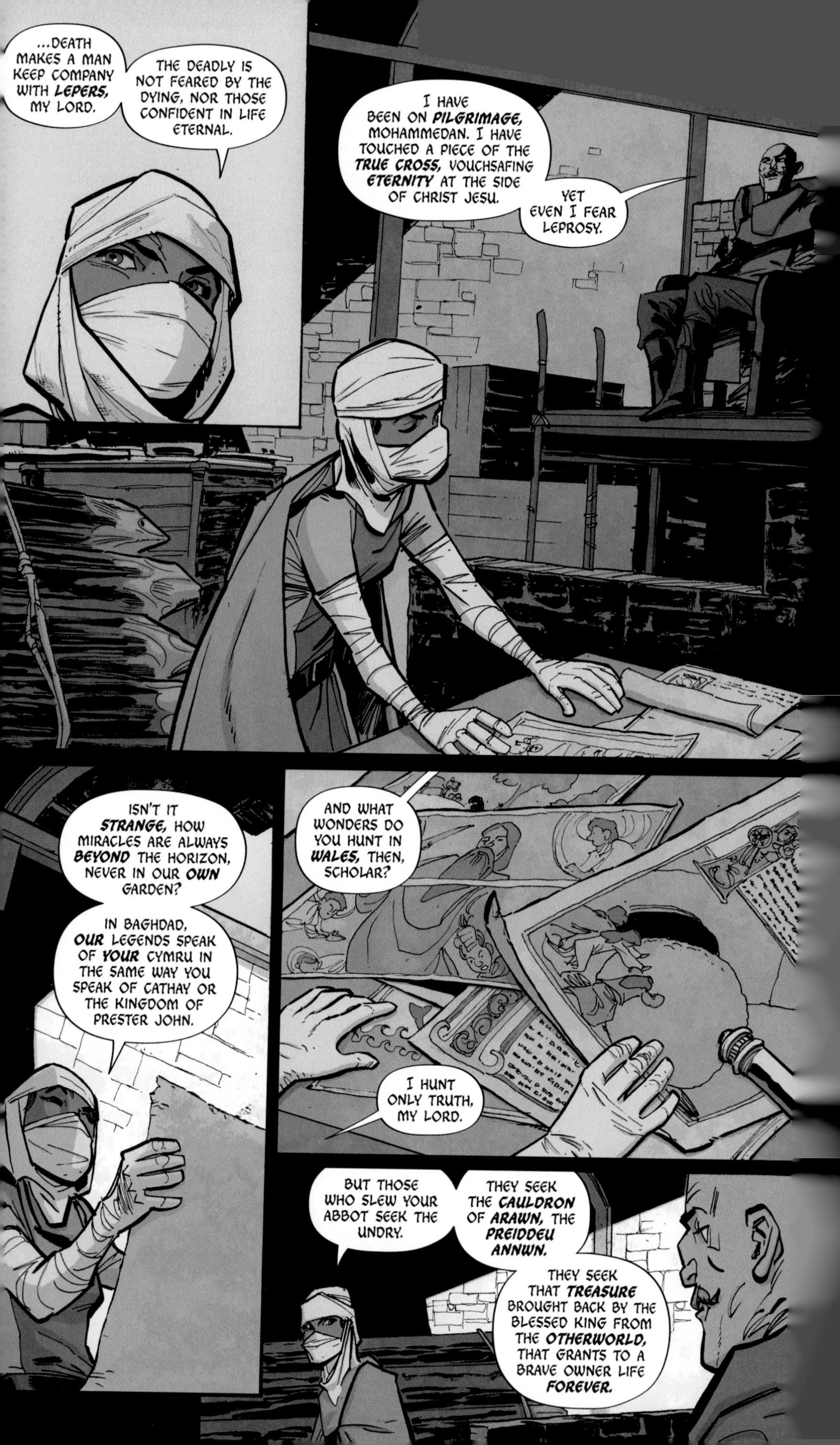
...DEATH MAKES A MAN KEEP COMPANY WITH LEPERS, MY LORD.
THE DEADLY IS NOT FEARED BY THE DYING, NOR THOSE CONFIDENT IN LIFE ETERNAL.
I HAVE BEEN ON PILGRIMAGE, MOHAMMEDAN. I HAVE TOUCHED A PIECE OF THE TRUE CROSS, VOUCHSAFING ETERNITY AT THE SIDE OF CHRIST JESU.
YET EVEN I FEAR LEPROSY.
ISN'T IT STRANGE, HOW MIRACLES ARE ALWAYS BEYOND THE HORIZON, NEVER IN OUR OWN GARDEN?
IN BAGHDAD, OUR LEGENDS SPEAK OF YOUR CYMRU IN THE SAME WAY YOU SPEAK OF CATHAY OR THE KINGDOM OF PRESTER JOHN.
AND WHAT WONDERS DO YOU HUNT IN WALES, THEN, SCHOLAR?
I HUNT ONLY TRUTH, MY LORD.
BUT THOSE WHO SLEW YOUR ABBOT SEEK THE UNDRY.
THEY SEEK THE CAULDRON OF ARAWN, THE PREIDDEU ANNWN.
THEY SEEK THAT TREASURE BROUGHT BACK BY THE BLESSED KING FROM THE OTHERWORLD, THAT GRANTS TO A BRAVE OWNER LIFE FOREVER.

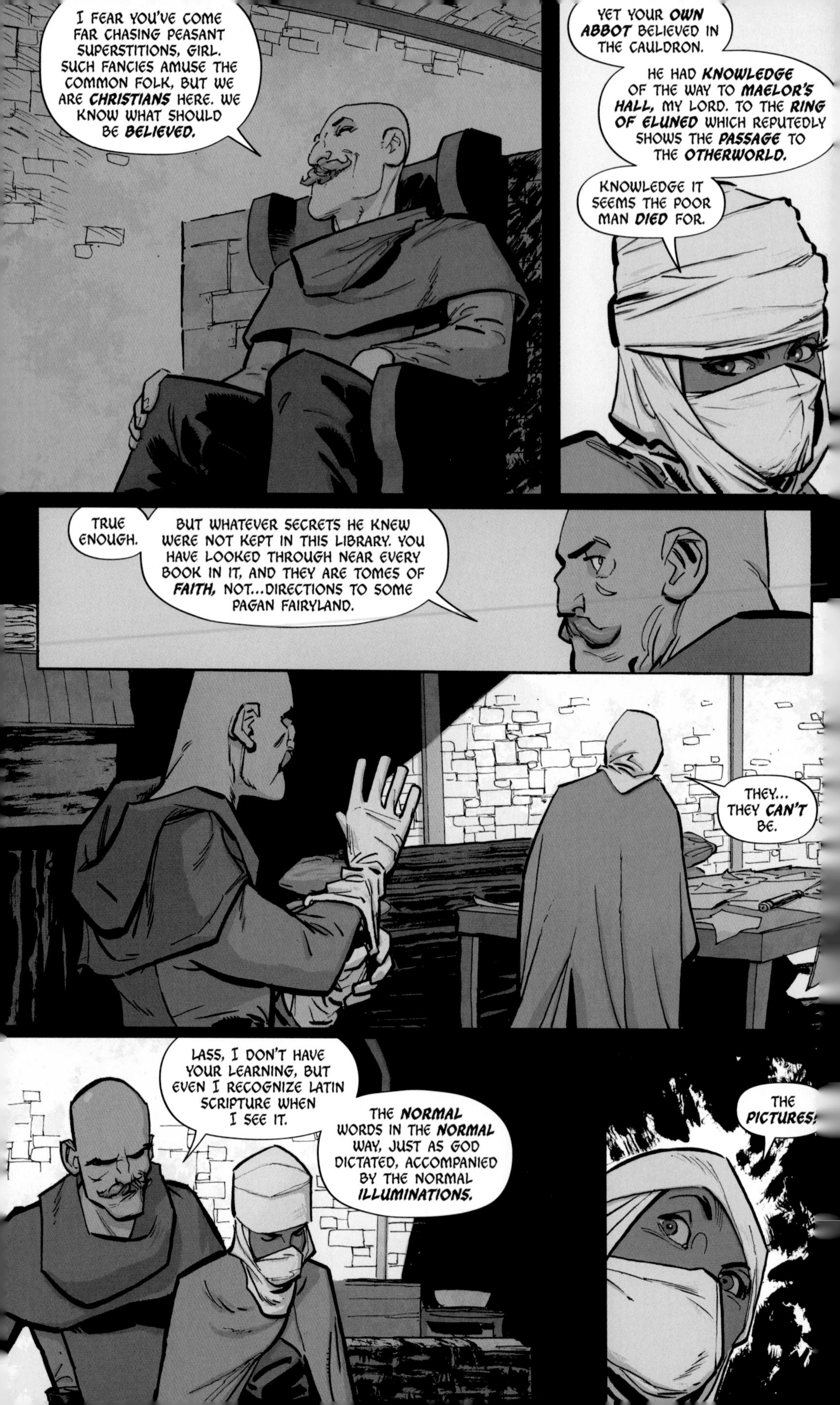
I FEAR YOU'VE COME FAR CHASING PEASANT SUPERSTITIONS, GIRL. SUCH FANCIES AMUSE THE COMMON FOLK, BUT WE ARE CHRISTIANS HERE. WE KNOW WHAT SHOULD BE BELIEVED.
YET YOUR OWN ABBOT BELIEVED IN THE CAULDRON.
HE HAD KNOWLEDGE OF THE WAY TO MAELOR'S HALL, MY LORD. TO THE RING OF ELUNED WHICH REPUTEDLY SHOWS THE PASSAGE TO THE OTHERWORLD.
KNOWLEDGE IT SEEMS THE POOR MAN DIED FOR.
TRUE ENOUGH.
BUT WHATEVER SECRETS HE KNEW WERE NOT KEPT IN THIS LIBRARY. YOU HAVE LOOKED THROUGH NEAR EVERY BOOK IN IT, AND THEY ARE TOMES OF FAITH, NOT...DIRECTIONS TO SOME PAGAN FAIRYLAND.
THEY... THEY CAN'T BE.
LASS, I DON'T HAVE YOUR LEARNING, BUT EVEN I RECOGNIZE LATIN SCRIPTURE WHEN I SEE IT.
THE NORMAL WORDS IN THE NORMAL WAY, JUST AS GOD DICTATED, ACCOMPANIED BY THE NORMAL ILLUMINATIONS.
THE PICTURES!

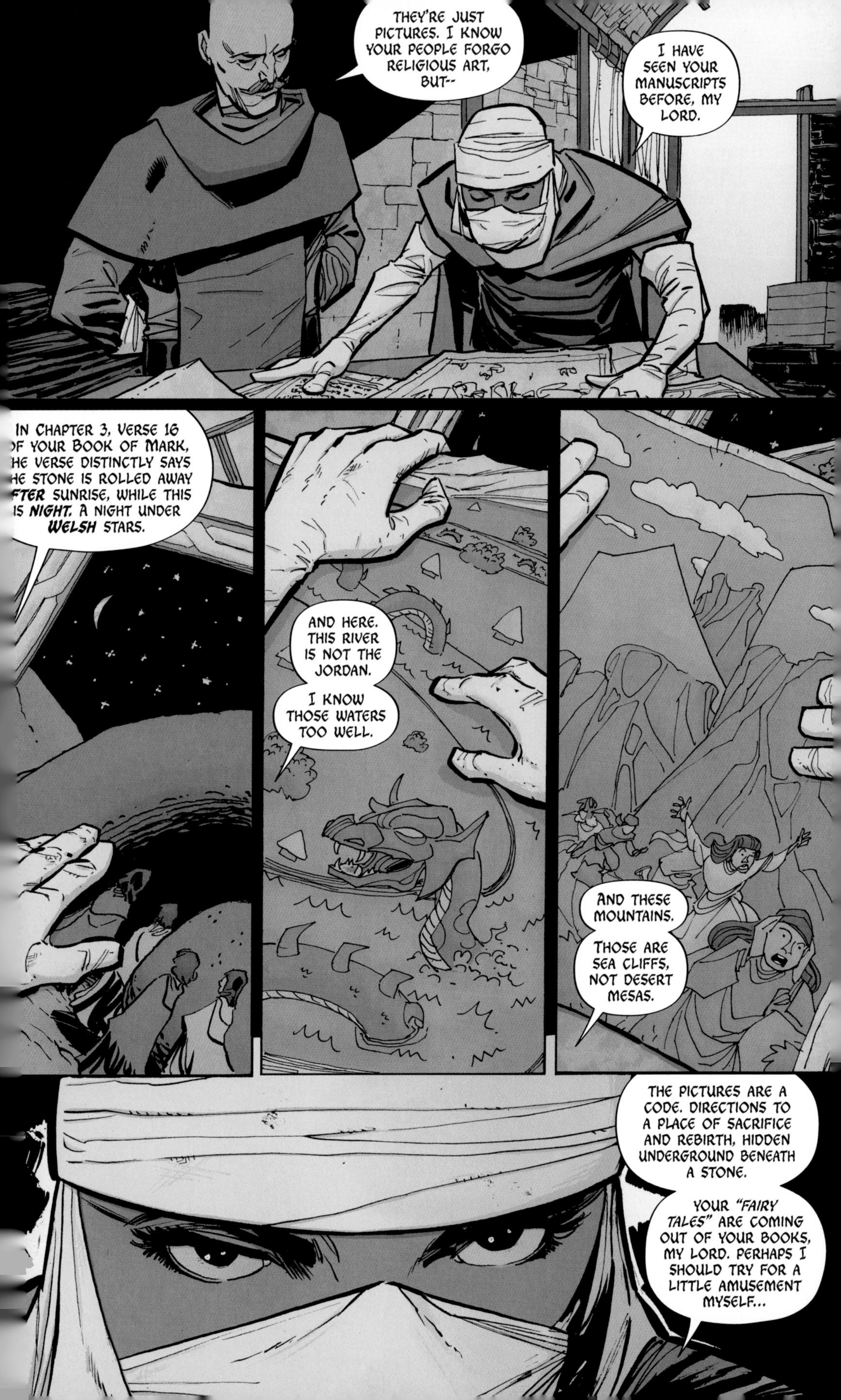
THEY'RE JUST PICTURES. I KNOW YOUR PEOPLE FORGO RELIGIOUS ART, BUT--
I HAVE SEEN YOUR MANUSCRIPTS BEFORE, MY LORD.
IN CHAPTER 3, VERSE 16 OF YOUR BOOK OF MARK, THE VERSE DISTINCTLY SAYS THE STONE IS ROLLED AWAY AFTER SUNRISE, WHILE THIS IS NIGHT. A NIGHT UNDER WELSH STARS.
AND HERE. THIS RIVER IS NOT THE JORDAN.
I KNOW THOSE WATERS TOO WELL.
AND THESE MOUNTAINS.
THOSE ARE SEA CLIFFS, NOT DESERT MESAS.
THE PICTURES ARE A CODE. DIRECTIONS TO A PLACE OF SACRIFICE AND REBIRTH, HIDDEN UNDERGROUND BENEATH A STONE.
YOUR "FAIRY TALES" ARE COMING OUT OF YOUR BOOKS, MY LORD. PERHAPS I SHOULD TRY FOR A LITTLE AMUSEMENT MYSELF...

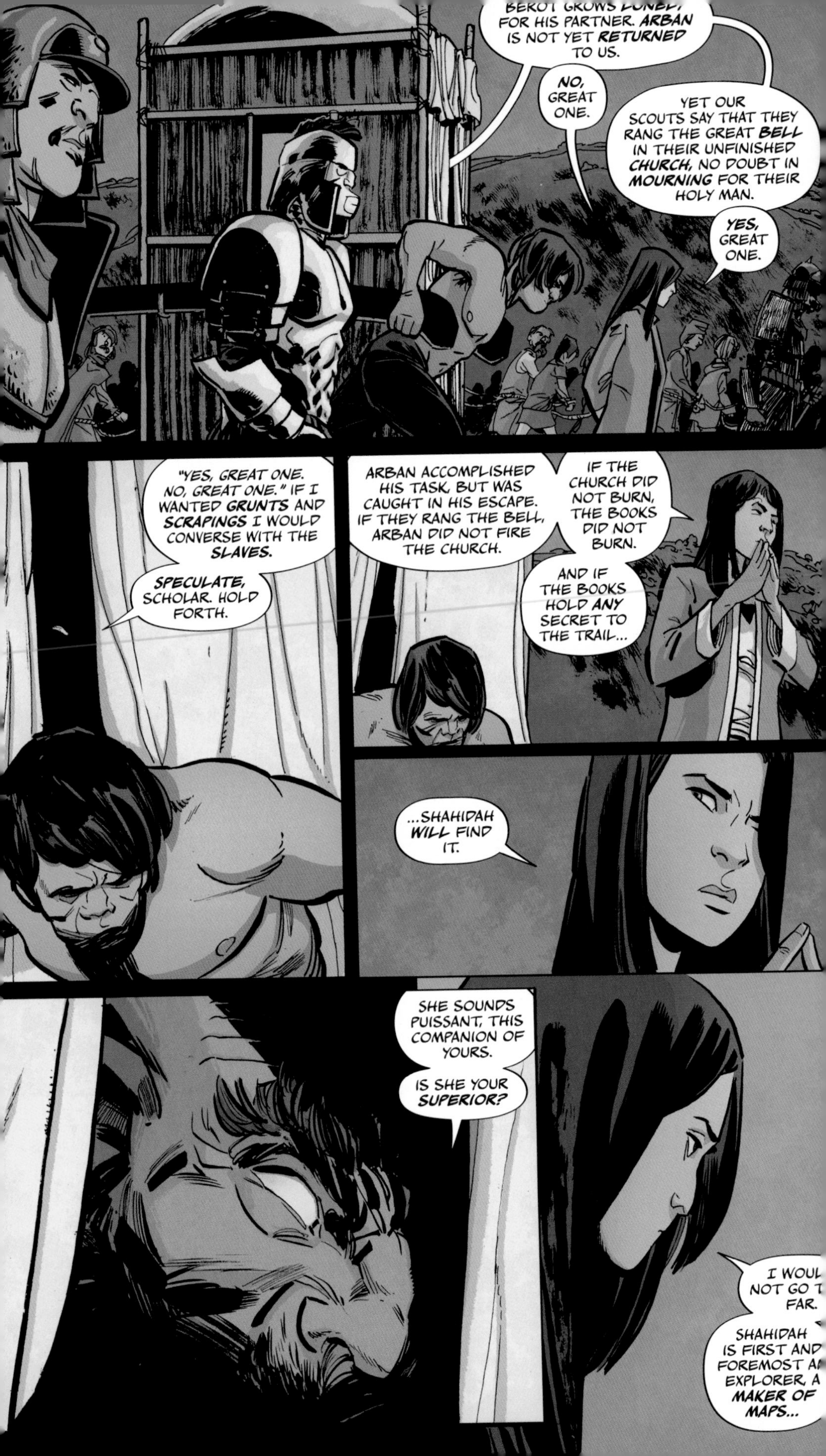
BEROT GROWS
FOR HIS PARTNER. ARBAN IS NOT YET RETURNED TO US.
NO, GREAT ONE.
YET OUR SCOUTS SAY THAT THEY RANG THE GREAT BELL IN THEIR UNFINISHED CHURCH, NO DOUBT IN MOURNING FOR THEIR HOLY MAN.
YES, GREAT ONE.
"YES, GREAT ONE. NO, GREAT ONE." IF I WANTED GRUNTS AND SCRAPINGS I WOULD CONVERSE WITH THE SLAVES.
SPECULATE, SCHOLAR. HOLD FORTH.
ARBAN ACCOMPLISHED HIS TASK, BUT WAS CAUGHT IN HIS ESCAPE. IF THEY RANG THE BELL, ARBAN DID NOT FIRE THE CHURCH.
IF THE CHURCH DID NOT BURN, THE BOOKS DID NOT BURN.
AND IF THE BOOKS HOLD ANY SECRET TO THE TRAIL...
...SHAHIDAH WILL FIND IT.
SHE SOUNDS PUISSANT, THIS COMPANION OF YOURS.
IS SHE YOUR SUPERIOR?
I WOUL NOT GO T FAR.
SHAHIDAH IS FIRST AND FOREMOST A EXPLORER, A MAKER OF MAPS...

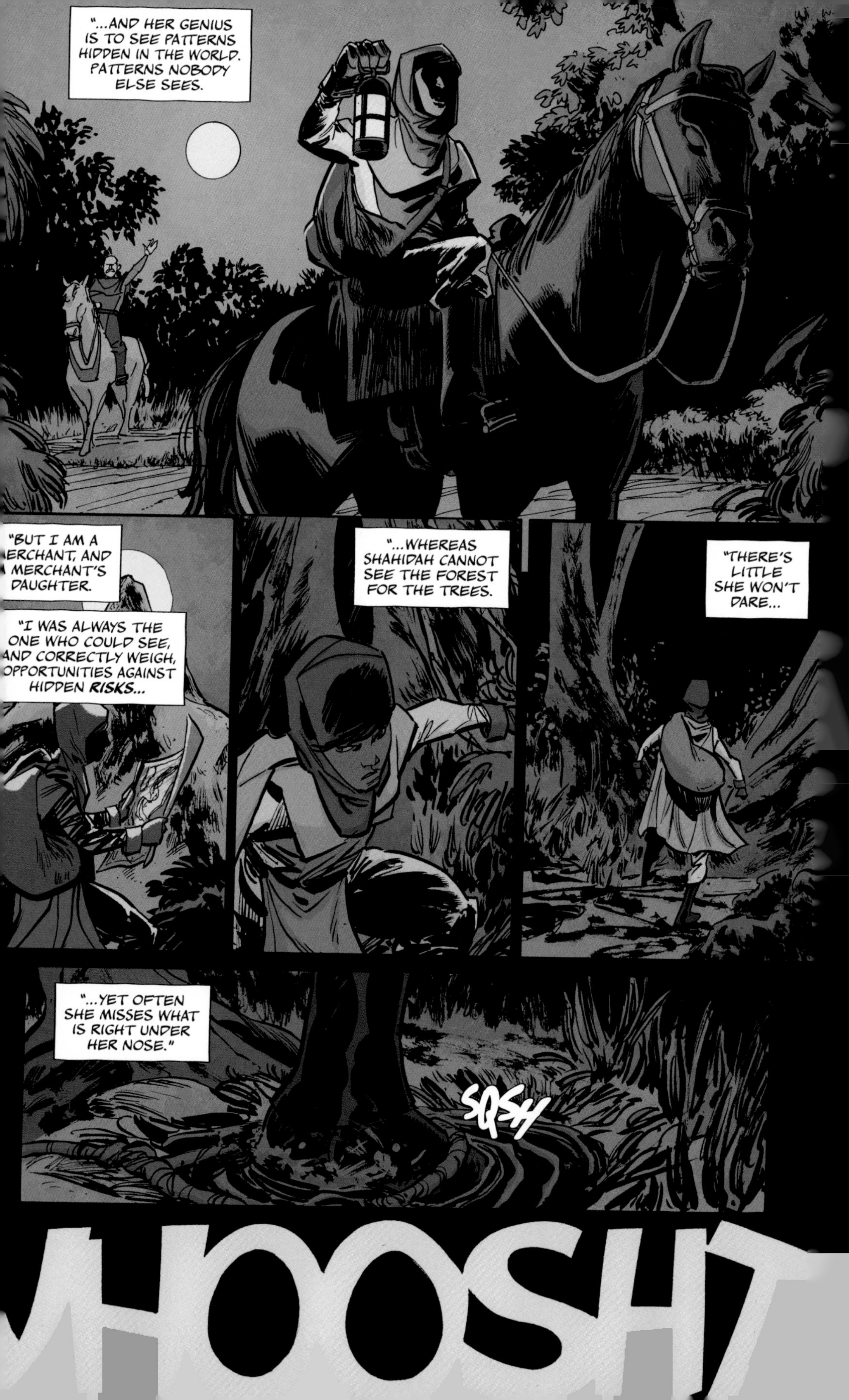
"...AND HER GENIUS IS TO SEE PATTERNS HIDDEN IN THE WORLD. PATTERNS NOBODY ELSE SEES.
"BUT I AM A ERCHANT, AND MERCHANT'S DAUGHTER.
"I WAS ALWAYS THE ONE WHO COULD SEE, ND CORRECTLY WEIGH, PPORTUNITIES AGAINST HIDDEN RISKS...
"...WHEREAS SHAHIDAH CANNOT SEE THE FOREST FOR THE TREES.
"THERE'S LITTLE SHE WON'T DARE...
"...YET OFTEN SHE MISSES WHAT IS RIGHT UNDER HER NOSE."
SQSH
HOOSH

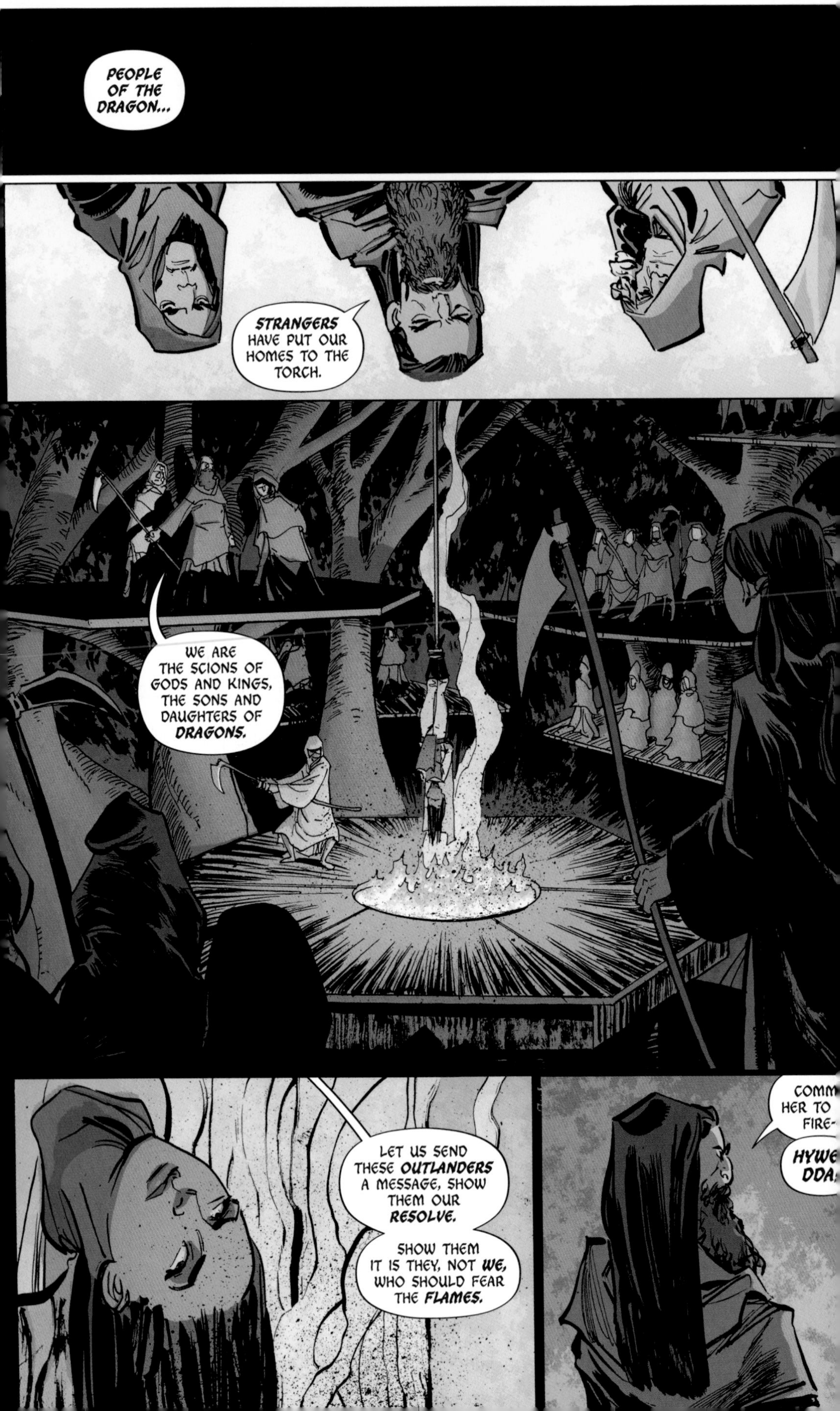
PEOPLE OF THE DRAGON...
STRANGERS HAVE PUT OUR HOMES TO THE TORCH.
WE ARE THE SCIONS OF GODS AND KINGS, THE SONS AND DAUGHTERS OF DRAGONS.
LET US SEND THESE OUTLANDERS A MESSAGE, SHOW THEM OUR RESOLVE.
SHOW THEM IT IS THEY, NOT WE, WHO SHOULD FEAR THE FLAMES.
COMM HER TO FIRE-
HYWE DDA

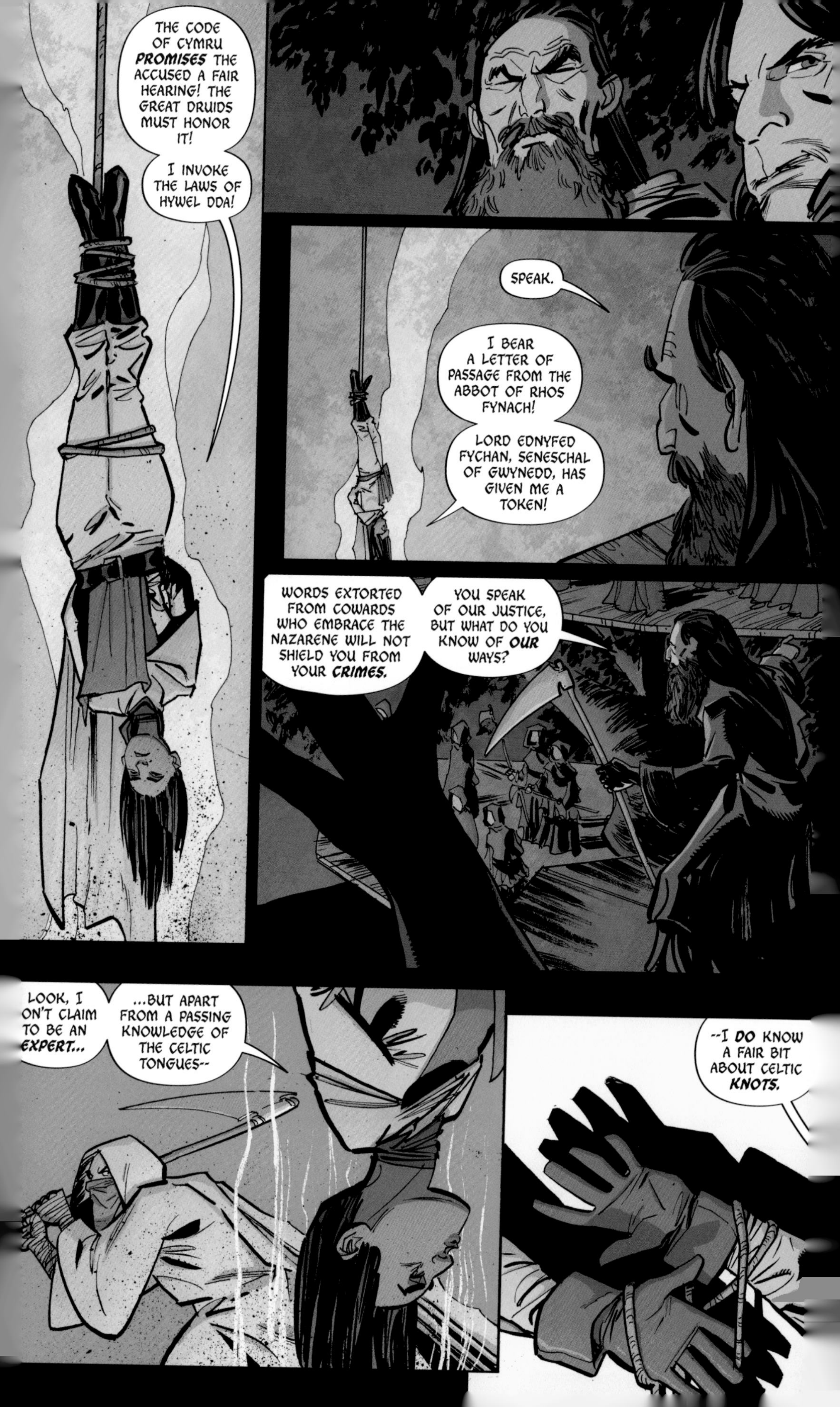
THE CODE OF CYMRU *PROMISES* THE ACCUSED A FAIR HEARING! THE GREAT DRUIDS MUST HONOR IT!
I INVOKE THE LAWS OF HYWEL DDA!
SPEAK.
I BEAR A LETTER OF PASSAGE FROM THE ABBOT OF RHOS FYNACH!
LORD EDNYFED FYCHAN, SENESCHAL OF GWYNEDD, HAS GIVEN ME A TOKEN!
WORDS EXTORTED FROM COWARDS WHO EMBRACE THE NAZARENE WILL NOT SHIELD YOU FROM YOUR *CRIMES.*
YOU SPEAK OF OUR JUSTICE, BUT WHAT DO YOU KNOW OF *OUR* WAYS?
LOOK, I ON'T CLAIM TO BE AN *EXPERT...*
...BUT APART FROM A PASSING KNOWLEDGE OF THE CELTIC TONGUES--
--I *DO* KNOW A FAIR BIT ABOUT CELTIC *KNOTS.*

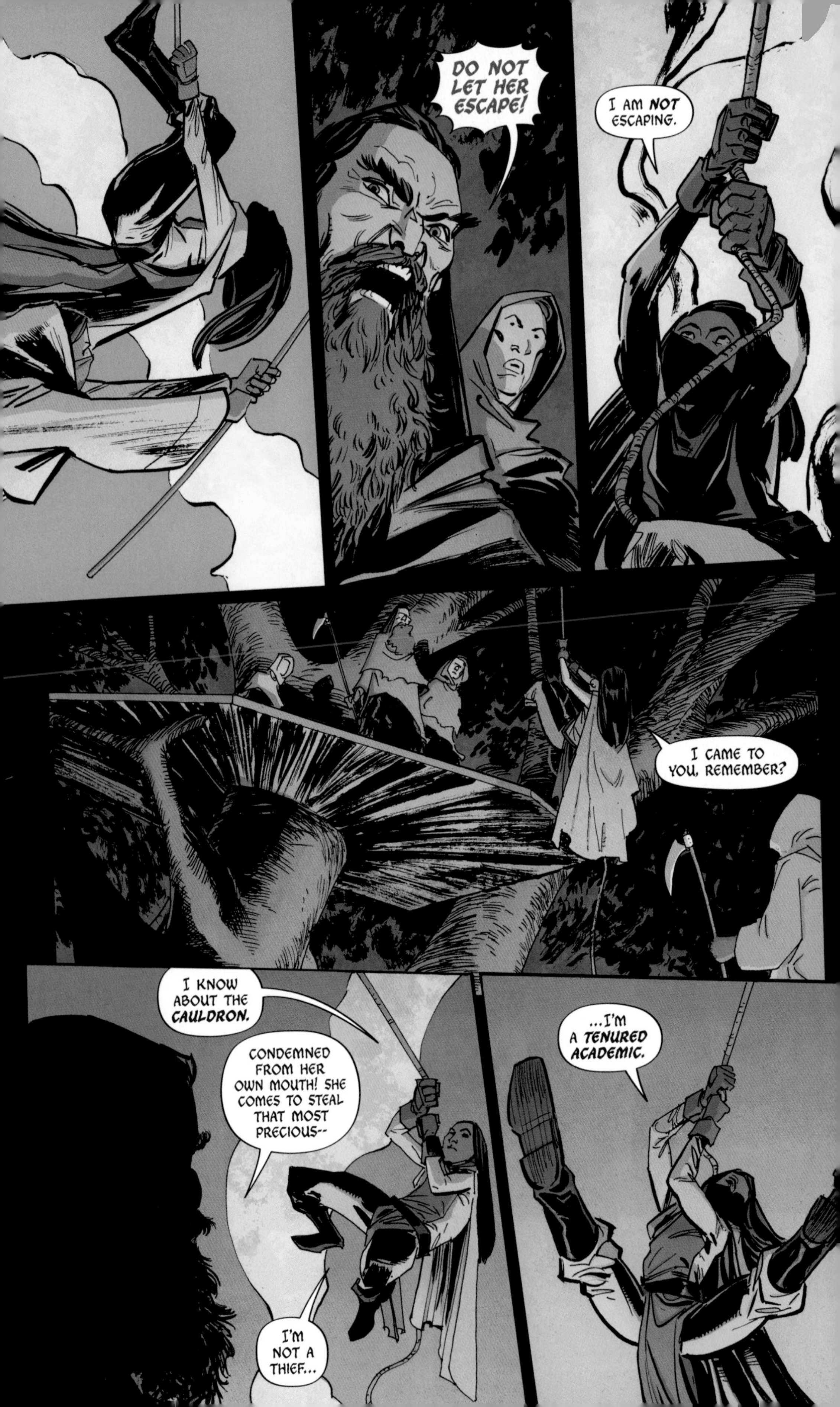
DO NOT LET HER ESCAPE!
I AM NOT ESCAPING.
I CAME TO YOU, REMEMBER?
I KNOW ABOUT THE CAULDRON.
CONDEMNED FROM HER OWN MOUTH! SHE COMES TO STEAL THAT MOST PRECIOUS--
I'M NOT A THIEF...
...I'M A TENURED ACADEMIC.

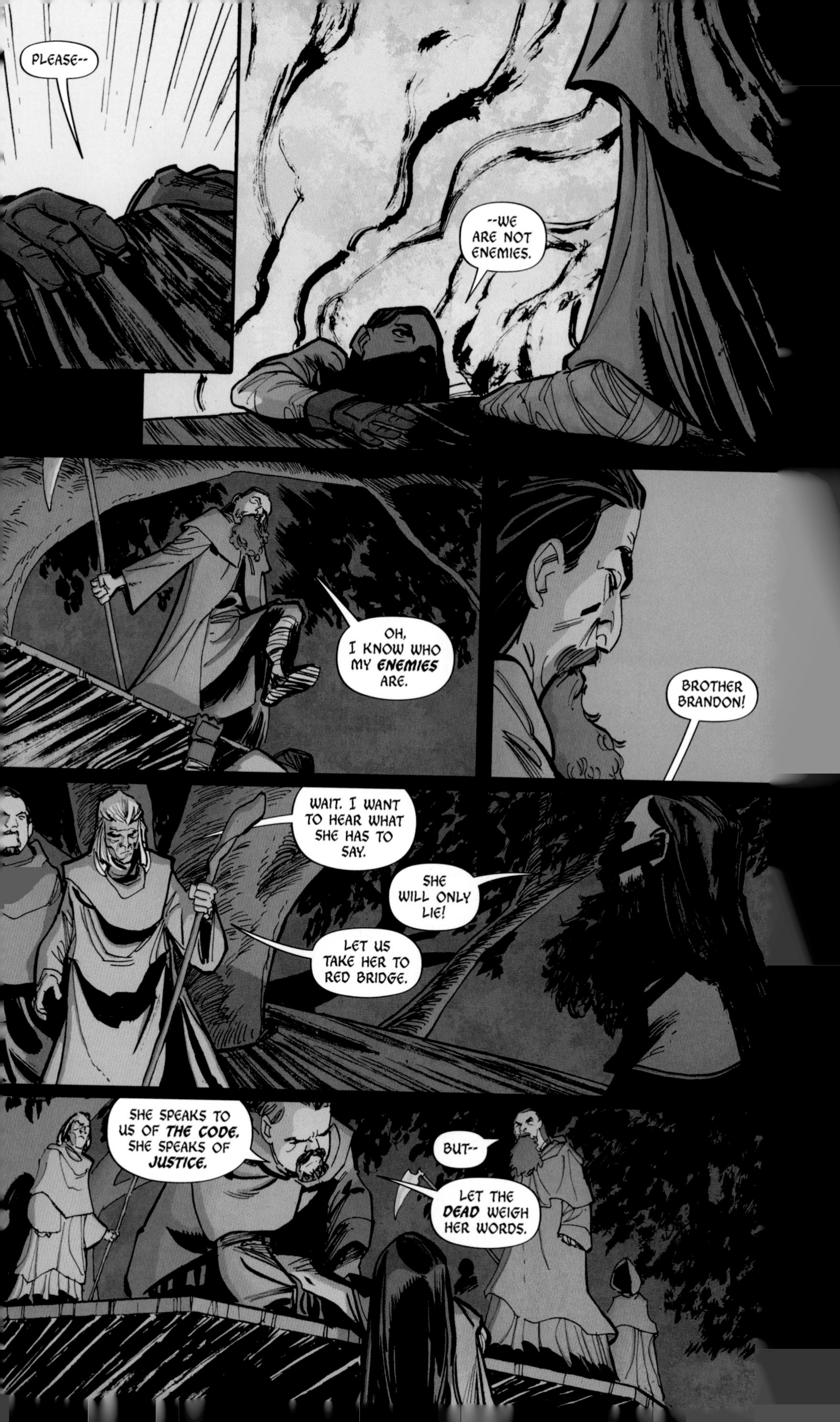
PLEASE--
--WE ARE NOT ENEMIES.
OH, I KNOW WHO MY ENEMIES ARE.
BROTHER BRANDON!
WAIT. I WANT TO HEAR WHAT SHE HAS TO SAY.
SHE WILL ONLY LIE!
LET US TAKE HER TO RED BRIDGE.
SHE SPEAKS TO US OF THE CODE. SHE SPEAKS OF JUSTICE.
BUT--
LET THE DEAD WEIGH HER WORDS.

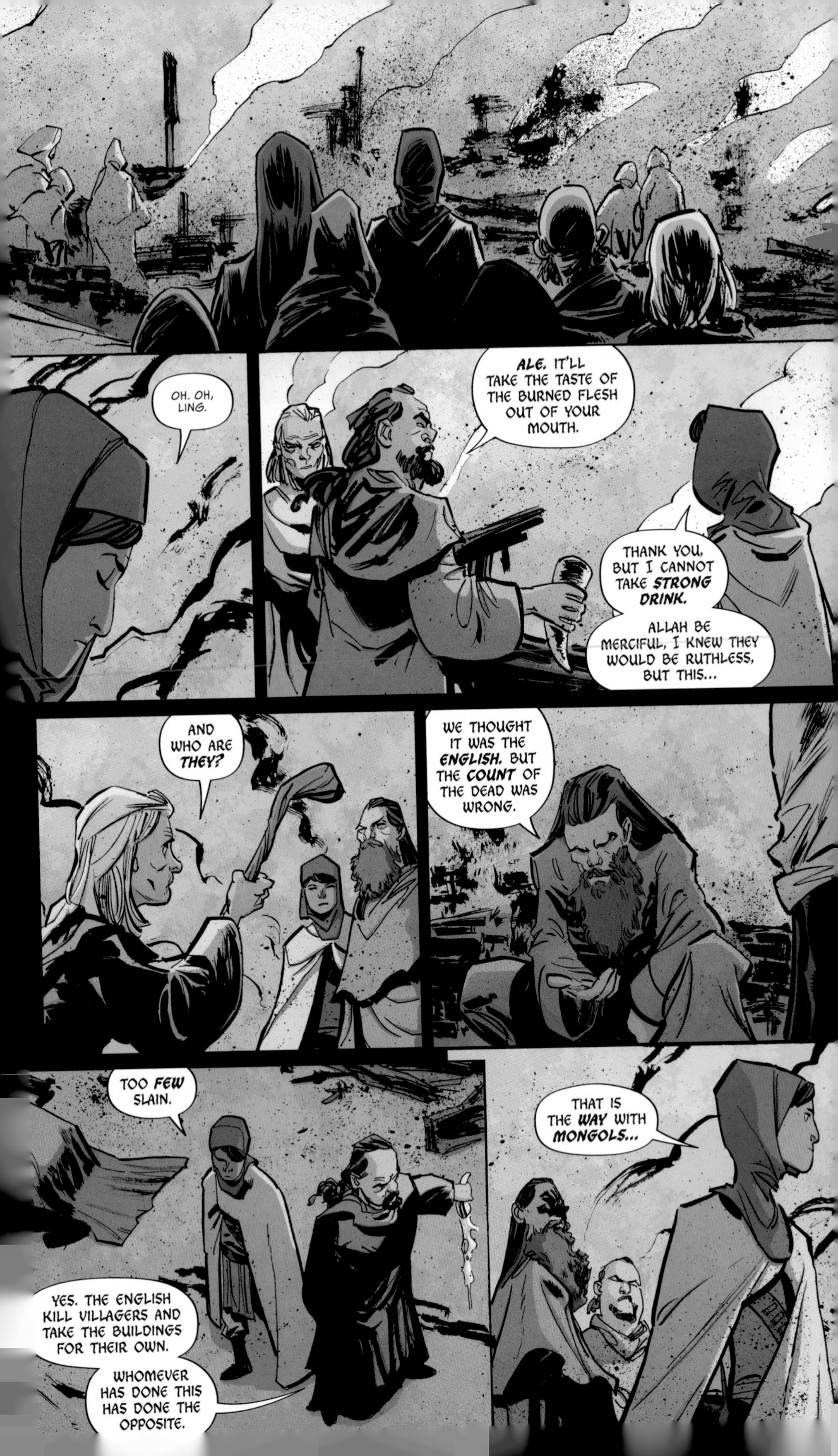
OH. OH, LING.
ALE. IT'LL TAKE THE TASTE OF THE BURNED FLESH OUT OF YOUR MOUTH.
THANK YOU, BUT I CANNOT TAKE STRONG DRINK.
ALLAH BE MERCIFUL, I KNEW THEY WOULD BE RUTHLESS, BUT THIS...
AND WHO ARE THEY?
WE THOUGHT IT WAS THE ENGLISH. BUT THE COUNT OF THE DEAD WAS WRONG.
TOO FEW SLAIN.
YES. THE ENGLISH KILL VILLAGERS AND TAKE THE BUILDINGS FOR THEIR OWN.
WHOMEVER HAS DONE THIS HAS DONE THE OPPOSITE.
THAT IS THE WAY WITH MONGOLS...

ARE **CONQUERORS,** BUT THEY HAVE NOT COME FOR **LAND.**

"THEY ARE **SLAVERS,** BUT THEIR INTEREST IN YOUR PEOPLE IS ONLY IN SO FAR AS IT LEADS TO THE **TREASURE** YOU GUARD."

YEEAAAAARGH!

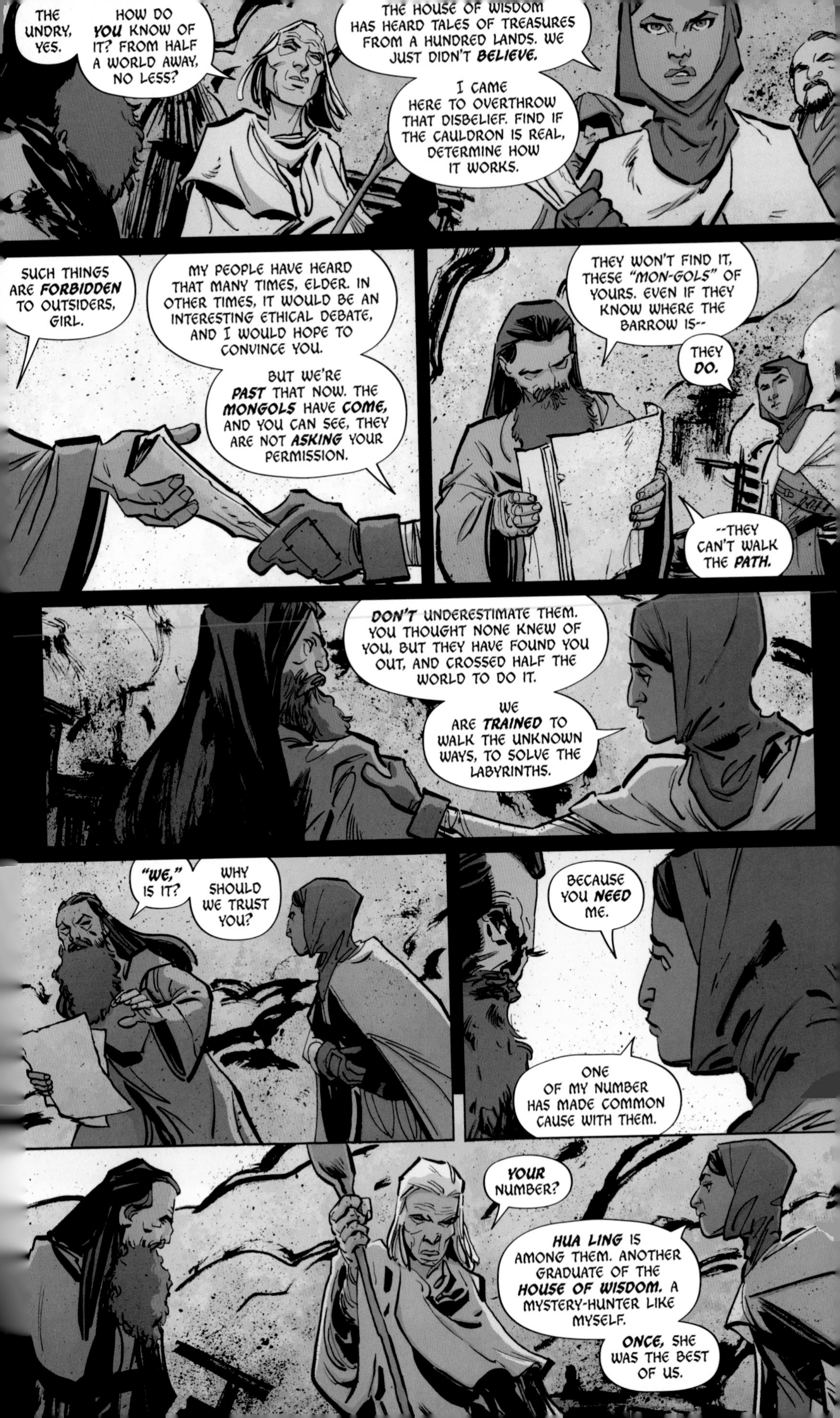

THE UNDRY, YES.
HOW DO YOU KNOW OF IT? FROM HALF A WORLD AWAY, NO LESS?
THE HOUSE OF WISDOM HAS HEARD TALES OF TREASURES FROM A HUNDRED LANDS. WE JUST DIDN'T BELIEVE.
I CAME HERE TO OVERTHROW THAT DISBELIEF. FIND IF THE CAULDRON IS REAL, DETERMINE HOW IT WORKS.
SUCH THINGS ARE FORBIDDEN TO OUTSIDERS, GIRL.
MY PEOPLE HAVE HEARD THAT MANY TIMES, ELDER. IN OTHER TIMES, IT WOULD BE AN INTERESTING ETHICAL DEBATE, AND I WOULD HOPE TO CONVINCE YOU.
BUT WE'RE PAST THAT NOW. THE MONGOLS HAVE COME, AND YOU CAN SEE, THEY ARE NOT ASKING YOUR PERMISSION.
THEY WON'T FIND IT, THESE "MON-GOLS" OF YOURS. EVEN IF THEY KNOW WHERE THE BARROW IS--
THEY DO.
--THEY CAN'T WALK THE PATH.
DON'T UNDERESTIMATE THEM. YOU THOUGHT NONE KNEW OF YOU, BUT THEY HAVE FOUND YOU OUT, AND CROSSED HALF THE WORLD TO DO IT.
WE ARE TRAINED TO WALK THE UNKNOWN WAYS, TO SOLVE THE LABYRINTHS.
"WE," IS IT?
WHY SHOULD WE TRUST YOU?
BECAUSE YOU NEED ME.
ONE OF MY NUMBER HAS MADE COMMON CAUSE WITH THEM.
YOUR NUMBER?
HUA LING IS AMONG THEM. ANOTHER GRADUATE OF THE HOUSE OF WISDOM. A MYSTERY-HUNTER LIKE MYSELF.
ONCE, SHE WAS THE BEST OF US.

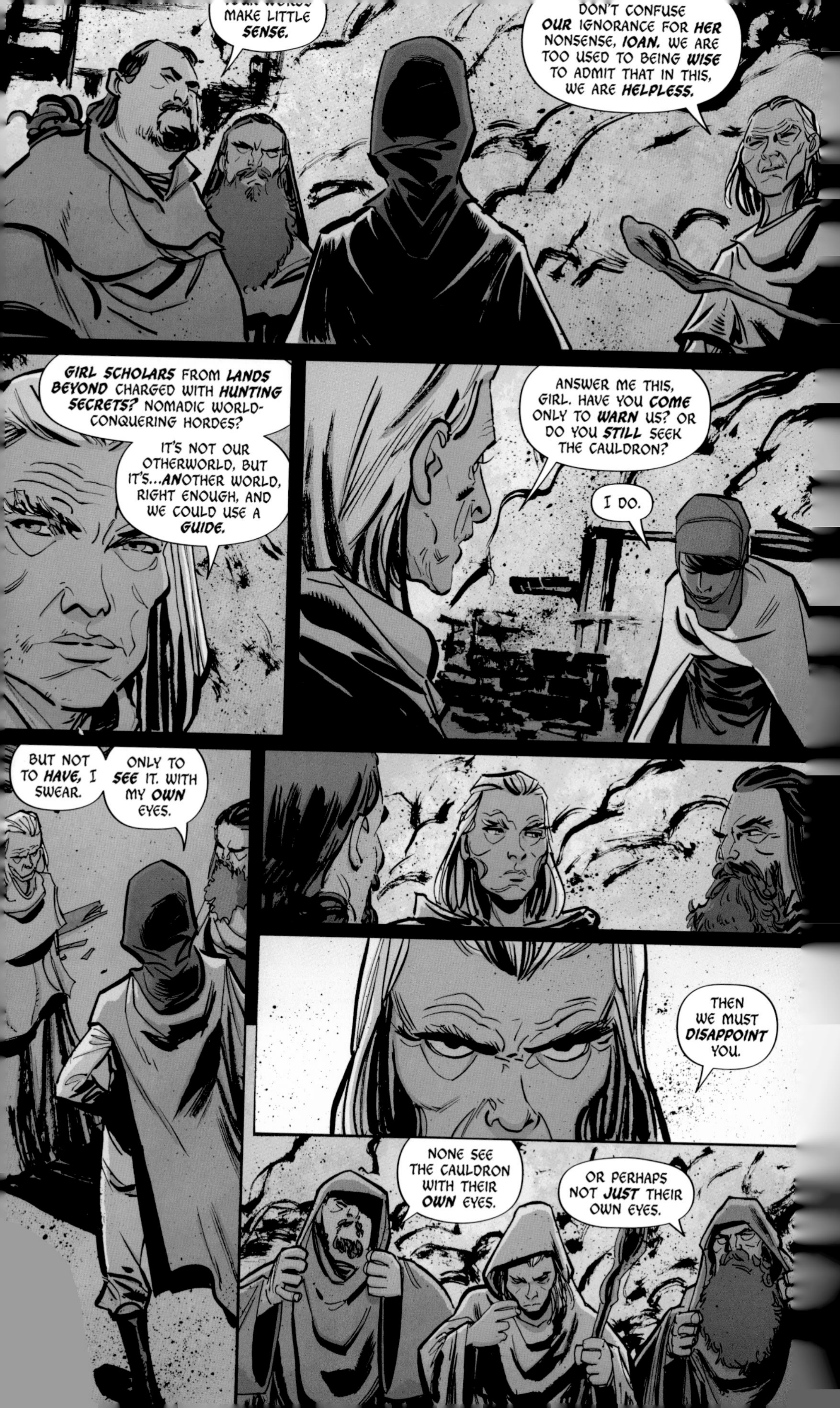
MAKE LITTLE SENSE.
DON'T CONFUSE OUR IGNORANCE FOR HER NONSENSE, IOAN. WE ARE TOO USED TO BEING WISE TO ADMIT THAT IN THIS, WE ARE HELPLESS.
GIRL SCHOLARS FROM LANDS BEYOND CHARGED WITH HUNTING SECRETS? NOMADIC WORLD-CONQUERING HORDES?
IT'S NOT OUR OTHERWORLD, BUT IT'S...ANOTHER WORLD, RIGHT ENOUGH, AND WE COULD USE A GUIDE.
ANSWER ME THIS, GIRL. HAVE YOU COME ONLY TO WARN US? OR DO YOU STILL SEEK THE CAULDRON?
I DO.
BUT NOT TO HAVE, I SWEAR.
ONLY TO SEE IT. WITH MY OWN EYES.
THEN WE MUST DISAPPOINT YOU.
NONE SEE THE CAULDRON WITH THEIR OWN EYES.
OR PERHAPS NOT JUST THEIR OWN EYES.

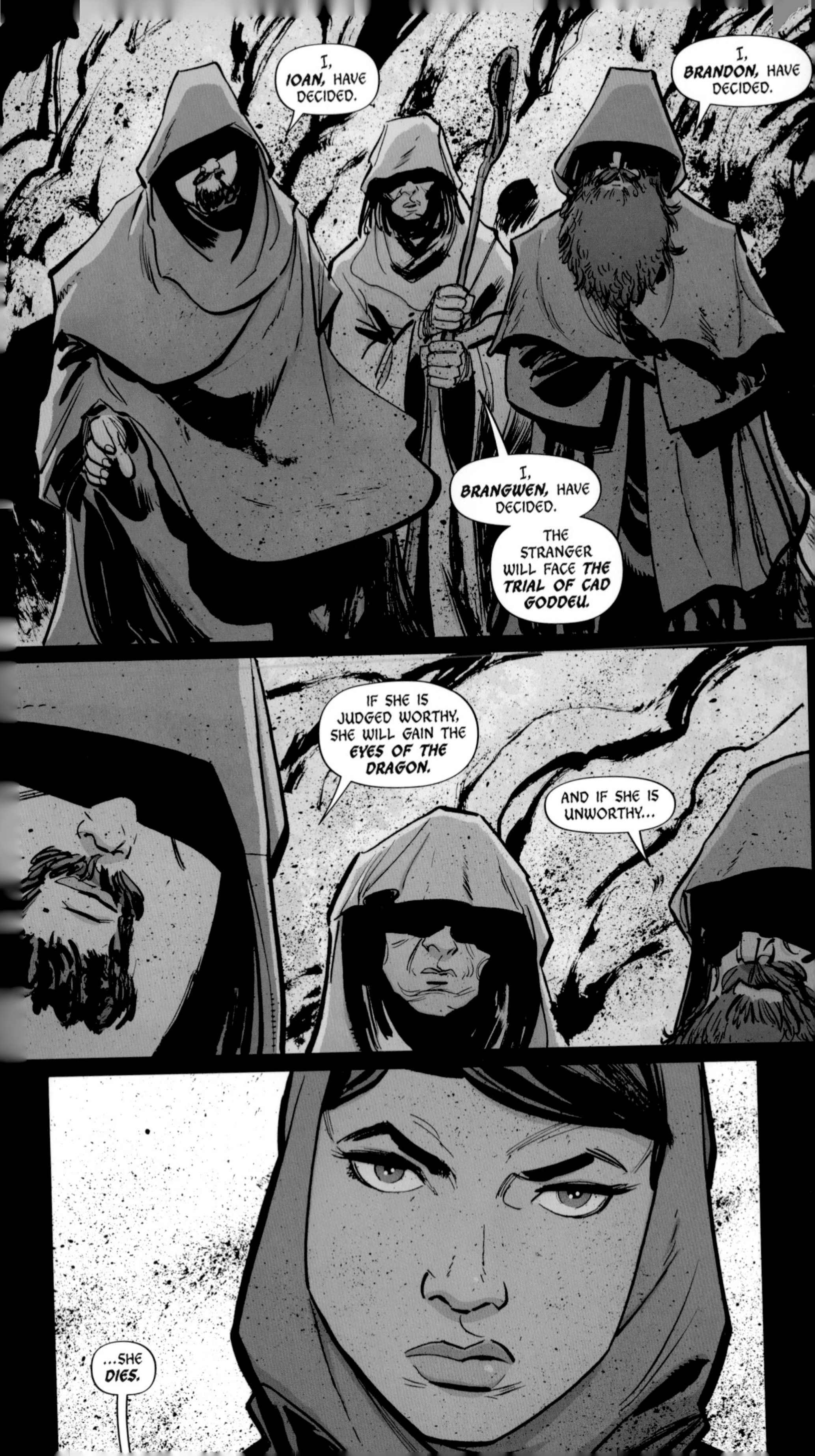
I, IOAN, HAVE DECIDED.
I, BRANDON, HAVE DECIDED.
I, BRANGWEN, HAVE DECIDED.
THE STRANGER WILL FACE THE TRIAL OF CAD GODDEU.
IF SHE IS JUDGED WORTHY, SHE WILL GAIN THE EYES OF THE DRAGON.
AND IF SHE IS UNWORTHY...
...SHE DIES.

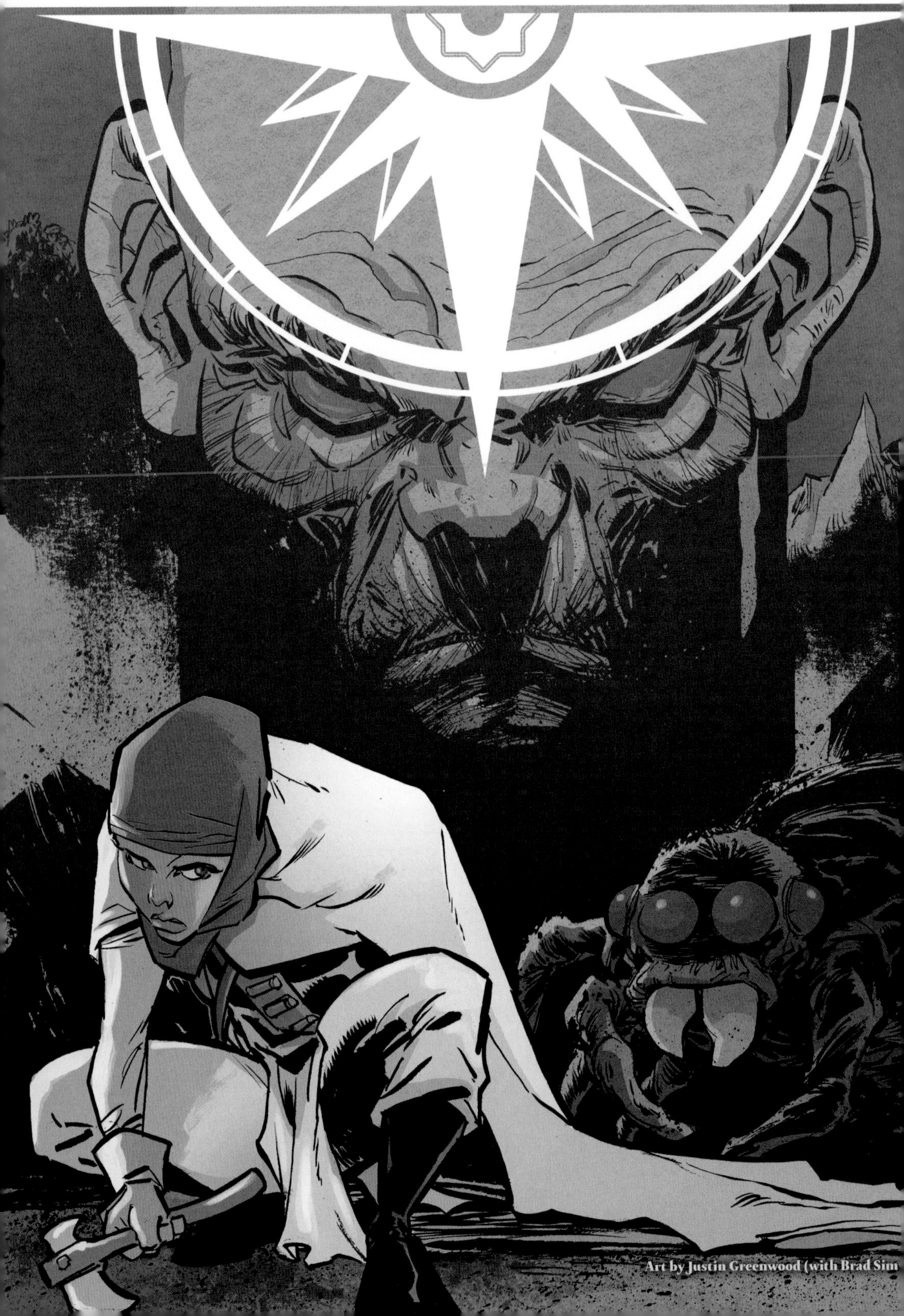

Art by Justin Greenwood (with Brad Sim

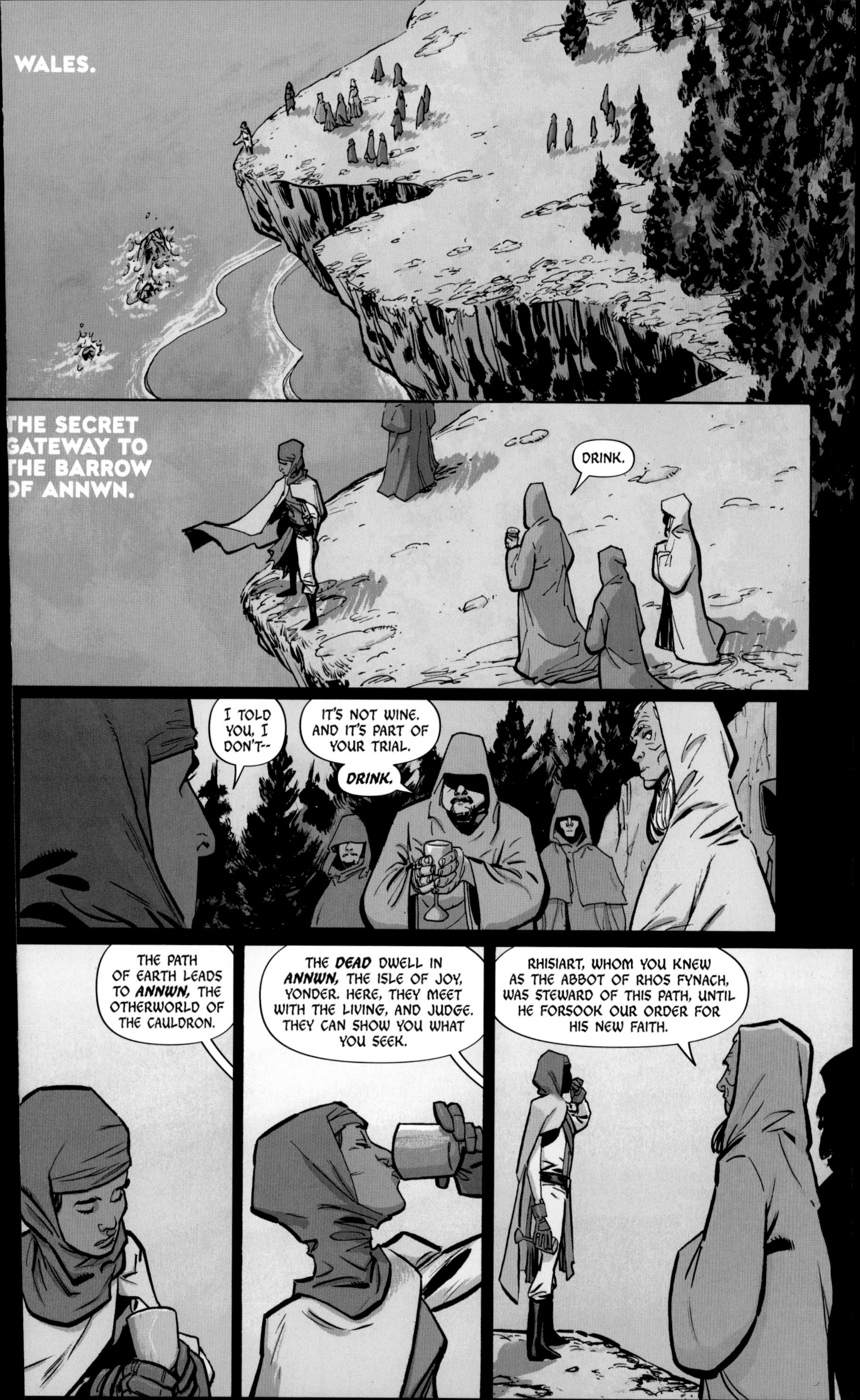
WALES.
THE SECRET GATEWAY TO THE BARROW OF ANNWN.
DRINK.
I TOLD YOU, I DON'T--
IT'S NOT WINE. AND IT'S PART OF YOUR TRIAL.
DRINK.
THE PATH OF EARTH LEADS TO ANNWN, THE OTHERWORLD OF THE CAULDRON.
THE DEAD DWELL IN ANNWN, THE ISLE OF JOY, YONDER. HERE, THEY MEET WITH THE LIVING, AND JUDGE. THEY CAN SHOW YOU WHAT YOU SEEK.
RHISIART, WHOM YOU KNEW AS THE ABBOT OF RHOS FYNACH, WAS STEWARD OF THIS PATH, UNTIL HE FORSOOK OUR ORDER FOR HIS NEW FAITH.

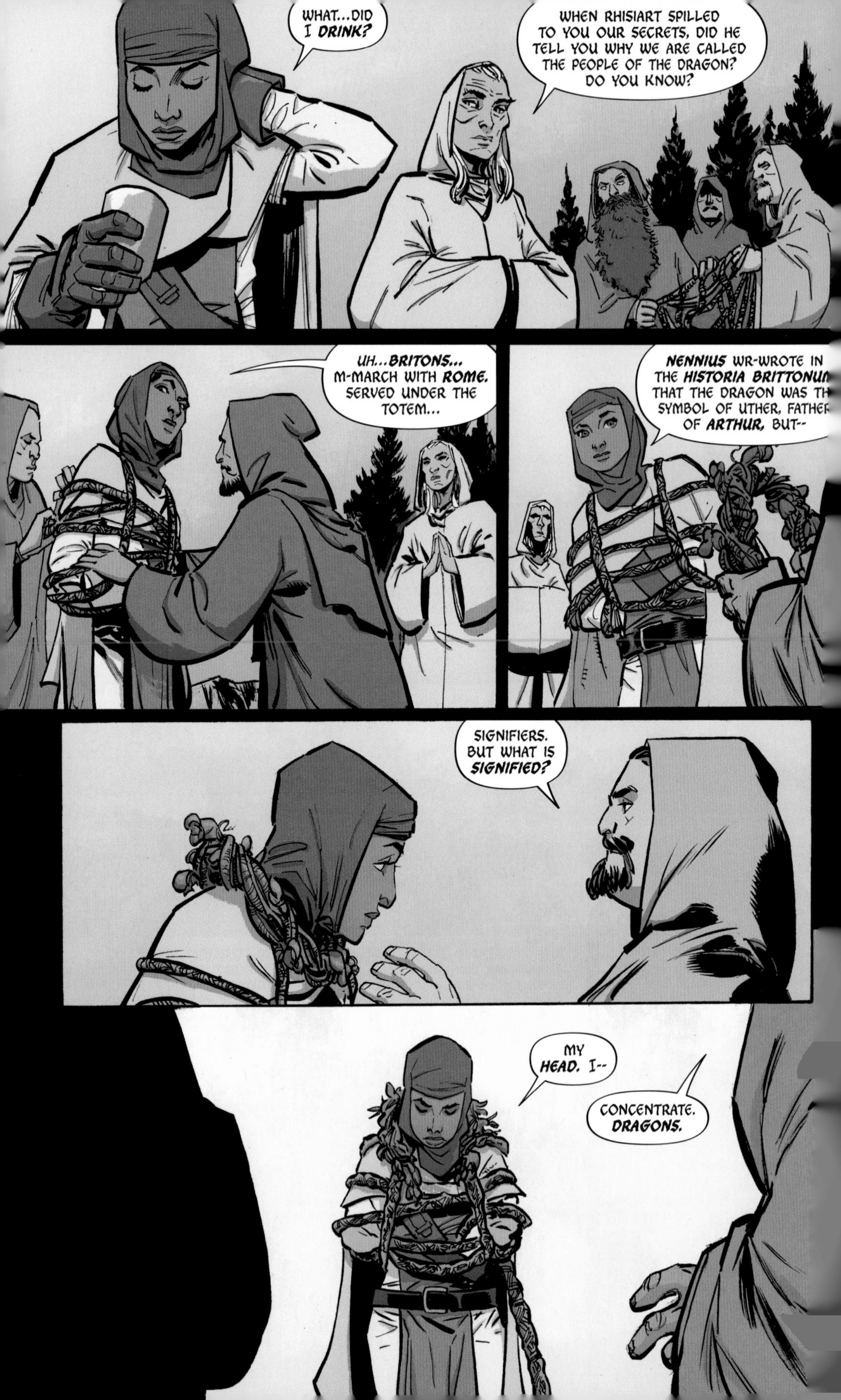
WHAT...DID I DRINK?
WHEN RHISIART SPILLED TO YOU OUR SECRETS, DID HE TELL YOU WHY WE ARE CALLED THE PEOPLE OF THE DRAGON? DO YOU KNOW?
UH...BRITONS... M-MARCH WITH ROME. SERVED UNDER THE TOTEM...
NENNIUS WR-WROTE IN THE HISTORIA BRITTONUM THAT THE DRAGON WAS THE SYMBOL OF UTHER, FATHER OF ARTHUR, BUT--
SIGNIFIERS. BUT WHAT IS SIGNIFIED?
MY HEAD. I--
CONCENTRATE. DRAGONS.

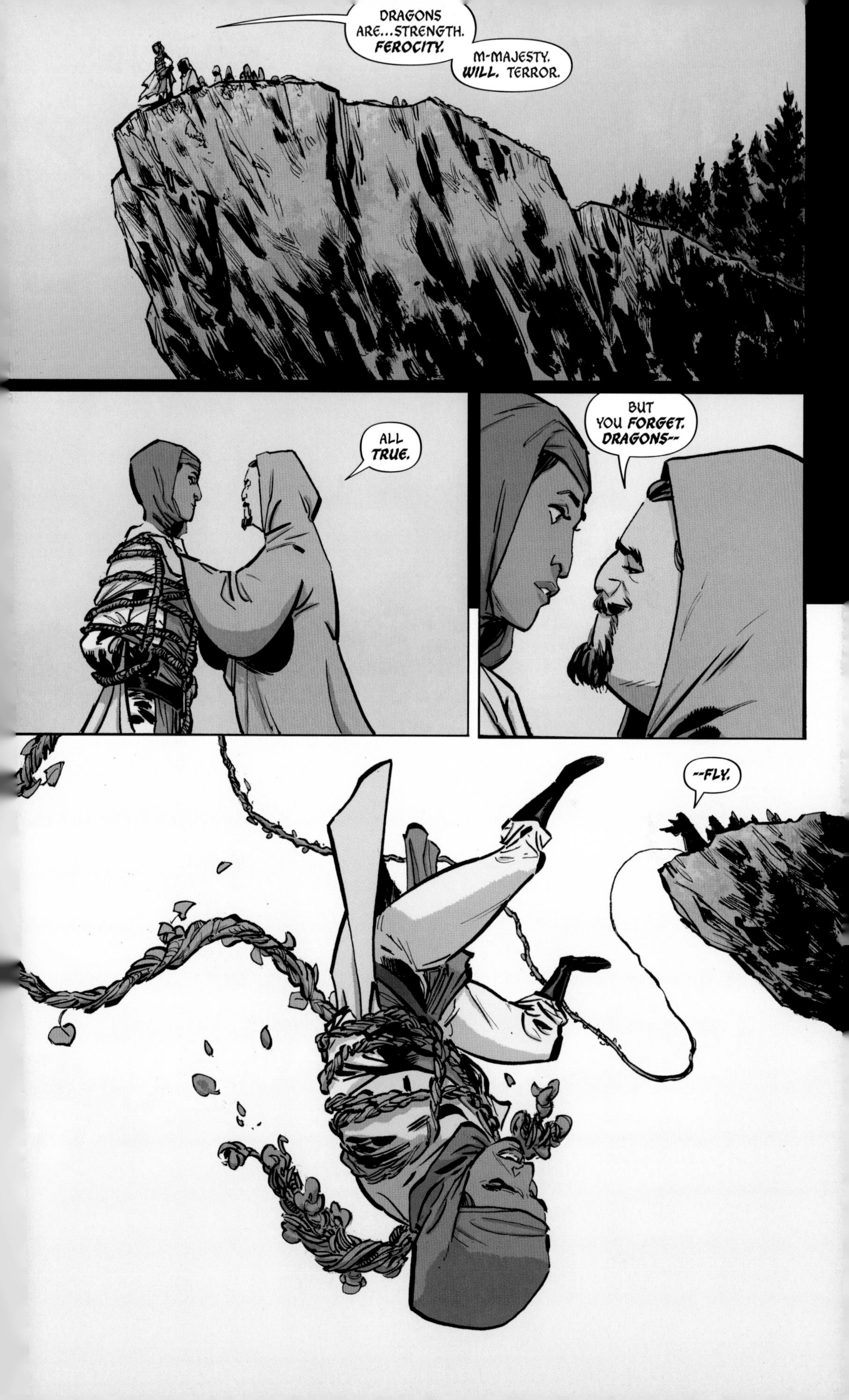
DRAGONS ARE...STRENGTH. FEROCITY.
M-MAJESTY. WILL. TERROR.
ALL TRUE.
BUT YOU FORGET. DRAGONS--
--FLY.

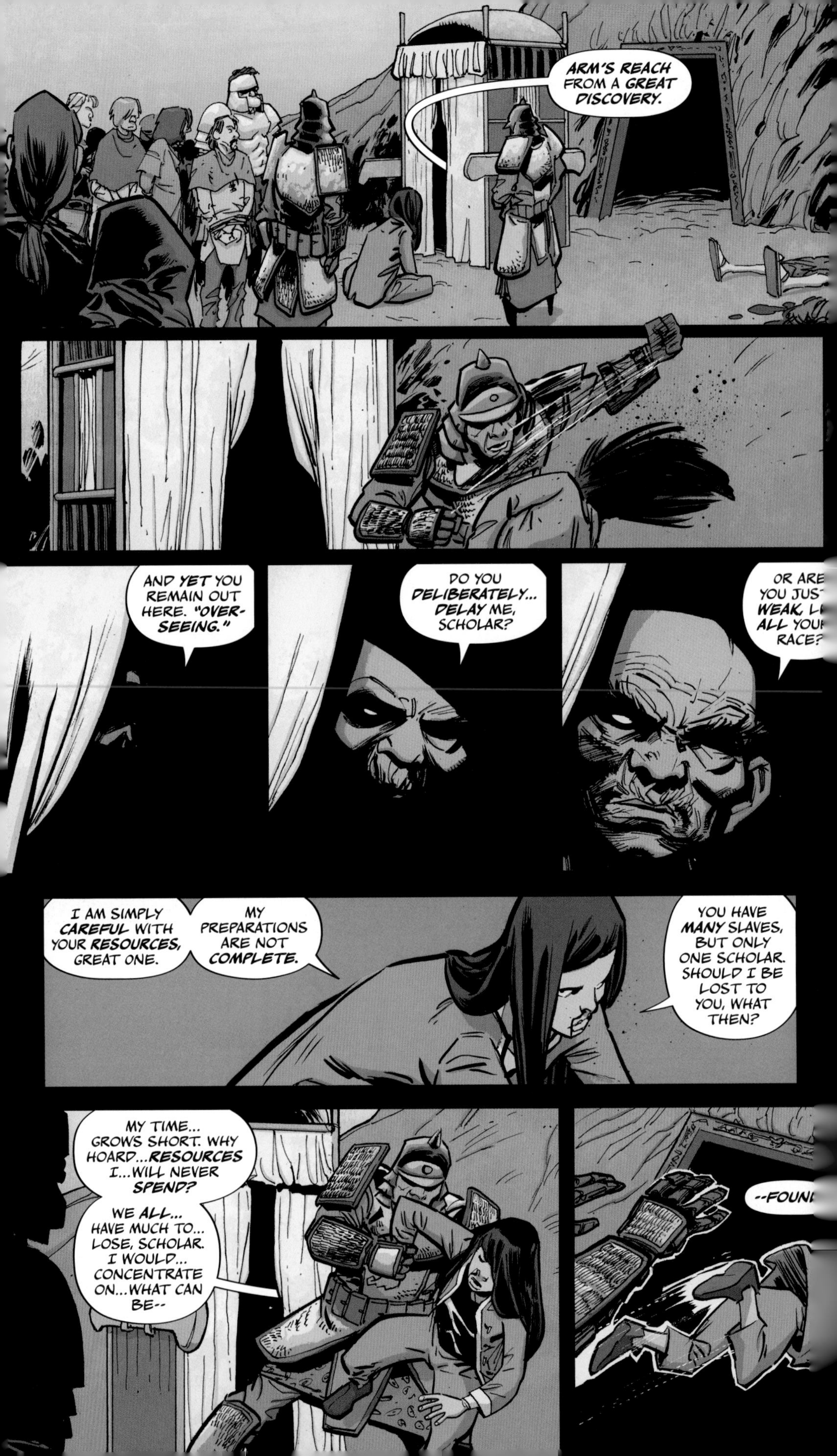
ARM'S REACH FROM A GREAT DISCOVERY.
AND YET YOU REMAIN OUT HERE. "OVER-SEEING."
DO YOU DELIBERATELY... DELAY ME, SCHOLAR?
OR ARE YOU JUST WEAK, L ALL YOUR RACE?
I AM SIMPLY CAREFUL WITH YOUR RESOURCES, GREAT ONE.
MY PREPARATIONS ARE NOT COMPLETE.
YOU HAVE MANY SLAVES, BUT ONLY ONE SCHOLAR. SHOULD I BE LOST TO YOU, WHAT THEN?
MY TIME... GROWS SHORT. WHY HOARD...RESOURCES I...WILL NEVER SPEND?
WE ALL... HAVE MUCH TO... LOSE, SCHOLAR. I WOULD... CONCENTRATE ON...WHAT CAN BE--
--FOUN

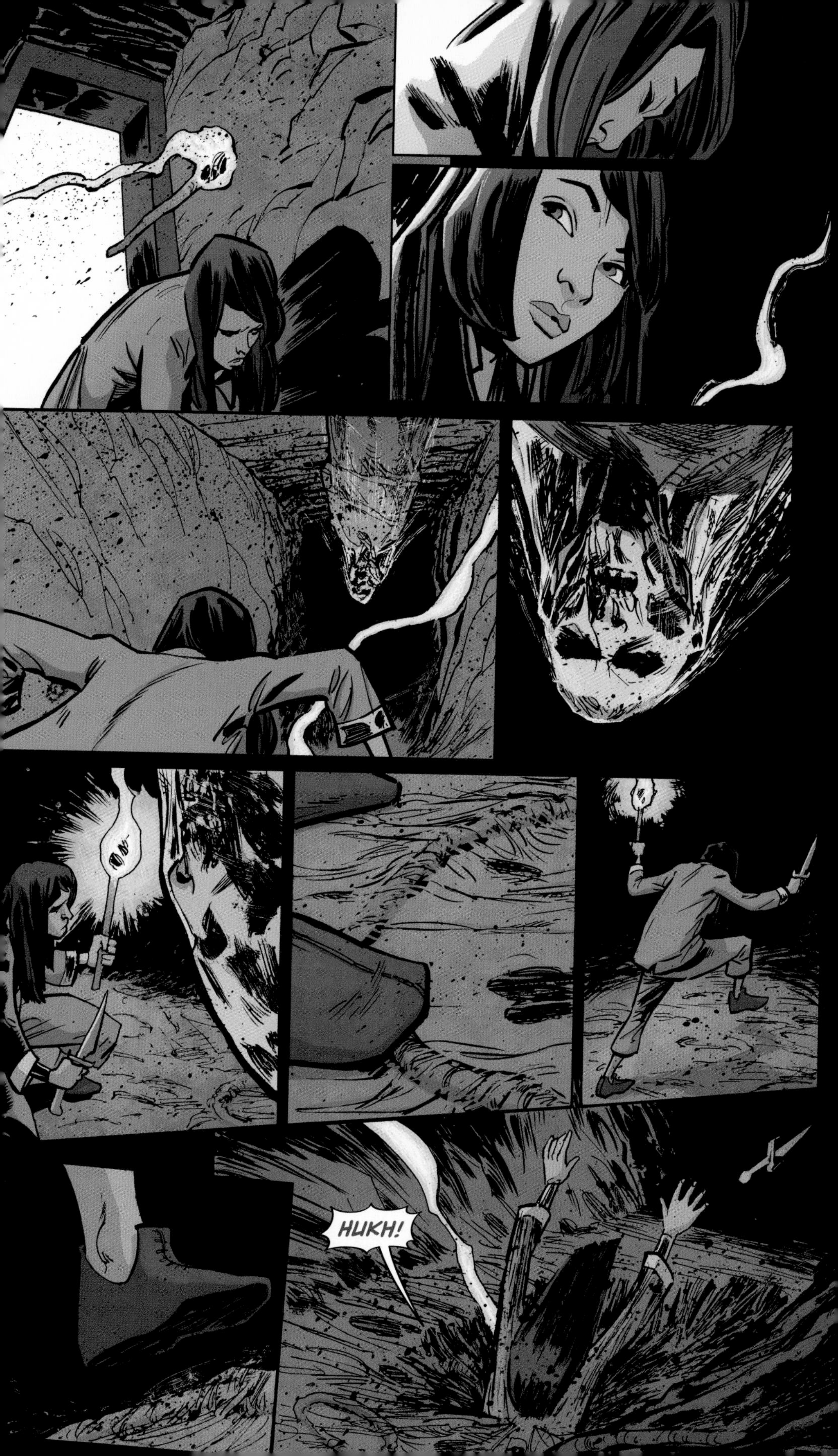
HUKH!

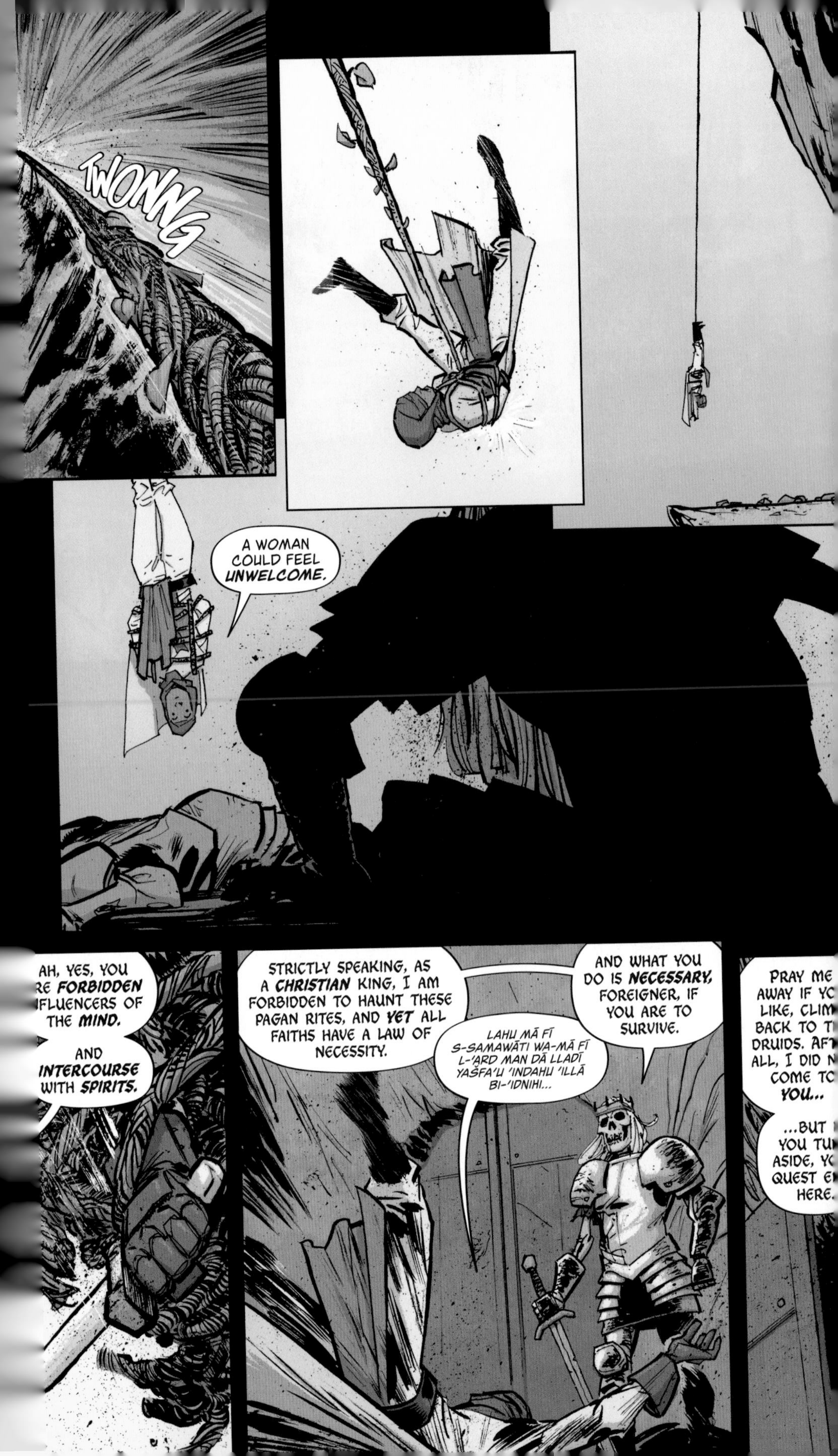
TWONNG
A WOMAN COULD FEEL UNWELCOME.
AH, YES, YOU RE FORBIDDEN FLUENCERS OF THE MIND.
AND INTERCOURSE WITH SPIRITS.
STRICTLY SPEAKING, AS A CHRISTIAN KING, I AM FORBIDDEN TO HAUNT THESE PAGAN RITES, AND YET ALL FAITHS HAVE A LAW OF NECESSITY.
AND WHAT YOU DO IS NECESSARY, FOREIGNER, IF YOU ARE TO SURVIVE.
LAHU MĀ FĪ S-SAMAWĀTI WA-MĀ FĪ L-'ARD MAN DĀ LLADĪ YAŠFA'U 'INDAHU 'ILLĀ BI-'IDNIHI...
PRAY ME AWAY IF YO LIKE, CLIM BACK TO T DRUIDS. AFT ALL, I DID N COME TO YOU...
...BUT YOU TU ASIDE, YO QUEST E HERE.

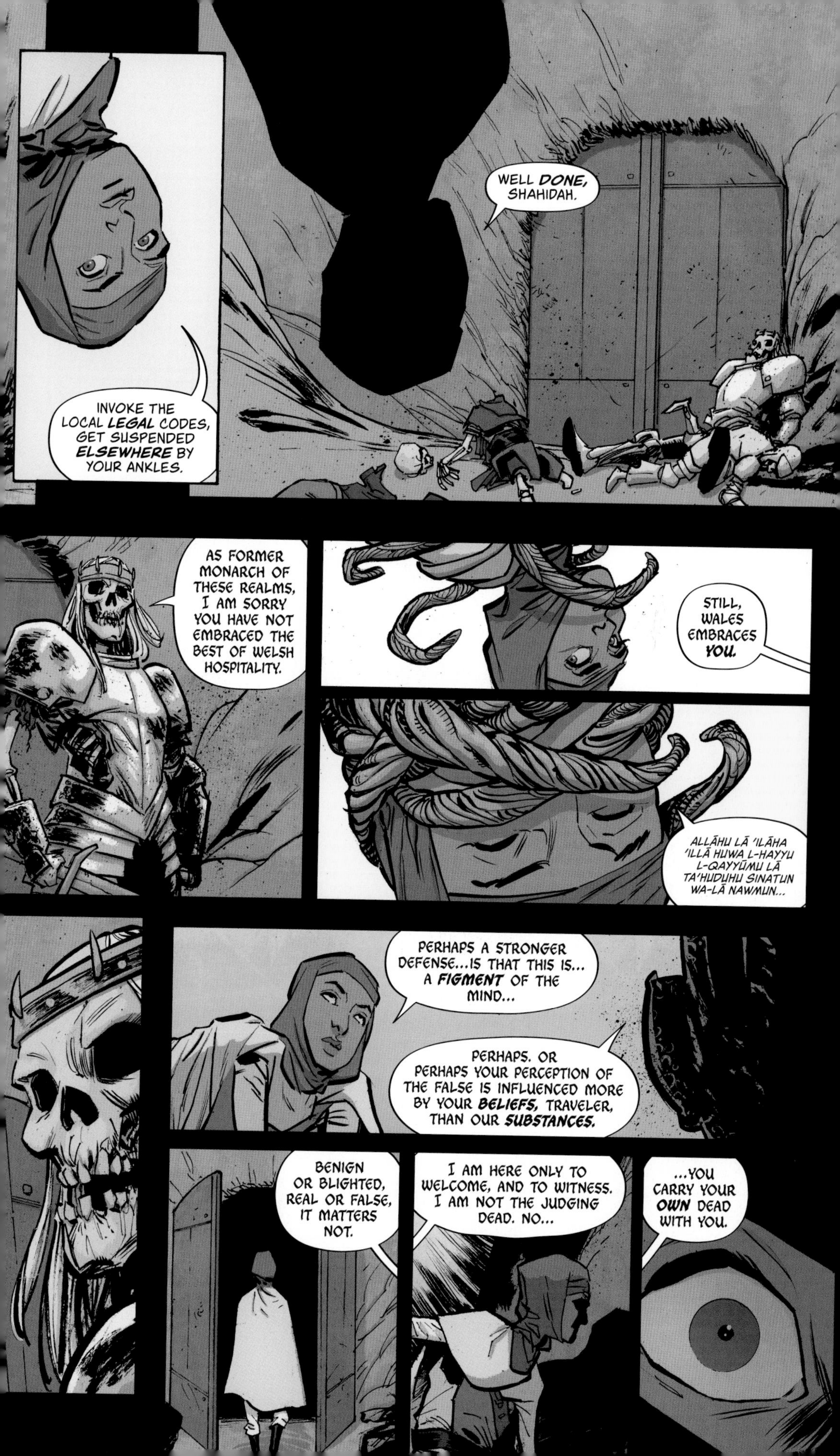
WELL DONE, SHAHIDAH.
INVOKE THE LOCAL LEGAL CODES, GET SUSPENDED ELSEWHERE BY YOUR ANKLES.
AS FORMER MONARCH OF THESE REALMS, I AM SORRY YOU HAVE NOT EMBRACED THE BEST OF WELSH HOSPITALITY.
STILL, WALES EMBRACES YOU.
ALLĀHU LĀ 'ILĀHA 'ILLĀ HUWA L-HAYYU L-QAYYŪMU LĀ TA'HUDUHU SINATUN WA-LĀ NAWMUN...
PERHAPS A STRONGER DEFENSE...IS THAT THIS IS... A FIGMENT OF THE MIND...
PERHAPS. OR PERHAPS YOUR PERCEPTION OF THE FALSE IS INFLUENCED MORE BY YOUR BELIEFS, TRAVELER, THAN OUR SUBSTANCES.
BENIGN OR BLIGHTED, REAL OR FALSE, IT MATTERS NOT.
I AM HERE ONLY TO WELCOME, AND TO WITNESS. I AM NOT THE JUDGING DEAD. NO...
...YOU CARRY YOUR OWN DEAD WITH YOU.

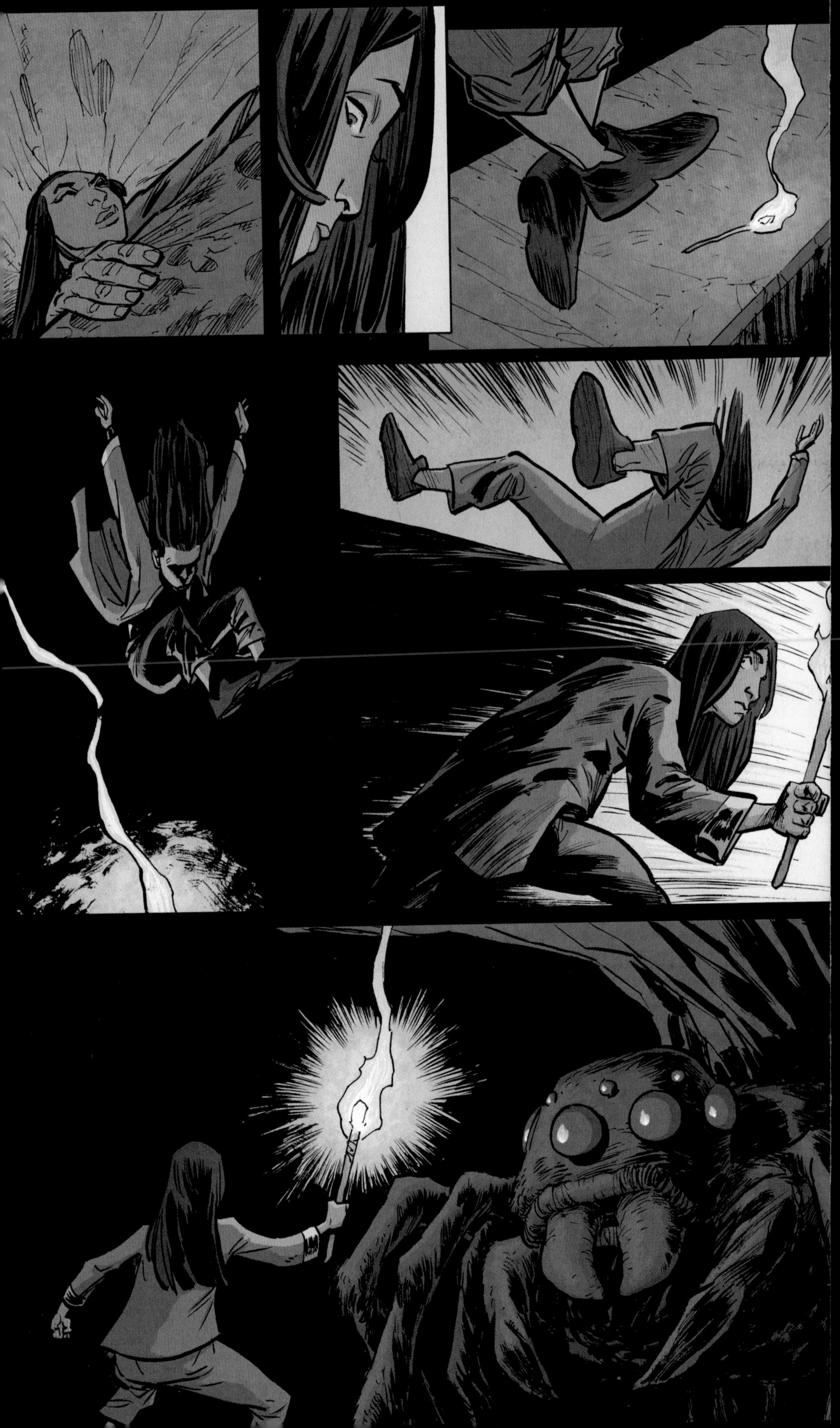

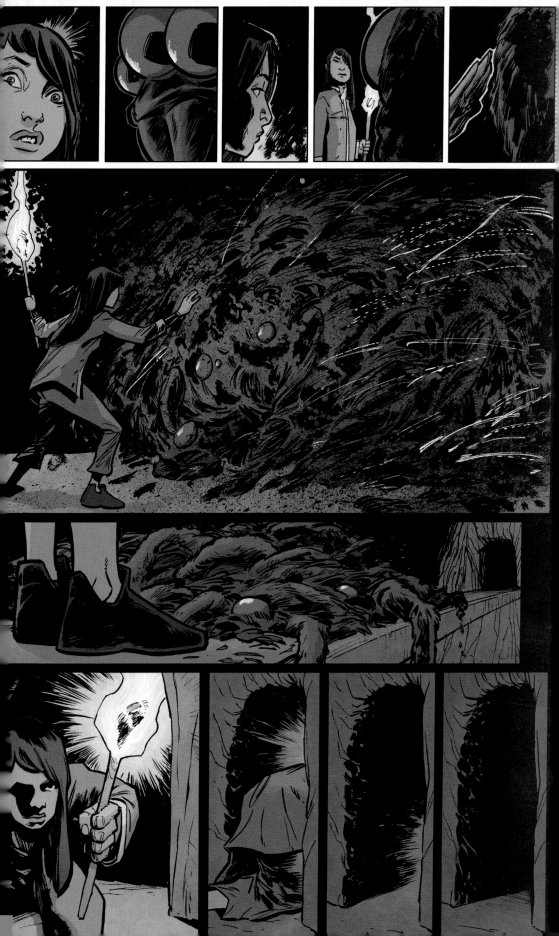

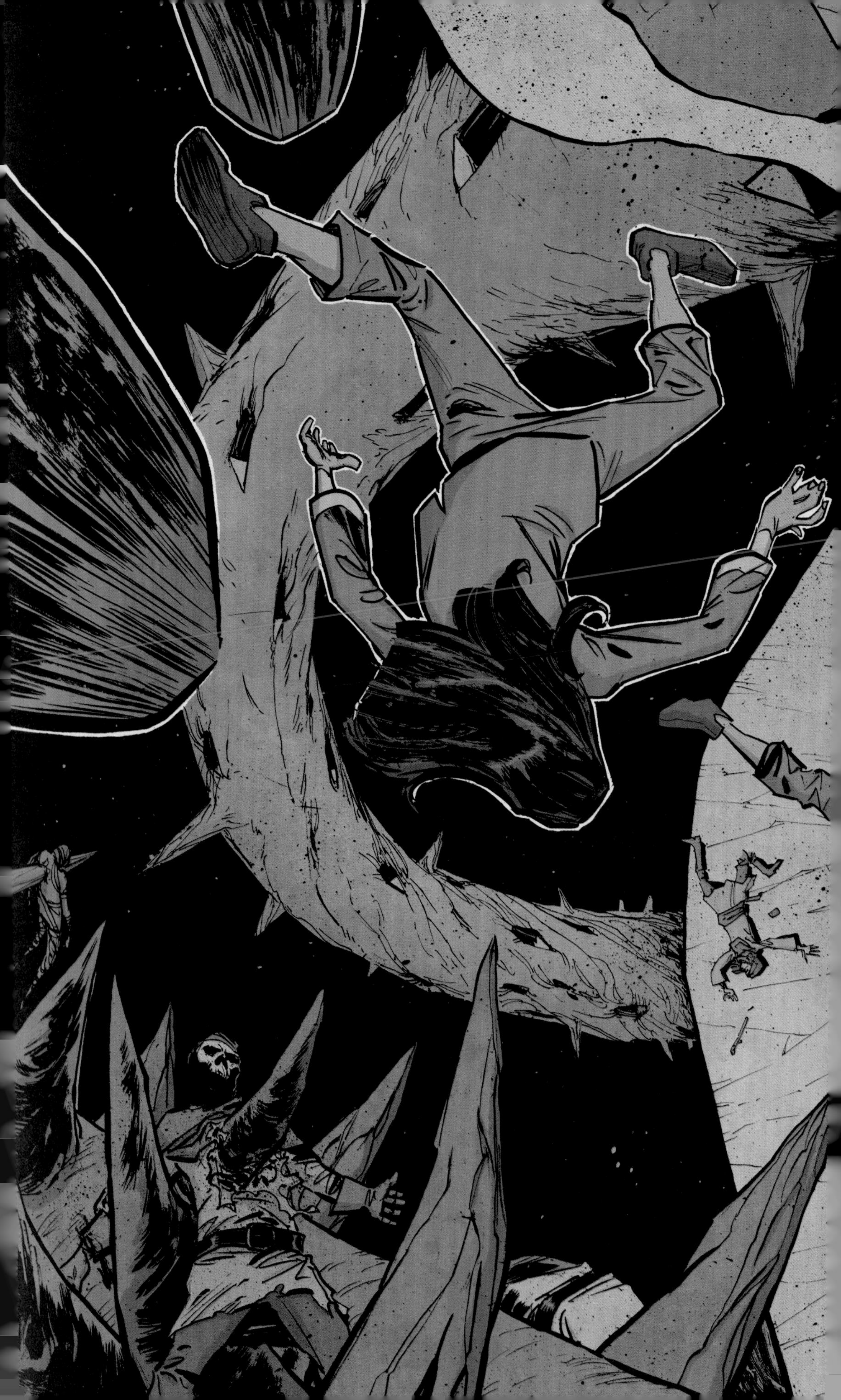

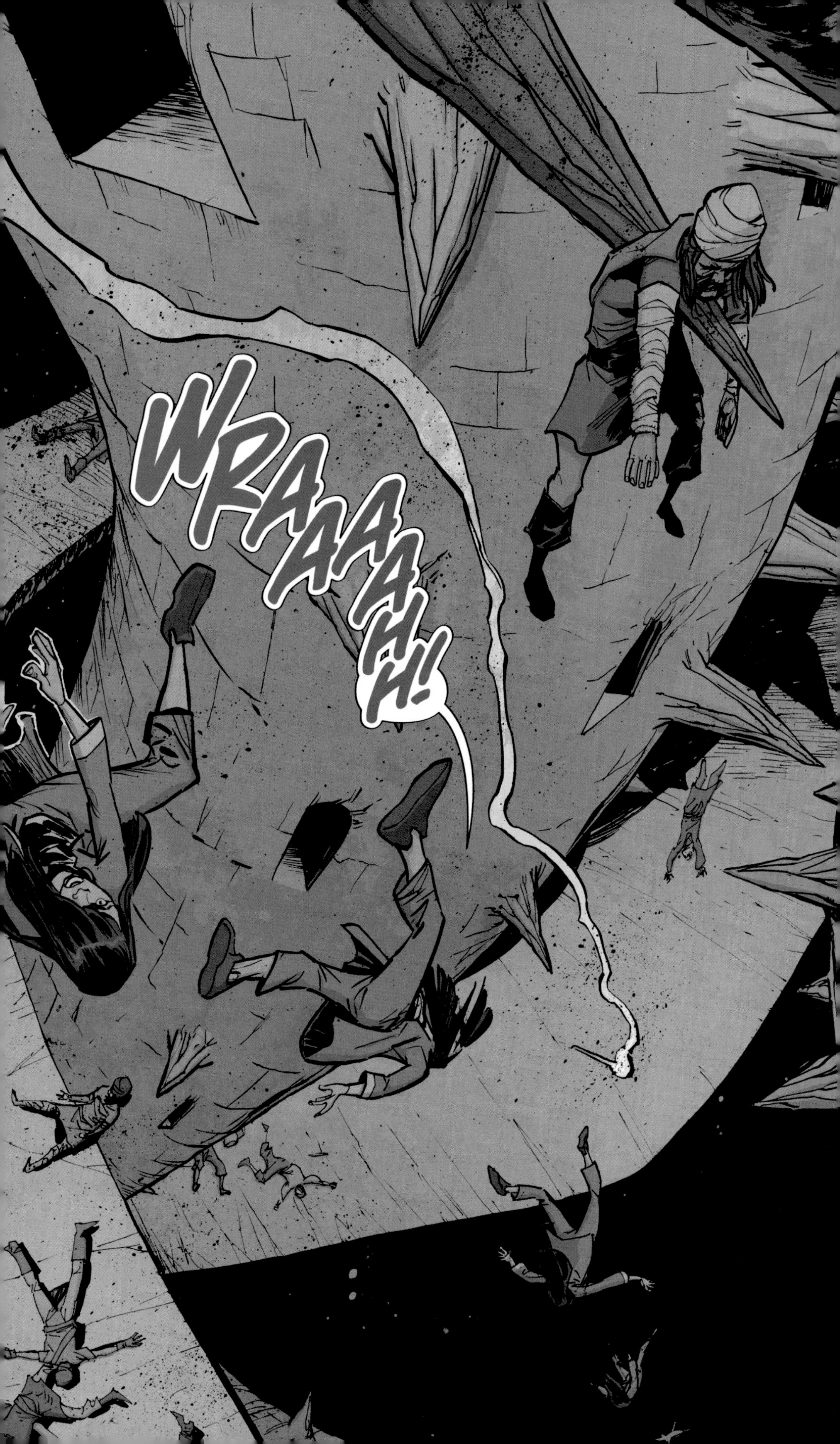
WRAAAAAHH!

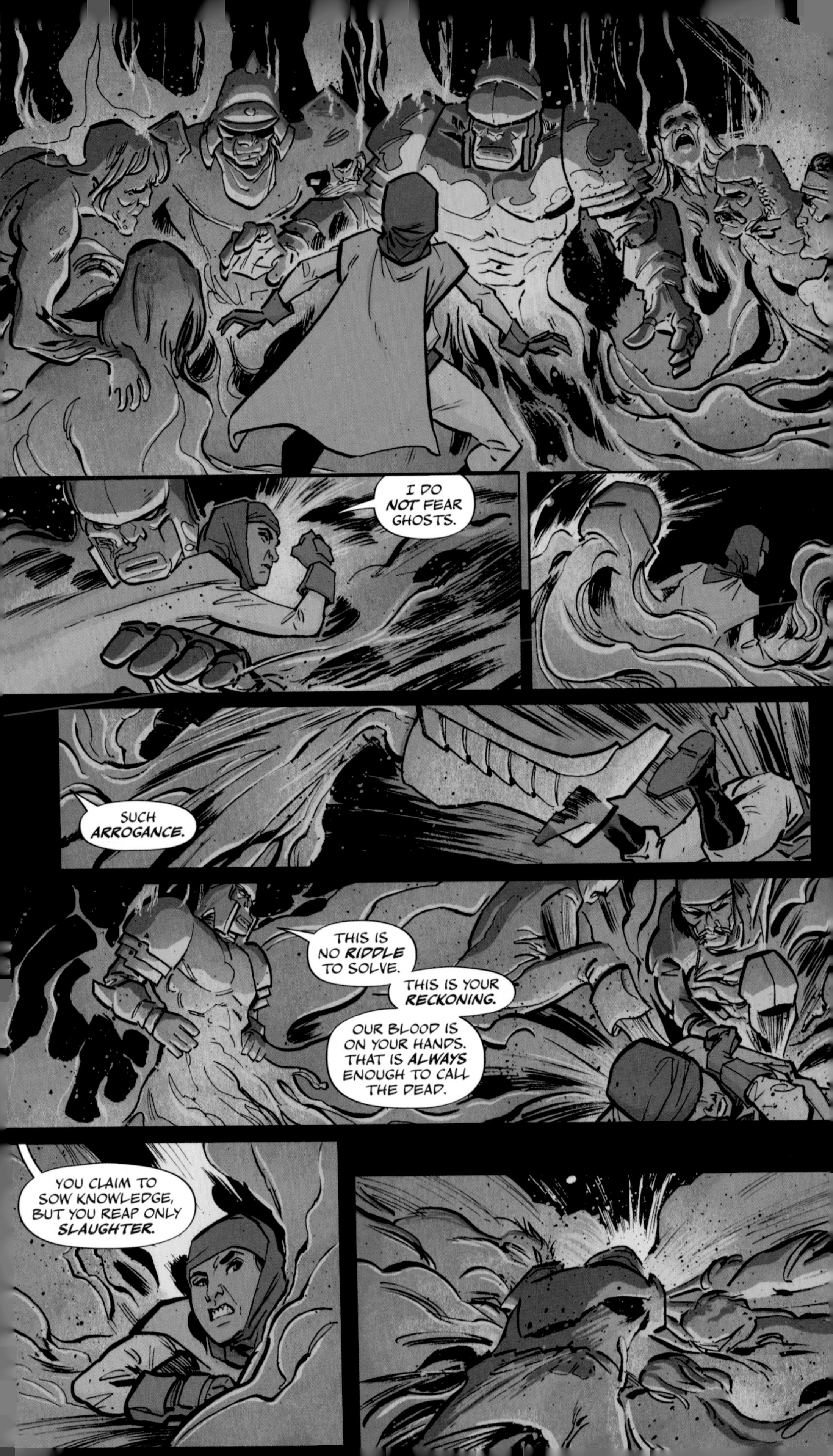

I DO NOT FEAR GHOSTS.
SUCH ARROGANCE.
THIS IS NO RIDDLE TO SOLVE.
THIS IS YOUR RECKONING.
OUR BLOOD IS ON YOUR HANDS. THAT IS ALWAYS ENOUGH TO CALL THE DEAD.
YOU CLAIM TO SOW KNOWLEDGE, BUT YOU REAP ONLY SLAUGHTER.

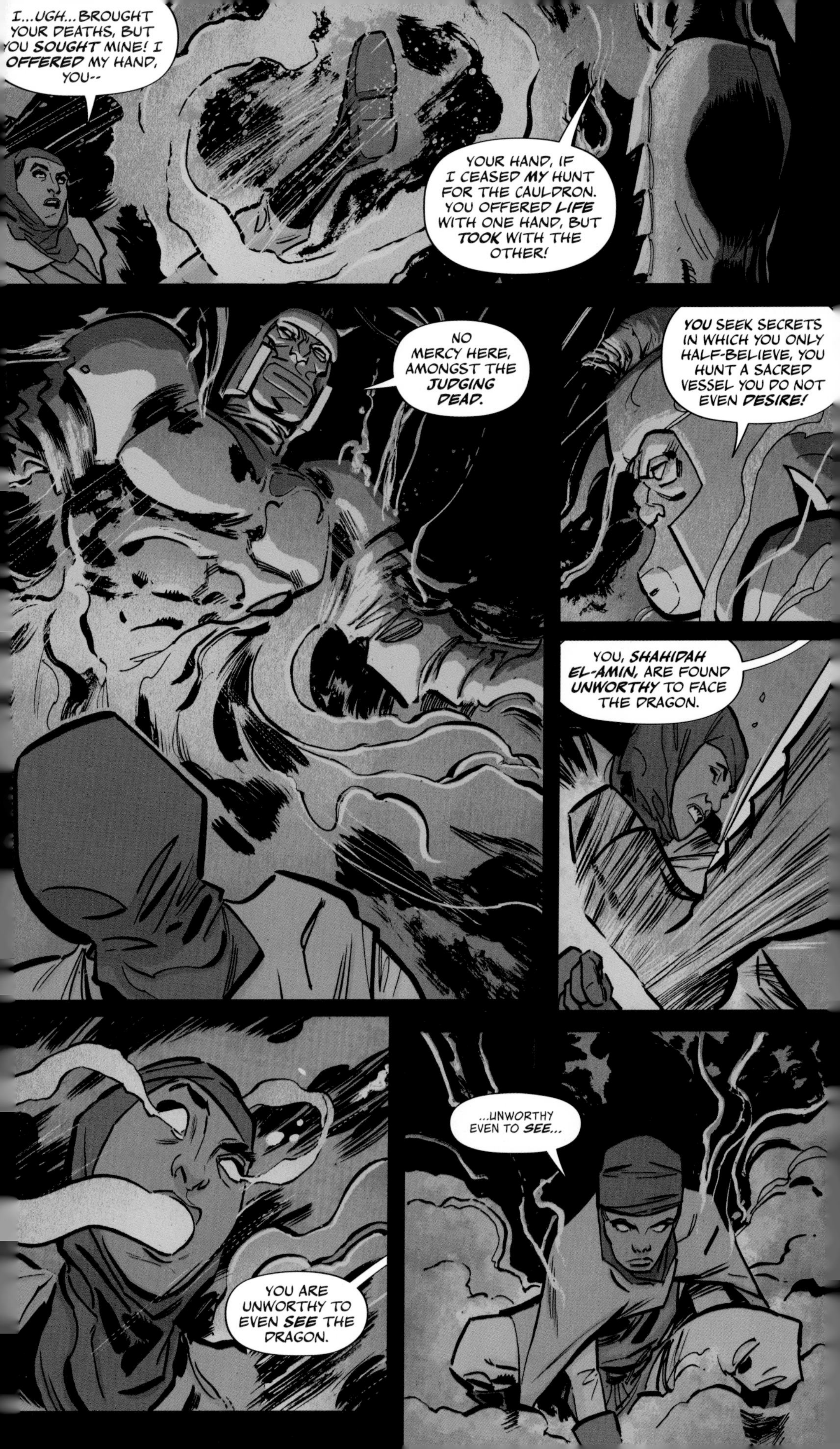
I...UGH...BROUGHT YOUR DEATHS, BUT YOU SOUGHT MINE! I OFFERED MY HAND, YOU--
YOUR HAND, IF I CEASED MY HUNT FOR THE CAULDRON. YOU OFFERED LIFE WITH ONE HAND, BUT TOOK WITH THE OTHER!
NO MERCY HERE, AMONGST THE JUDGING DEAD.
YOU SEEK SECRETS IN WHICH YOU ONLY HALF-BELIEVE, YOU HUNT A SACRED VESSEL YOU DO NOT EVEN DESIRE!
YOU, SHAHIDAH EL-AMIN, ARE FOUND UNWORTHY TO FACE THE DRAGON.
YOU ARE UNWORTHY TO EVEN SEE THE DRAGON.
...UNWORTHY EVEN TO SEE...

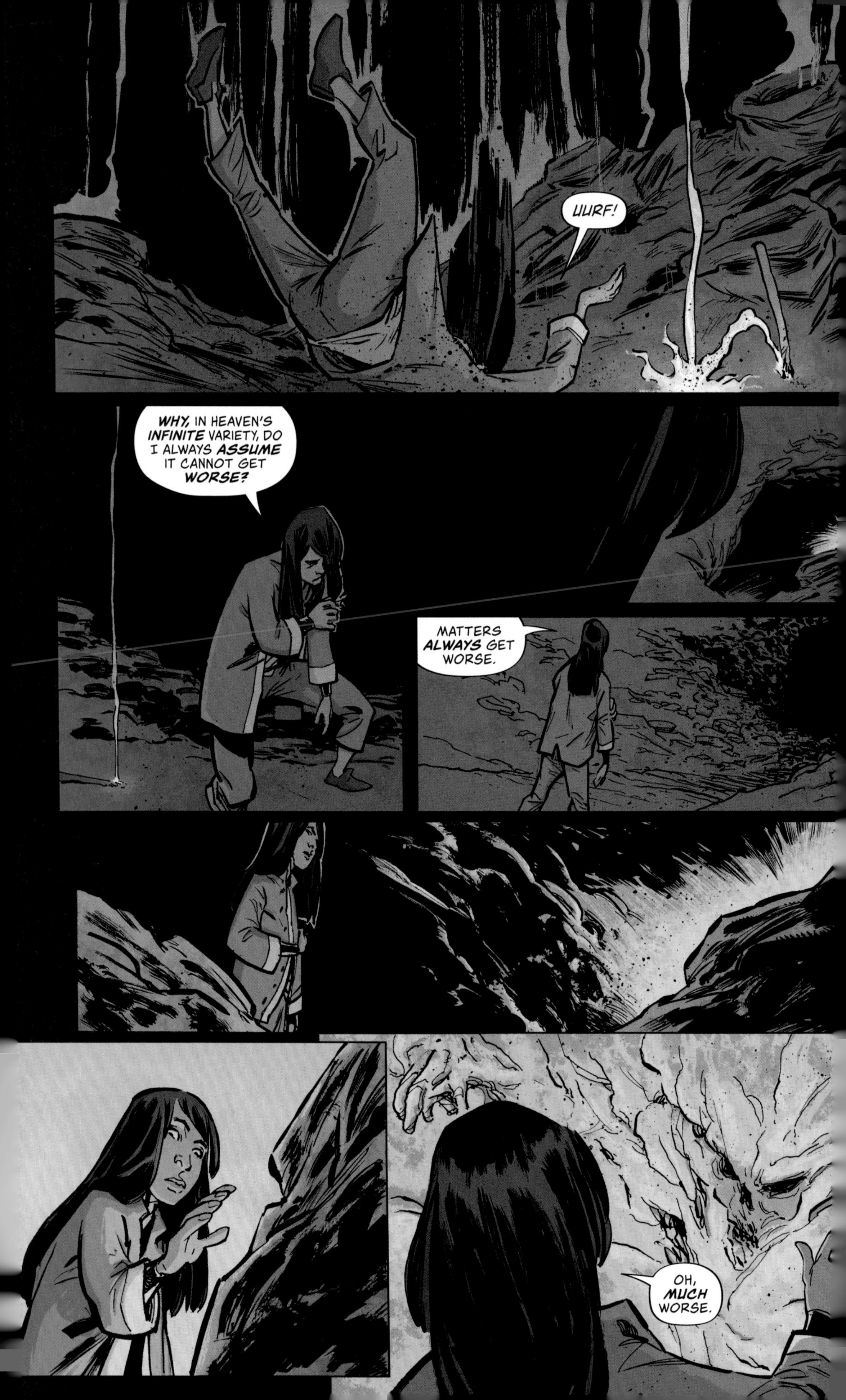
UURF!
WHY, IN HEAVEN'S INFINITE VARIETY, DO I ALWAYS ASSUME IT CANNOT GET WORSE?
MATTERS ALWAYS GET WORSE.
OH, MUCH WORSE.

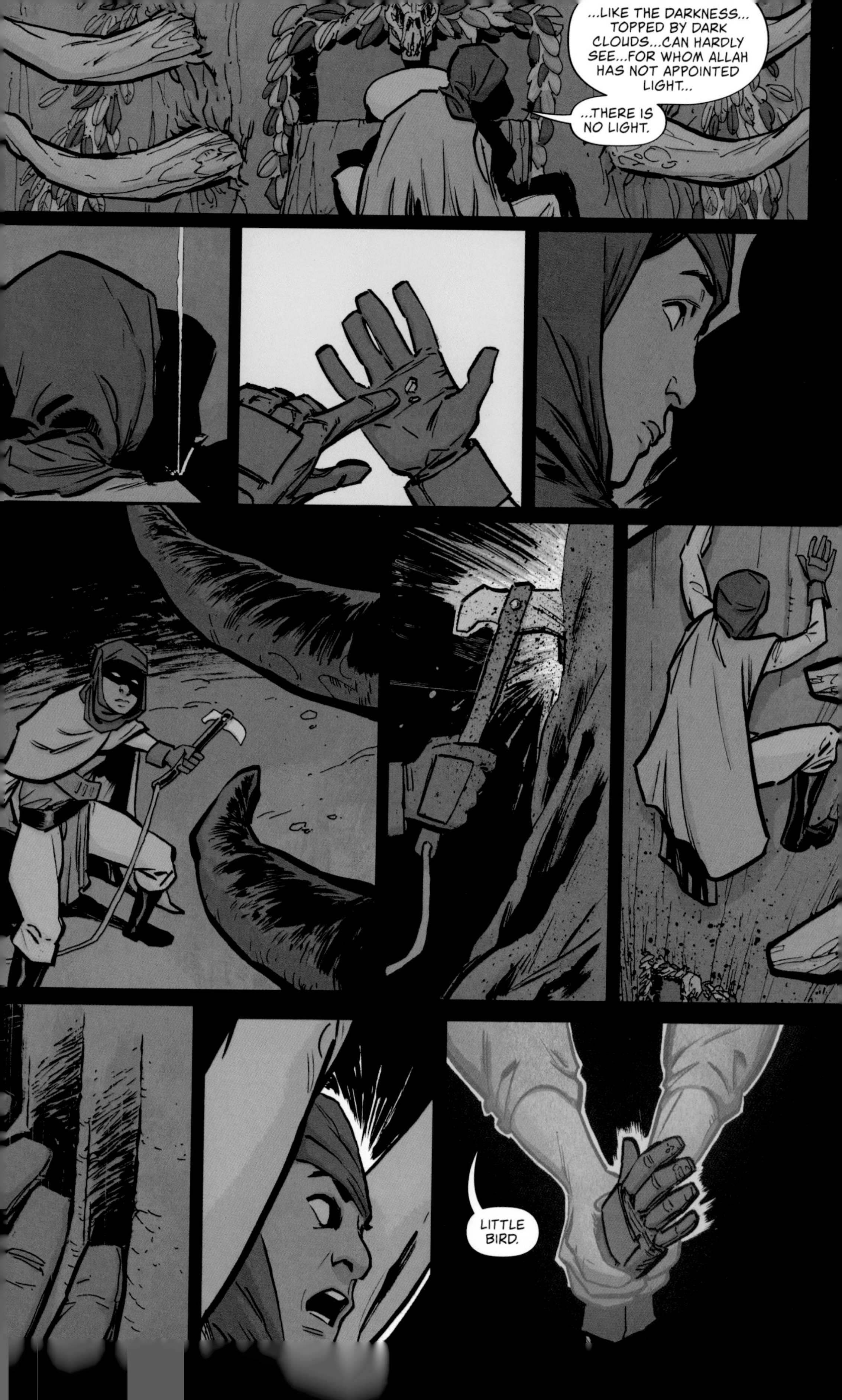
...LIKE THE DARKNESS... TOPPED BY DARK CLOUDS...CAN HARDLY SEE...FOR WHOM ALLAH HAS NOT APPOINTED LIGHT...
...THERE IS NO LIGHT.
LITTLE BIRD.

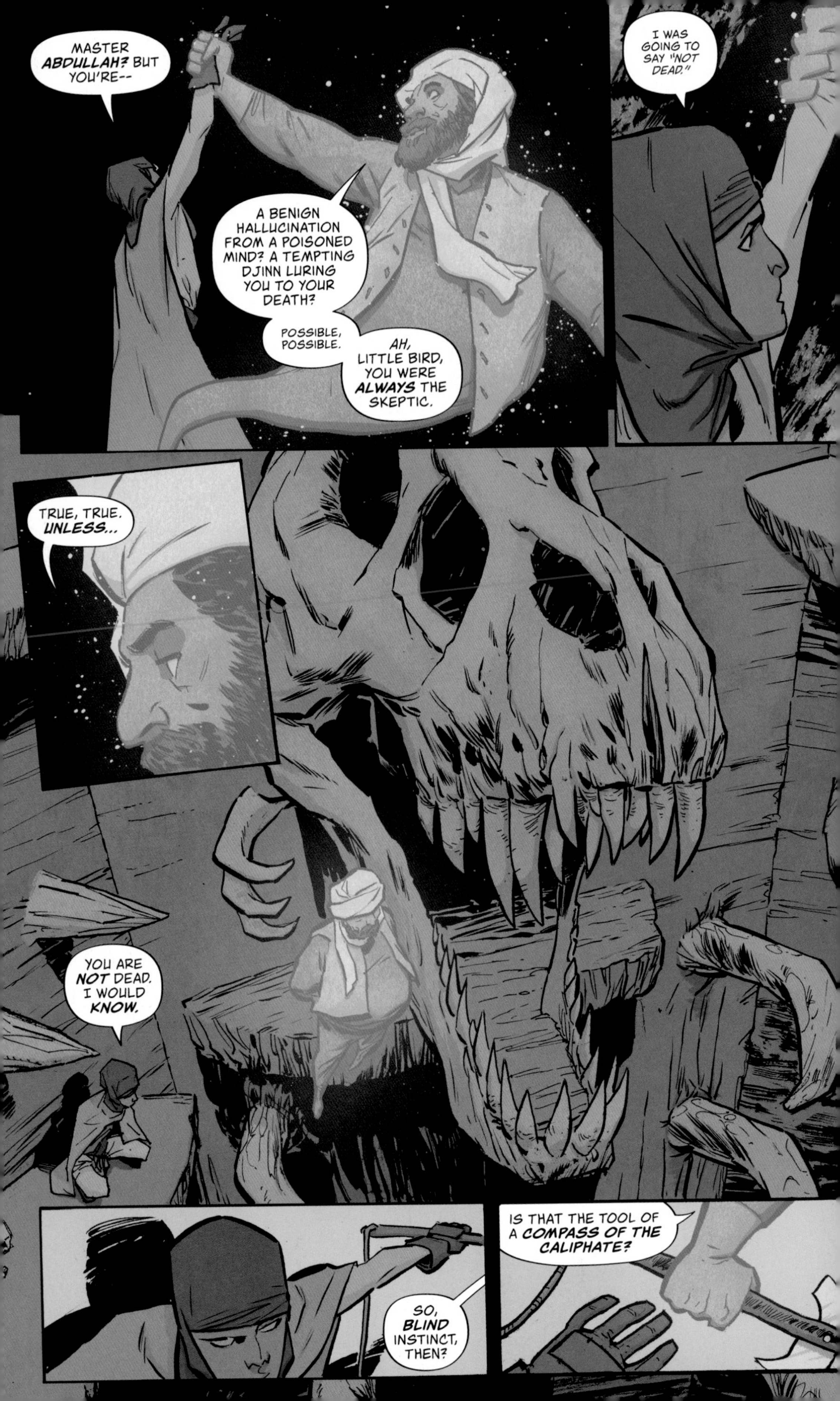

MASTER **ABDULLAH?** BUT YOU'RE--
A BENIGN HALLUCINATION FROM A POISONED MIND? A TEMPTING DJINN LURING YOU TO YOUR DEATH?
POSSIBLE, POSSIBLE.
AH, LITTLE BIRD, YOU WERE ***ALWAYS*** THE SKEPTIC.
I WAS GOING TO SAY *"NOT DEAD."*
TRUE, TRUE. ***UNLESS...***
YOU ARE ***NOT*** DEAD. I WOULD ***KNOW.***
SO, ***BLIND*** INSTINCT, THEN?
IS THAT THE TOOL OF A ***COMPASS OF THE CALIPHATE?***

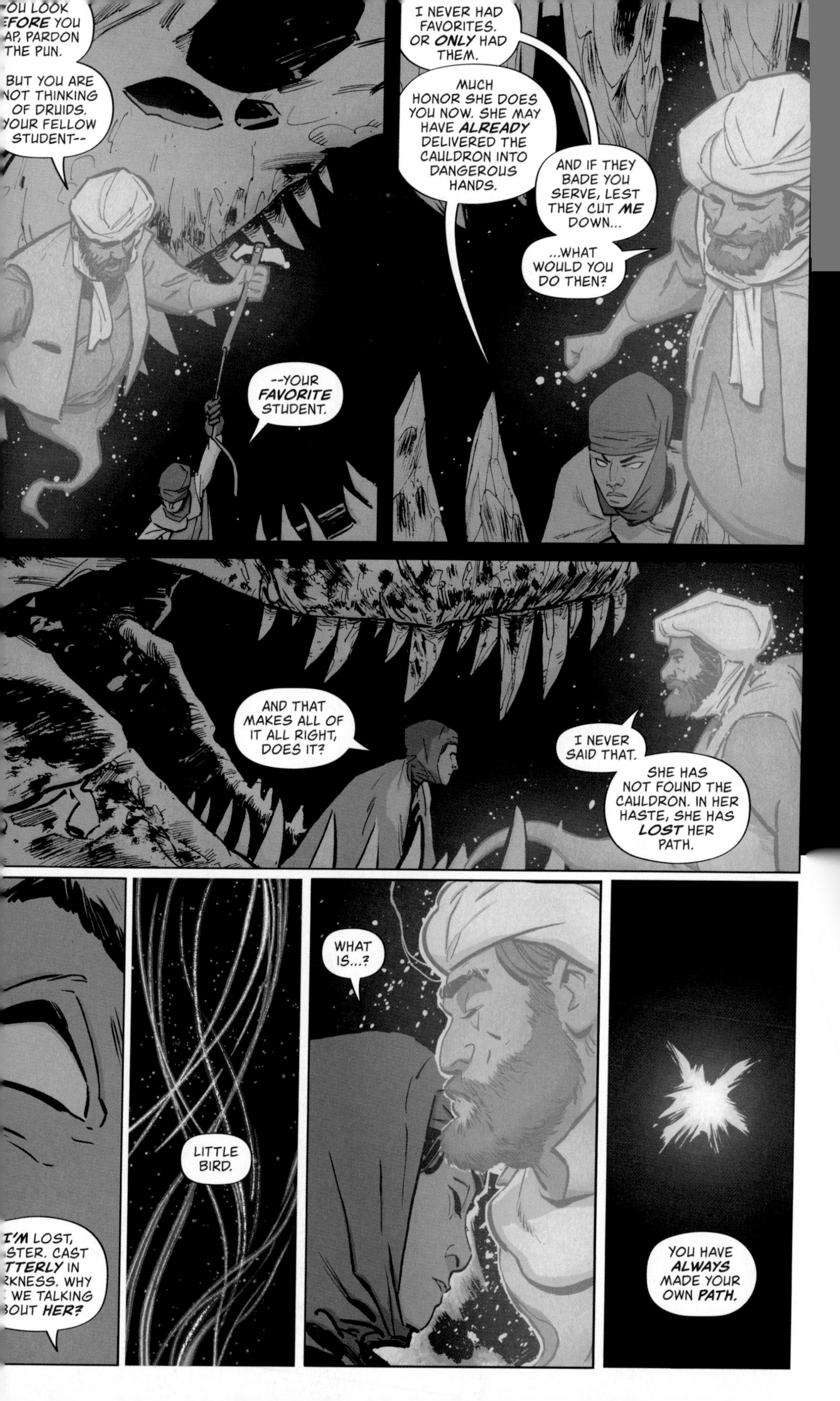

OU LOOK EFORE YOU AP, PARDON THE PUN.
BUT YOU ARE NOT THINKING OF DRUIDS. YOUR FELLOW STUDENT--
--YOUR **FAVORITE** STUDENT.
I NEVER HAD FAVORITES. OR **ONLY** HAD THEM.
MUCH HONOR SHE DOES YOU NOW. SHE MAY HAVE **ALREADY** DELIVERED THE CAULDRON INTO DANGEROUS HANDS.
AND IF THEY BADE YOU SERVE, LEST THEY CUT **ME** DOWN...
...WHAT WOULD YOU DO THEN?
AND THAT MAKES ALL OF IT ALL RIGHT, DOES IT?
I NEVER SAID THAT.
SHE HAS NOT FOUND THE CAULDRON. IN HER HASTE, SHE HAS **LOST** HER PATH.
I'M LOST, STER. CAST **TTERLY** IN RKNESS. WHY WE TALKING BOUT **HER?**
LITTLE BIRD.
WHAT IS...?
YOU HAVE **ALWAYS** MADE YOUR OWN **PATH.**

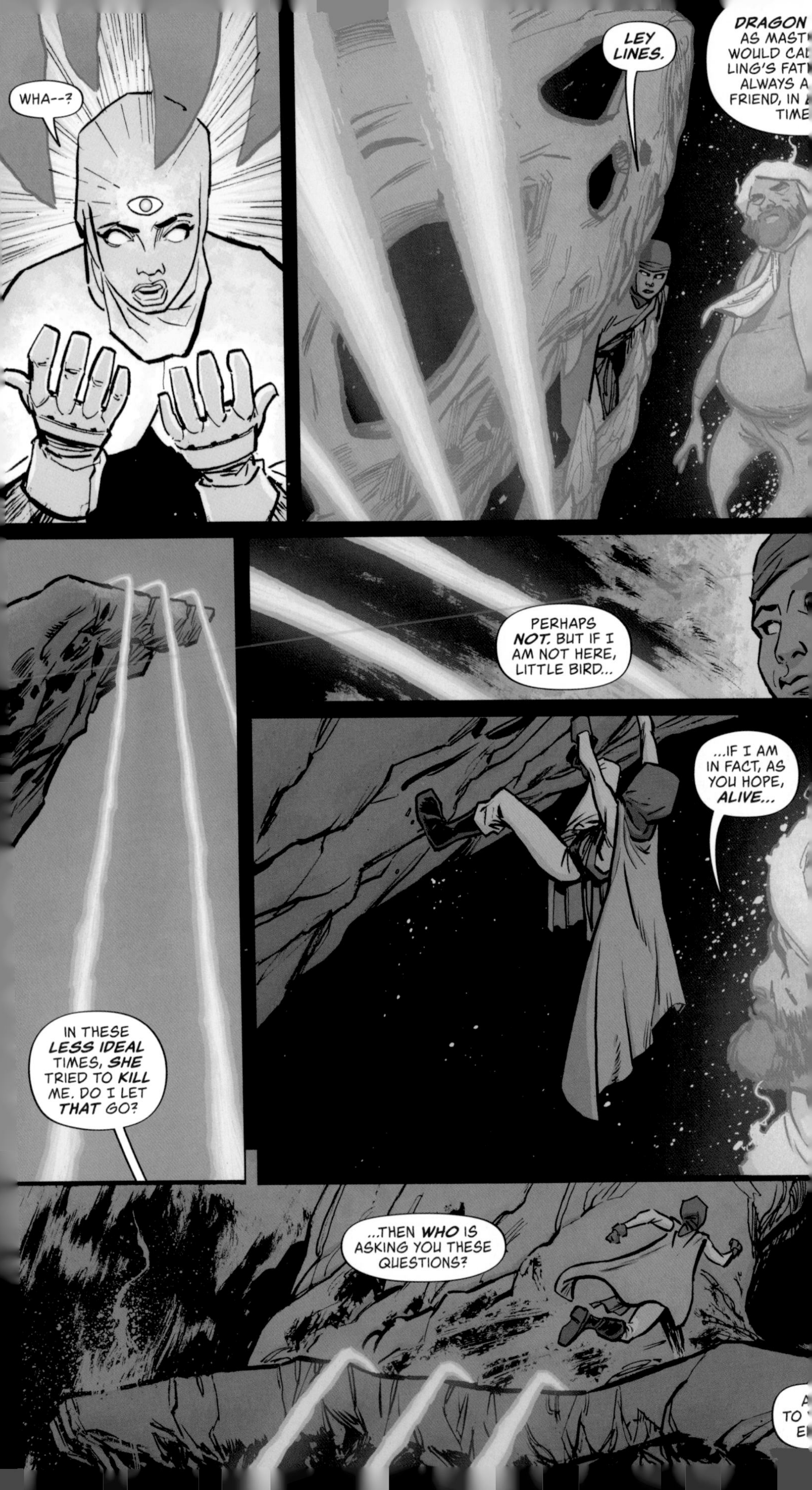
WHA--?
LEY LINES.
PERHAPS NOT. BUT IF I AM NOT HERE, LITTLE BIRD...
...IF I AM IN FACT, AS YOU HOPE, ALIVE...
IN THESE LESS IDEAL TIMES, SHE TRIED TO KILL ME. DO I LET THAT GO?
...THEN WHO IS ASKING YOU THESE QUESTIONS?

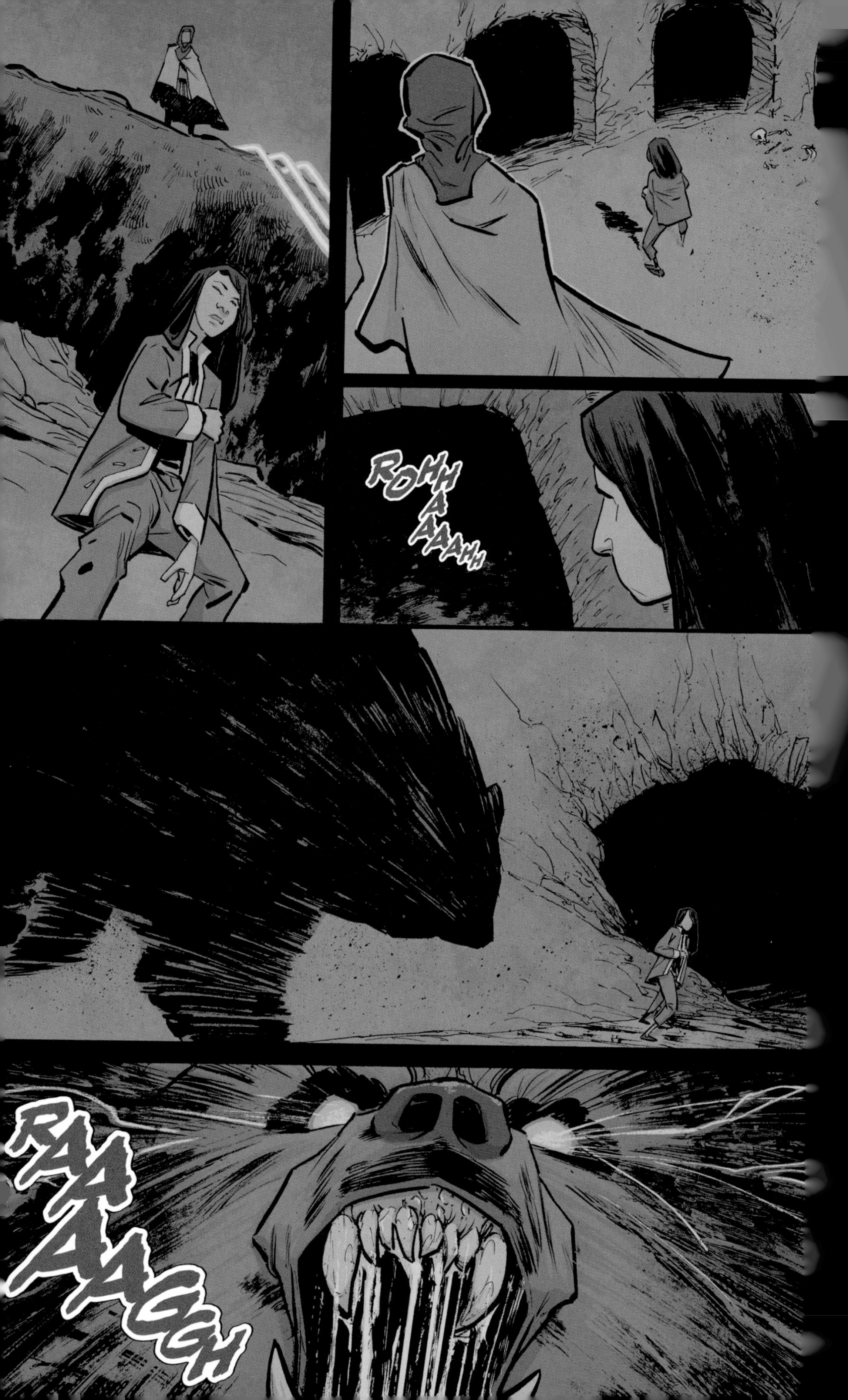
ROHHAAAAHH
RAAAAGGH

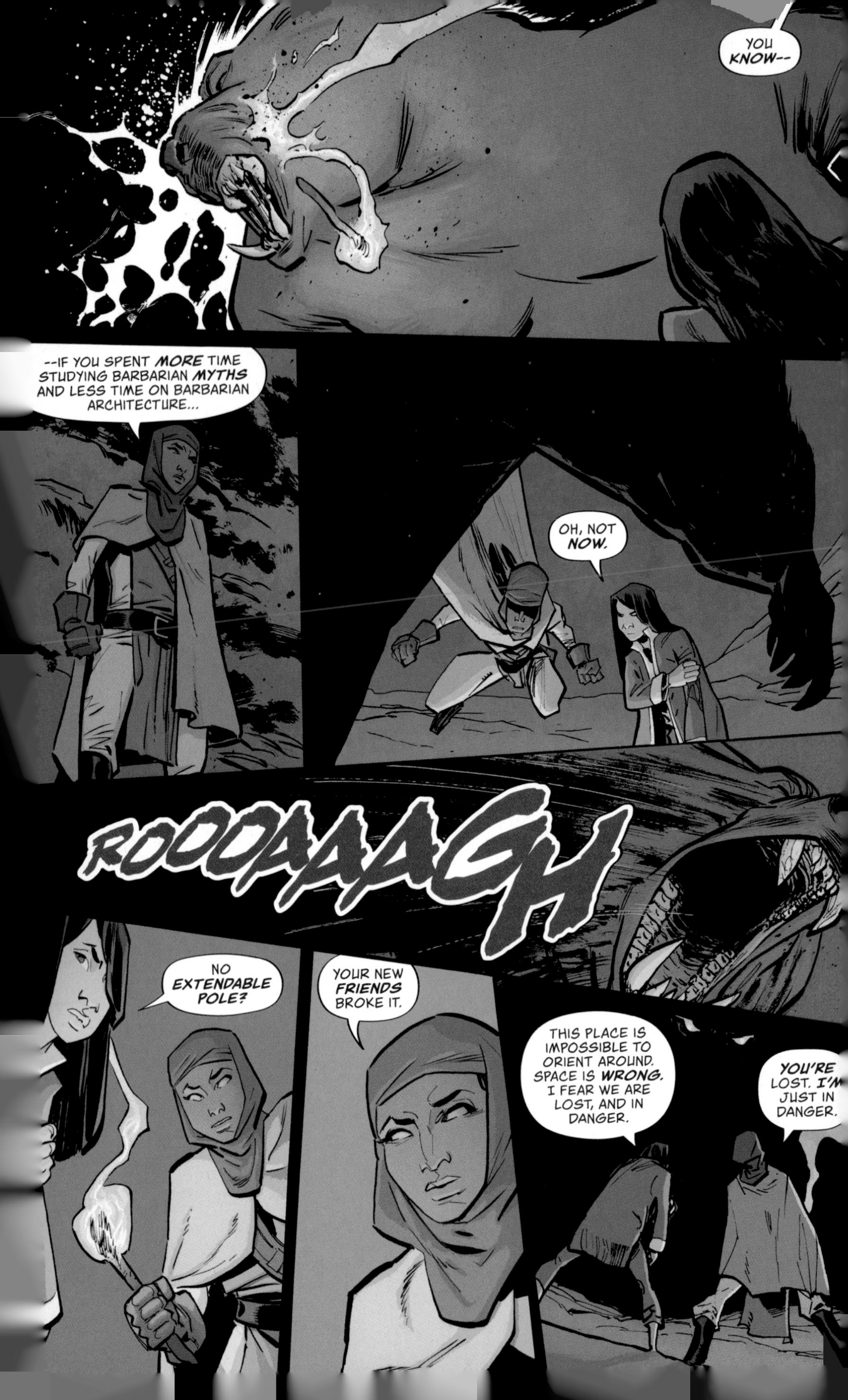
YOU KNOW--
--IF YOU SPENT MORE TIME STUDYING BARBARIAN MYTHS AND LESS TIME ON BARBARIAN ARCHITECTURE...
OH, NOT NOW.
ROOOAAAGH
NO EXTENDABLE POLE?
YOUR NEW FRIENDS BROKE IT.
THIS PLACE IS IMPOSSIBLE TO ORIENT AROUND. SPACE IS WRONG. I FEAR WE ARE LOST, AND IN DANGER.
YOU'RE LOST. I'M JUST IN DANGER.

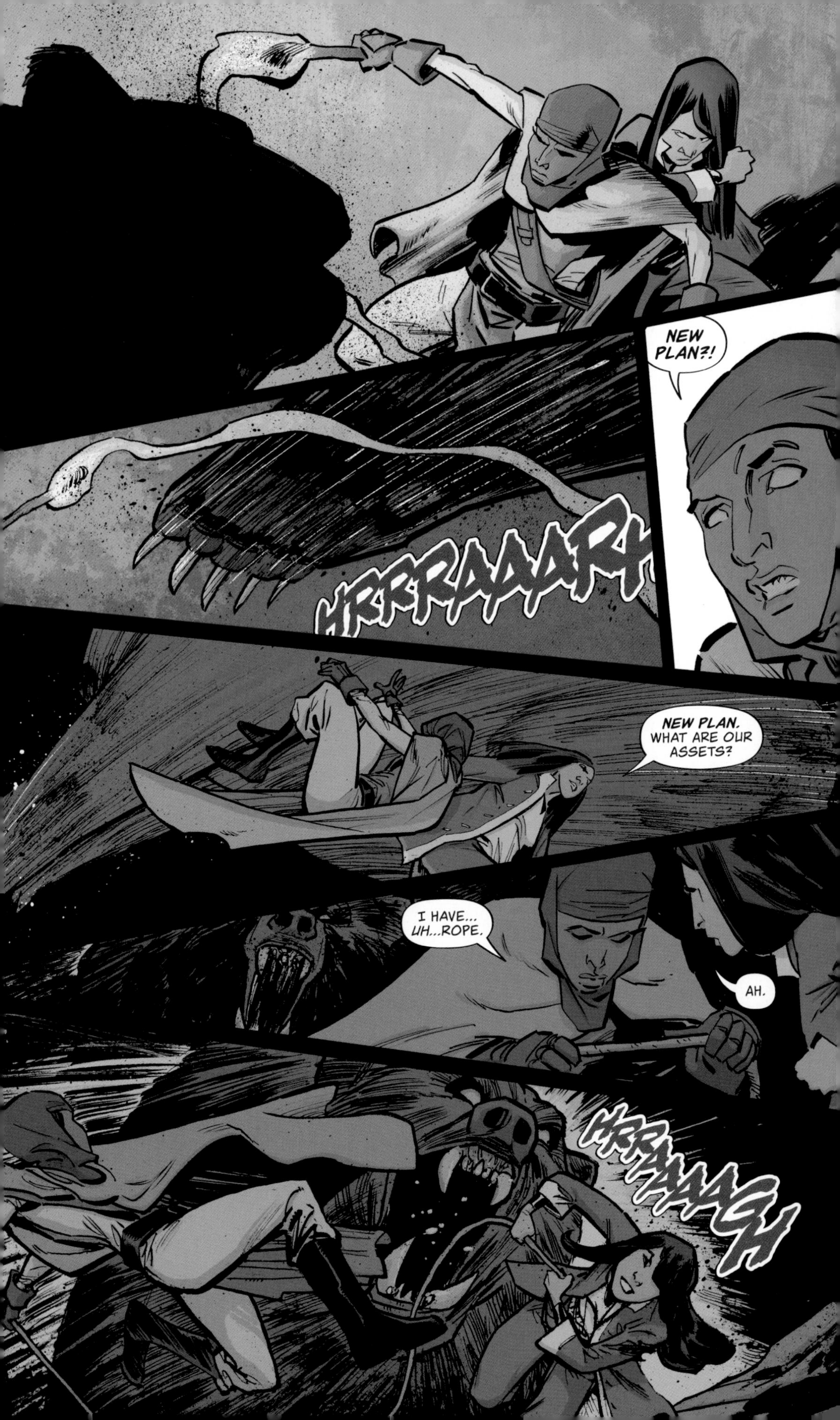
NEW PLAN?!
HRRRAAARK
NEW PLAN. WHAT ARE OUR ASSETS?
I HAVE... UH...ROPE.
AH.
HRRAAAGH

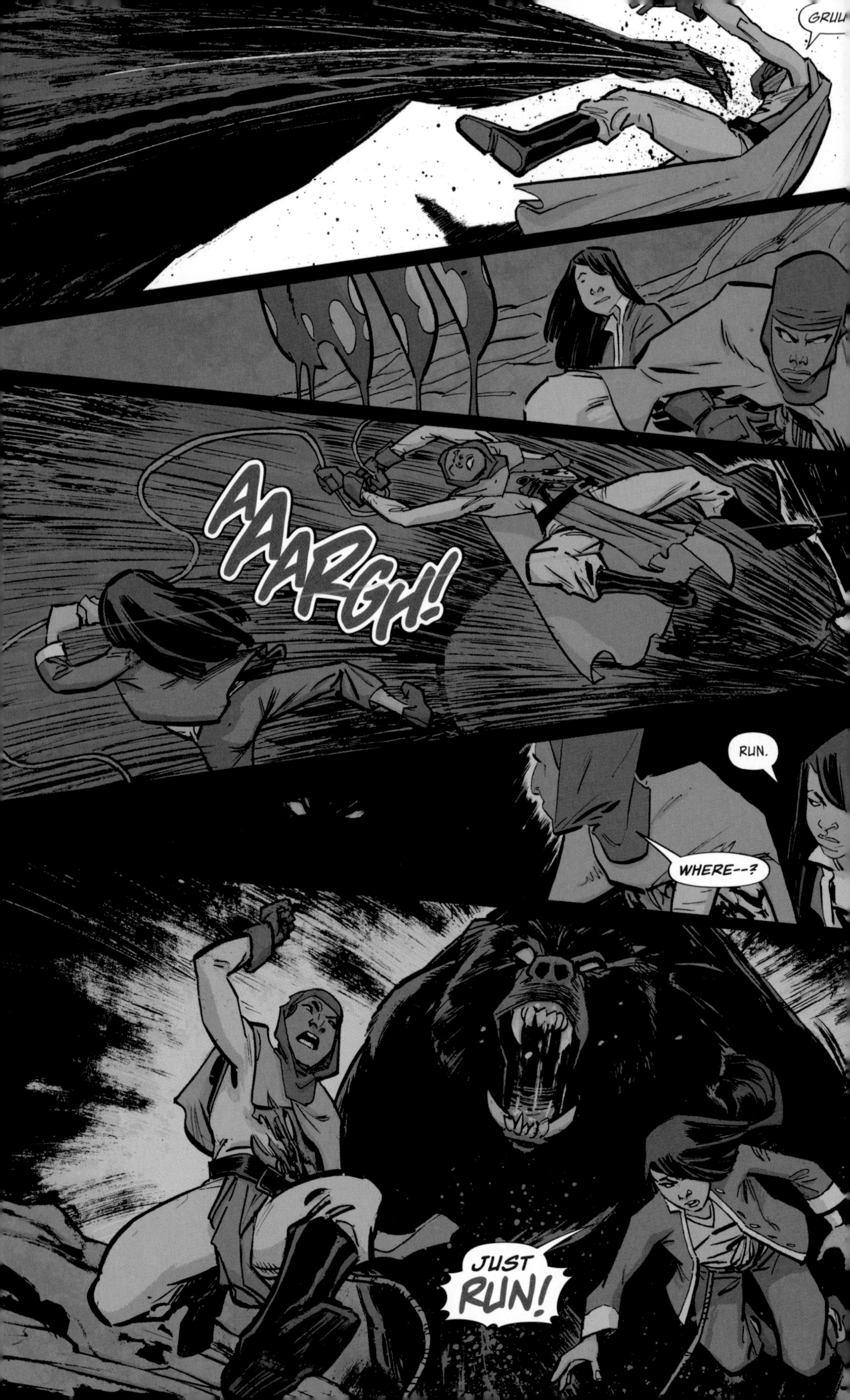
GRUL
AAARGH!
RUN.
WHERE--?
JUST RUN!

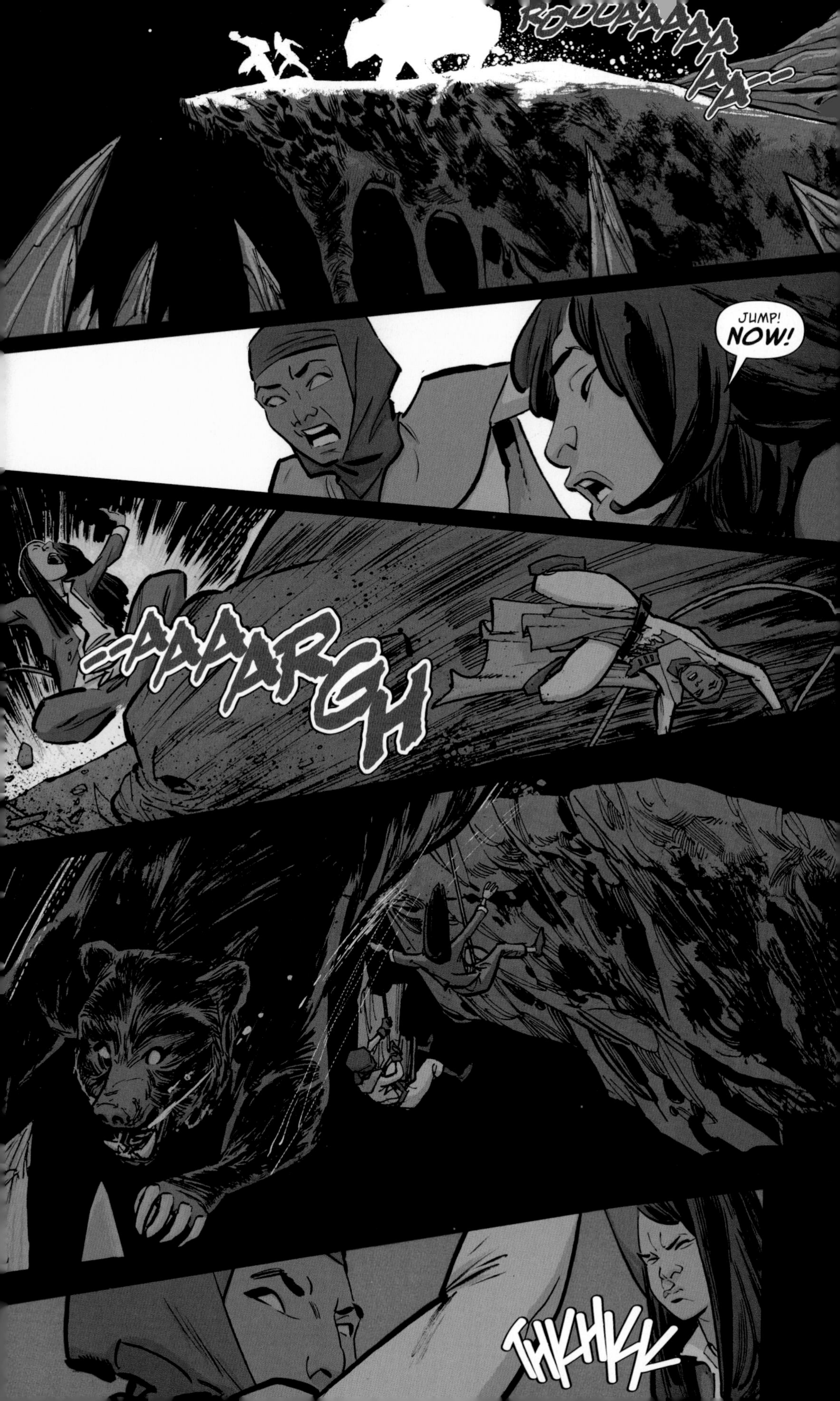

ROOOAAAAAAAA--
JUMP! NOW!
--AAAARGH
THKHKK

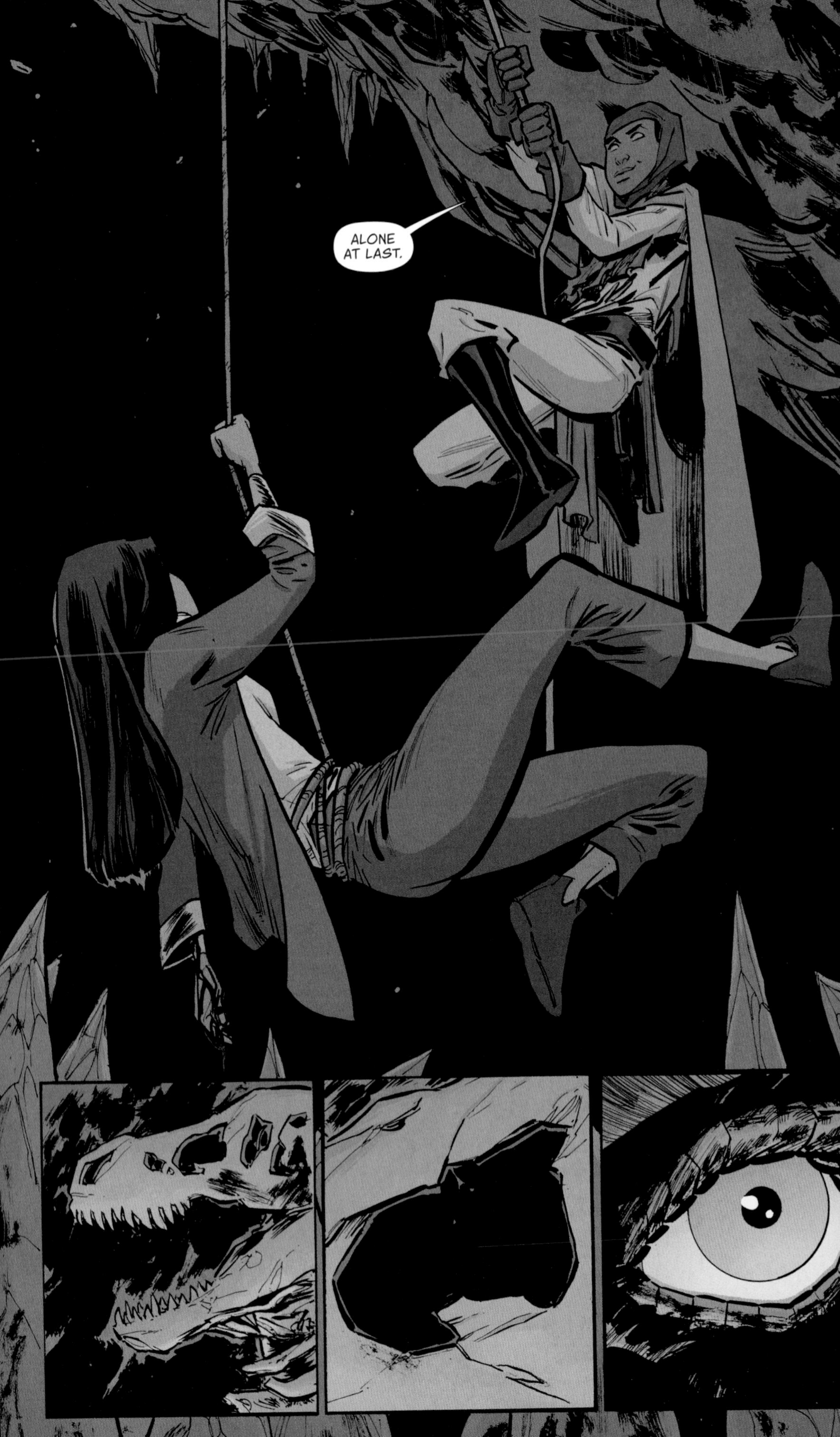
ALONE AT LAST.

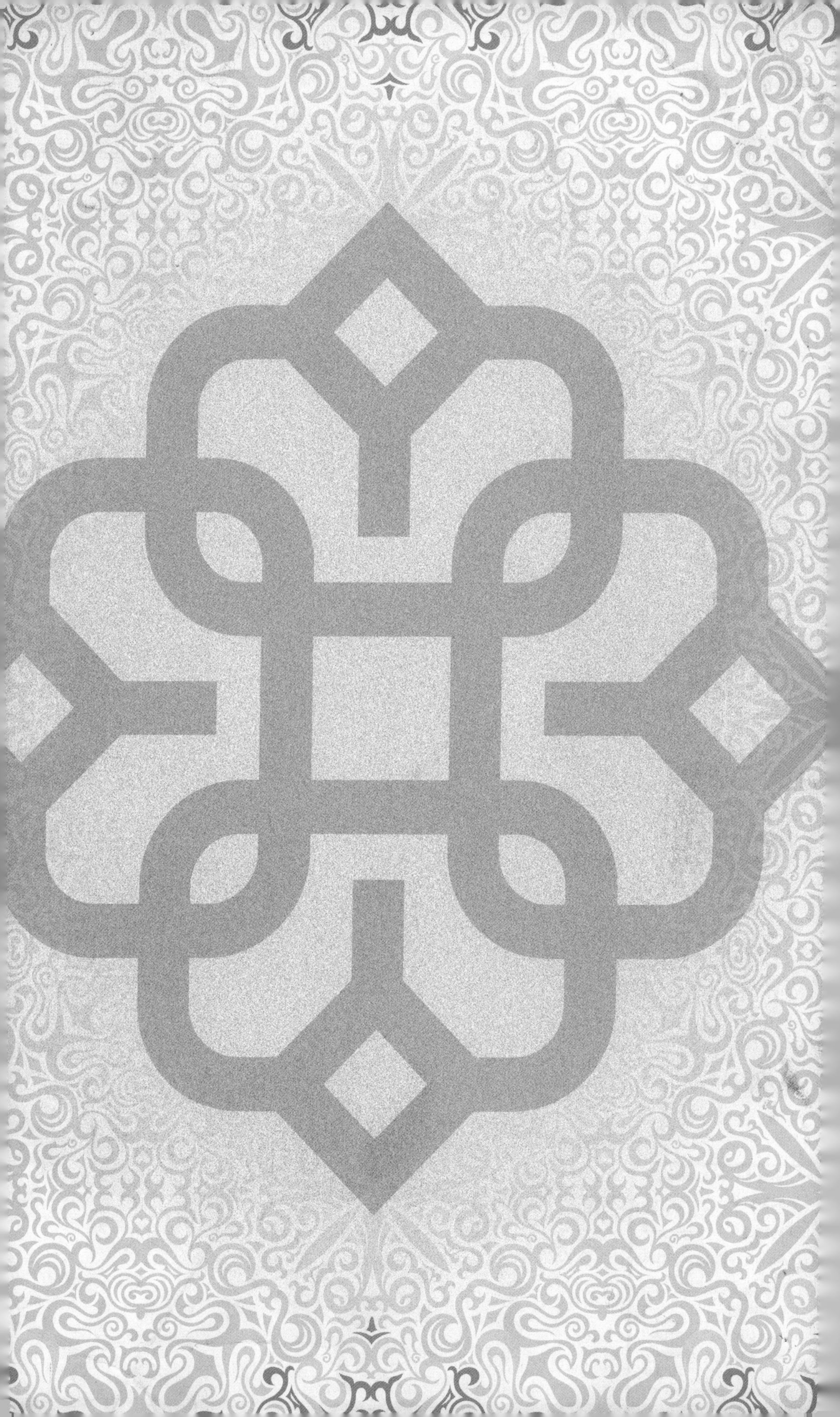

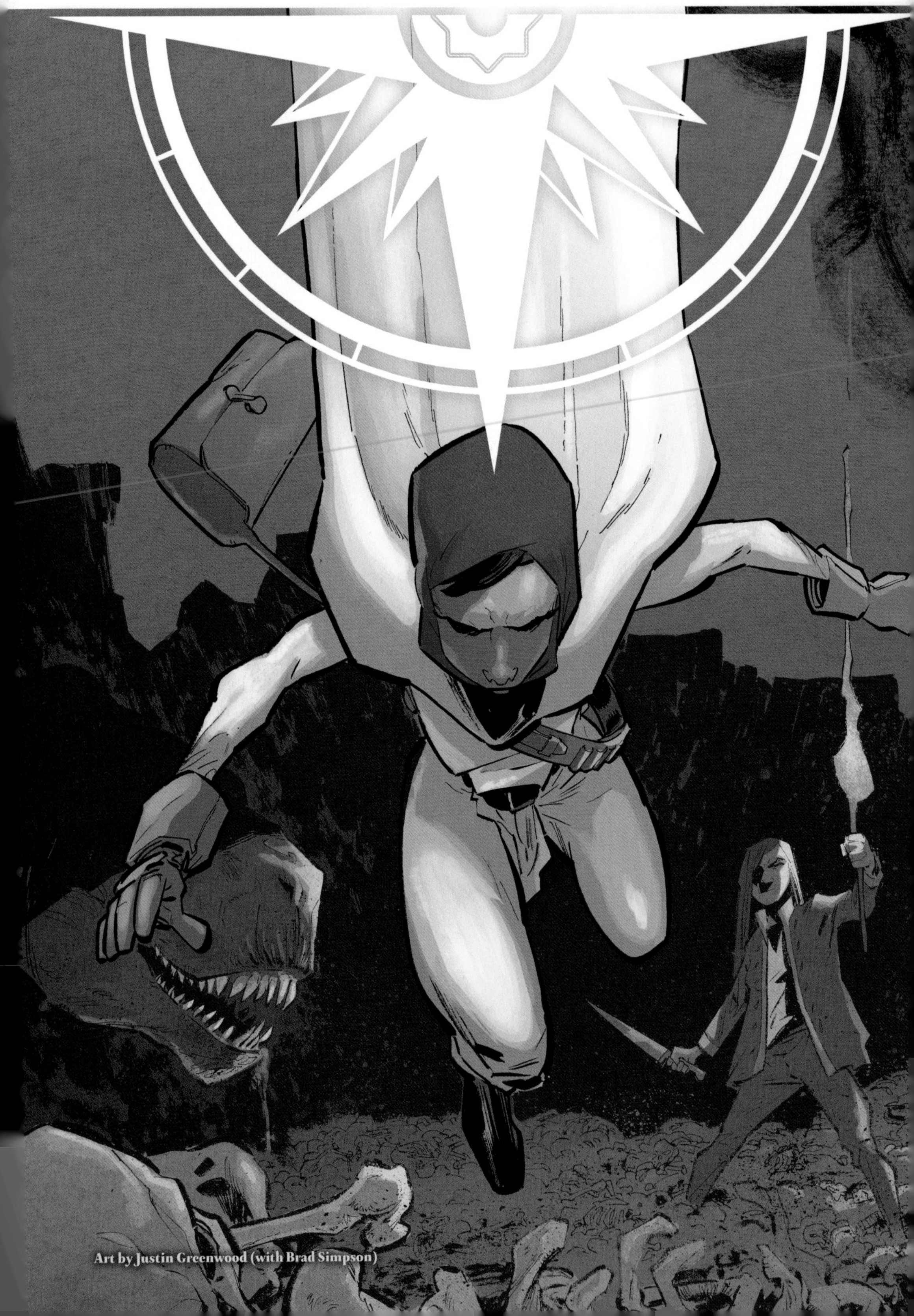
Art by Justin Greenwood (with Brad Simpson)

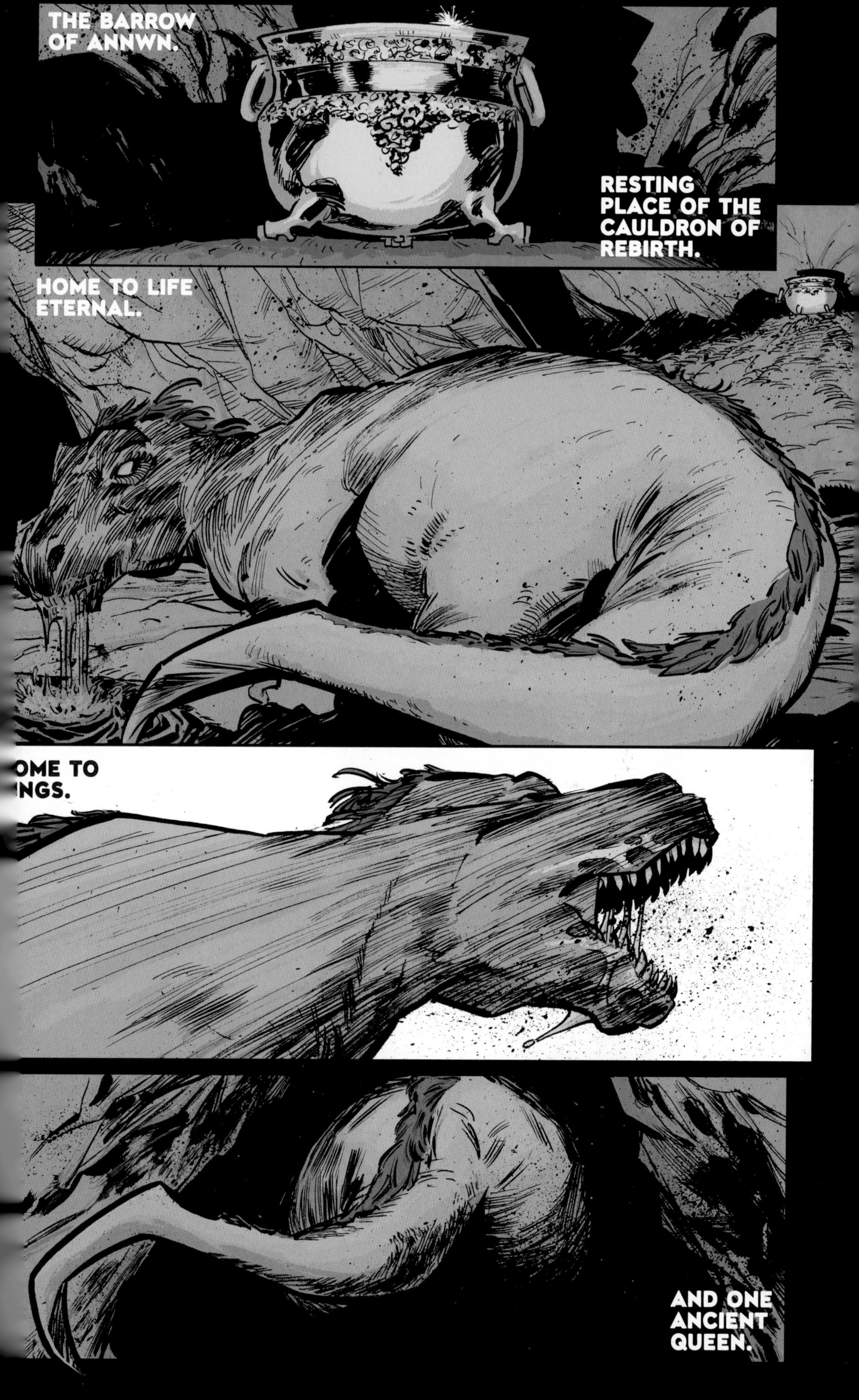

THE BARROW OF ANNWN.
RESTING PLACE OF THE CAULDRON OF REBIRTH.
HOME TO LIFE ETERNAL.
OME TO
NGS.
AND ONE ANCIENT QUEEN.

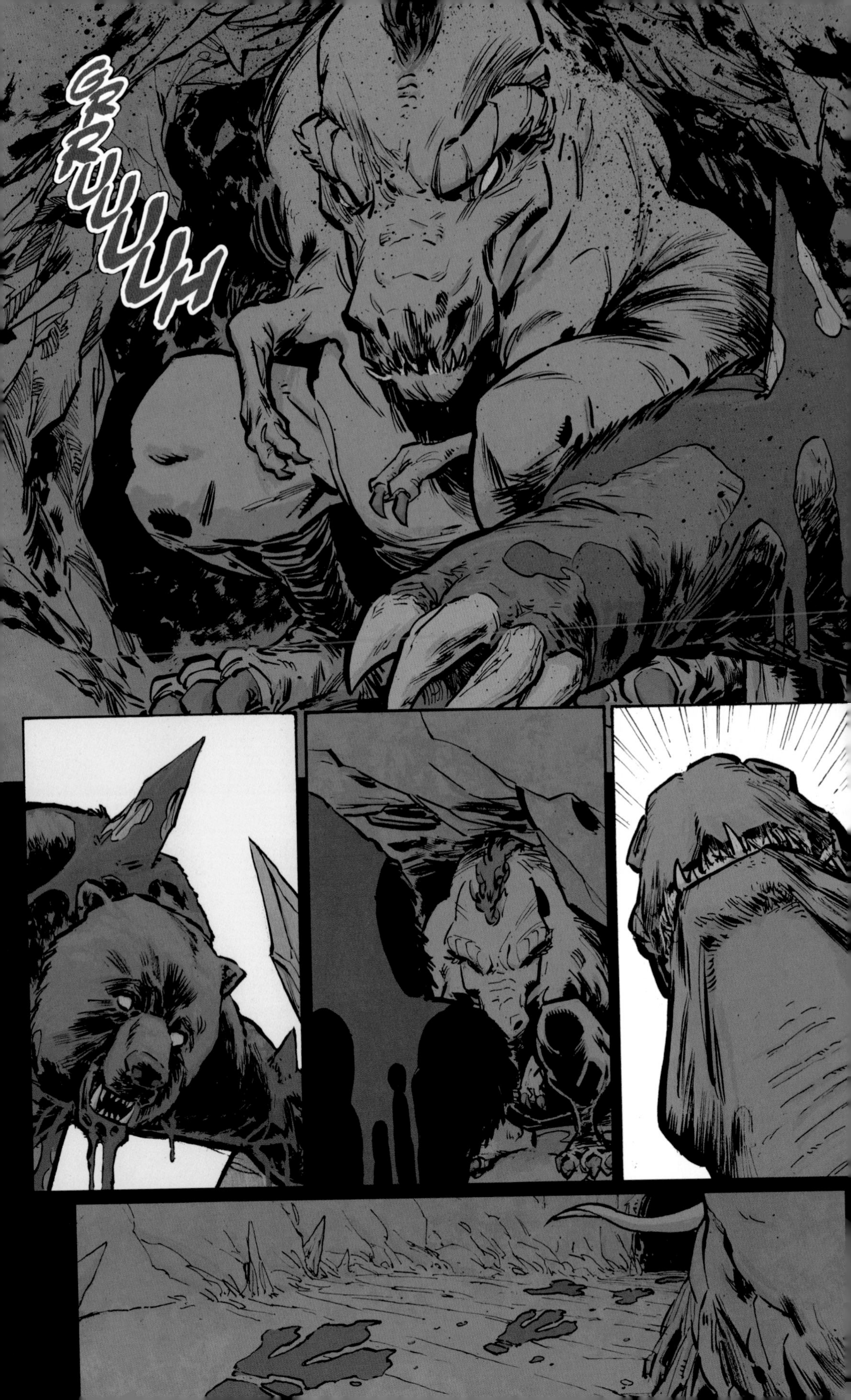
GRUUUH

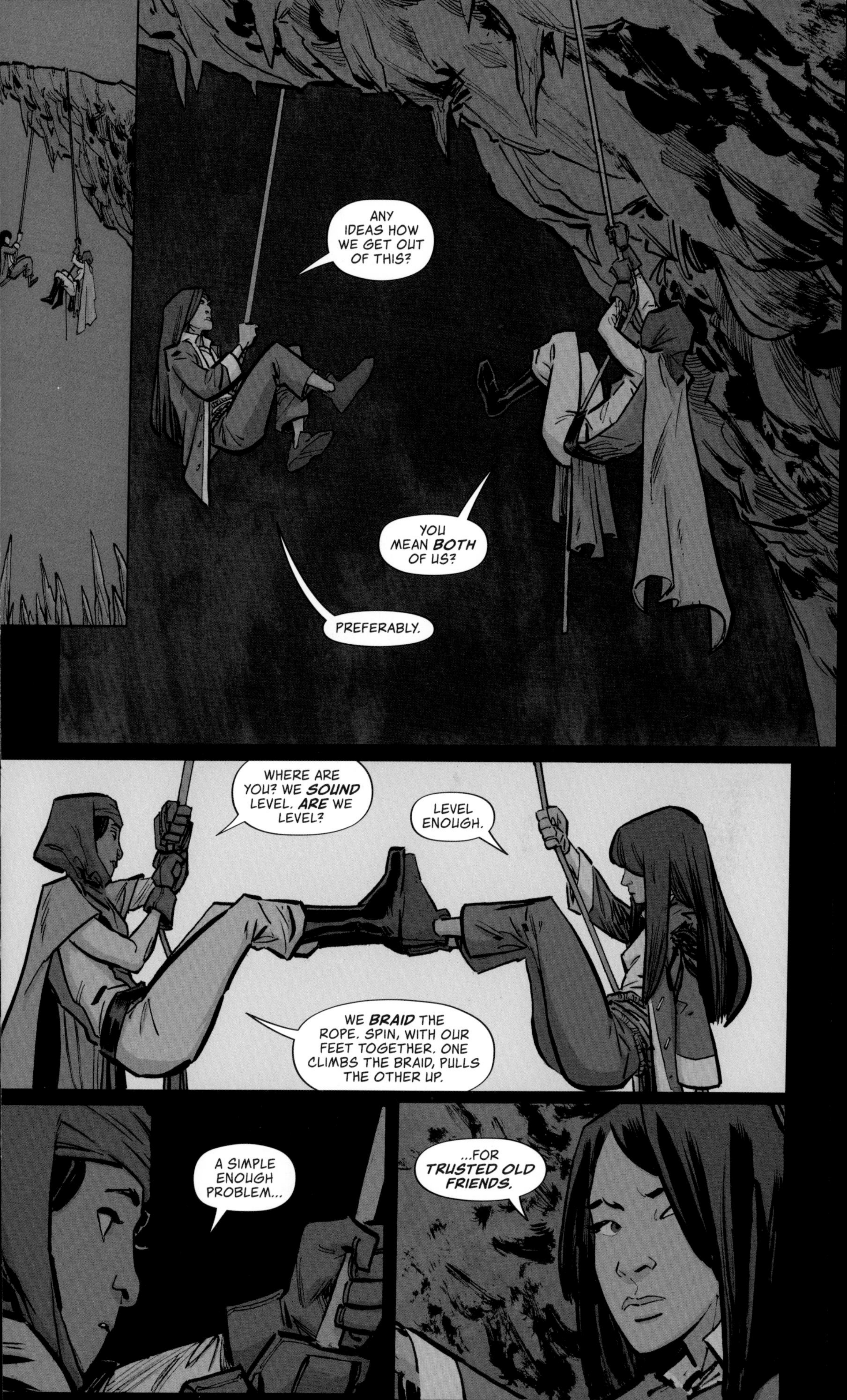
ANY IDEAS HOW WE GET OUT OF THIS?
YOU MEAN BOTH OF US?
PREFERABLY.
WHERE ARE YOU? WE SOUND LEVEL. ARE WE LEVEL?
LEVEL ENOUGH.
WE BRAID THE ROPE. SPIN, WITH OUR FEET TOGETHER. ONE CLIMBS THE BRAID, PULLS THE OTHER UP.
A SIMPLE ENOUGH PROBLEM...
...FOR TRUSTED OLD FRIENDS.

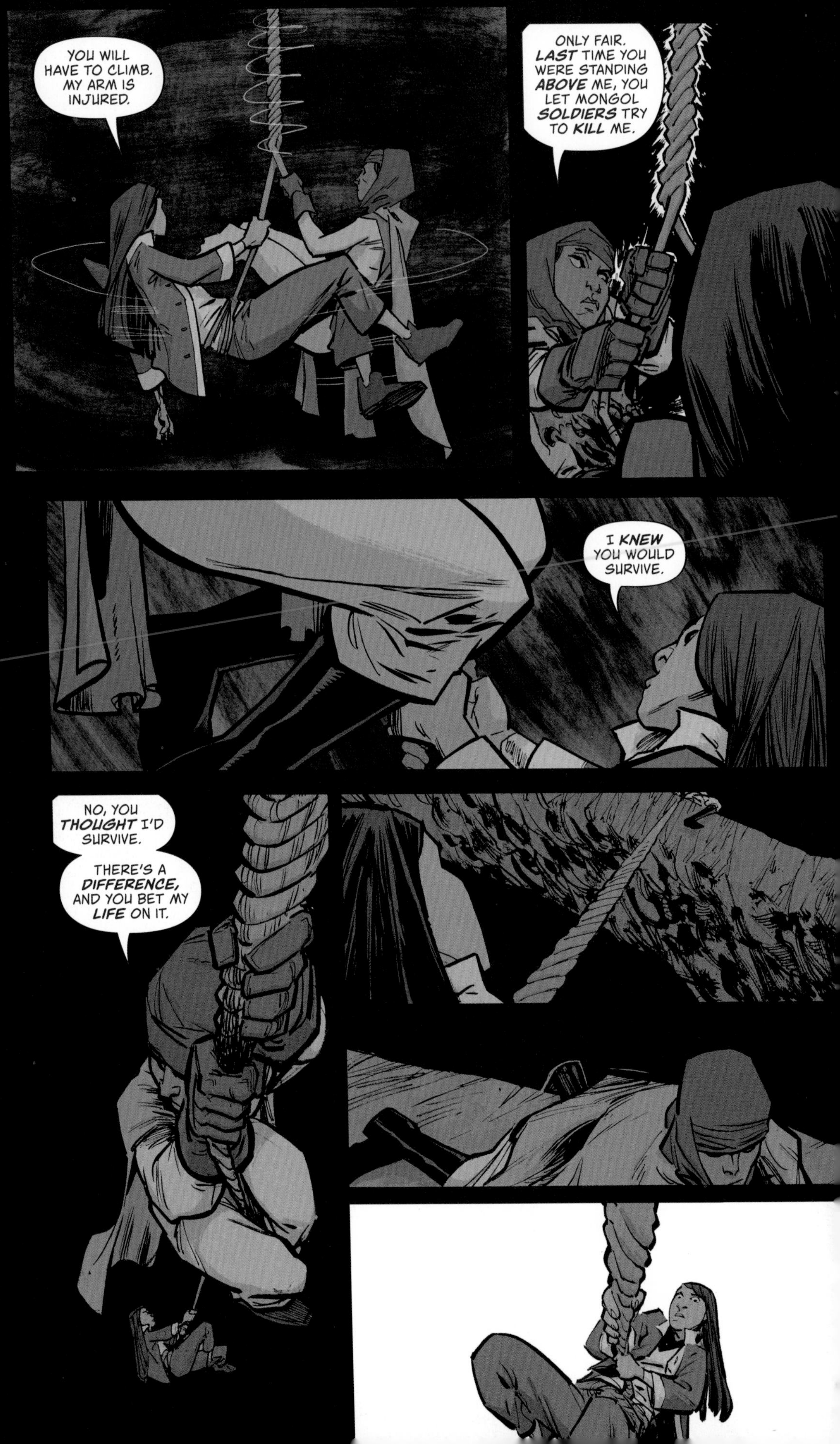

YOU WILL HAVE TO CLIMB. MY ARM IS INJURED.
ONLY FAIR. LAST TIME YOU WERE STANDING ABOVE ME, YOU LET MONGOL SOLDIERS TRY TO KILL ME.
I KNEW YOU WOULD SURVIVE.
NO, YOU THOUGHT I'D SURVIVE.
THERE'S A DIFFERENCE, AND YOU BET MY LIFE ON IT.

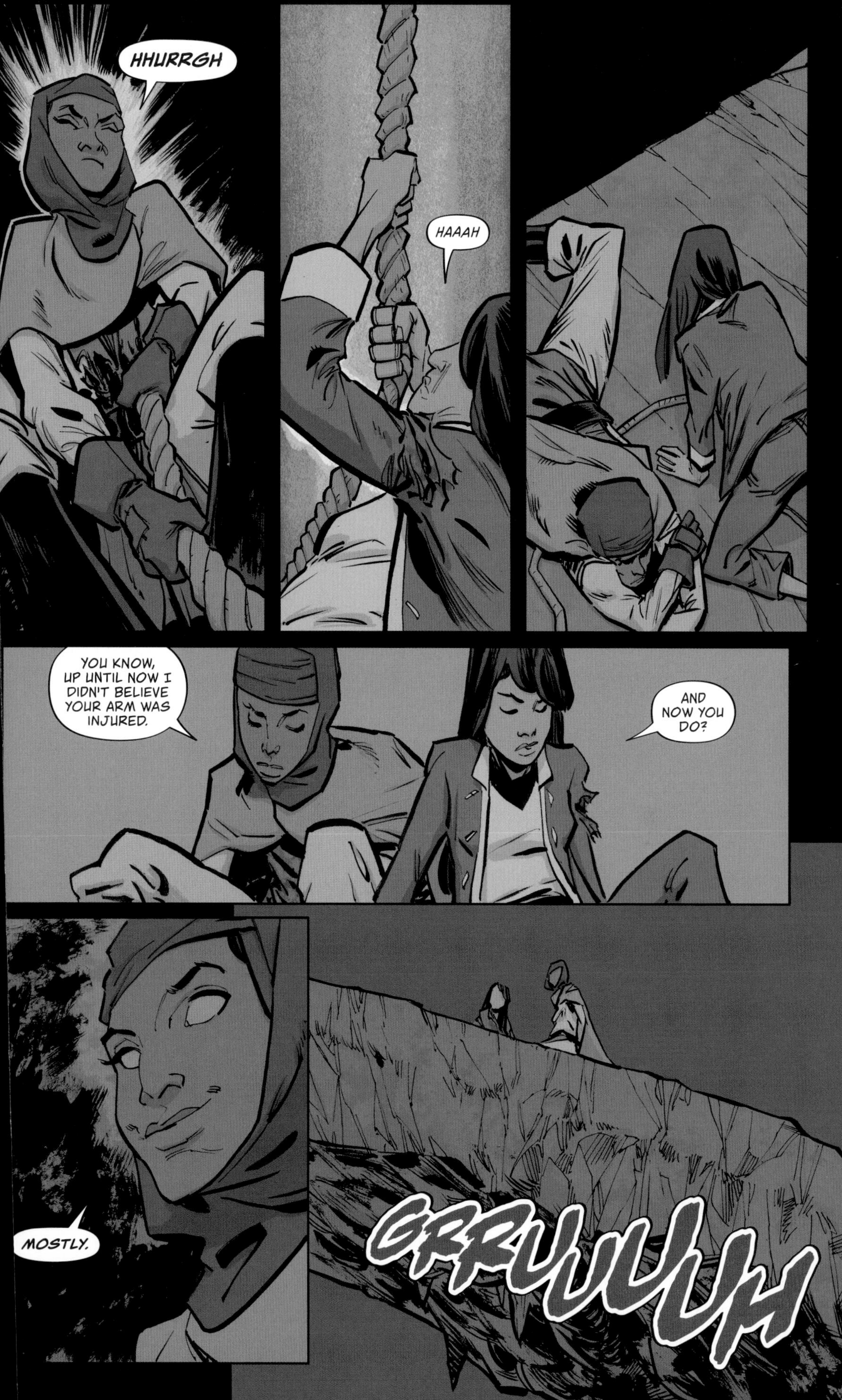
HHURRGH
HAAAH
YOU KNOW, UP UNTIL NOW I DIDN'T BELIEVE YOUR ARM WAS INJURED.
AND NOW YOU DO?
MOSTLY.
GRRUUUUH

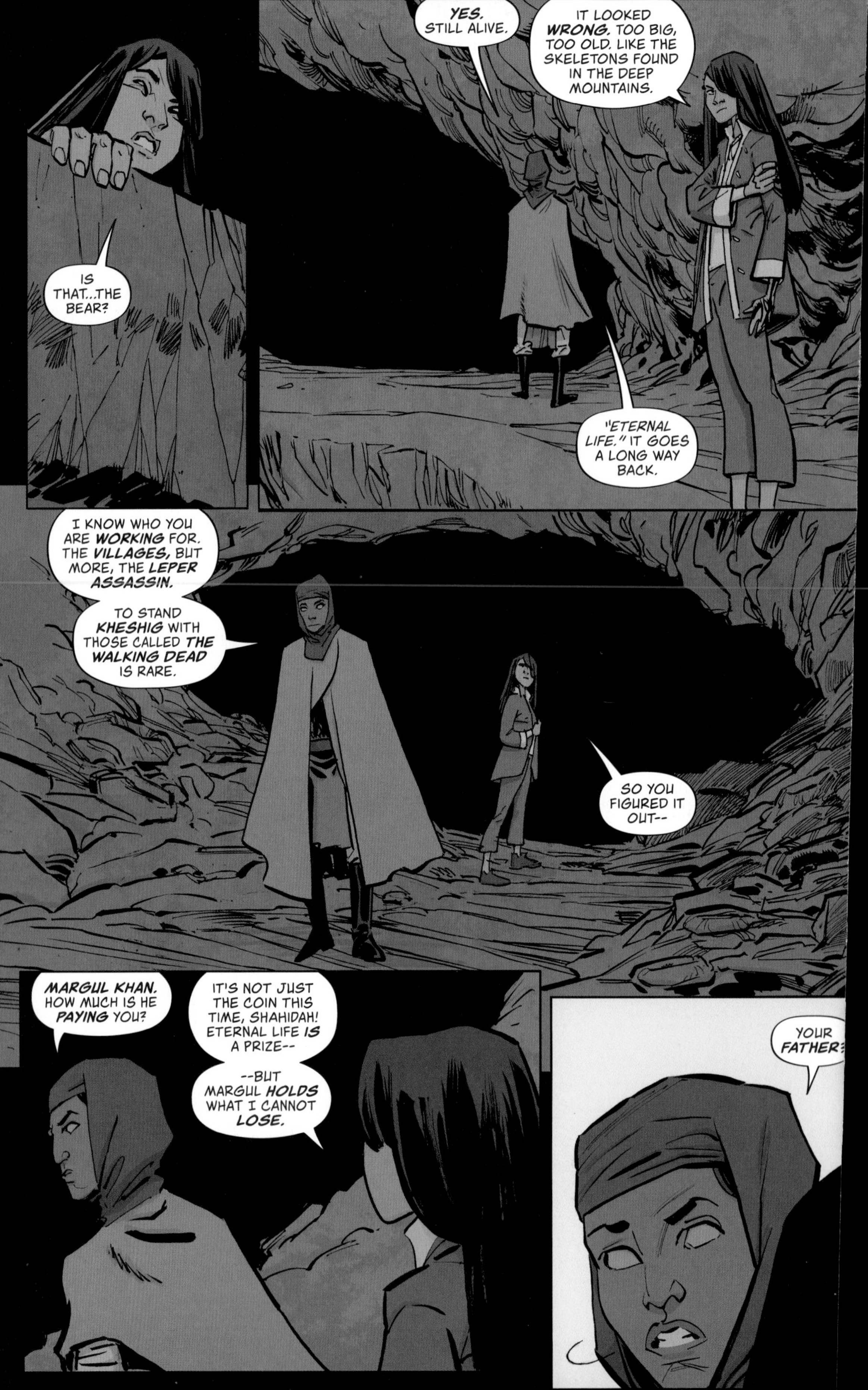
IS THAT...THE BEAR?
YES. STILL ALIVE.
IT LOOKED WRONG. TOO BIG, TOO OLD. LIKE THE SKELETONS FOUND IN THE DEEP MOUNTAINS.
"ETERNAL LIFE." IT GOES A LONG WAY BACK.
I KNOW WHO YOU ARE WORKING FOR. THE VILLAGES, BUT MORE, THE LEPER ASSASSIN.
TO STAND KHESHIG WITH THOSE CALLED THE WALKING DEAD IS RARE.
SO YOU FIGURED IT OUT--
MARGUL KHAN. HOW MUCH IS HE PAYING YOU?
IT'S NOT JUST THE COIN THIS TIME, SHAHIDAH! ETERNAL LIFE IS A PRIZE--
--BUT MARGUL HOLDS WHAT I CANNOT LOSE.
YOUR FATHER?

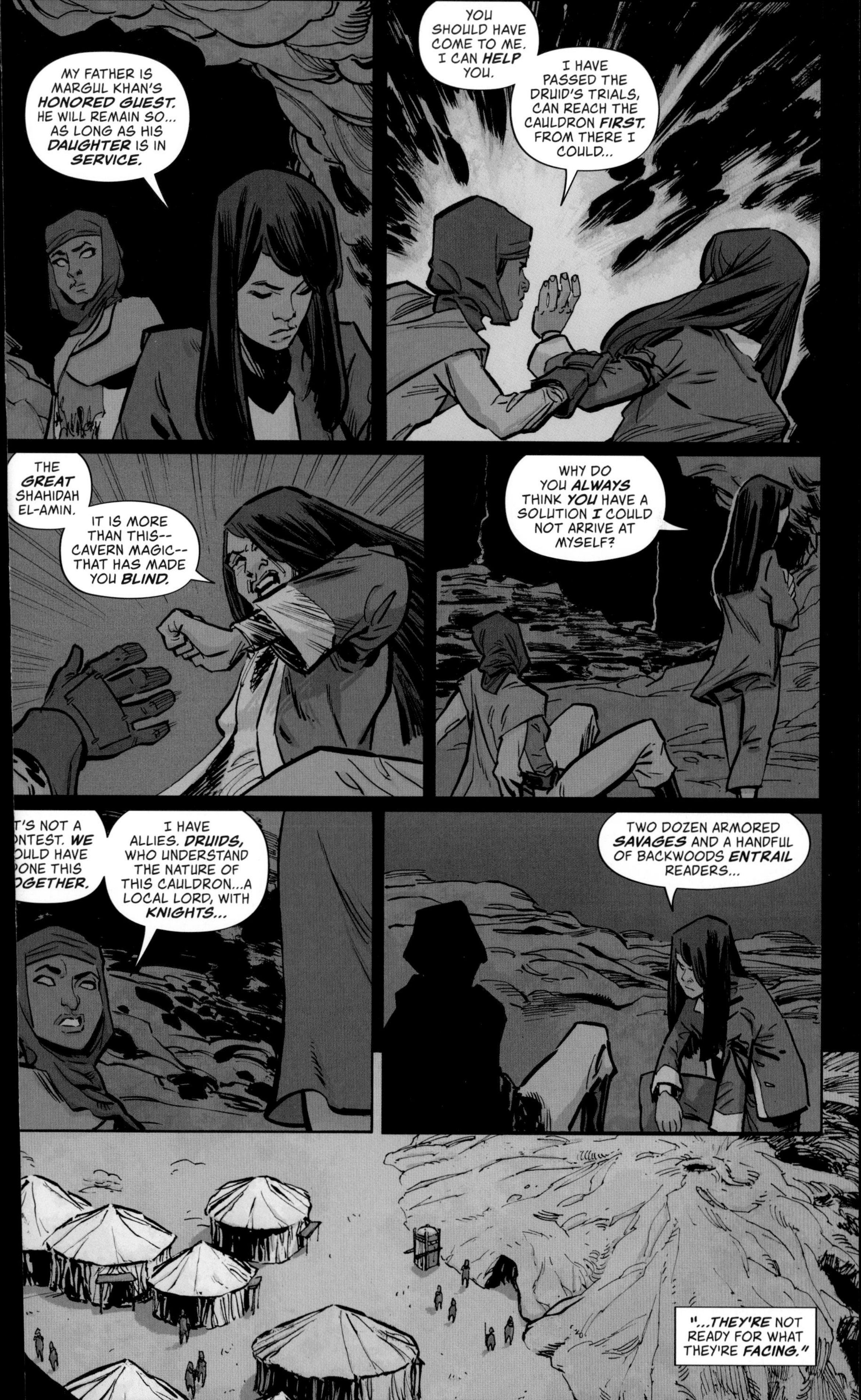

MY FATHER IS MARGUL KHAN'S HONORED GUEST. HE WILL REMAIN SO... AS LONG AS HIS DAUGHTER IS IN SERVICE.
YOU SHOULD HAVE COME TO ME. I CAN HELP YOU.
I HAVE PASSED THE DRUID'S TRIALS, CAN REACH THE CAULDRON FIRST. FROM THERE I COULD...
THE GREAT SHAHIDAH EL-AMIN.
IT IS MORE THAN THIS-- CAVERN MAGIC-- THAT HAS MADE YOU BLIND.
WHY DO YOU ALWAYS THINK YOU HAVE A SOLUTION I COULD NOT ARRIVE AT MYSELF?
T'S NOT A ONTEST. WE OULD HAVE ONE THIS OGETHER.
I HAVE ALLIES. DRUIDS, WHO UNDERSTAND THE NATURE OF THIS CAULDRON...A LOCAL LORD, WITH KNIGHTS...
TWO DOZEN ARMORED SAVAGES AND A HANDFUL OF BACKWOODS ENTRAIL READERS...
"...THEY'RE NOT READY FOR WHAT THEY'RE FACING."

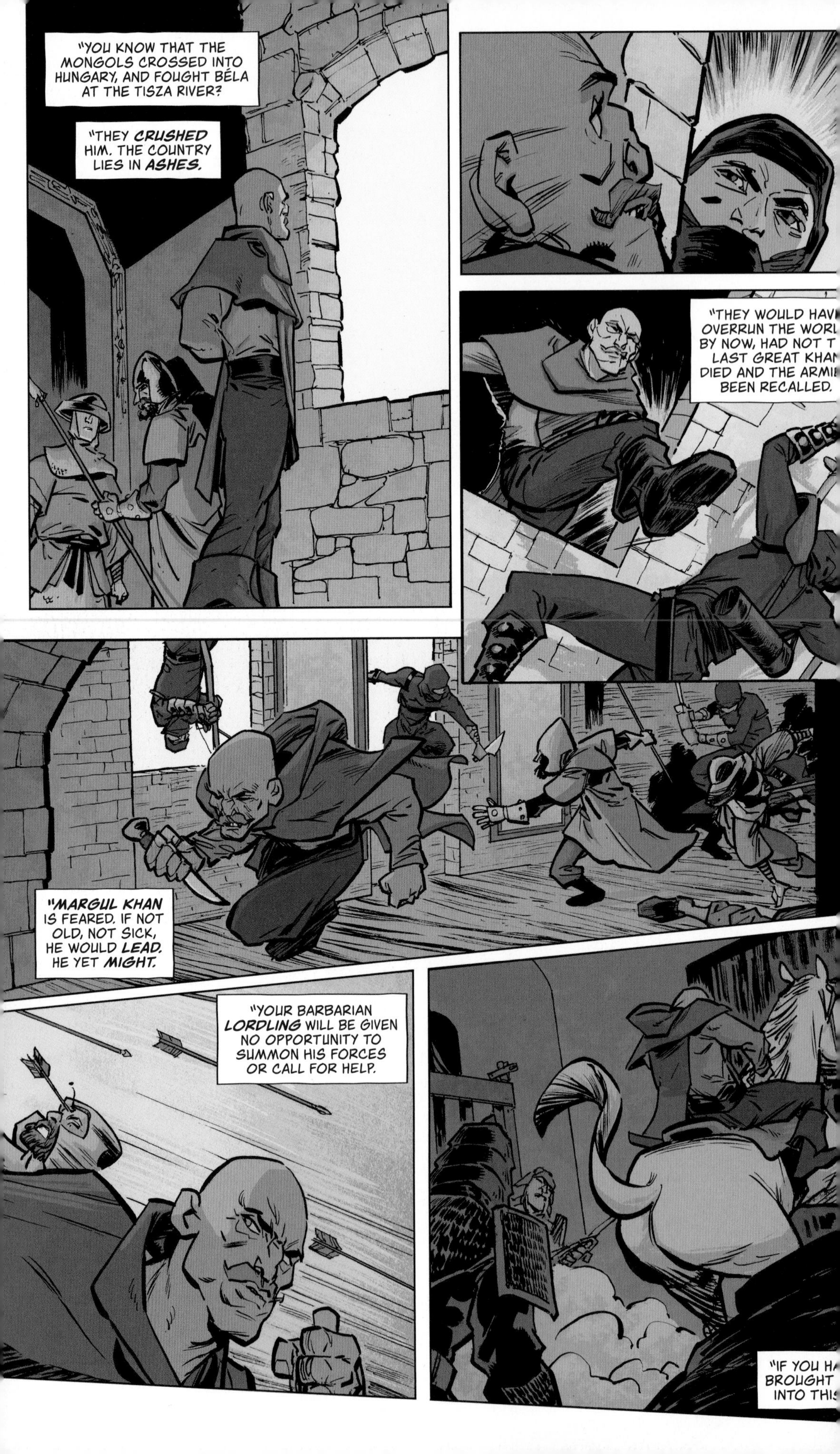
"YOU KNOW THAT THE MONGOLS CROSSED INTO HUNGARY, AND FOUGHT BÉLA AT THE TISZA RIVER?
"THEY CRUSHED HIM. THE COUNTRY LIES IN ASHES.
"THEY WOULD HAV OVERRUN THE WORL BY NOW, HAD NOT T LAST GREAT KHAN DIED AND THE ARMI BEEN RECALLED.
"MARGUL KHAN IS FEARED. IF NOT OLD, NOT SICK, HE WOULD LEAD. HE YET MIGHT.
"YOUR BARBARIAN LORDLING WILL BE GIVEN NO OPPORTUNITY TO SUMMON HIS FORCES OR CALL FOR HELP.
"IF YOU H BROUGHT INTO THIS

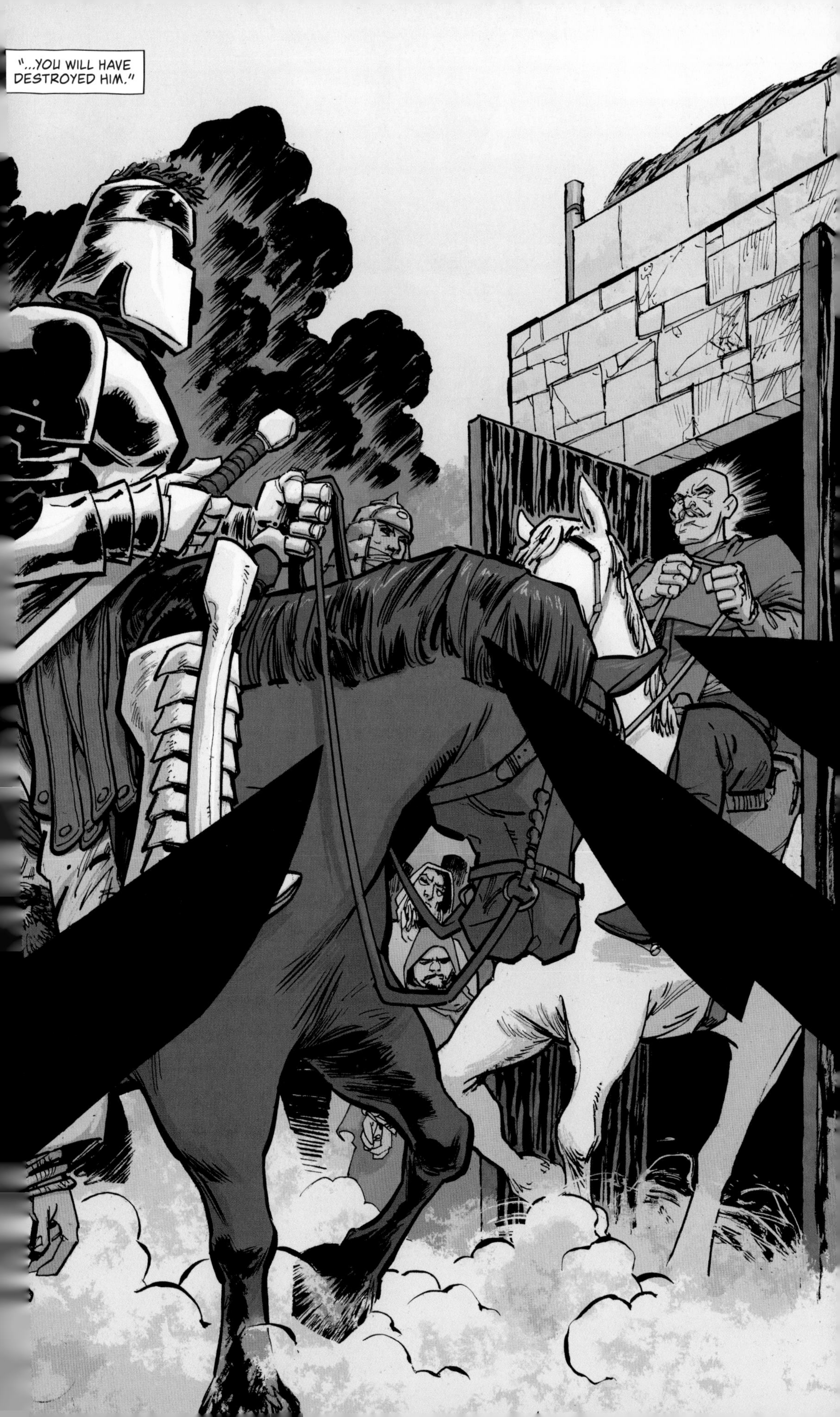
"...YOU WILL HAVE DESTROYED HIM."

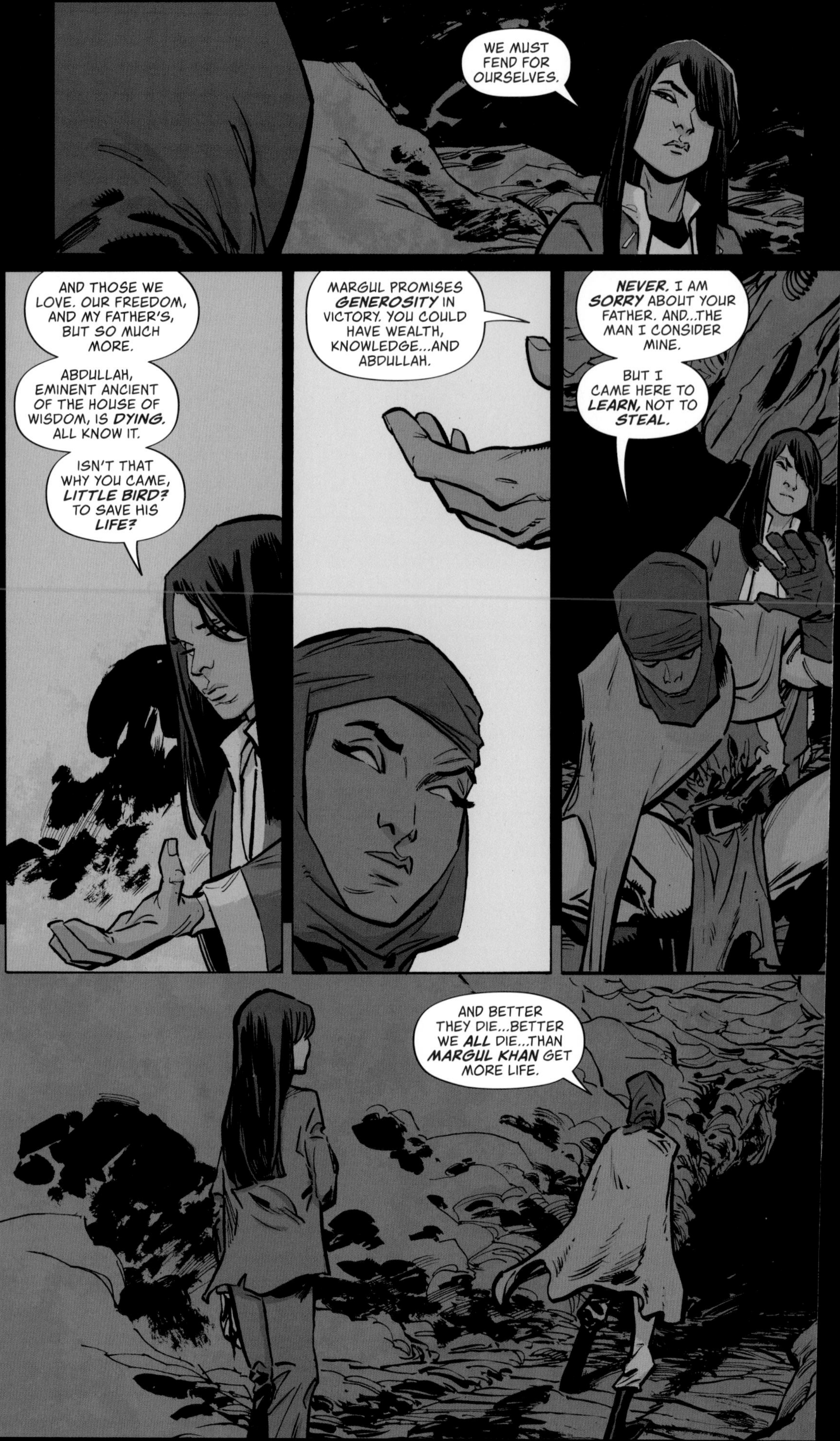
WE MUST FEND FOR OURSELVES.
AND THOSE WE LOVE. OUR FREEDOM, AND MY FATHER'S, BUT SO MUCH MORE.
ABDULLAH, EMINENT ANCIENT OF THE HOUSE OF WISDOM, IS DYING. ALL KNOW IT.
ISN'T THAT WHY YOU CAME, LITTLE BIRD? TO SAVE HIS LIFE?
MARGUL PROMISES GENEROSITY IN VICTORY. YOU COULD HAVE WEALTH, KNOWLEDGE...AND ABDULLAH.
NEVER. I AM SORRY ABOUT YOUR FATHER. AND...THE MAN I CONSIDER MINE.
BUT I CAME HERE TO LEARN, NOT TO STEAL.
AND BETTER THEY DIE...BETTER WE ALL DIE...THAN MARGUL KHAN GET MORE LIFE.

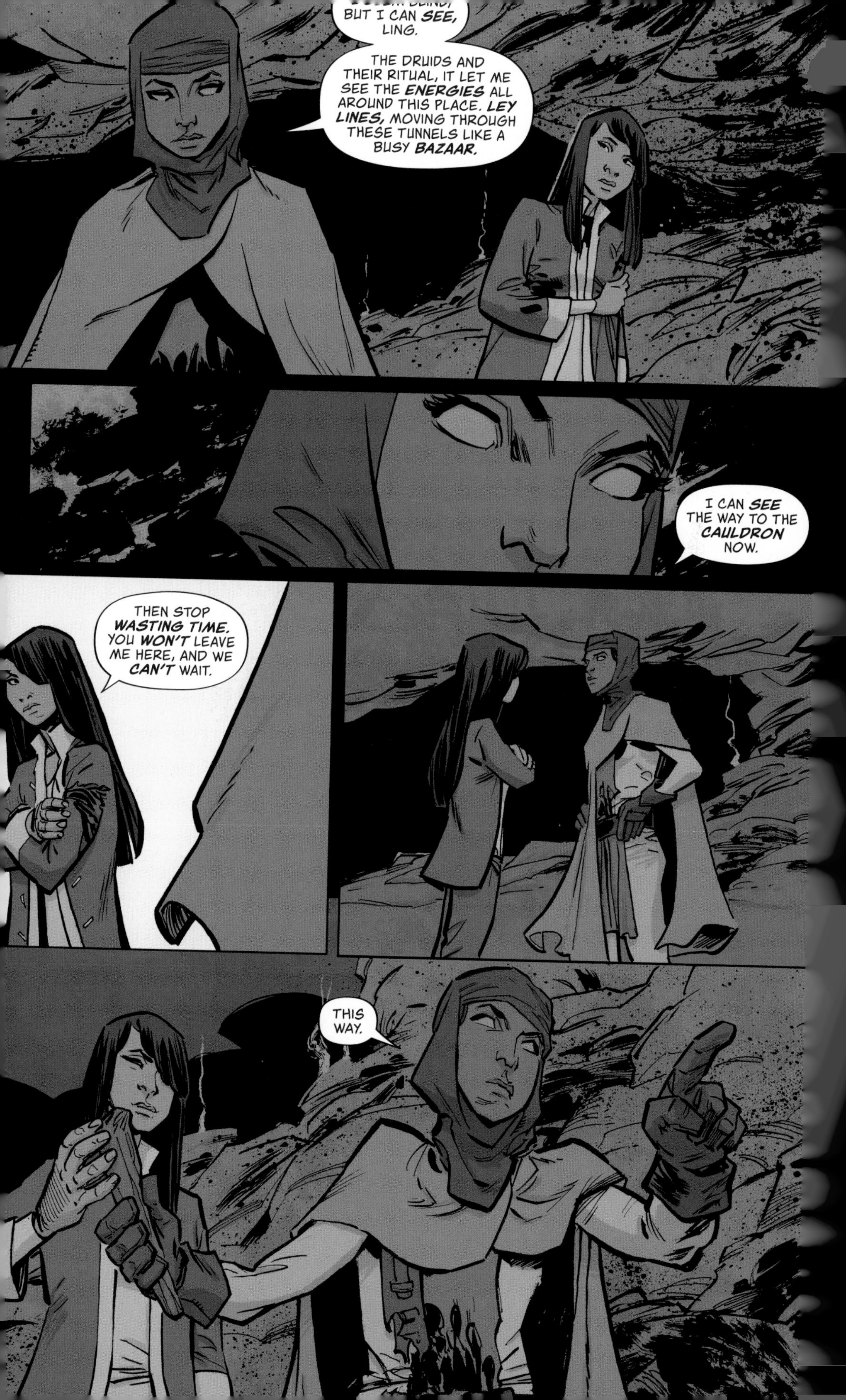

BUT I CAN SEE, LING.
THE DRUIDS AND THEIR RITUAL, IT LET ME SEE THE ENERGIES ALL AROUND THIS PLACE. LEY LINES, MOVING THROUGH THESE TUNNELS LIKE A BUSY BAZAAR.
I CAN SEE THE WAY TO THE CAULDRON NOW.
THEN STOP WASTING TIME. YOU WON'T LEAVE ME HERE, AND WE CAN'T WAIT.
THIS WAY.

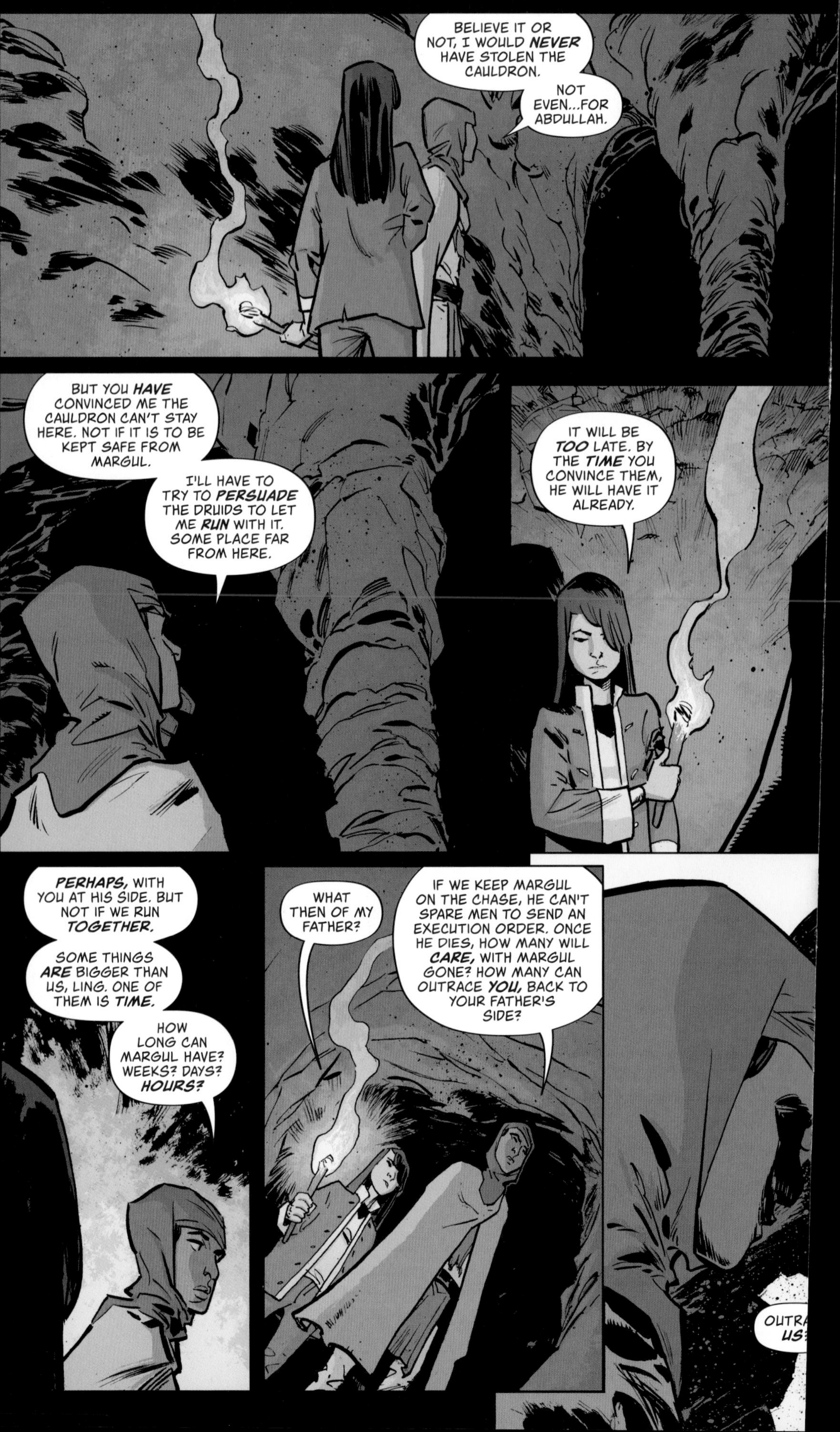
BELIEVE IT OR NOT, I WOULD NEVER HAVE STOLEN THE CAULDRON.
NOT EVEN...FOR ABDULLAH.
BUT YOU HAVE CONVINCED ME THE CAULDRON CAN'T STAY HERE. NOT IF IT IS TO BE KEPT SAFE FROM MARGUL.
I'LL HAVE TO TRY TO PERSUADE THE DRUIDS TO LET ME RUN WITH IT. SOME PLACE FAR FROM HERE.
IT WILL BE TOO LATE. BY THE TIME YOU CONVINCE THEM, HE WILL HAVE IT ALREADY.
PERHAPS, WITH YOU AT HIS SIDE. BUT NOT IF WE RUN TOGETHER.
SOME THINGS ARE BIGGER THAN US, LING. ONE OF THEM IS TIME.
HOW LONG CAN MARGUL HAVE? WEEKS? DAYS? HOURS?
WHAT THEN OF MY FATHER?
IF WE KEEP MARGUL ON THE CHASE, HE CAN'T SPARE MEN TO SEND AN EXECUTION ORDER. ONCE HE DIES, HOW MANY WILL CARE, WITH MARGUL GONE? HOW MANY CAN OUTRACE YOU, BACK TO YOUR FATHER'S SIDE?

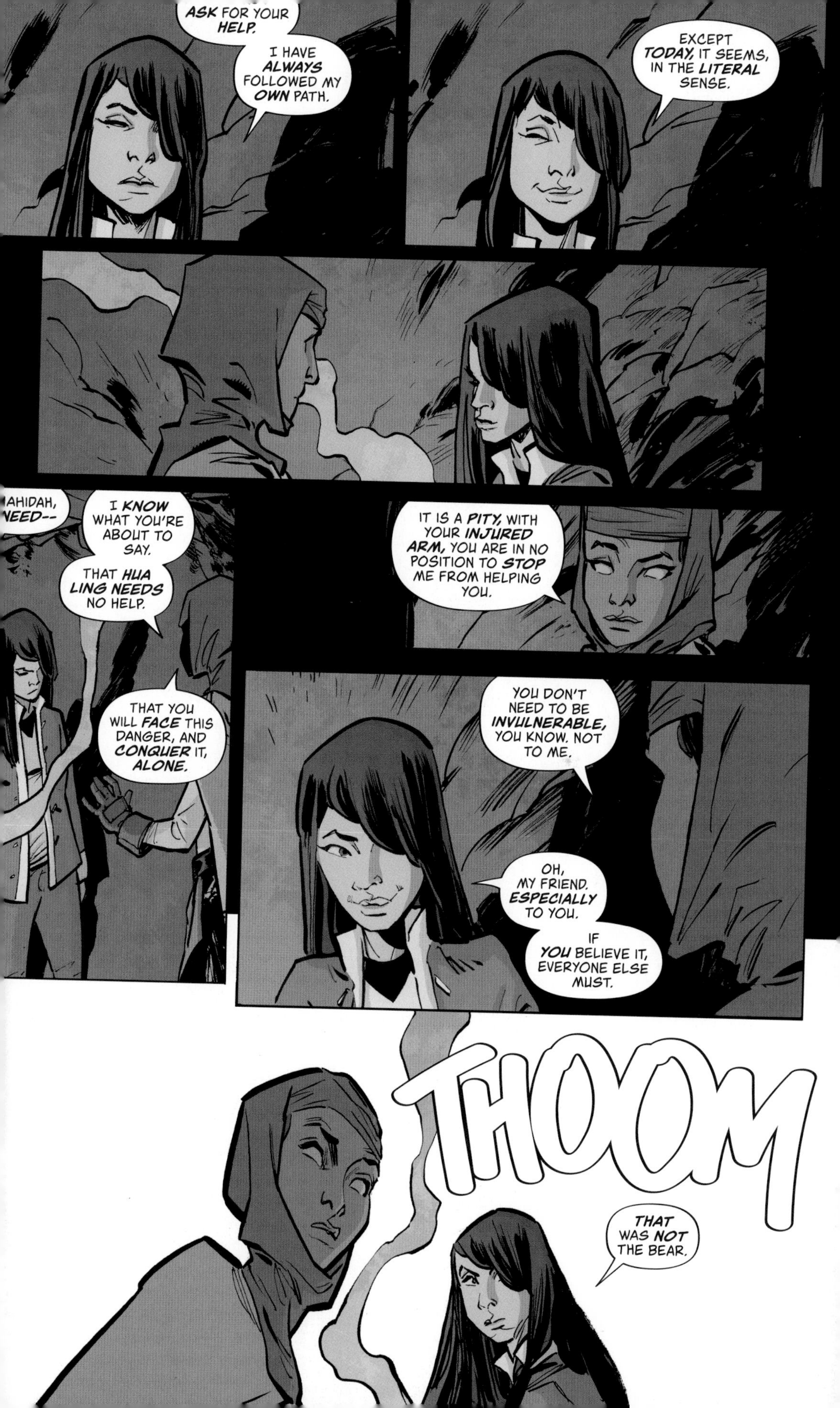

ASK FOR YOUR HELP.
I HAVE ALWAYS FOLLOWED MY OWN PATH.
EXCEPT TODAY, IT SEEMS, IN THE LITERAL SENSE.
AHIDAH, NEED--
I KNOW WHAT YOU'RE ABOUT TO SAY.
THAT HUA LING NEEDS NO HELP.
THAT YOU WILL FACE THIS DANGER, AND CONQUER IT, ALONE.
IT IS A PITY, WITH YOUR INJURED ARM, YOU ARE IN NO POSITION TO STOP ME FROM HELPING YOU.
YOU DON'T NEED TO BE INVULNERABLE, YOU KNOW. NOT TO ME.
OH, MY FRIEND. ESPECIALLY TO YOU.
IF YOU BELIEVE IT, EVERYONE ELSE MUST.
THOOM
THAT WAS NOT THE BEAR.

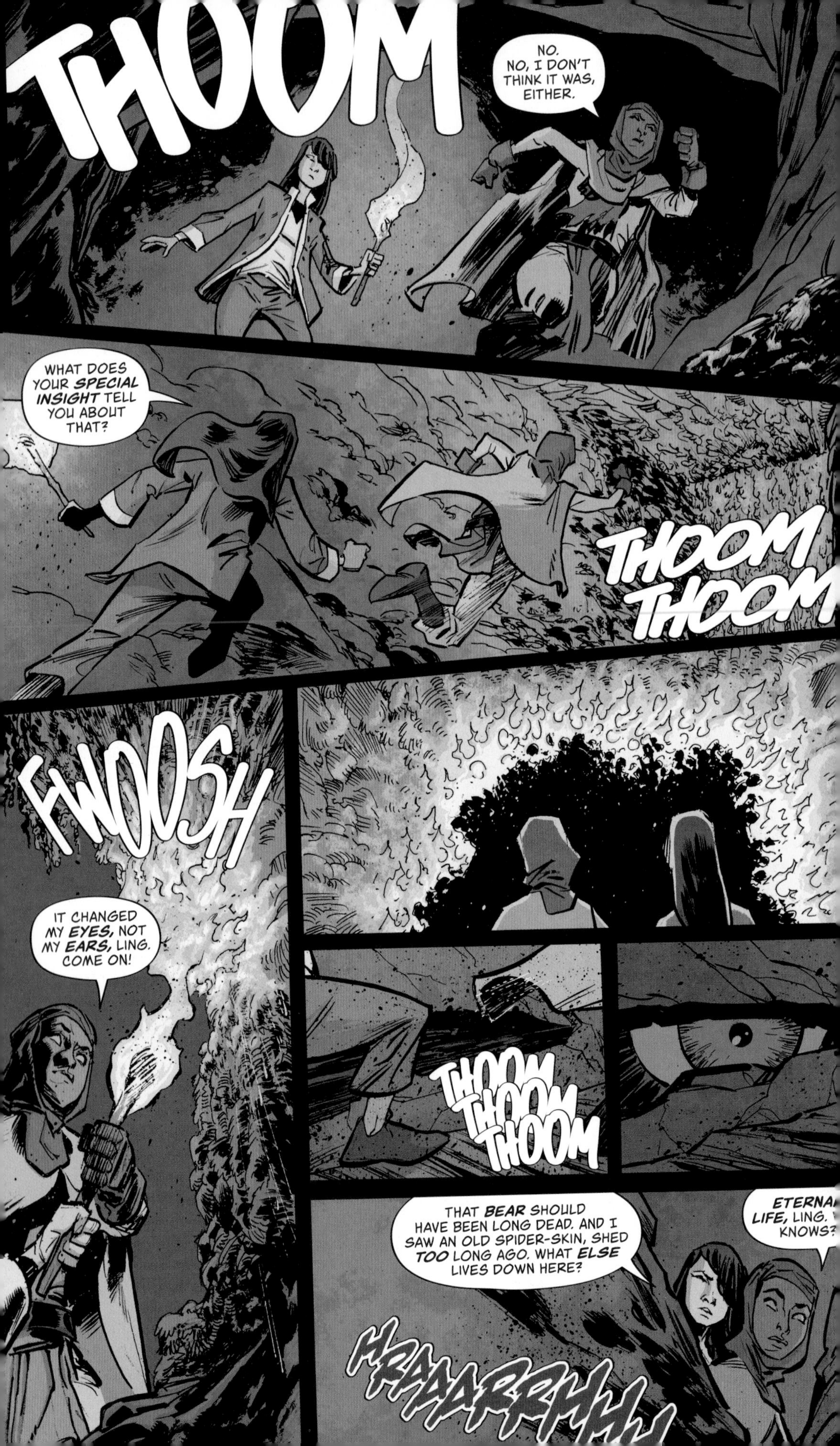
THOOM
NO. NO, I DON'T THINK IT WAS, EITHER.
WHAT DOES YOUR SPECIAL INSIGHT TELL YOU ABOUT THAT?
THOOM THOOM
FWOOSH
IT CHANGED MY EYES, NOT MY EARS, LING. COME ON!
THOOM THOOM THOOM
THAT BEAR SHOULD HAVE BEEN LONG DEAD. AND I SAW AN OLD SPIDER-SKIN, SHED TOO LONG AGO. WHAT ELSE LIVES DOWN HERE?

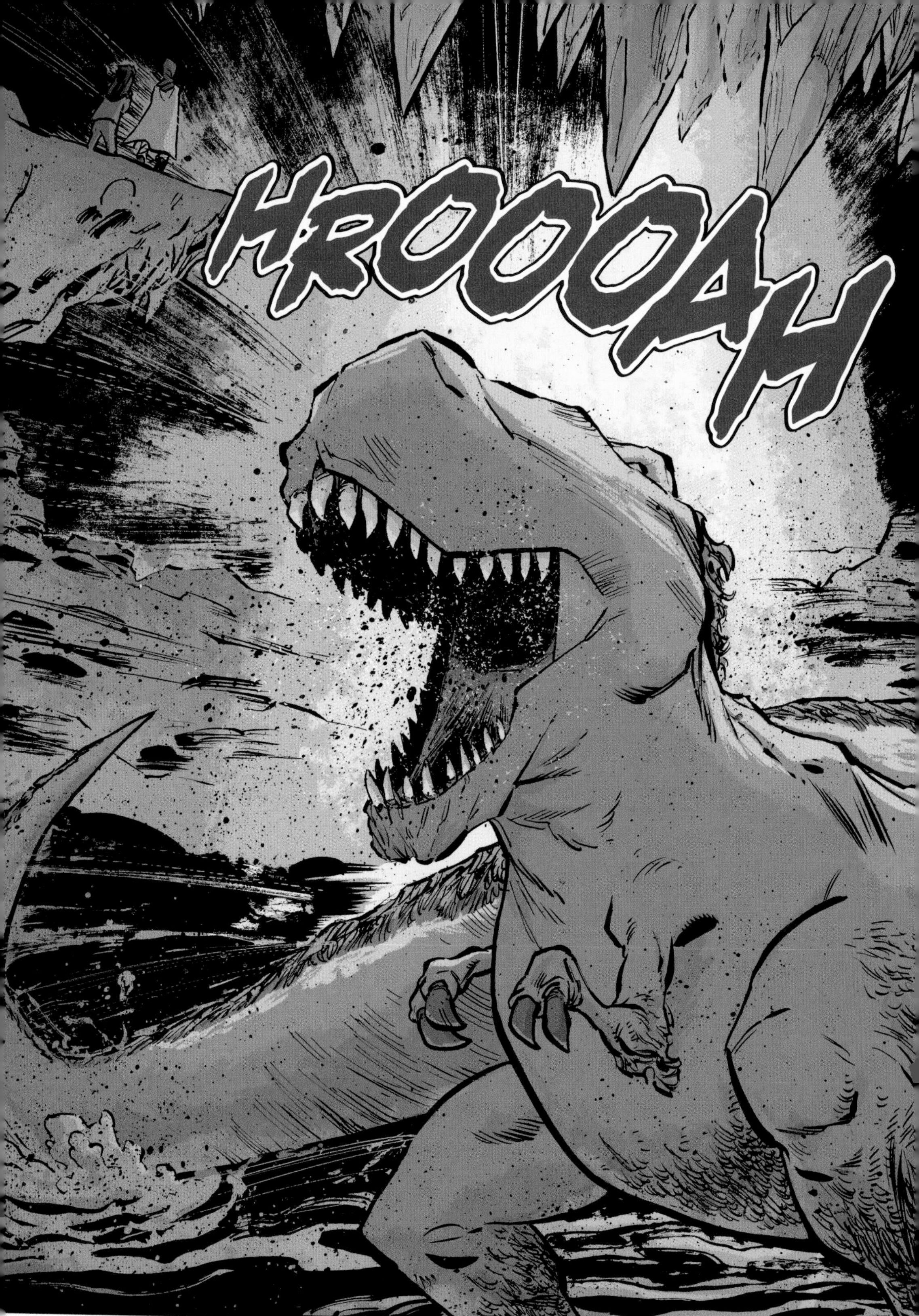
HROOOAH

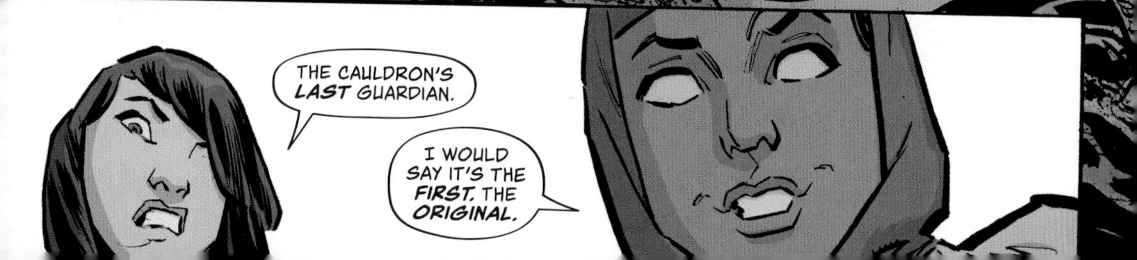
THE CAULDRON'S LAST GUARDIAN.
I WOULD SAY IT'S THE FIRST. THE ORIGINAL.

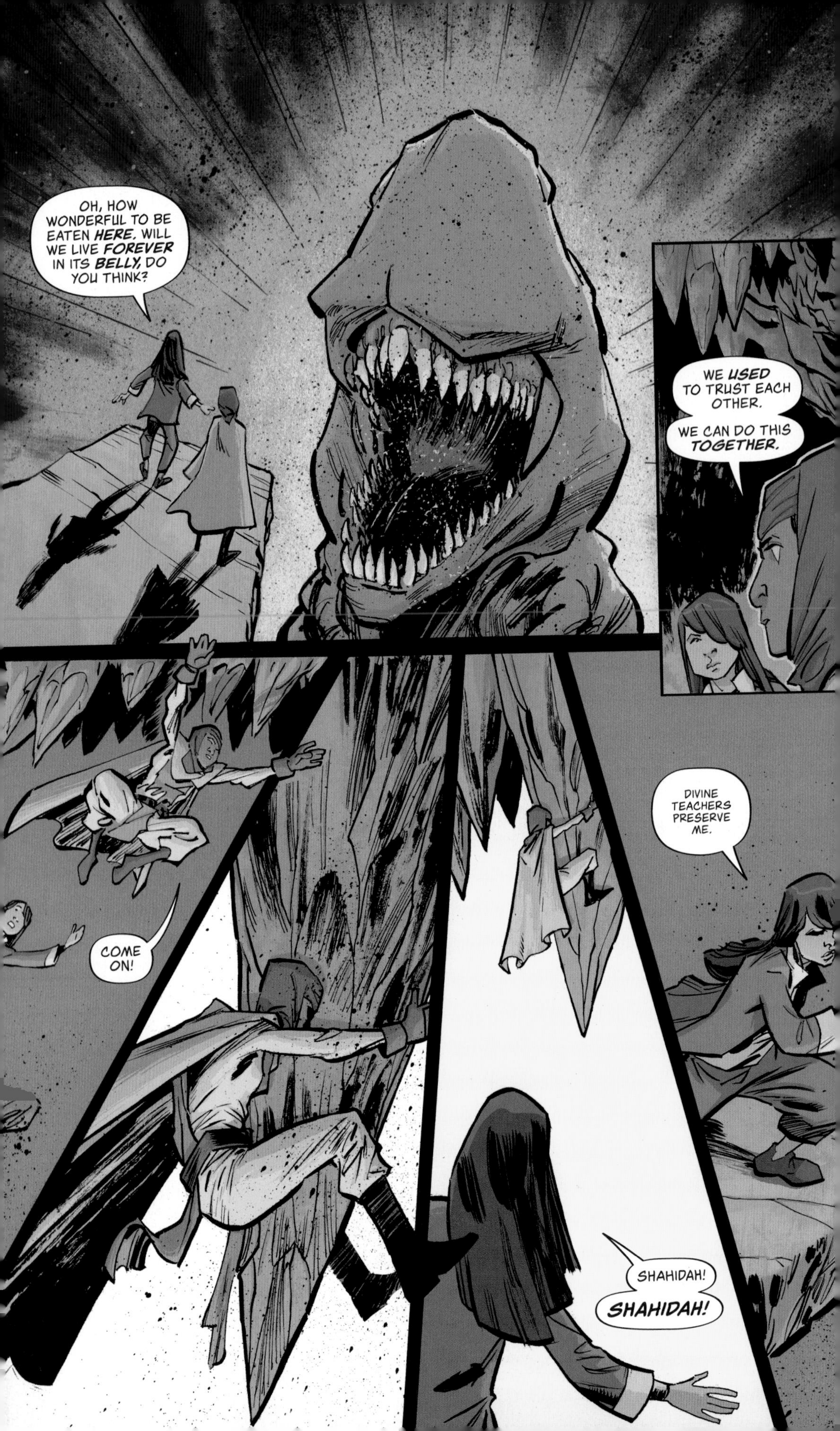
OH, HOW WONDERFUL TO BE EATEN HERE. WILL WE LIVE FOREVER IN ITS BELLY, DO YOU THINK?
WE USED TO TRUST EACH OTHER.
WE CAN DO THIS TOGETHER.
COME ON!
DIVINE TEACHERS PRESERVE ME.
SHAHIDAH!
SHAHIDAH!

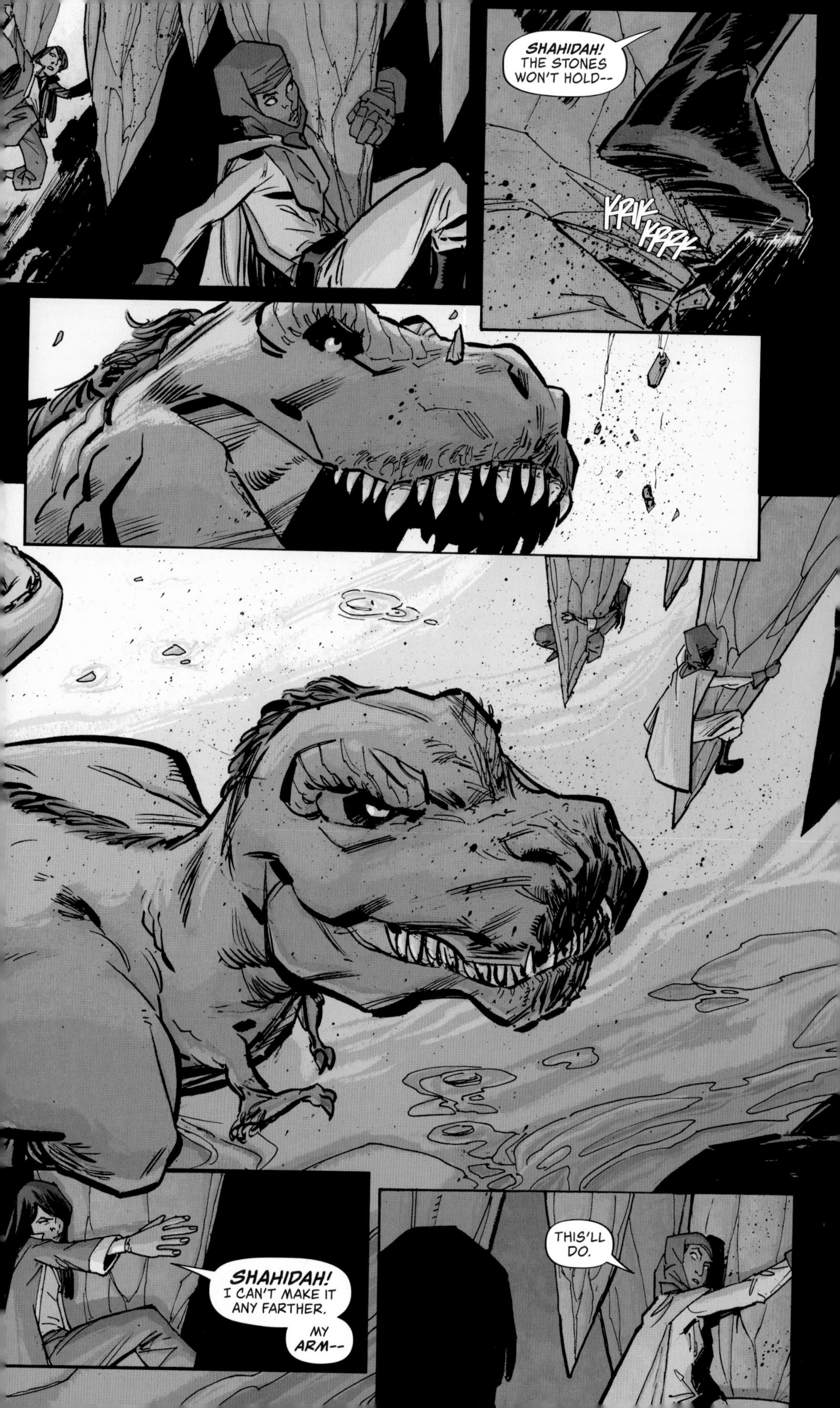
SHAHIDAH! THE STONES WON'T HOLD--
KRAK KRRRK
SHAHIDAH! I CAN'T MAKE IT ANY FARTHER.
MY ARM--
THIS'LL DO.

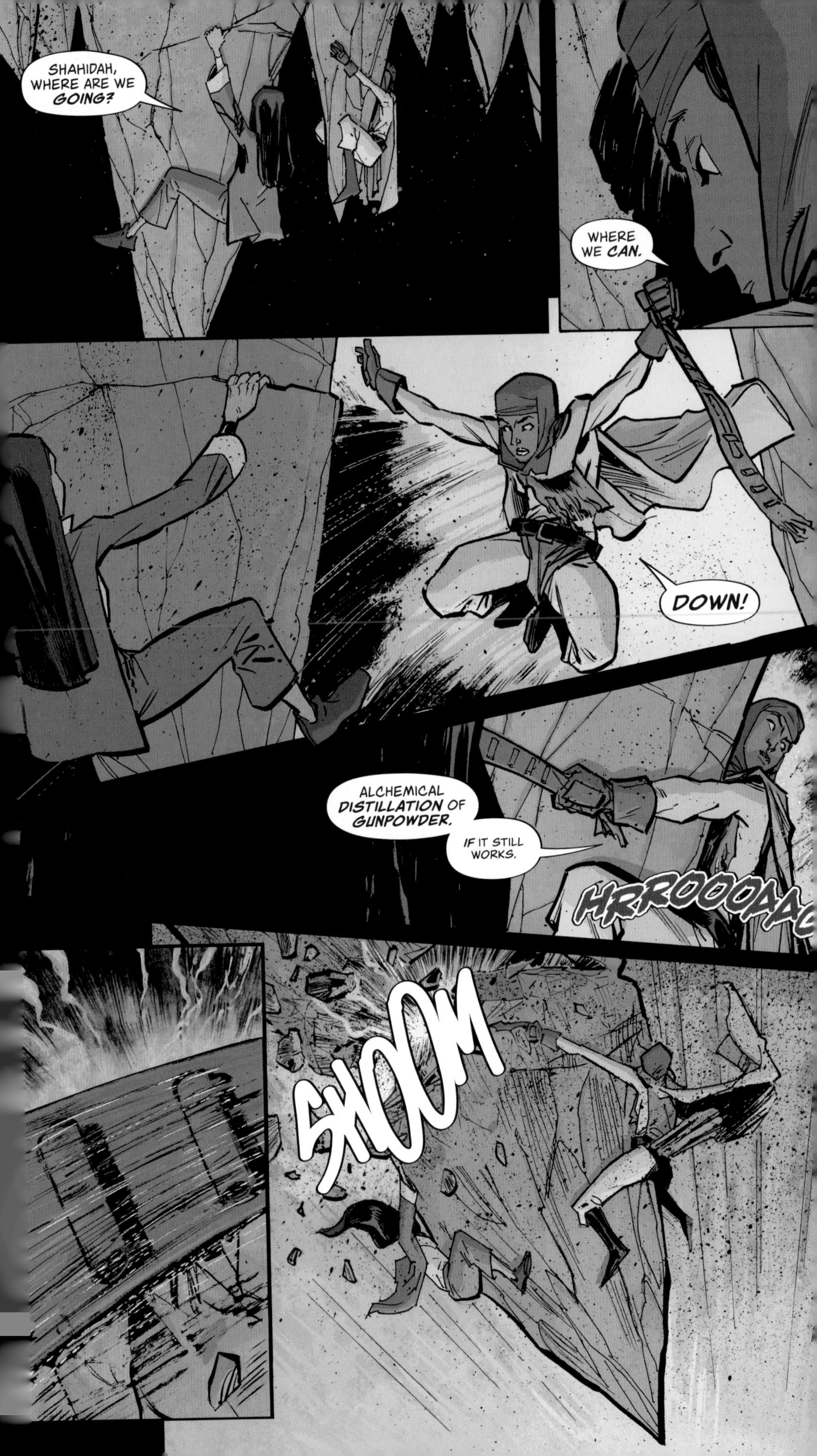

SHAHIDAH, WHERE ARE WE GOING?
WHERE WE CAN.
DOWN!
ALCHEMICAL DISTILLATION OF GUNPOWDER.
IF IT STILL WORKS.
HRROOOAA
SHOOM

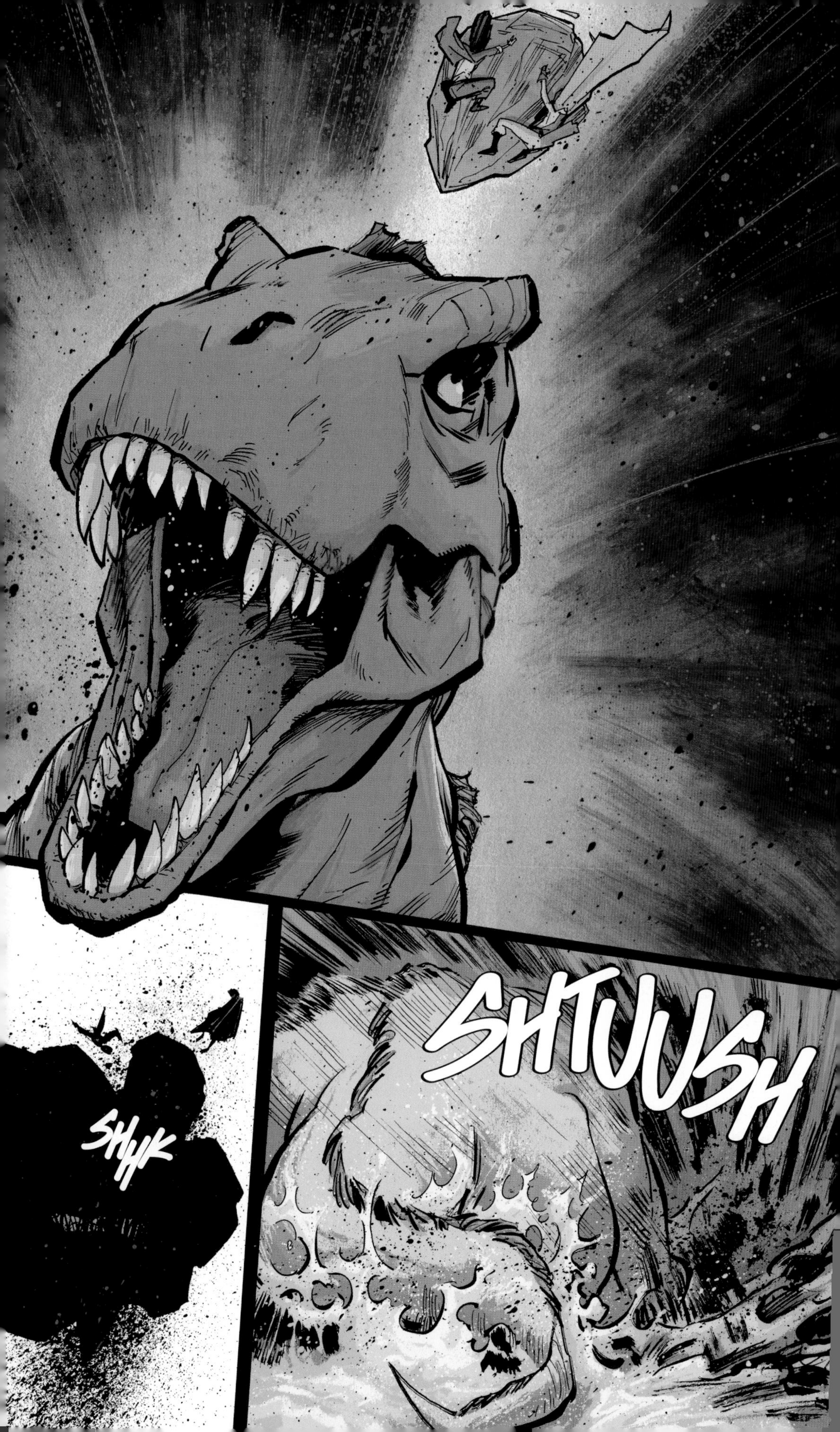
SHHK
SHTUUSH

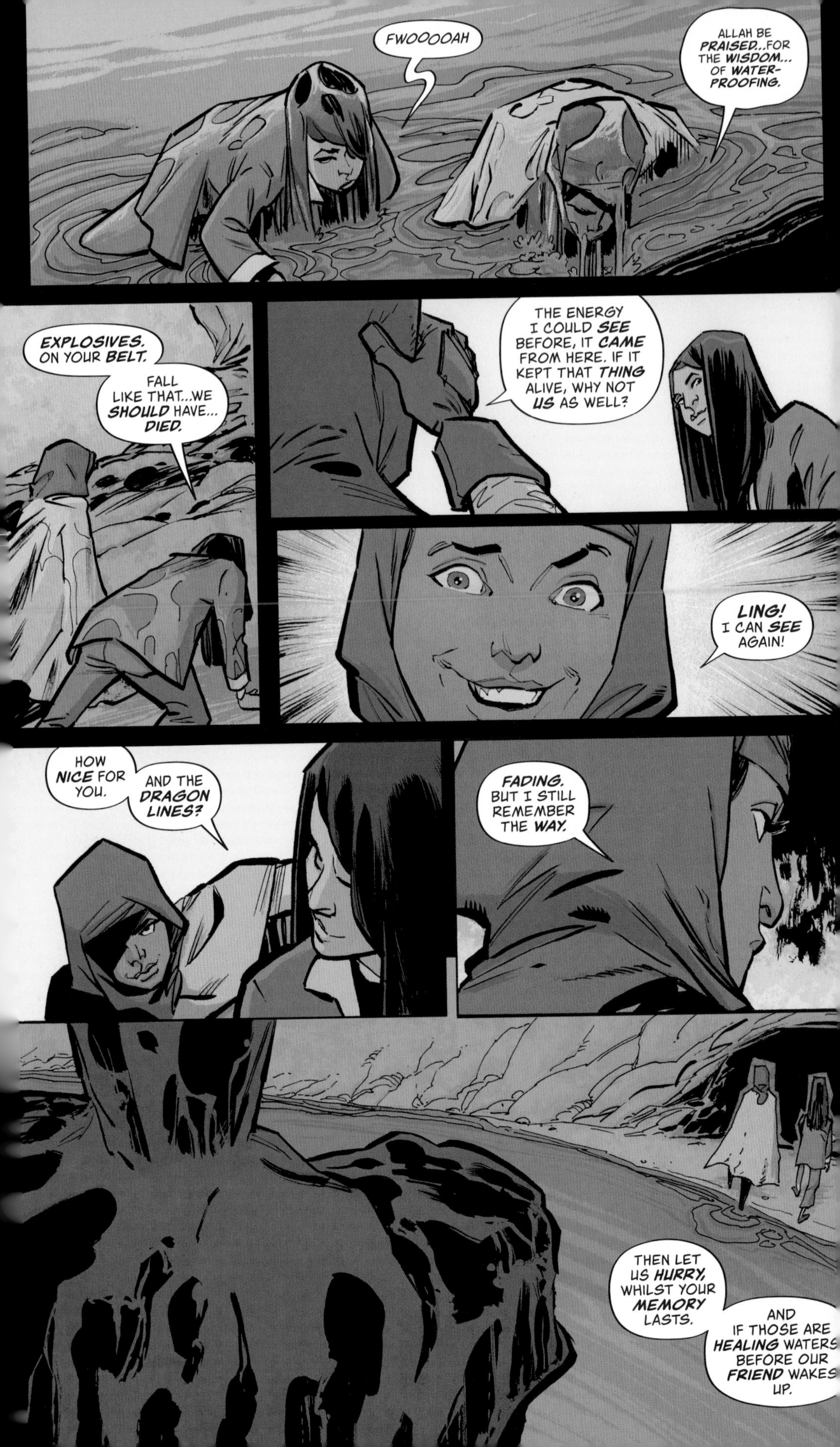
FWOOOOAH
ALLAH BE PRAISED...FOR THE WISDOM... OF WATER-PROOFING.
EXPLOSIVES. ON YOUR BELT.
FALL LIKE THAT...WE SHOULD HAVE... DIED.
THE ENERGY I COULD SEE BEFORE, IT CAME FROM HERE. IF IT KEPT THAT THING ALIVE, WHY NOT US AS WELL?
LING! I CAN SEE AGAIN!
HOW NICE FOR YOU.
AND THE DRAGON LINES?
FADING. BUT I STILL REMEMBER THE WAY.
THEN LET US HURRY, WHILST YOUR MEMORY LASTS.
AND IF THOSE ARE HEALING WATERS BEFORE OUR FRIEND WAKES UP.

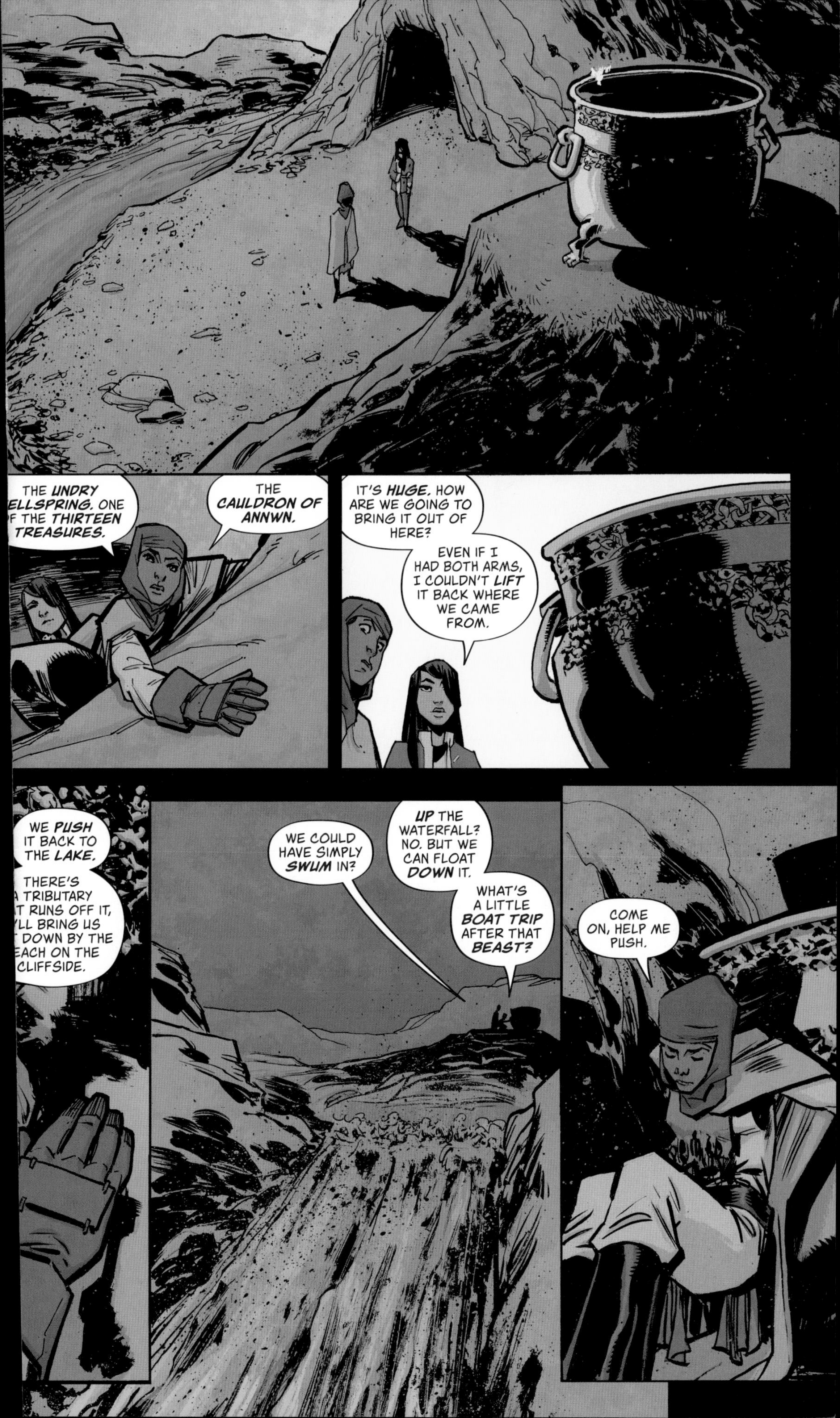
THE UNDRY WELLSPRING. ONE OF THE THIRTEEN TREASURES.
THE CAULDRON OF ANNWN.
IT'S HUGE. HOW ARE WE GOING TO BRING IT OUT OF HERE?
EVEN IF I HAD BOTH ARMS, I COULDN'T LIFT IT BACK WHERE WE CAME FROM.
WE PUSH IT BACK TO THE LAKE.
THERE'S A TRIBUTARY THAT RUNS OFF IT, IT'LL BRING US DOWN BY THE BEACH ON THE CLIFFSIDE.
WE COULD HAVE SIMPLY SWUM IN?
UP THE WATERFALL? NO. BUT WE CAN FLOAT DOWN IT.
WHAT'S A LITTLE BOAT TRIP AFTER THAT BEAST?
COME ON, HELP ME PUSH.

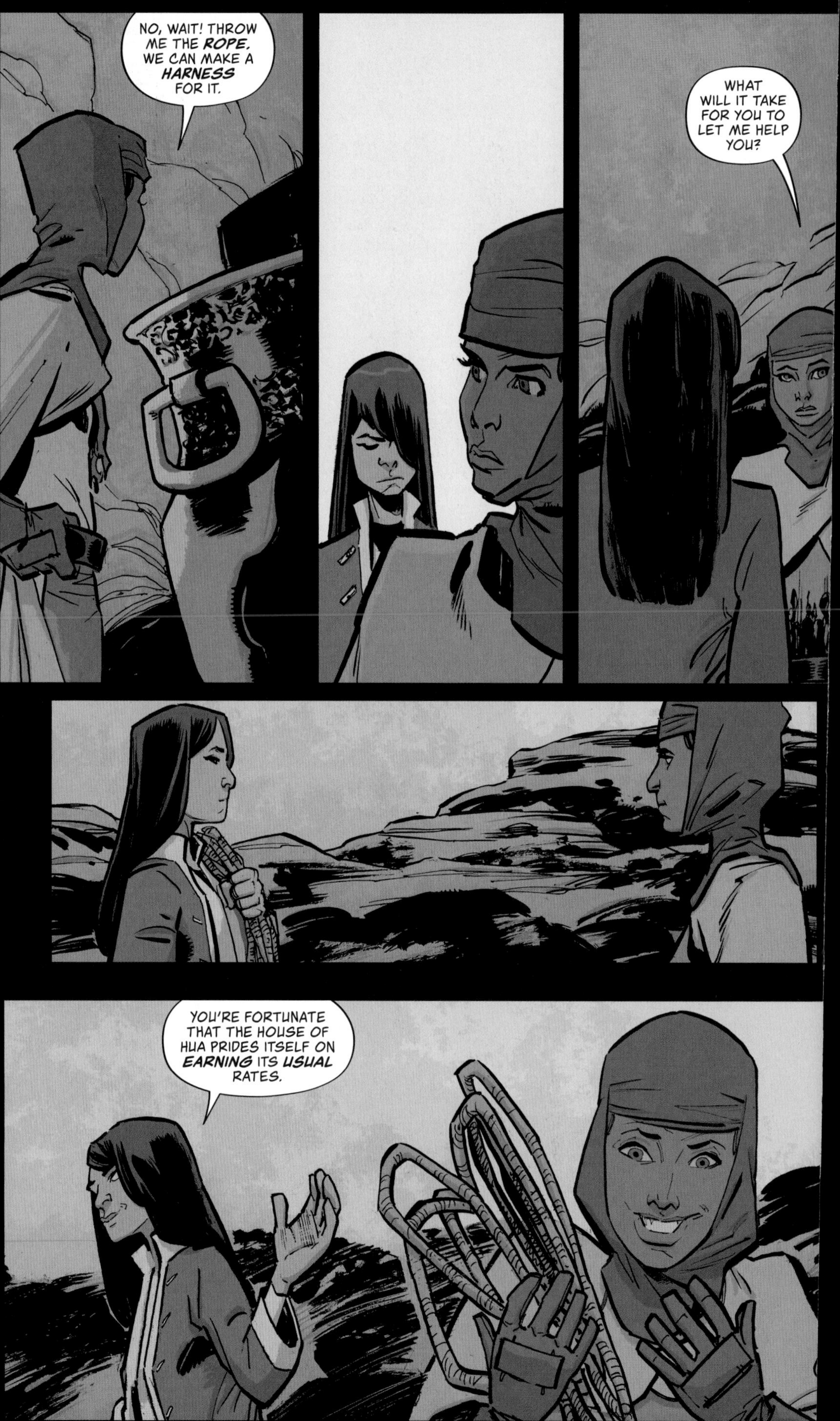
NO, WAIT! THROW ME THE ROPE. WE CAN MAKE A HARNESS FOR IT.
WHAT WILL IT TAKE FOR YOU TO LET ME HELP YOU?
YOU'RE FORTUNATE THAT THE HOUSE OF HUA PRIDES ITSELF ON EARNING ITS USUAL RATES.

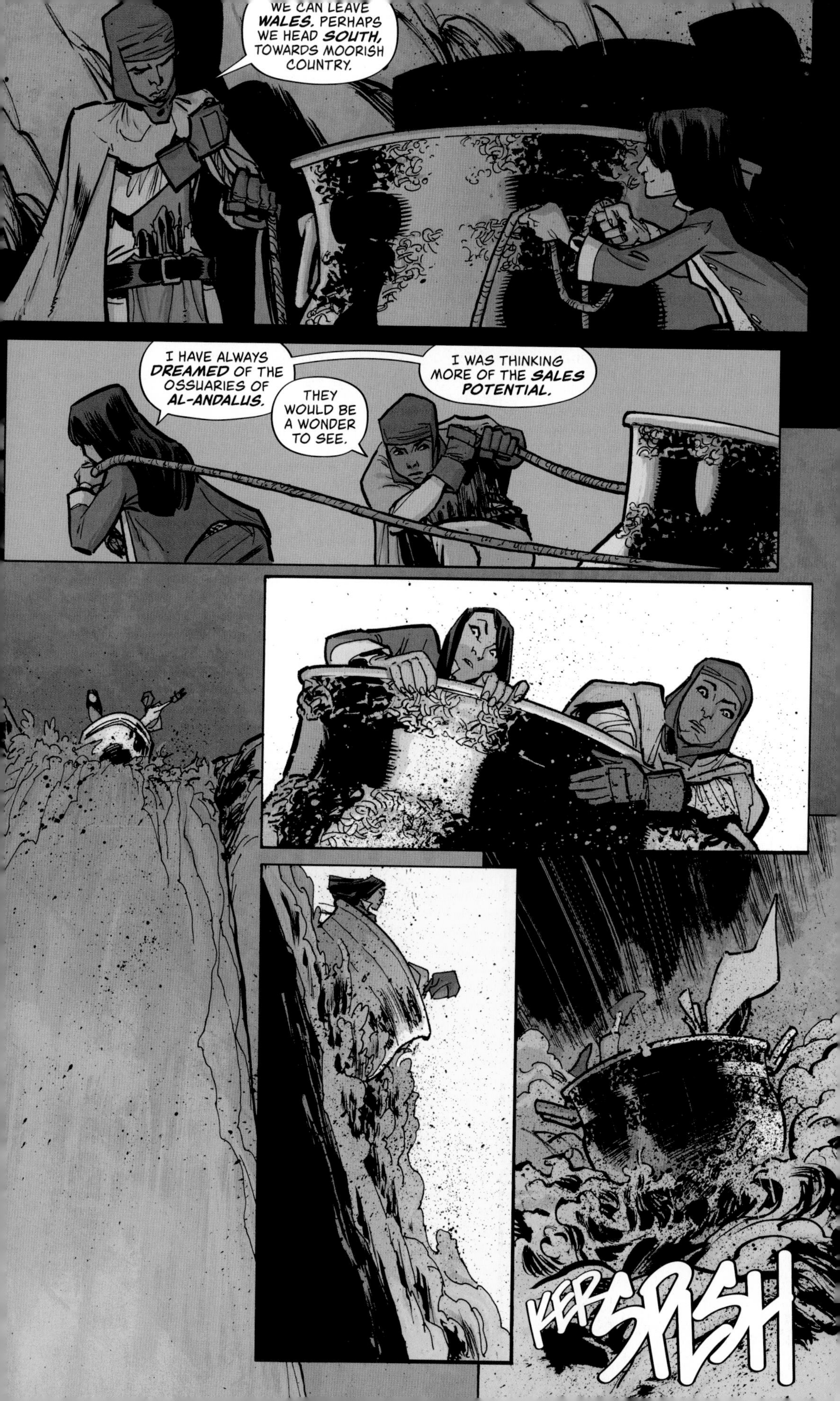

WE CAN LEAVE WALES. PERHAPS WE HEAD SOUTH, TOWARDS MOORISH COUNTRY.
I HAVE ALWAYS DREAMED OF THE OSSUARIES OF AL-ANDALUS.
THEY WOULD BE A WONDER TO SEE.
I WAS THINKING MORE OF THE SALES POTENTIAL.
KERSPLSH

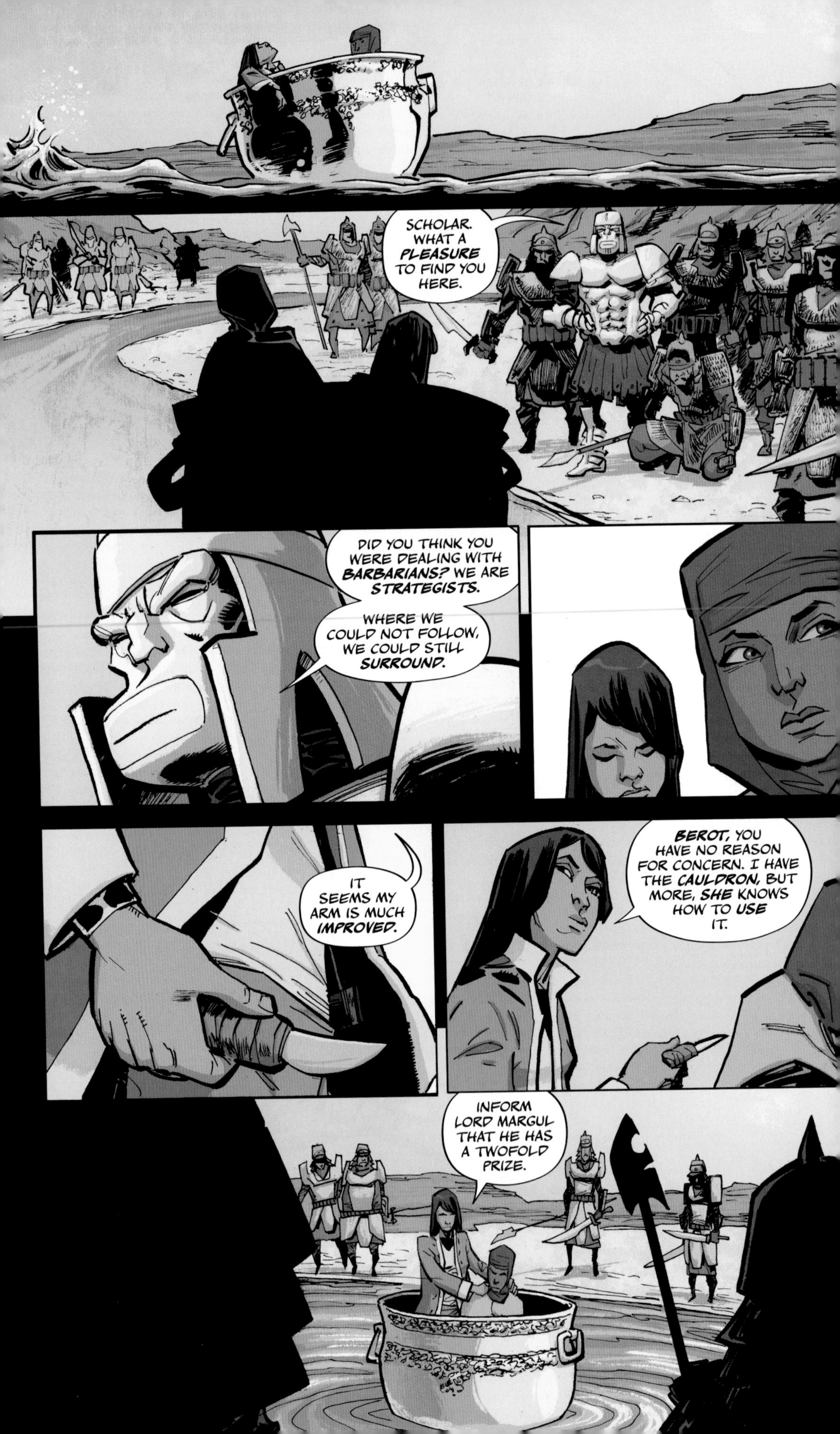
SCHOLAR. WHAT A PLEASURE TO FIND YOU HERE.
DID YOU THINK YOU WERE DEALING WITH BARBARIANS? WE ARE STRATEGISTS.
WHERE WE COULD NOT FOLLOW, WE COULD STILL SURROUND.
IT SEEMS MY ARM IS MUCH IMPROVED.
BEROT, YOU HAVE NO REASON FOR CONCERN. I HAVE THE CAULDRON, BUT MORE, SHE KNOWS HOW TO USE IT.
INFORM LORD MARGUL THAT HE HAS A TWOFOLD PRIZE.

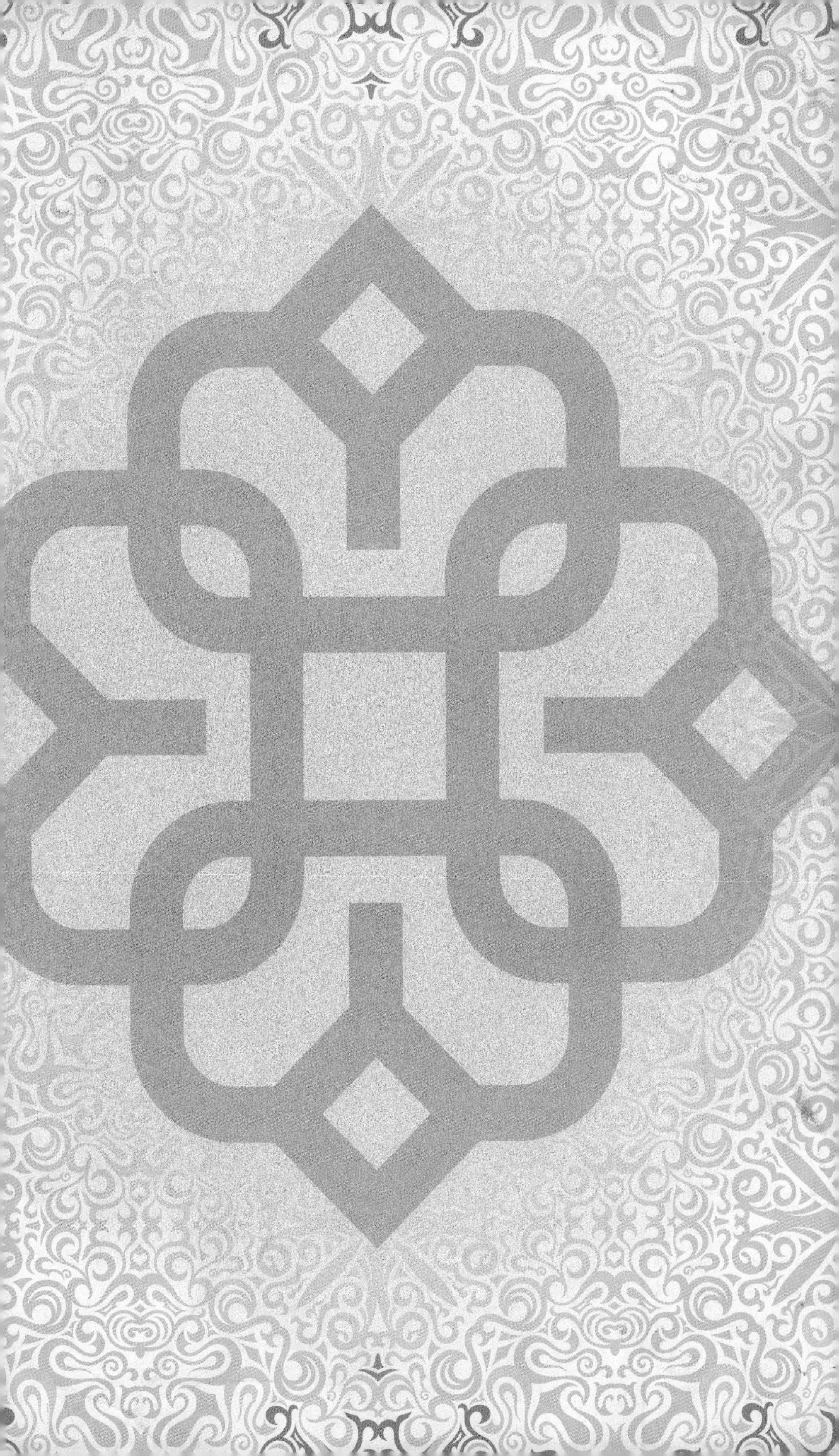

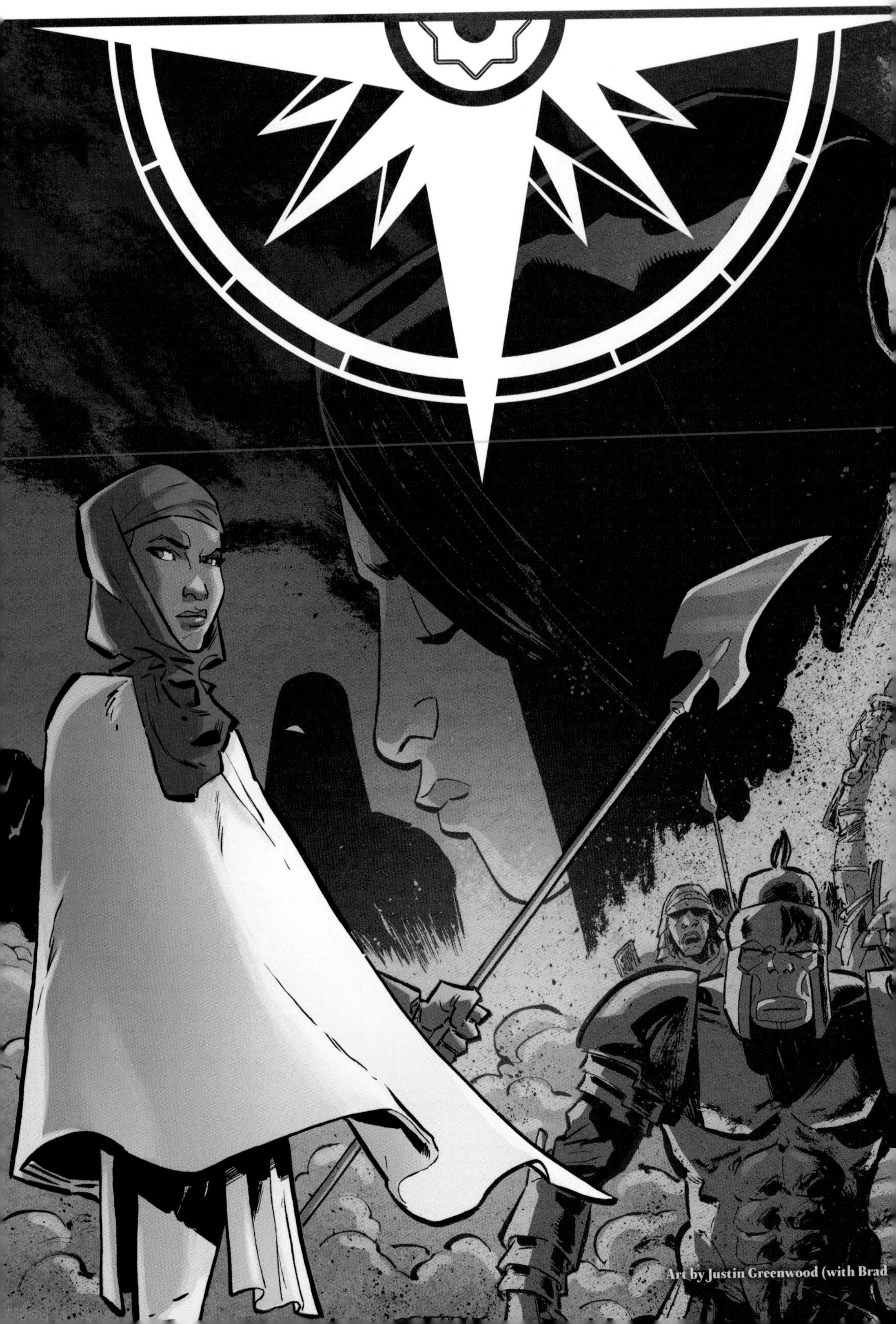

Art by Justin Greenwood (with Brad

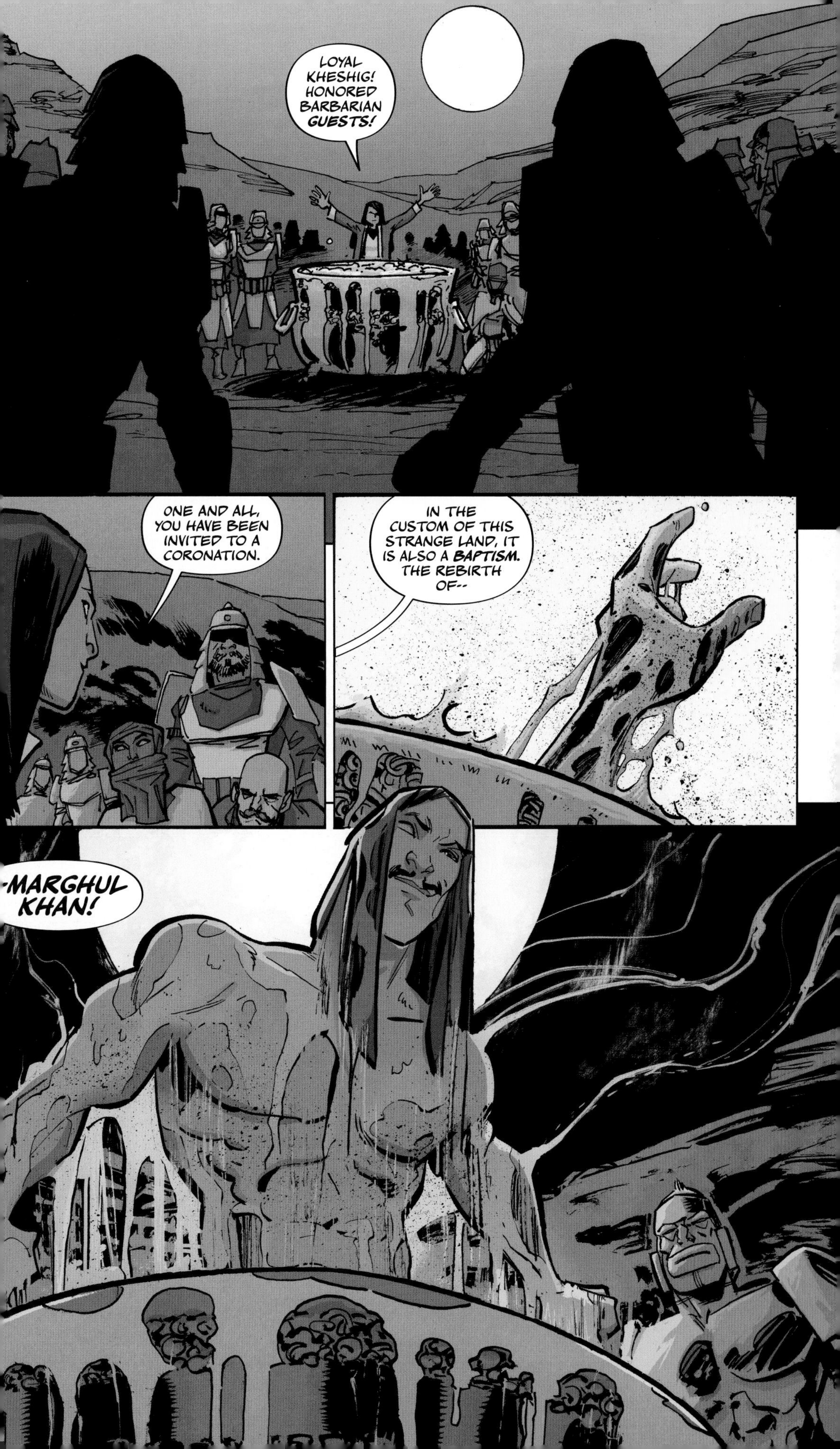
LOYAL KHESHIG! HONORED BARBARIAN GUESTS!
ONE AND ALL, YOU HAVE BEEN INVITED TO A CORONATION.
IN THE CUSTOM OF THIS STRANGE LAND, IT IS ALSO A BAPTISM. THE REBIRTH OF--
--MARGHUL KHAN!

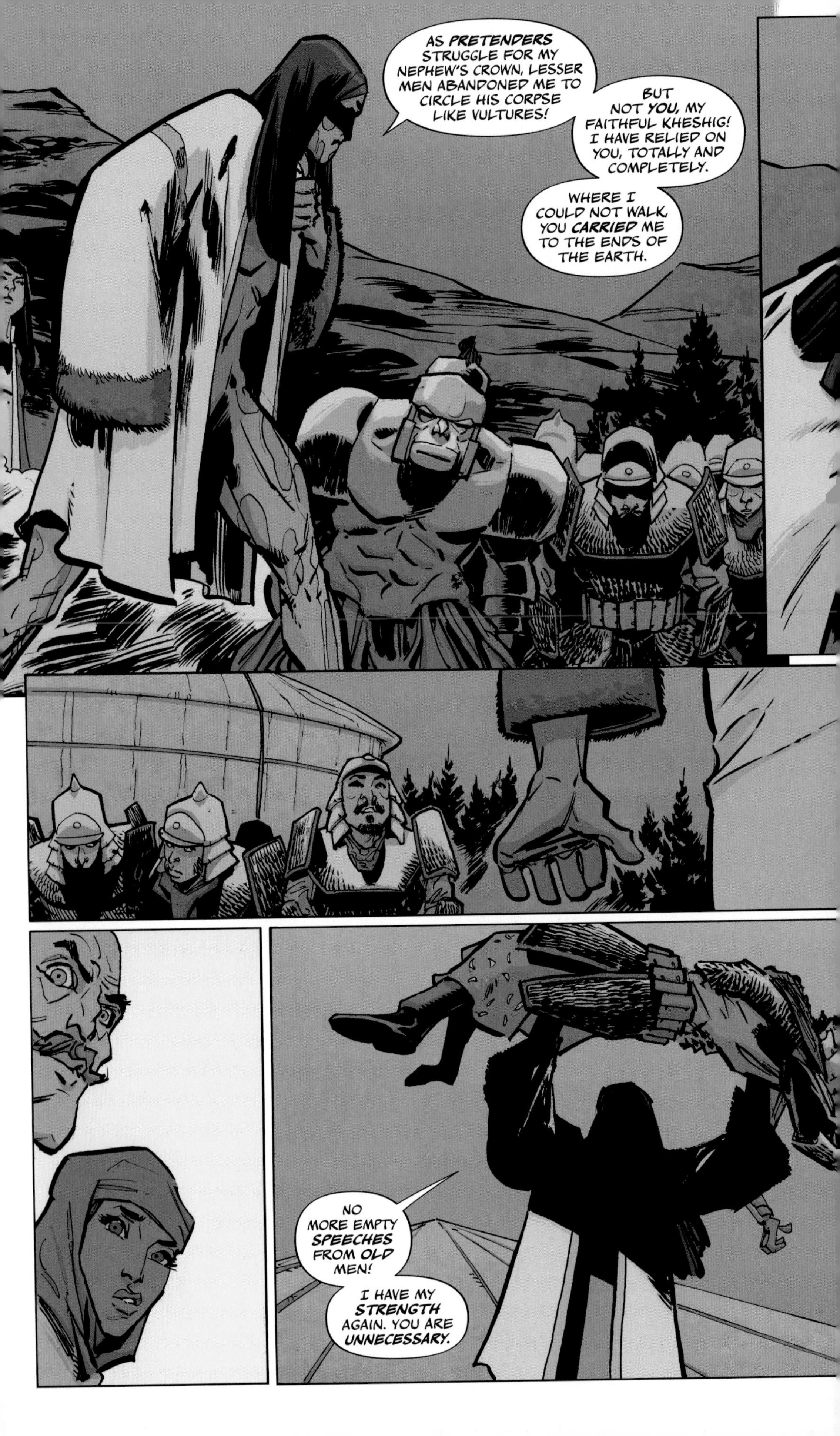
AS PRETENDERS STRUGGLE FOR MY NEPHEW'S CROWN, LESSER MEN ABANDONED ME TO CIRCLE HIS CORPSE LIKE VULTURES!
BUT NOT YOU, MY FAITHFUL KHESHIG! I HAVE RELIED ON YOU, TOTALLY AND COMPLETELY.
WHERE I COULD NOT WALK, YOU CARRIED ME TO THE ENDS OF THE EARTH.
NO MORE EMPTY SPEECHES FROM OLD MEN!
I HAVE MY STRENGTH AGAIN. YOU ARE UNNECESSARY.

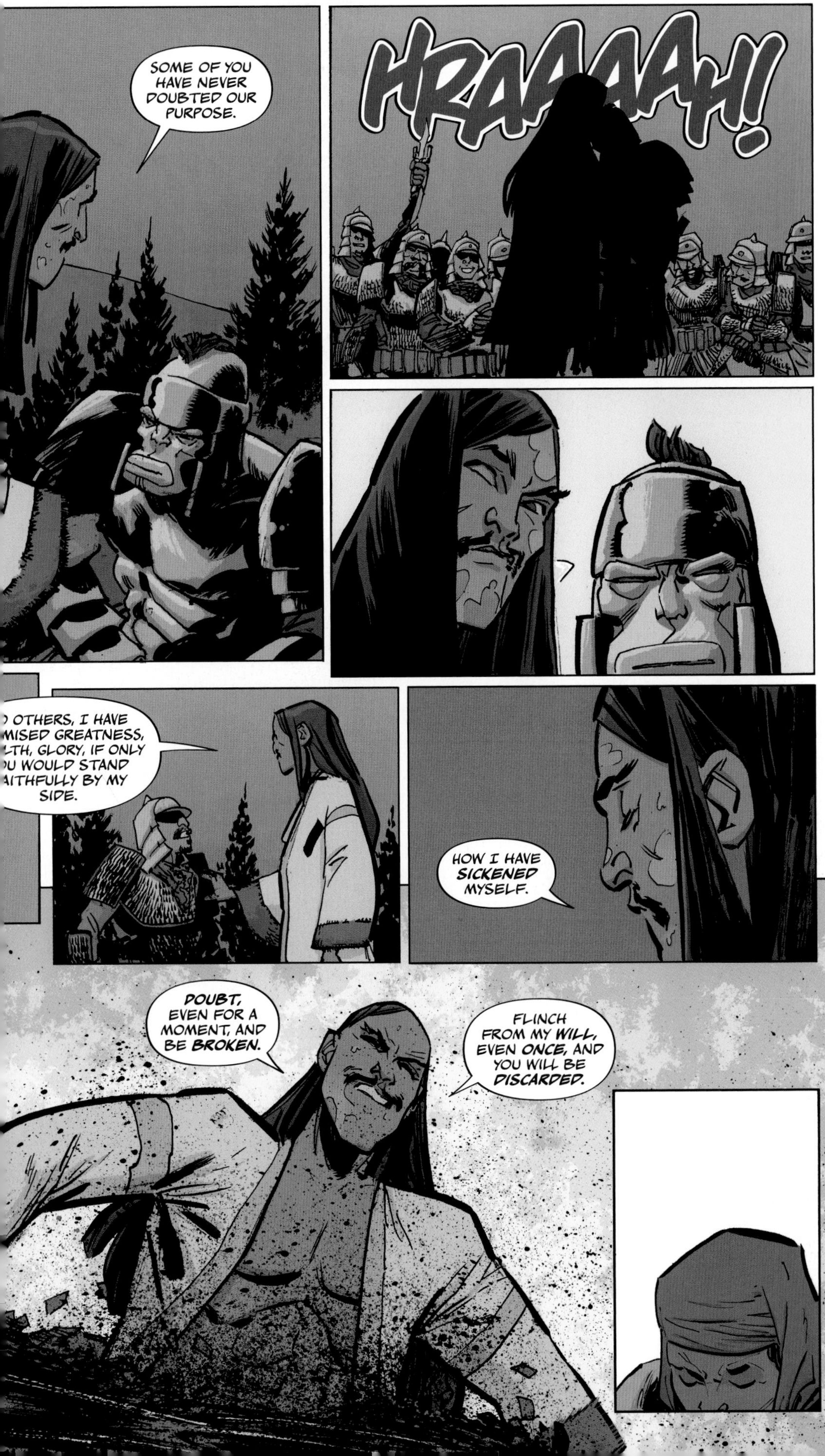

SOME OF YOU HAVE NEVER DOUBTED OUR PURPOSE.
HRAAAAH!
O OTHERS, I HAVE MISED GREATNESS, LTH, GLORY, IF ONLY OU WOULD STAND AITHFULLY BY MY SIDE.
HOW I HAVE SICKENED MYSELF.
DOUBT, EVEN FOR A MOMENT, AND BE BROKEN.
FLINCH FROM MY WILL, EVEN ONCE, AND YOU WILL BE DISCARDED.

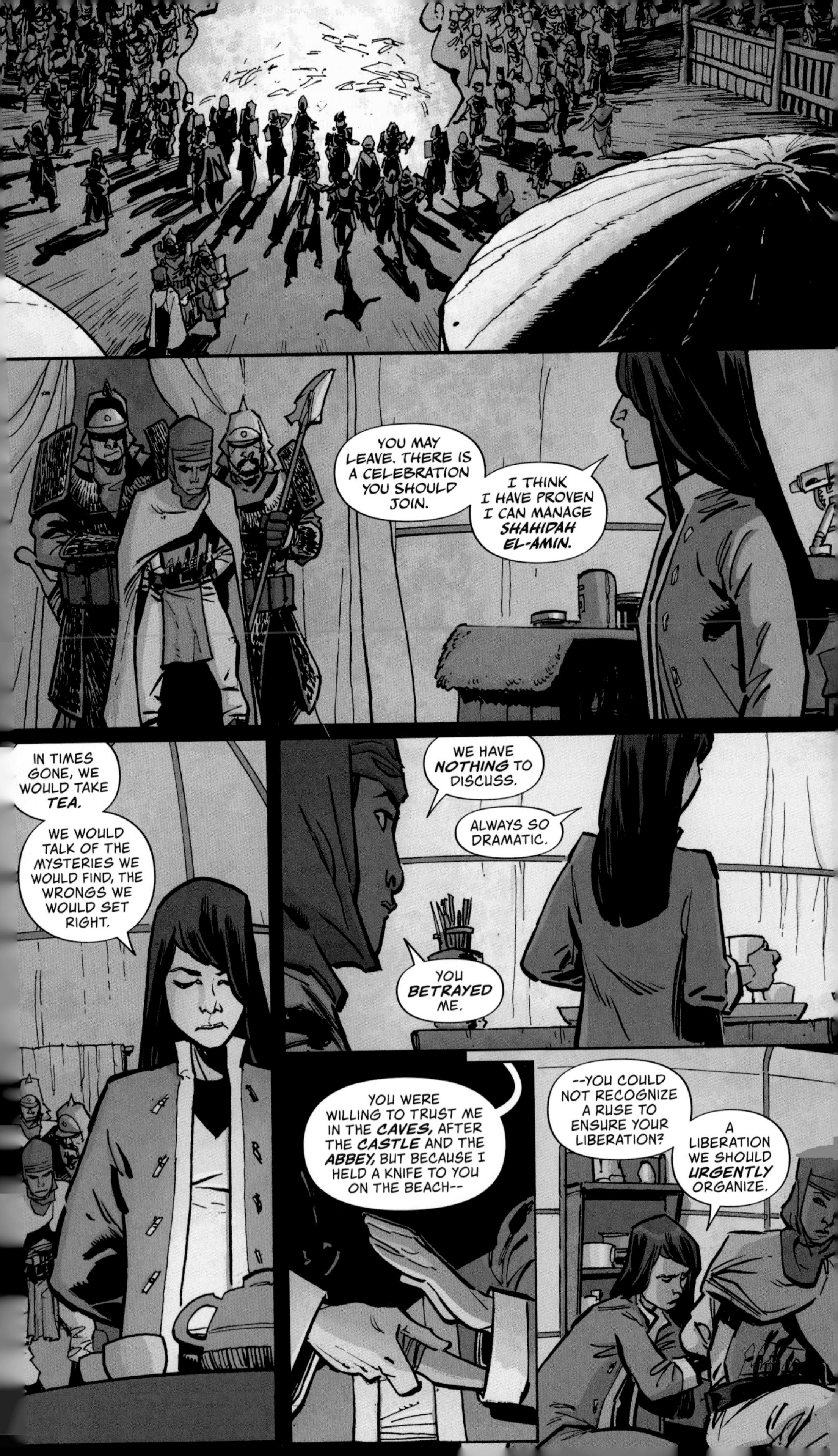
YOU MAY LEAVE. THERE IS A CELEBRATION YOU SHOULD JOIN.
I THINK I HAVE PROVEN I CAN MANAGE SHAHIDAH EL-AMIN.
IN TIMES GONE, WE WOULD TAKE TEA.
WE WOULD TALK OF THE MYSTERIES WE WOULD FIND, THE WRONGS WE WOULD SET RIGHT.
WE HAVE NOTHING TO DISCUSS.
ALWAYS SO DRAMATIC.
YOU BETRAYED ME.
YOU WERE WILLING TO TRUST ME IN THE CAVES, AFTER THE CASTLE AND THE ABBEY, BUT BECAUSE I HELD A KNIFE TO YOU ON THE BEACH--
--YOU COULD NOT RECOGNIZE A RUSE TO ENSURE YOUR LIBERATION?
A LIBERATION WE SHOULD URGENTLY ORGANIZE.

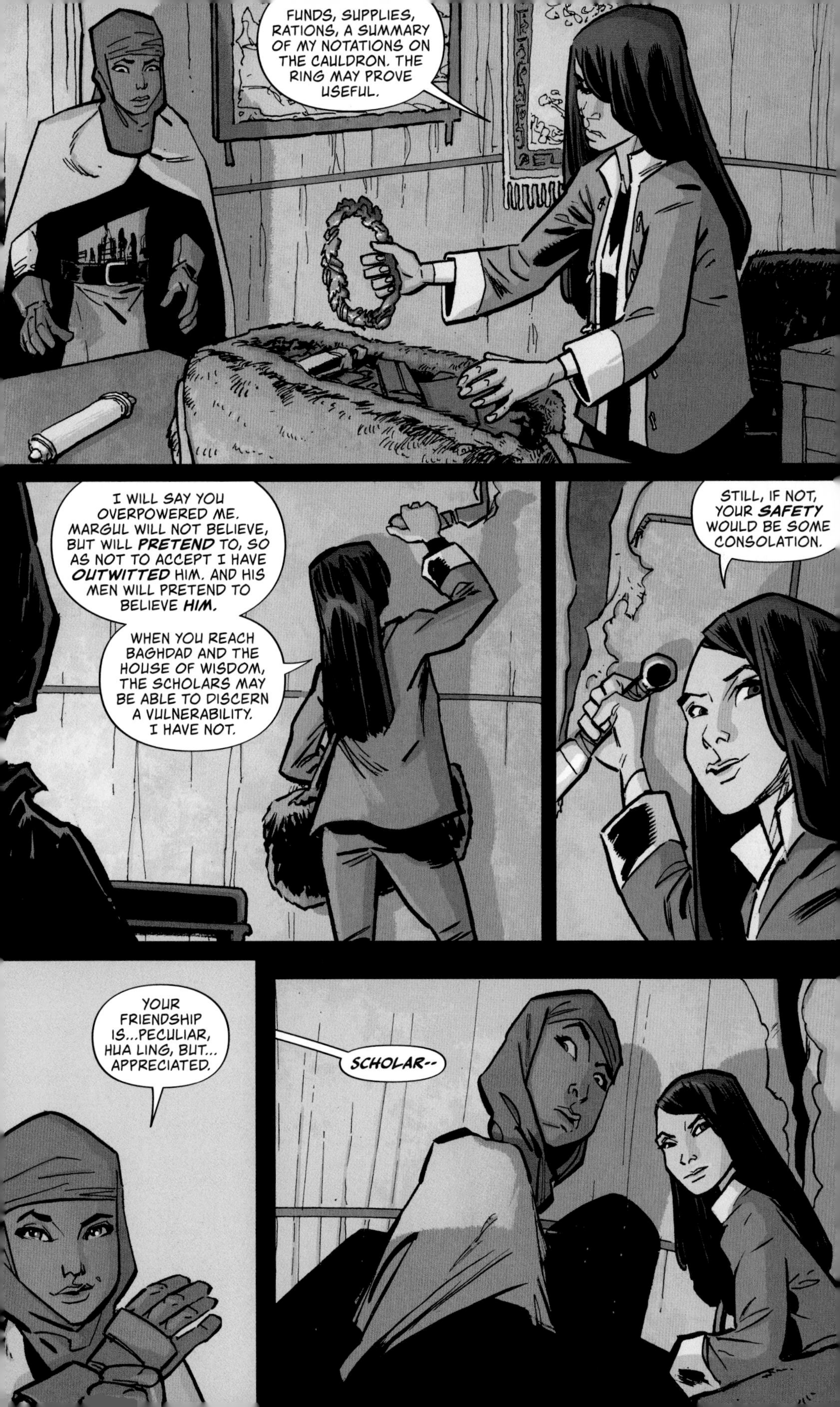

FUNDS, SUPPLIES, RATIONS, A SUMMARY OF MY NOTATIONS ON THE CAULDRON. THE RING MAY PROVE USEFUL.
I WILL SAY YOU OVERPOWERED ME. MARGUL WILL NOT BELIEVE, BUT WILL *PRETEND* TO, SO AS NOT TO ACCEPT I HAVE *OUTWITTED* HIM. AND HIS MEN WILL PRETEND TO BELIEVE *HIM.*
WHEN YOU REACH BAGHDAD AND THE HOUSE OF WISDOM, THE SCHOLARS MAY BE ABLE TO DISCERN A VULNERABILITY. I HAVE NOT.
STILL, IF NOT, YOUR *SAFETY* WOULD BE SOME CONSOLATION.
YOUR FRIENDSHIP IS...PECULIAR, HUA LING, BUT... APPRECIATED.
SCHOLAR--

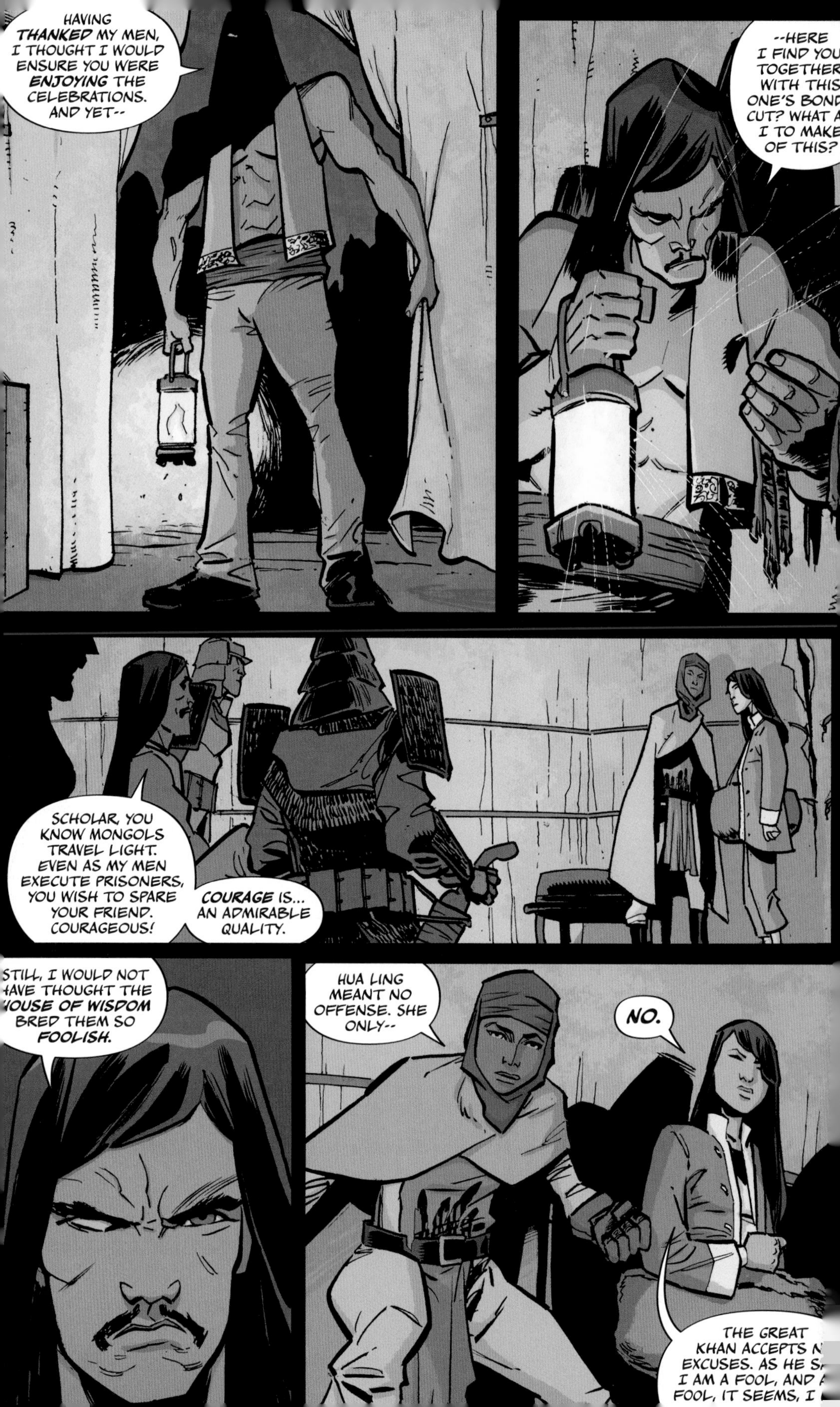

HAVING THANKED MY MEN, I THOUGHT I WOULD ENSURE YOU WERE ENJOYING THE CELEBRATIONS. AND YET--
--HERE I FIND YOU TOGETHER WITH THIS ONE'S BOND CUT? WHAT A I TO MAKE OF THIS?
SCHOLAR, YOU KNOW MONGOLS TRAVEL LIGHT. EVEN AS MY MEN EXECUTE PRISONERS, YOU WISH TO SPARE YOUR FRIEND. COURAGEOUS!
COURAGE IS... AN ADMIRABLE QUALITY.
STILL, I WOULD NOT HAVE THOUGHT THE HOUSE OF WISDOM BRED THEM SO FOOLISH.
HUA LING MEANT NO OFFENSE. SHE ONLY--
NO.
THE GREAT KHAN ACCEPTS N EXCUSES. AS HE S I AM A FOOL, AND A FOOL, IT SEEMS, I

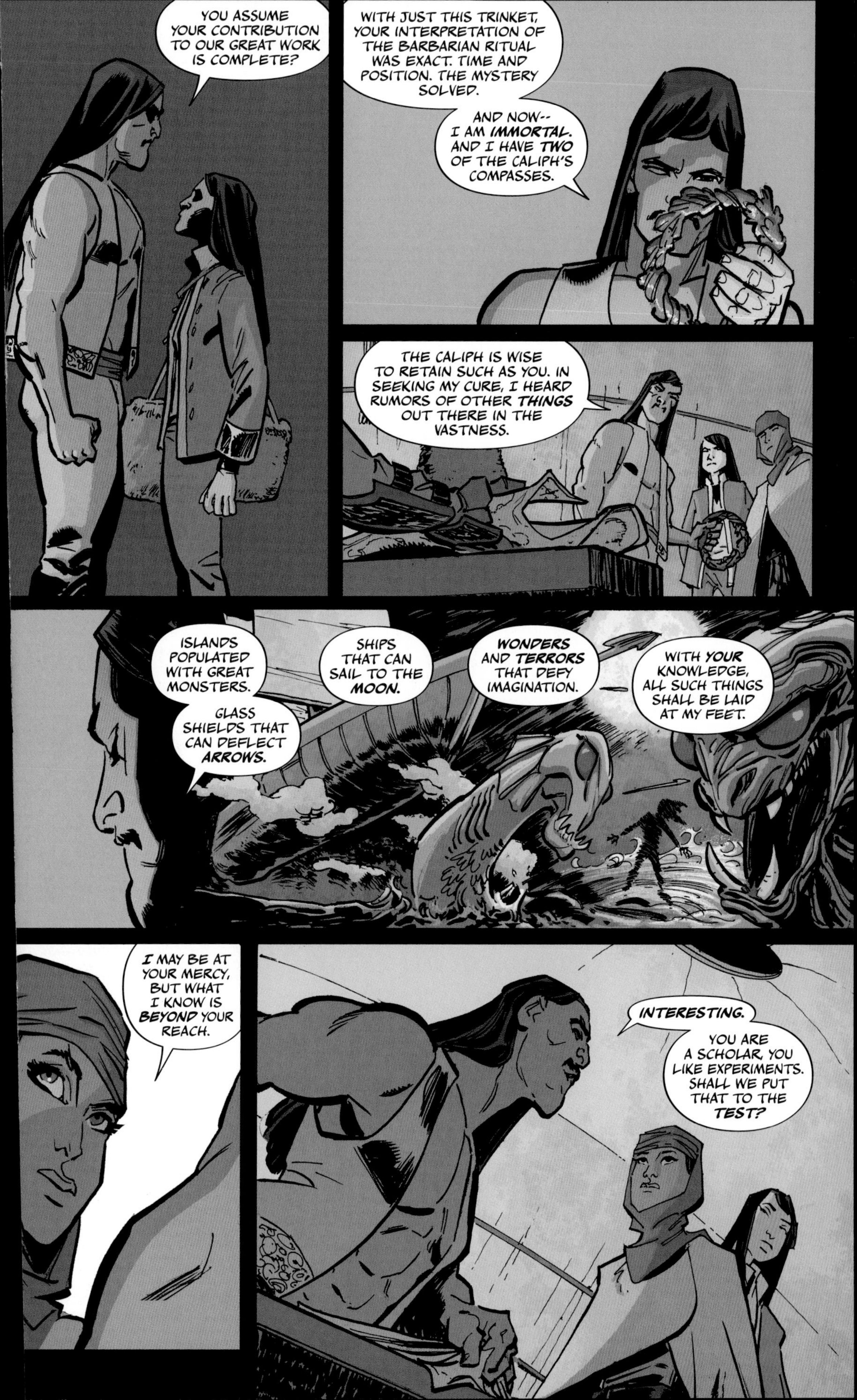
YOU ASSUME YOUR CONTRIBUTION TO OUR GREAT WORK IS COMPLETE?
WITH JUST THIS TRINKET, YOUR INTERPRETATION OF THE BARBARIAN RITUAL WAS EXACT. TIME AND POSITION. THE MYSTERY SOLVED.
AND NOW-- I AM IMMORTAL. AND I HAVE TWO OF THE CALIPH'S COMPASSES.
THE CALIPH IS WISE TO RETAIN SUCH AS YOU. IN SEEKING MY CURE, I HEARD RUMORS OF OTHER THINGS OUT THERE IN THE VASTNESS.
ISLANDS POPULATED WITH GREAT MONSTERS.
GLASS SHIELDS THAT CAN DEFLECT ARROWS.
SHIPS THAT CAN SAIL TO THE MOON.
WONDERS AND TERRORS THAT DEFY IMAGINATION.
WITH YOUR KNOWLEDGE, ALL SUCH THINGS SHALL BE LAID AT MY FEET.
I MAY BE AT YOUR MERCY, BUT WHAT I KNOW IS BEYOND YOUR REACH.
INTERESTING.
YOU ARE A SCHOLAR, YOU LIKE EXPERIMENTS. SHALL WE PUT THAT TO THE TEST?

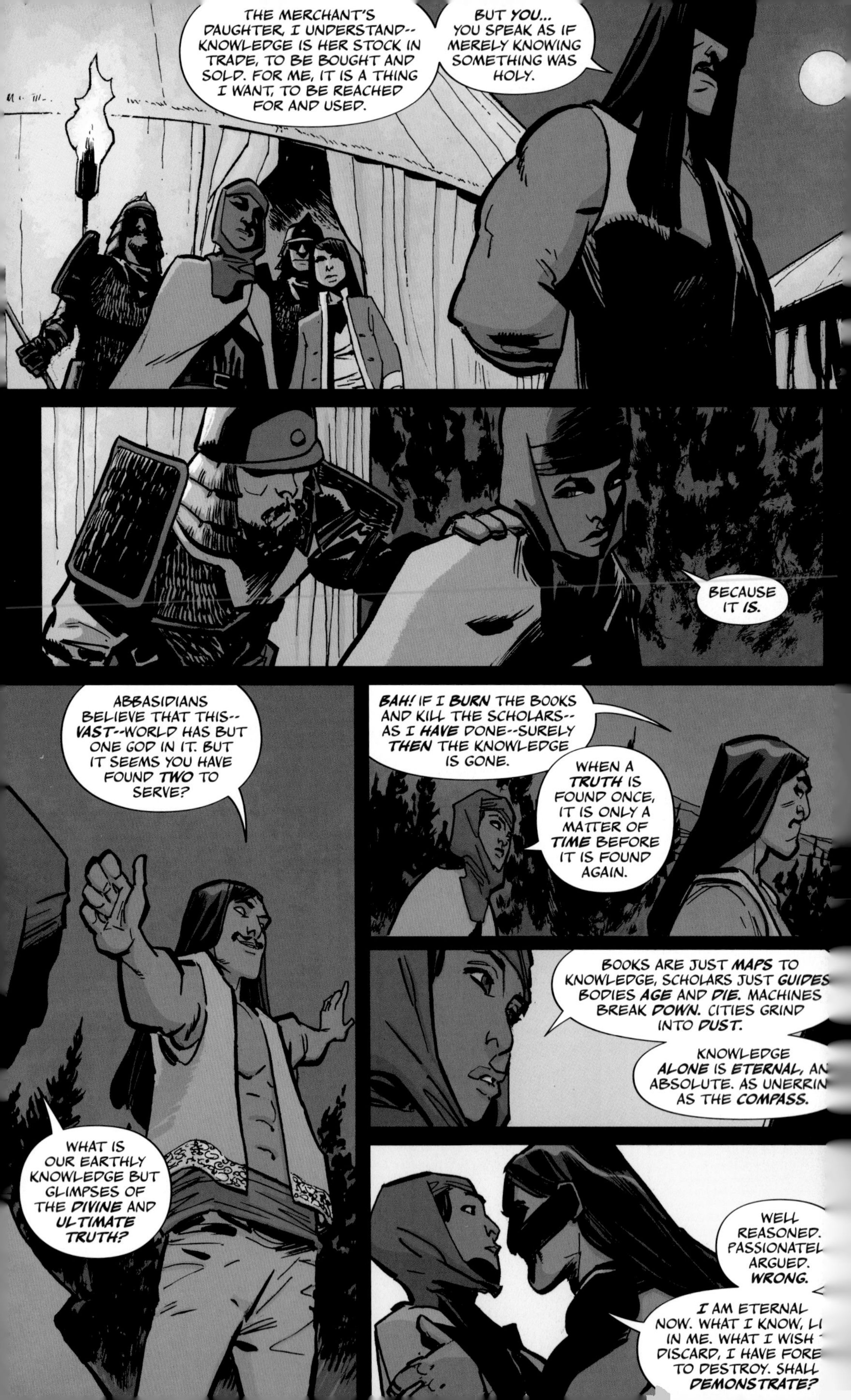
THE MERCHANT'S DAUGHTER, I UNDERSTAND-- KNOWLEDGE IS HER STOCK IN TRADE, TO BE BOUGHT AND SOLD. FOR ME, IT IS A THING I WANT, TO BE REACHED FOR AND USED.
BUT YOU... YOU SPEAK AS IF MERELY KNOWING SOMETHING WAS HOLY.
BECAUSE IT IS.
ABBASIDIANS BELIEVE THAT THIS--VAST--WORLD HAS BUT ONE GOD IN IT. BUT IT SEEMS YOU HAVE FOUND TWO TO SERVE?
WHAT IS OUR EARTHLY KNOWLEDGE BUT GLIMPSES OF THE DIVINE AND ULTIMATE TRUTH?
BAH! IF I BURN THE BOOKS AND KILL THE SCHOLARS-- AS I HAVE DONE--SURELY THEN THE KNOWLEDGE IS GONE.
WHEN A TRUTH IS FOUND ONCE, IT IS ONLY A MATTER OF TIME BEFORE IT IS FOUND AGAIN.
BOOKS ARE JUST MAPS TO KNOWLEDGE, SCHOLARS JUST GUIDES BODIES AGE AND DIE. MACHINES BREAK DOWN. CITIES GRIND INTO DUST.
KNOWLEDGE ALONE IS ETERNAL, AN ABSOLUTE. AS UNERRIN AS THE COMPASS.
WELL REASONED. PASSIONATEL ARGUED. WRONG.
I AM ETERNAL NOW. WHAT I KNOW, LI IN ME. WHAT I WISH DISCARD, I HAVE FORE TO DESTROY. SHALL DEMONSTRATE?

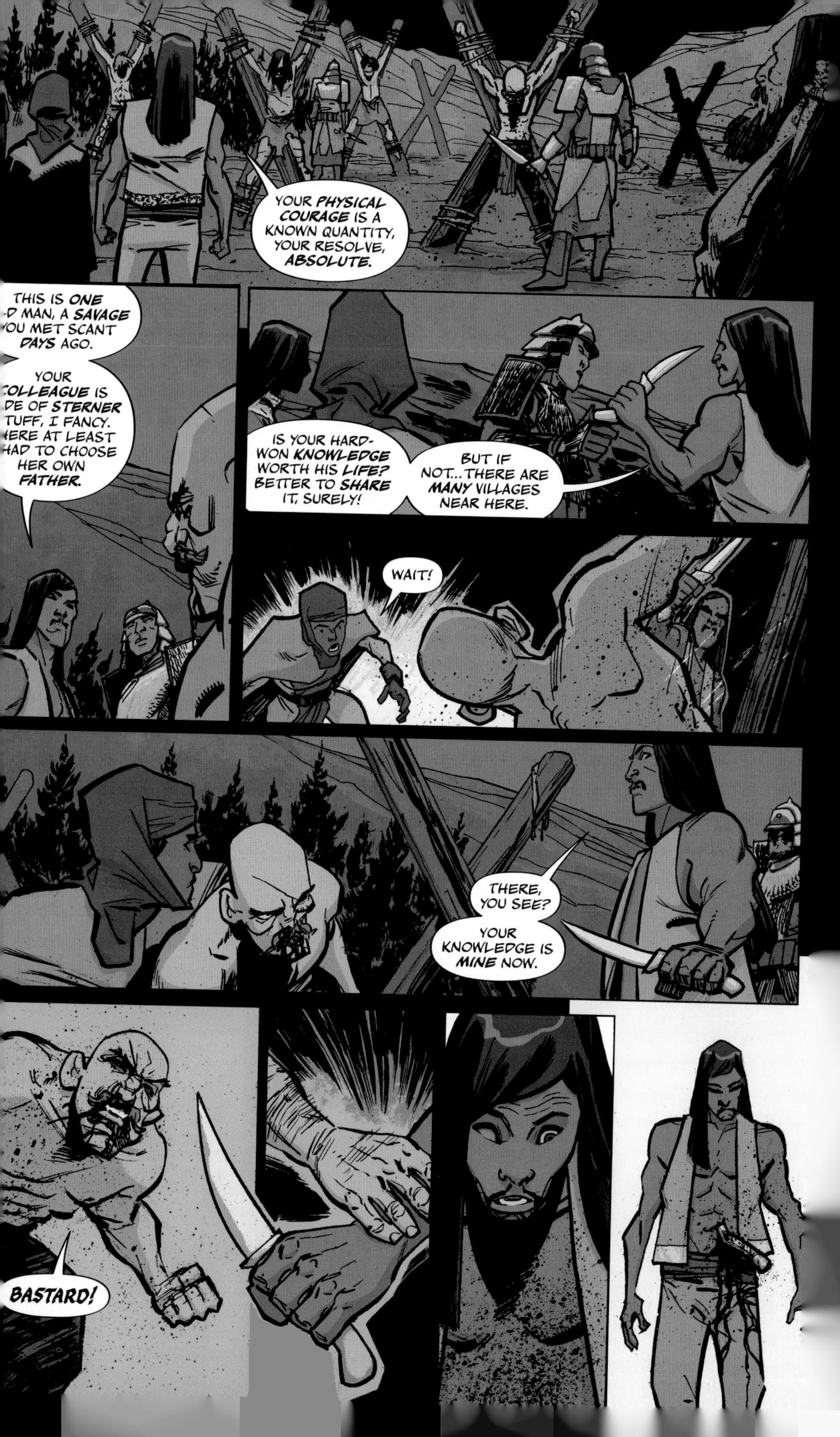
YOUR PHYSICAL COURAGE IS A KNOWN QUANTITY, YOUR RESOLVE, ABSOLUTE.
THIS IS ONE -D MAN, A SAVAGE YOU MET SCANT DAYS AGO.
YOUR COLLEAGUE IS -DE OF STERNER TUFF, I FANCY. HERE AT LEAST HAD TO CHOOSE HER OWN FATHER.
IS YOUR HARD-WON KNOWLEDGE WORTH HIS LIFE? BETTER TO SHARE IT, SURELY!
BUT IF NOT... THERE ARE MANY VILLAGES NEAR HERE.
WAIT!
THERE, YOU SEE?
YOUR KNOWLEDGE IS MINE NOW.
BASTARD!

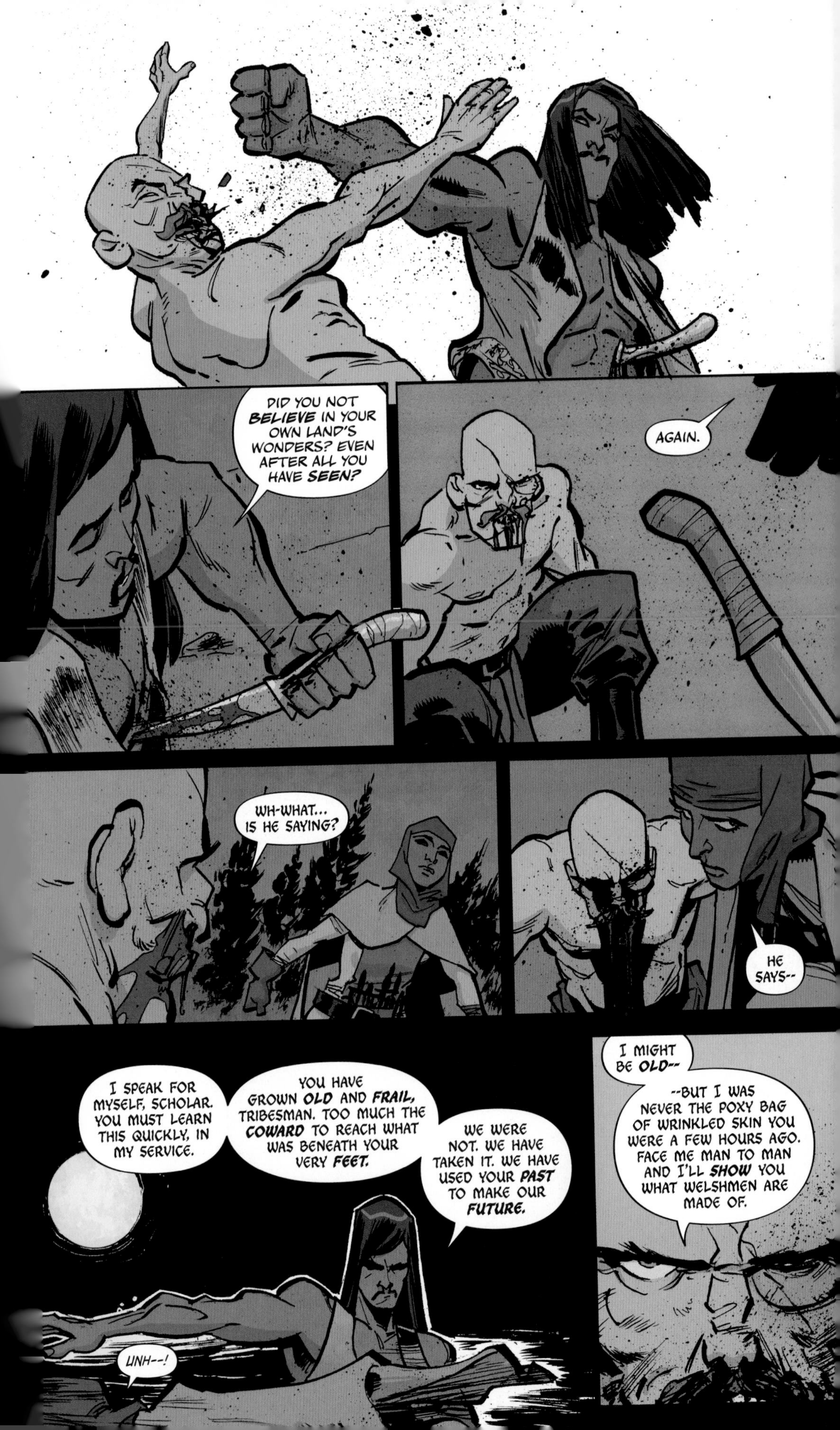
DID YOU NOT BELIEVE IN YOUR OWN LAND'S WONDERS? EVEN AFTER ALL YOU HAVE SEEN?
AGAIN.
WH-WHAT... IS HE SAYING?
HE SAYS--
I SPEAK FOR MYSELF, SCHOLAR. YOU MUST LEARN THIS QUICKLY, IN MY SERVICE.
YOU HAVE GROWN OLD AND FRAIL, TRIBESMAN. TOO MUCH THE COWARD TO REACH WHAT WAS BENEATH YOUR VERY FEET.
WE WERE NOT. WE HAVE TAKEN IT. WE HAVE USED YOUR PAST TO MAKE OUR FUTURE.
UNH--!
I MIGHT BE OLD--
--BUT I WAS NEVER THE POXY BAG OF WRINKLED SKIN YOU WERE A FEW HOURS AGO. FACE ME MAN TO MAN AND I'LL SHOW YOU WHAT WELSHMEN ARE MADE OF.

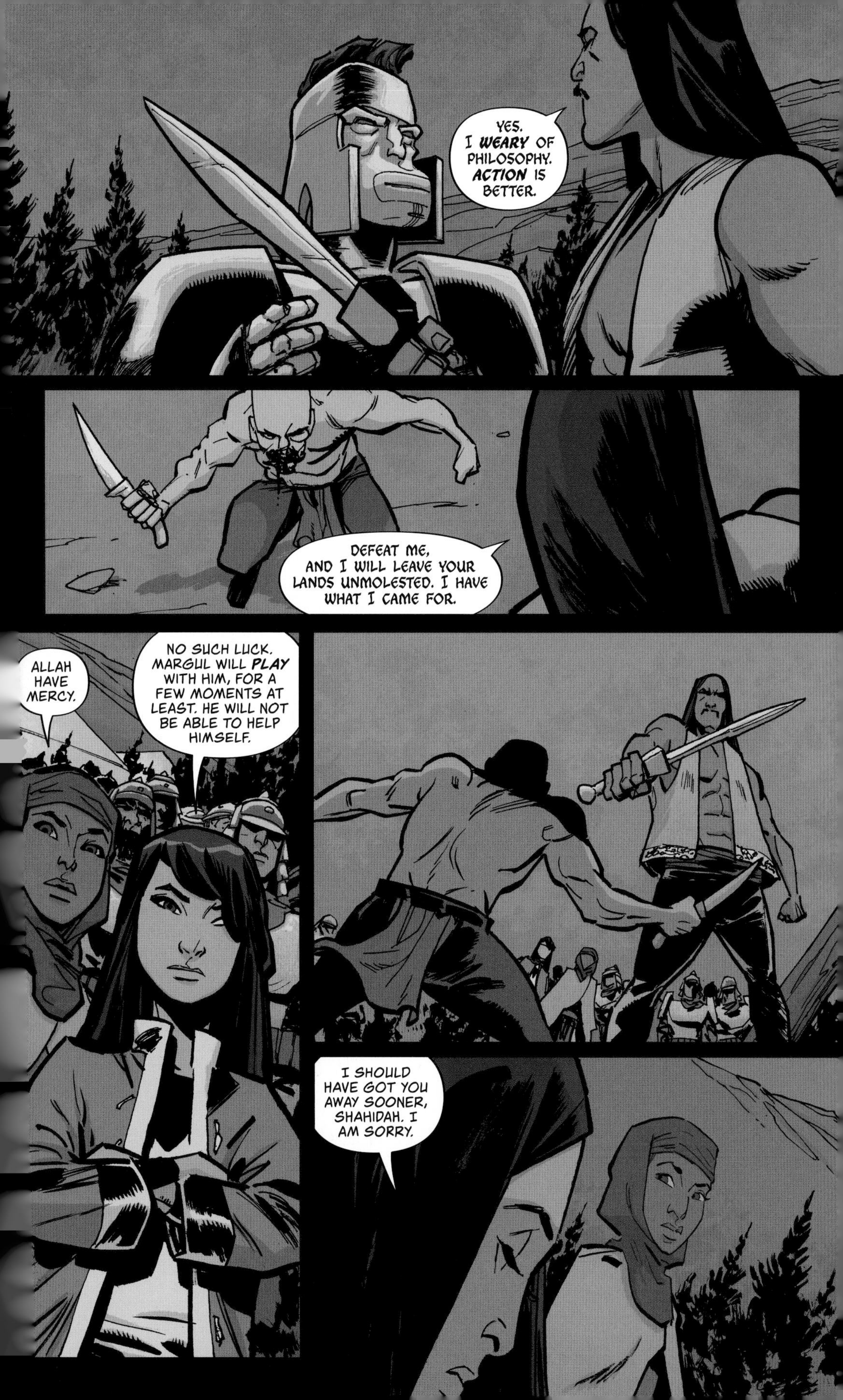
YES. I WEARY OF PHILOSOPHY. ACTION IS BETTER.
DEFEAT ME, AND I WILL LEAVE YOUR LANDS UNMOLESTED. I HAVE WHAT I CAME FOR.
ALLAH HAVE MERCY.
NO SUCH LUCK. MARGUL WILL PLAY WITH HIM, FOR A FEW MOMENTS AT LEAST. HE WILL NOT BE ABLE TO HELP HIMSELF.
I SHOULD HAVE GOT YOU AWAY SOONER, SHAHIDAH. I AM SORRY.

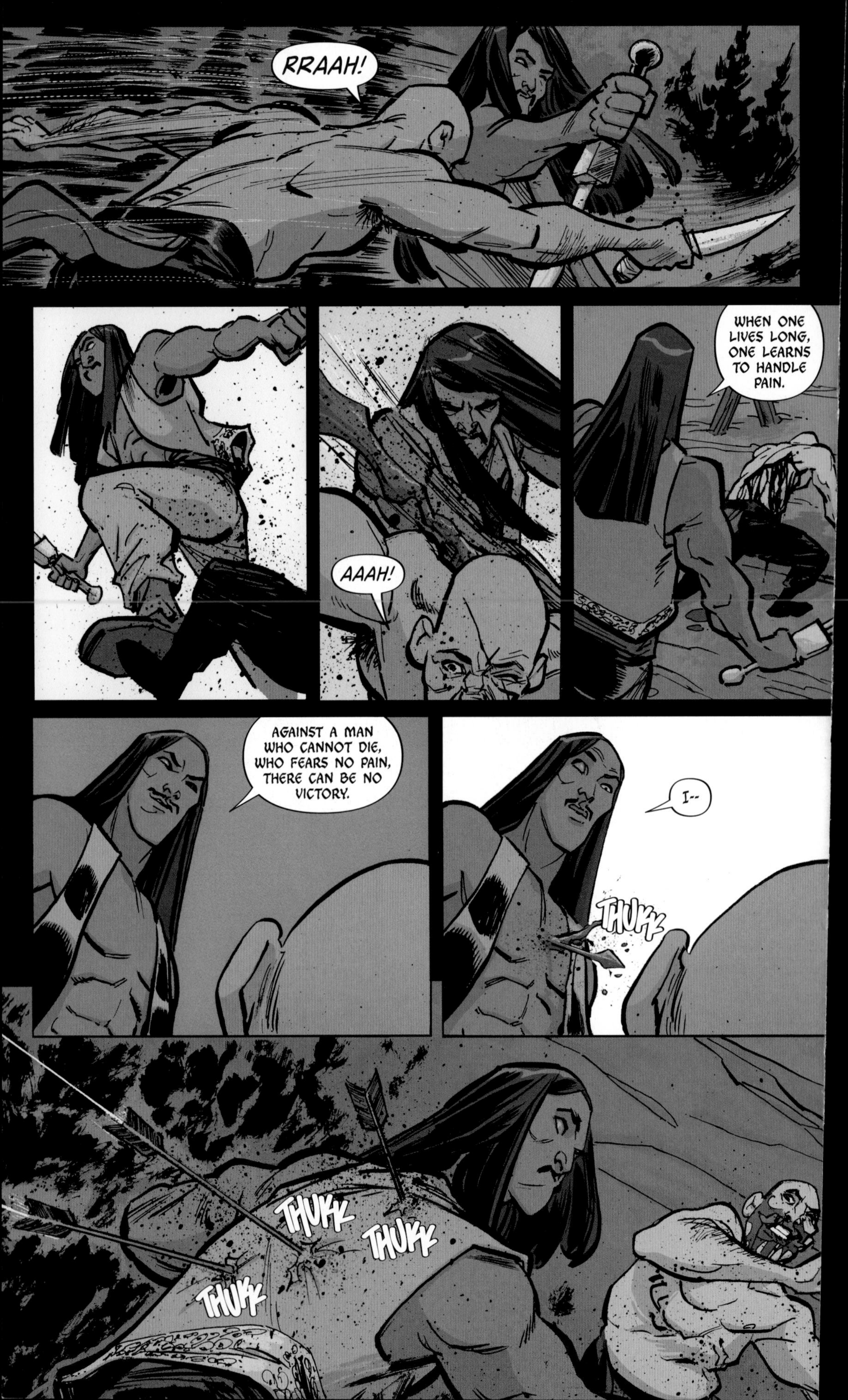
RRAAH!
AAAH!
WHEN ONE LIVES LONG, ONE LEARNS TO HANDLE PAIN.
AGAINST A MAN WHO CANNOT DIE, WHO FEARS NO PAIN, THERE CAN BE NO VICTORY.
I--
THUKK
THUKK
THUKK
THUKK

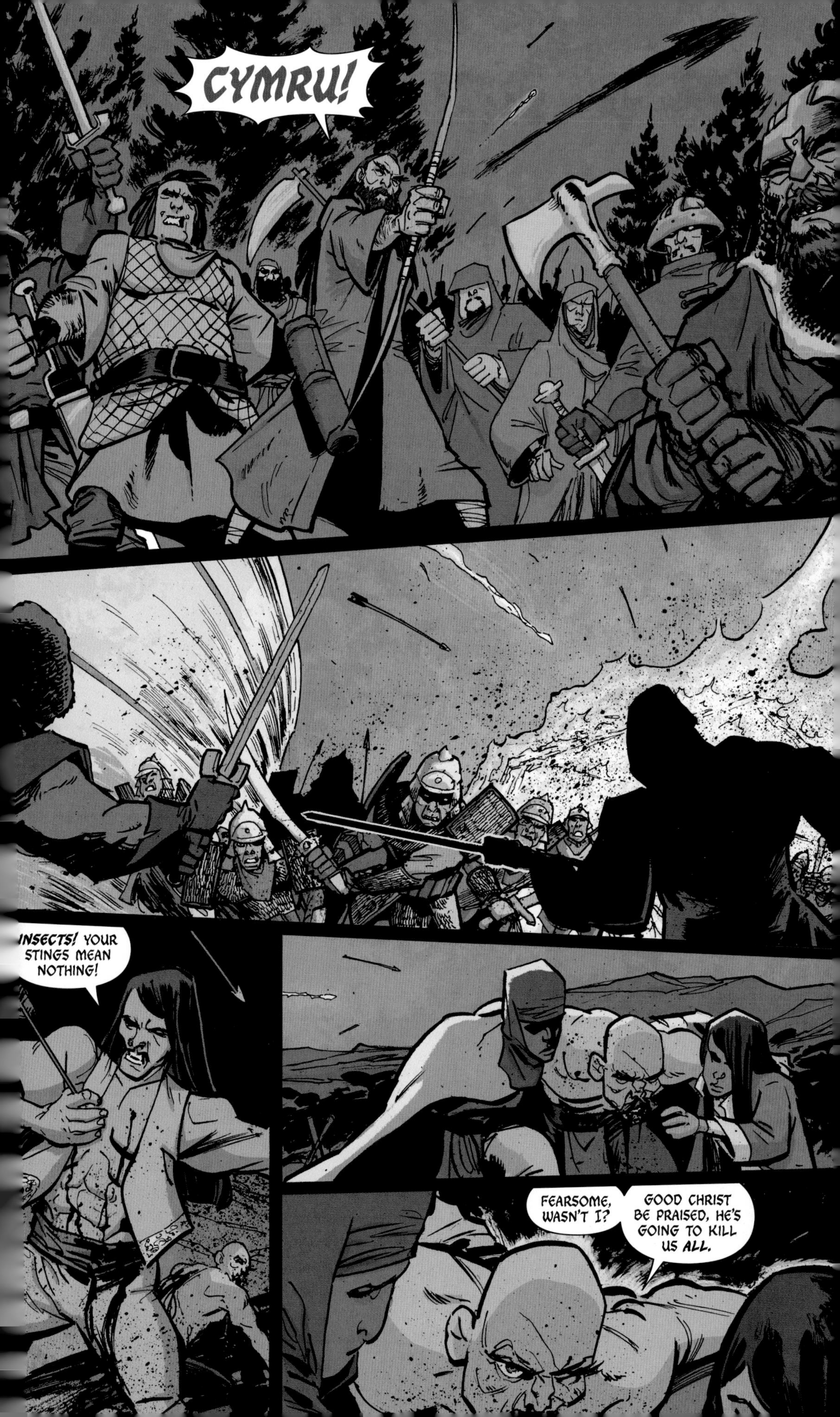
CYMRU!
INSECTS! YOUR STINGS MEAN NOTHING!
FEARSOME, WASN'T I?
GOOD CHRIST BE PRAISED, HE'S GOING TO KILL US ALL.

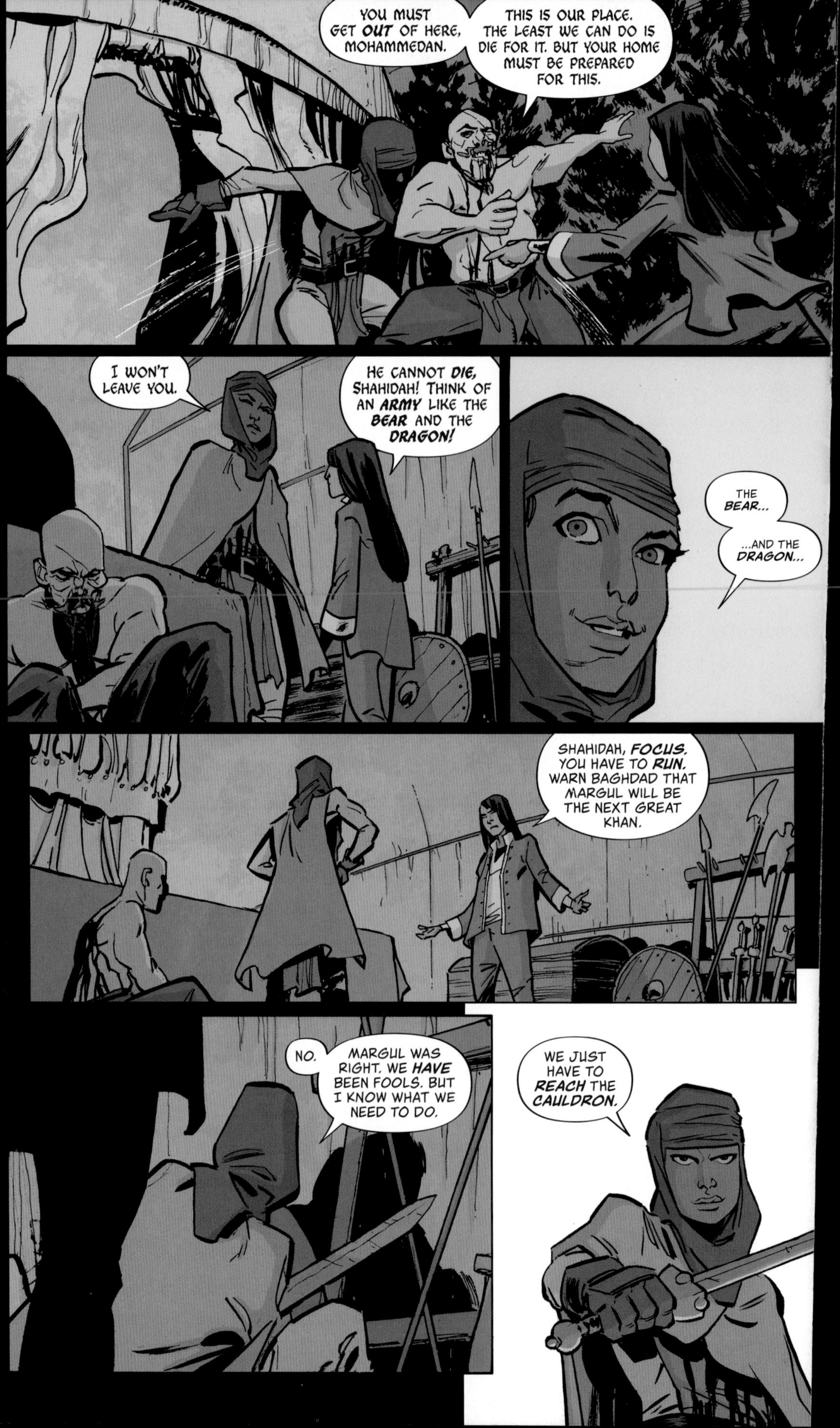
YOU MUST GET OUT OF HERE, MOHAMMEDAN.
THIS IS OUR PLACE. THE LEAST WE CAN DO IS DIE FOR IT. BUT YOUR HOME MUST BE PREPARED FOR THIS.
I WON'T LEAVE YOU.
HE CANNOT DIE, SHAHIDAH! THINK OF AN ARMY LIKE THE BEAR AND THE DRAGON!
THE BEAR...
...AND THE DRAGON...
SHAHIDAH, FOCUS. YOU HAVE TO RUN. WARN BAGHDAD THAT MARGUL WILL BE THE NEXT GREAT KHAN.
NO.
MARGUL WAS RIGHT. WE HAVE BEEN FOOLS. BUT I KNOW WHAT WE NEED TO DO.
WE JUST HAVE TO REACH THE CAULDRON.

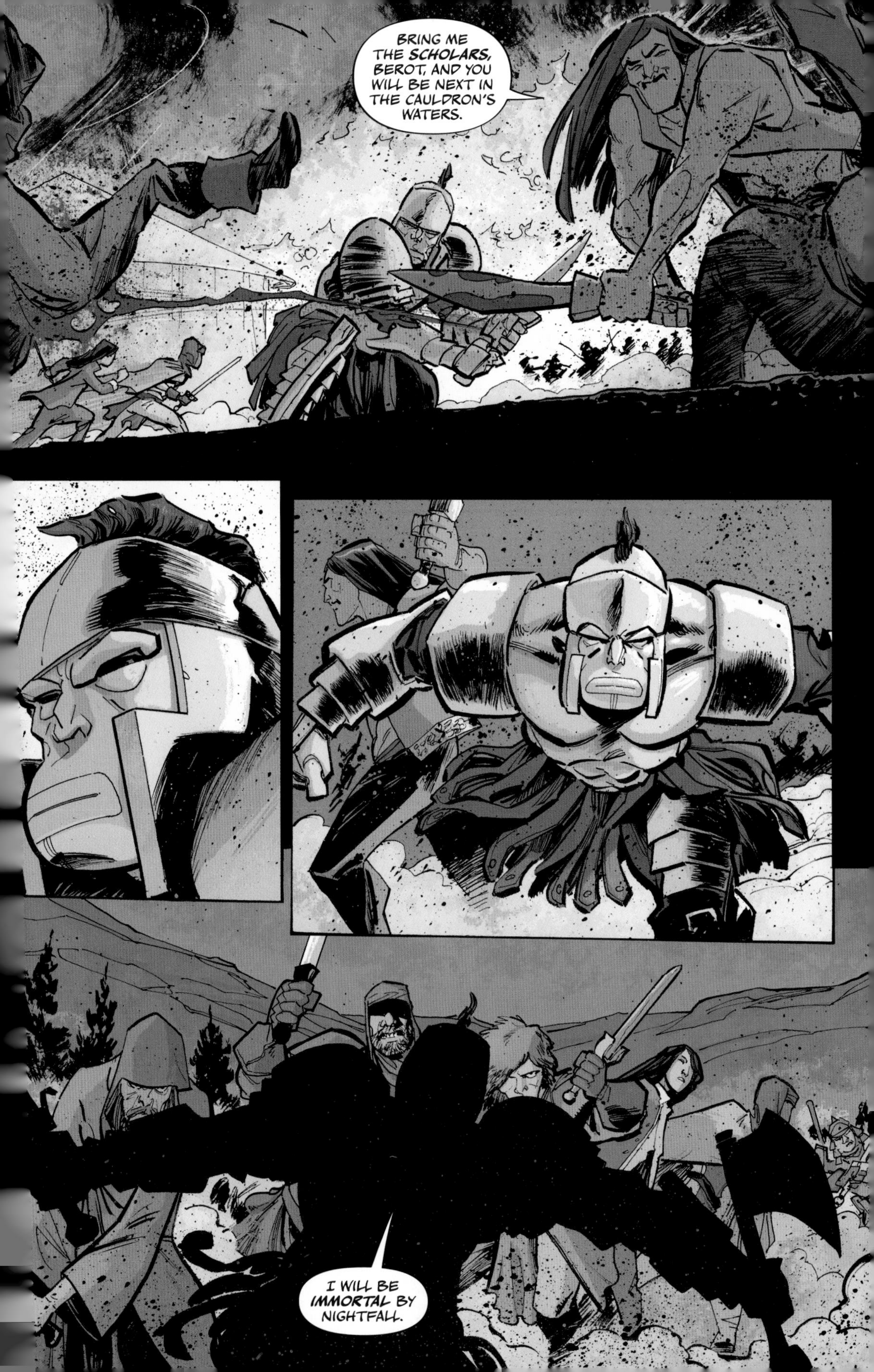
BRING ME THE SCHOLARS, BEROT, AND YOU WILL BE NEXT IN THE CAULDRON'S WATERS.
I WILL BE IMMORTAL BY NIGHTFALL.

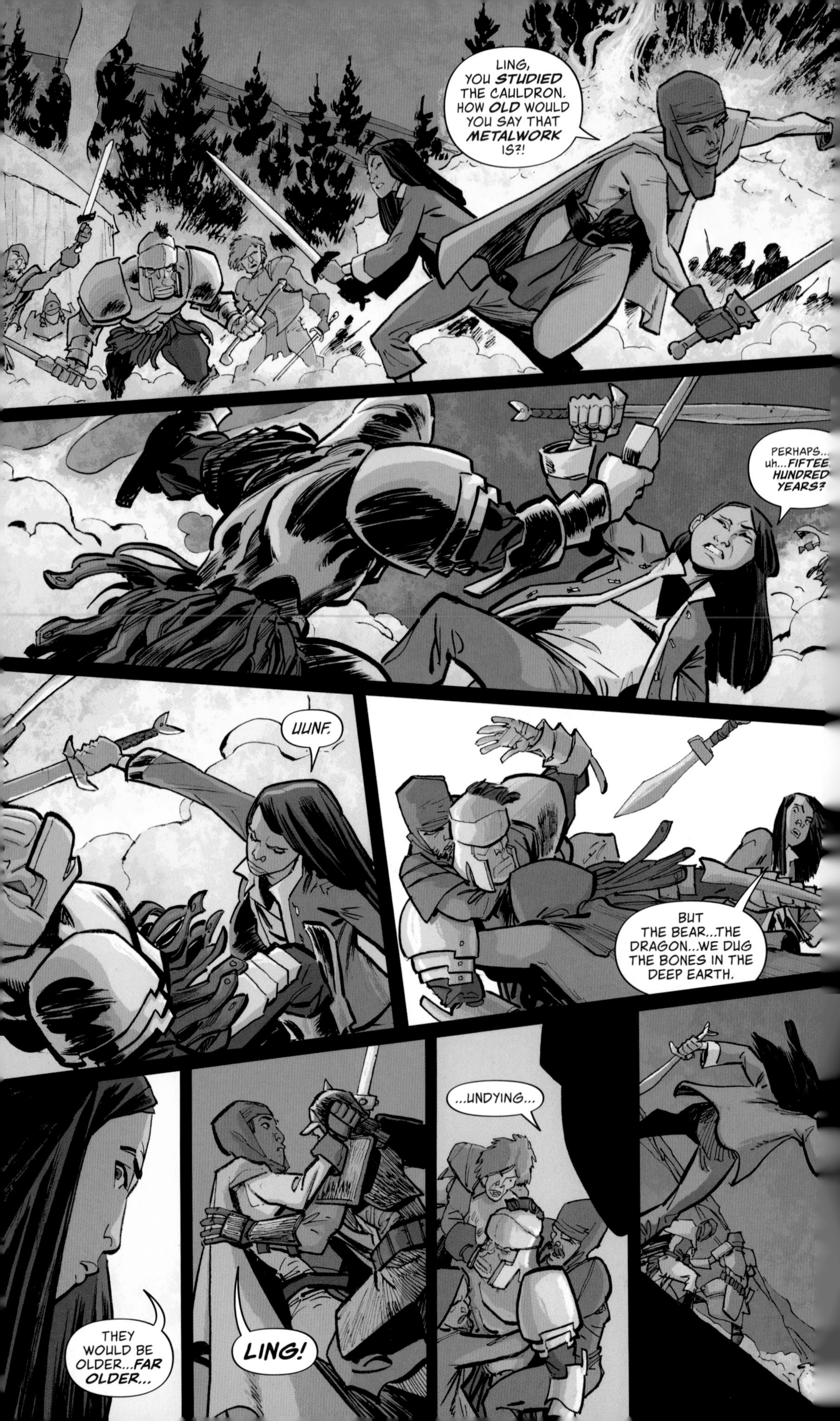
LING, YOU **STUDIED** THE CAULDRON. HOW **OLD** WOULD YOU SAY THAT **METALWORK** IS?!
PERHAPS... uh... **FIFTEE HUNDRED YEARS?**
UUNF.
BUT THE BEAR...THE DRAGON...WE DUG THE BONES IN THE DEEP EARTH.
THEY WOULD BE OLDER... **FAR OLDER...**
LING!
...UNDYING...

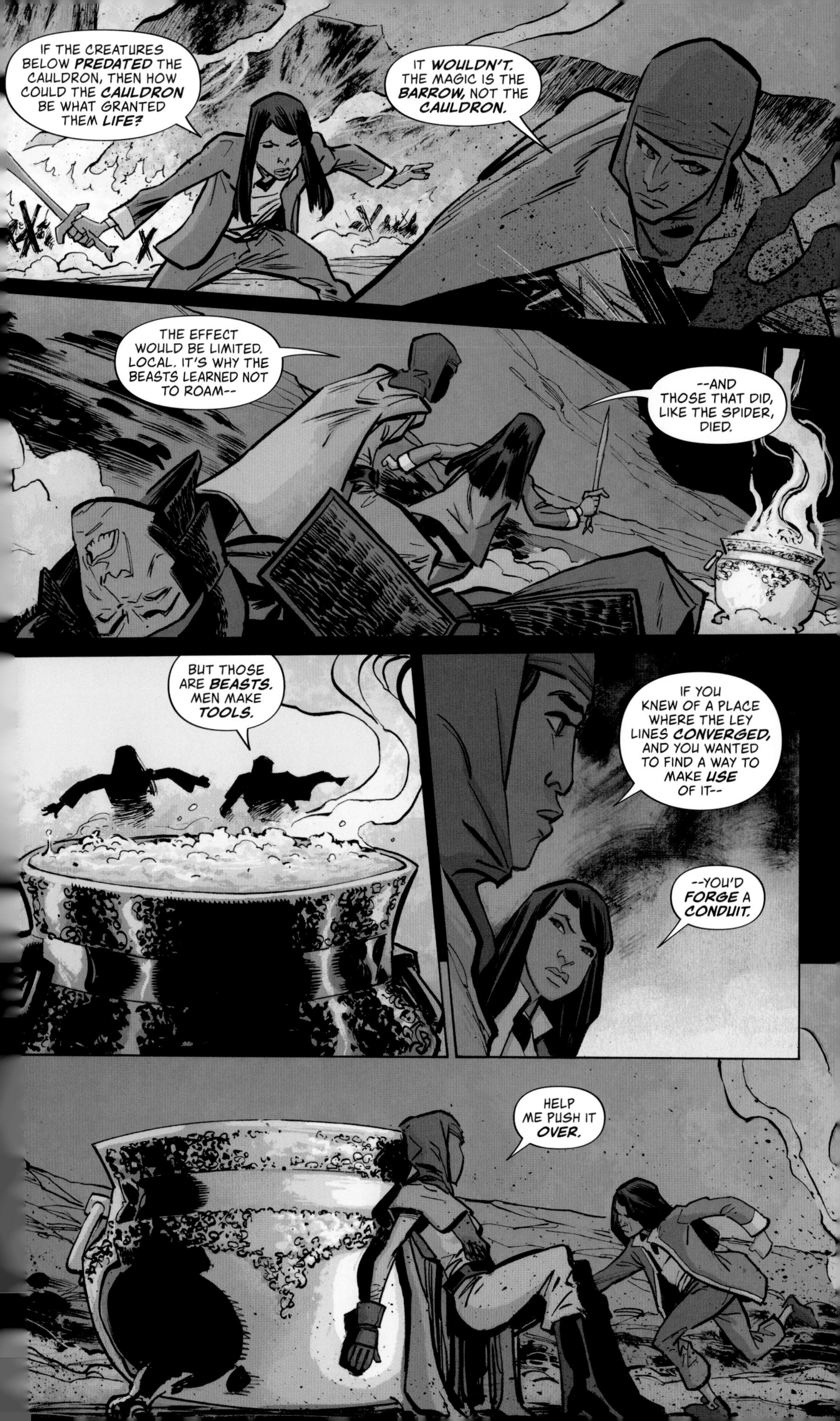
IF THE CREATURES BELOW PREDATED THE CAULDRON, THEN HOW COULD THE CAULDRON BE WHAT GRANTED THEM LIFE?
IT WOULDN'T. THE MAGIC IS THE BARROW, NOT THE CAULDRON.
THE EFFECT WOULD BE LIMITED. LOCAL. IT'S WHY THE BEASTS LEARNED NOT TO ROAM--
--AND THOSE THAT DID, LIKE THE SPIDER, DIED.
BUT THOSE ARE BEASTS. MEN MAKE TOOLS.
IF YOU KNEW OF A PLACE WHERE THE LEY LINES CONVERGED, AND YOU WANTED TO FIND A WAY TO MAKE USE OF IT--
--YOU'D FORGE A CONDUIT.
HELP ME PUSH IT OVER.

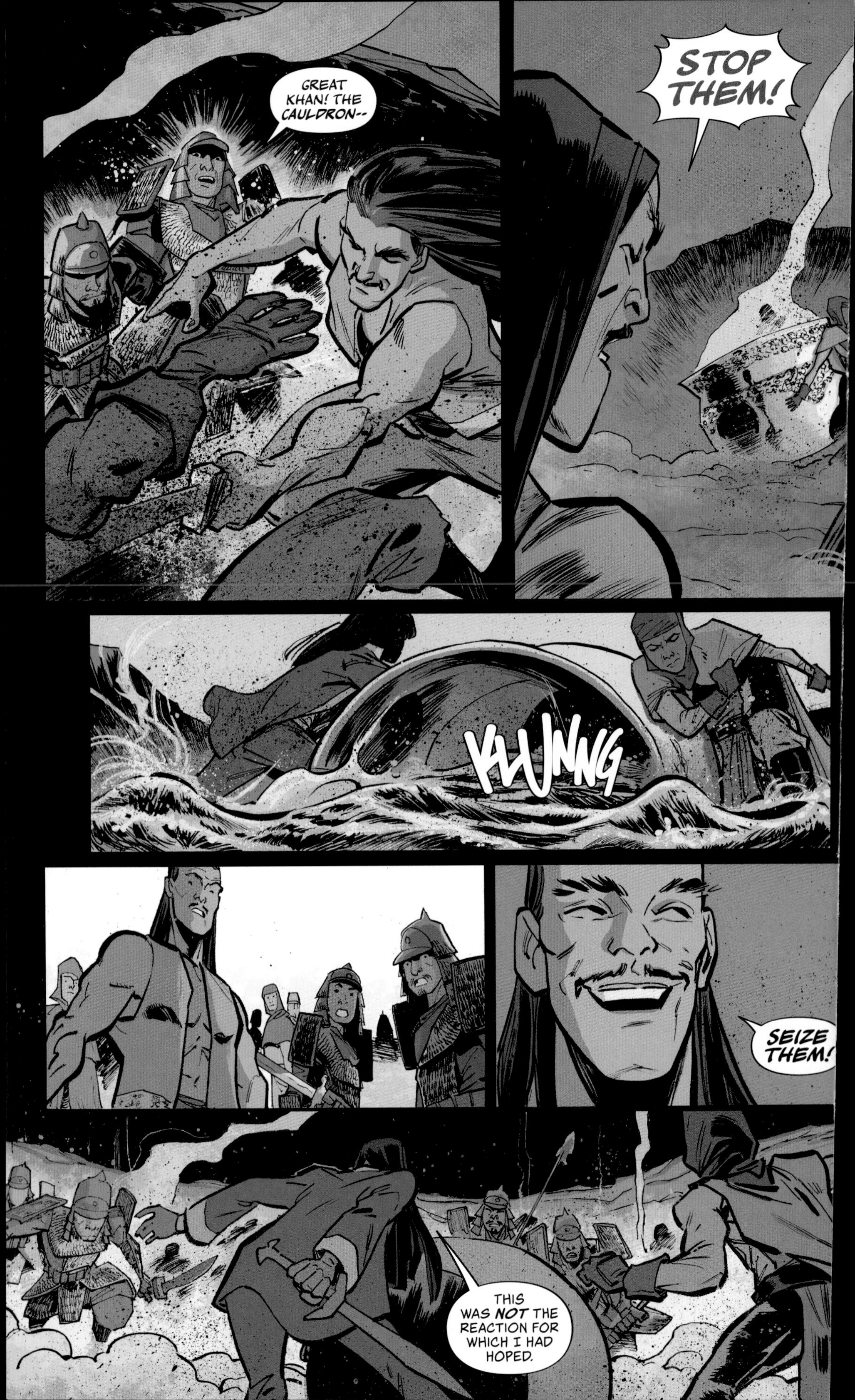
GREAT KHAN! THE CAULDRON--
STOP THEM!
KLUNNG
SEIZE THEM!
THIS WAS NOT THE REACTION FOR WHICH I HAD HOPED.

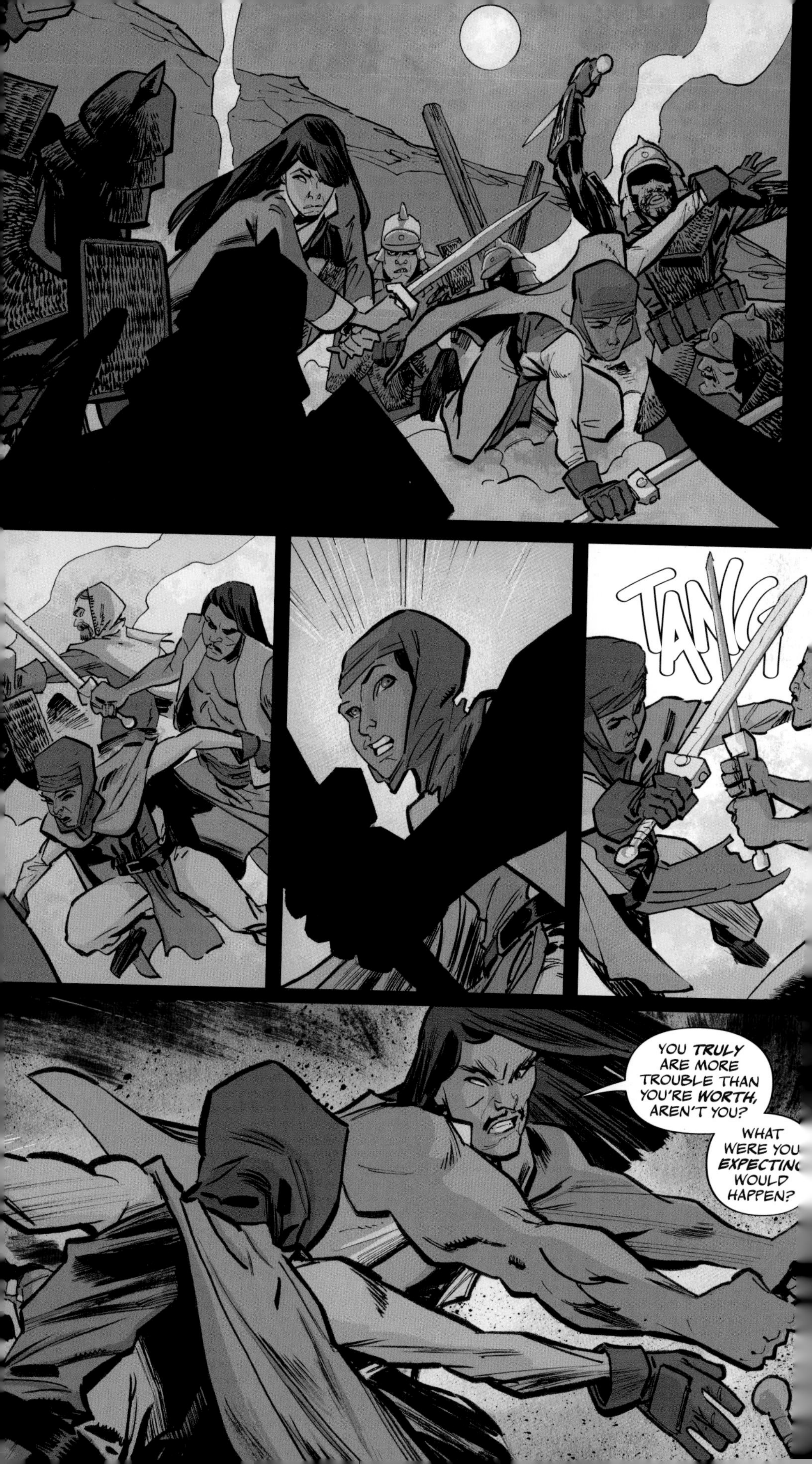
TANG
YOU TRULY ARE MORE TROUBLE THAN YOU'RE WORTH, AREN'T YOU?
WHAT WERE YOU EXPECTING WOULD HAPPEN?

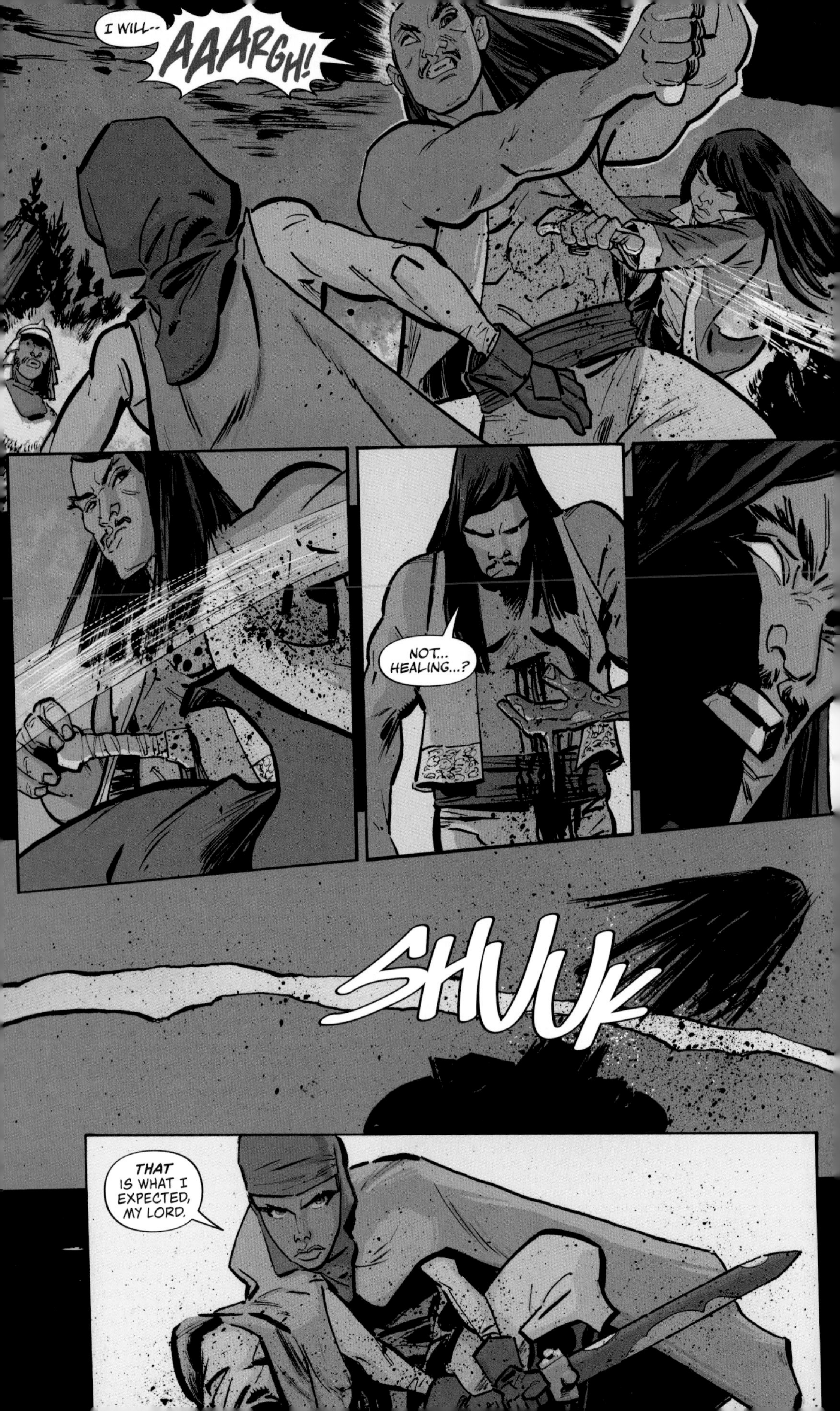
I WILL--
AAARGH!
NOT... HEALING...?
SHUUK
THAT IS WHAT I EXPECTED, MY LORD.

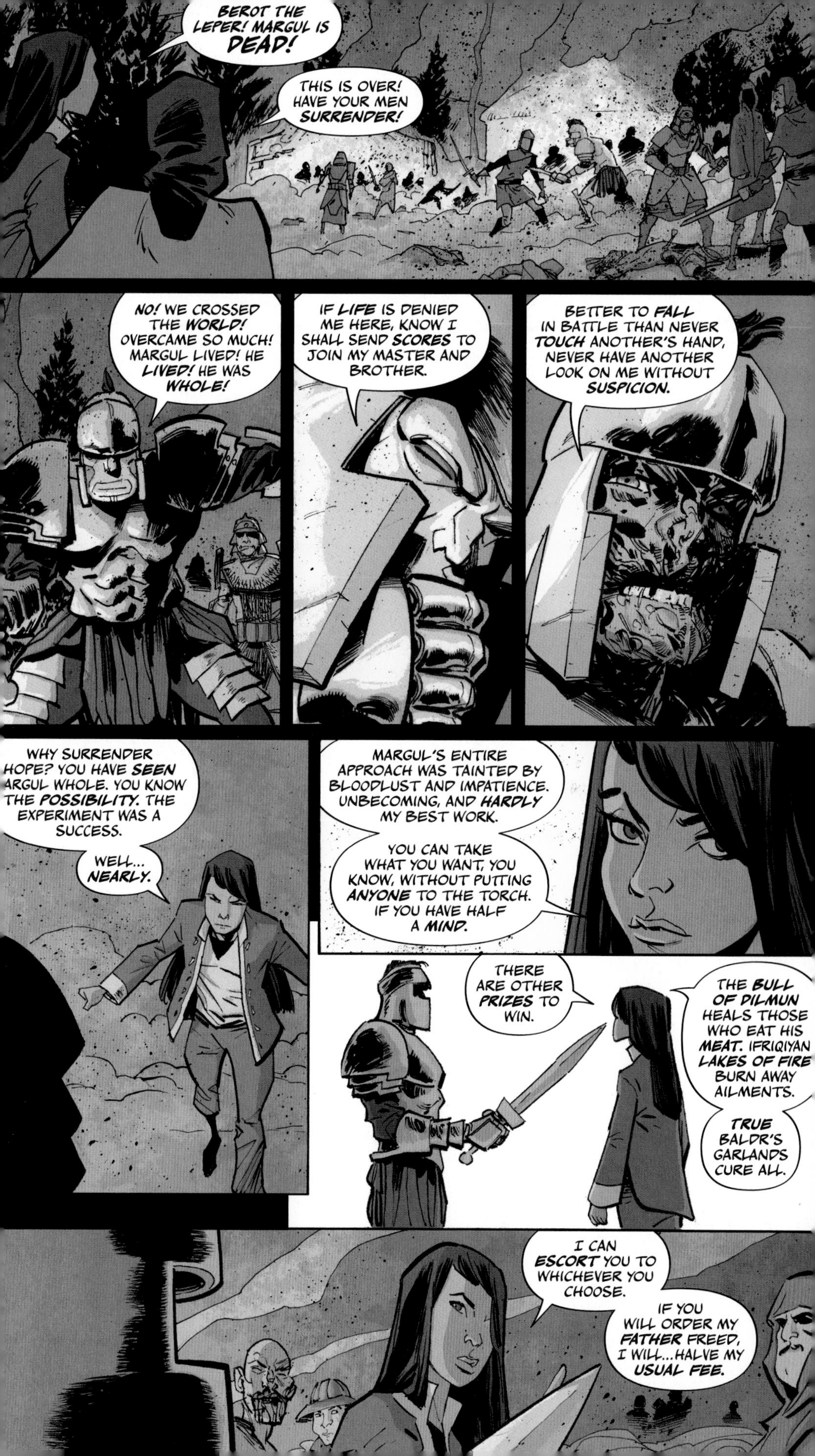
BEROT THE LEPER! MARGUL IS DEAD!
THIS IS OVER! HAVE YOUR MEN SURRENDER!
NO! WE CROSSED THE WORLD! OVERCAME SO MUCH! MARGUL LIVED! HE LIVED! HE WAS WHOLE!
IF LIFE IS DENIED ME HERE, KNOW I SHALL SEND SCORES TO JOIN MY MASTER AND BROTHER.
BETTER TO FALL IN BATTLE THAN NEVER TOUCH ANOTHER'S HAND, NEVER HAVE ANOTHER LOOK ON ME WITHOUT SUSPICION.
WHY SURRENDER HOPE? YOU HAVE SEEN ARGUL WHOLE. YOU KNOW THE POSSIBILITY. THE EXPERIMENT WAS A SUCCESS.
WELL... NEARLY.
MARGUL'S ENTIRE APPROACH WAS TAINTED BY BLOODLUST AND IMPATIENCE. UNBECOMING, AND HARDLY MY BEST WORK.
YOU CAN TAKE WHAT YOU WANT, YOU KNOW, WITHOUT PUTTING ANYONE TO THE TORCH. IF YOU HAVE HALF A MIND.
THERE ARE OTHER PRIZES TO WIN.
THE BULL OF DILMUN HEALS THOSE WHO EAT HIS MEAT. IFRIQIYAN LAKES OF FIRE BURN AWAY AILMENTS.
TRUE BALDR'S GARLANDS CURE ALL.
I CAN ESCORT YOU TO WHICHEVER YOU CHOOSE.
IF YOU WILL ORDER MY FATHER FREED, I WILL...HALVE MY USUAL FEE.

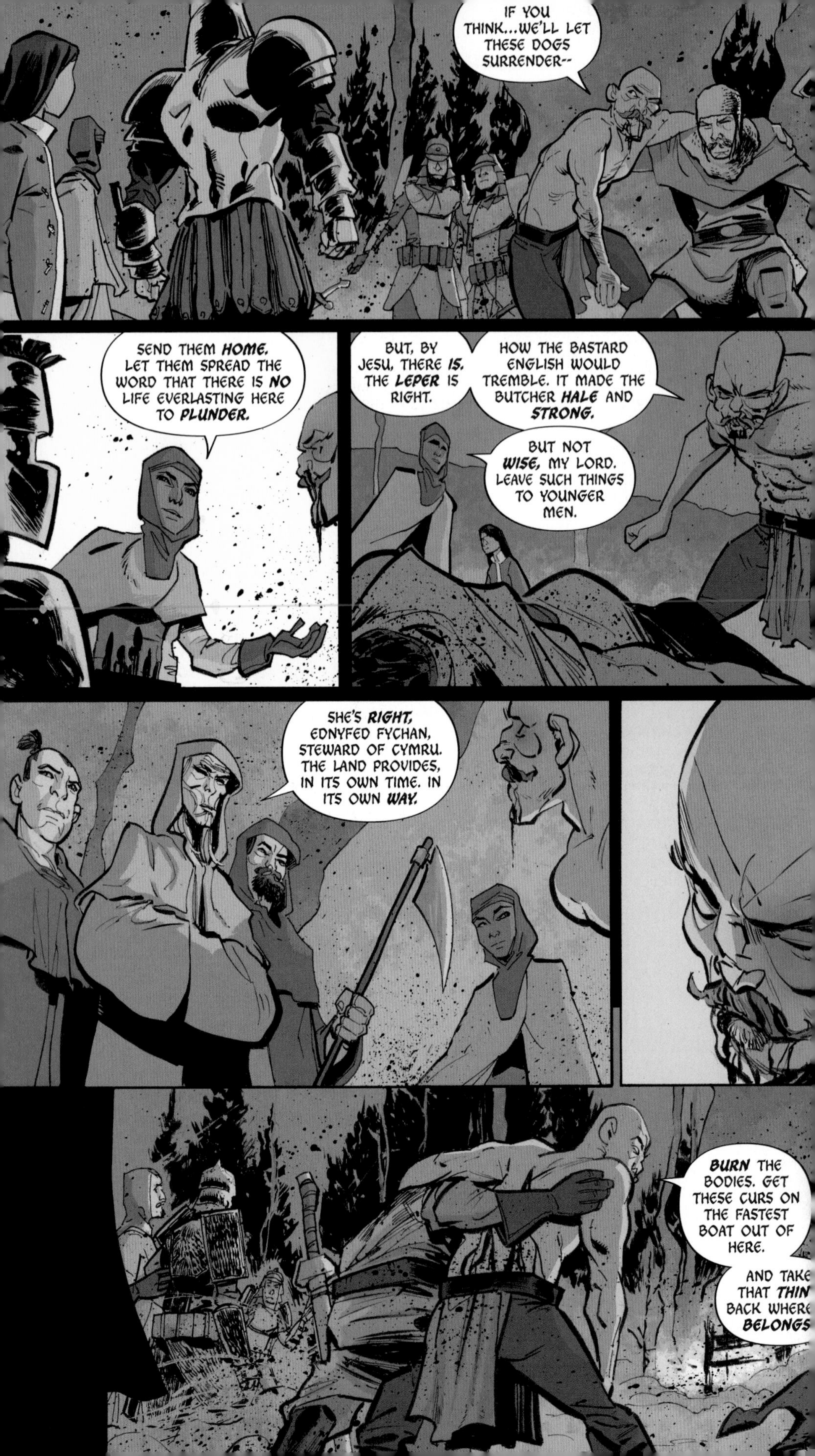
IF YOU THINK...WE'LL LET THESE DOGS SURRENDER--
SEND THEM HOME. LET THEM SPREAD THE WORD THAT THERE IS NO LIFE EVERLASTING HERE TO PLUNDER.
BUT, BY JESU, THERE IS. THE LEPER IS RIGHT.
HOW THE BASTARD ENGLISH WOULD TREMBLE. IT MADE THE BUTCHER HALE AND STRONG.
BUT NOT WISE, MY LORD. LEAVE SUCH THINGS TO YOUNGER MEN.
SHE'S RIGHT, EDNYFED FYCHAN, STEWARD OF CYMRU. THE LAND PROVIDES, IN ITS OWN TIME. IN ITS OWN WAY.
BURN THE BODIES. GET THESE CURS ON THE FASTEST BOAT OUT OF HERE.
AND TAKE THAT THIN BACK WHERE BELONGS

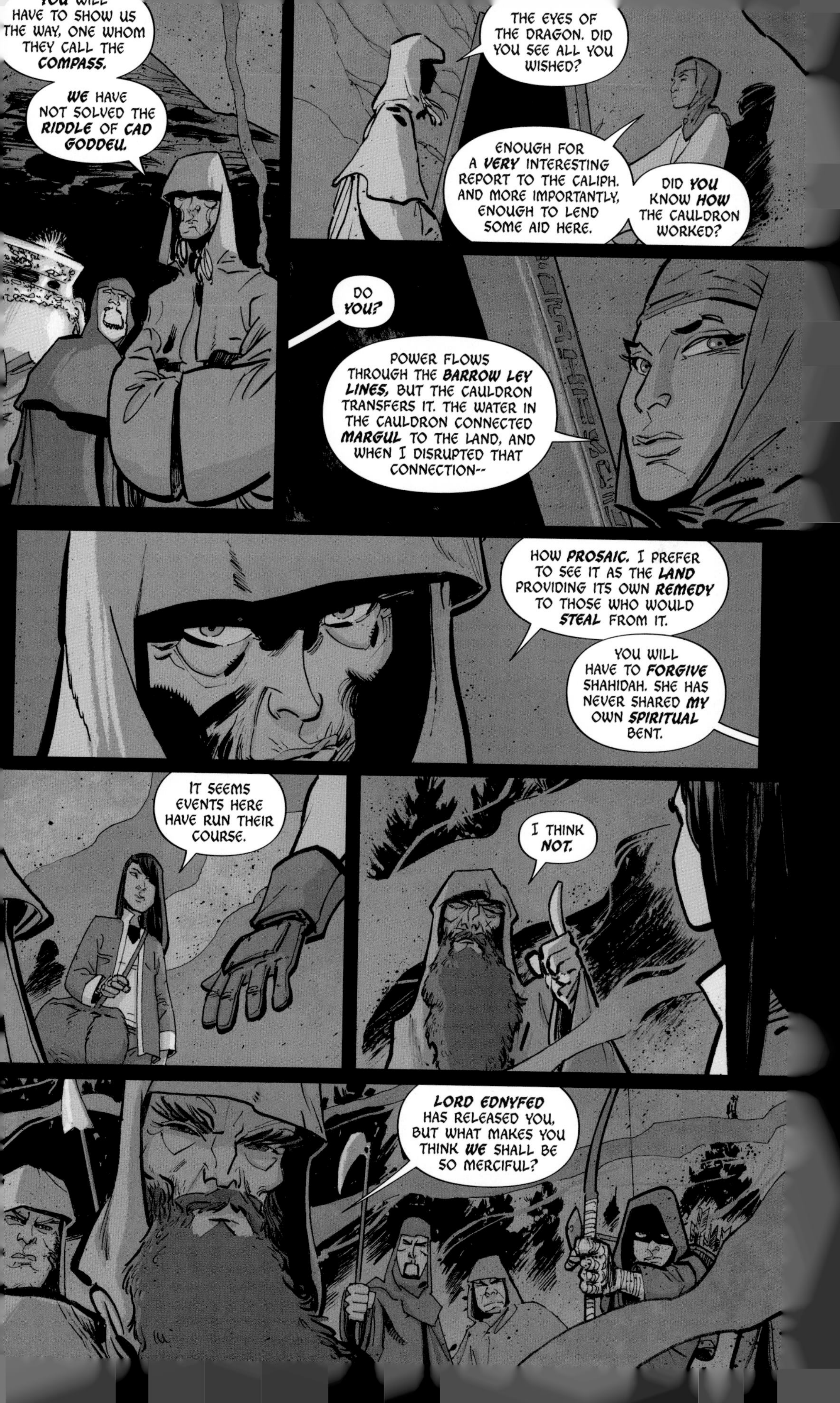
HAVE TO SHOW US THE WAY, ONE WHOM THEY CALL THE COMPASS.
WE HAVE NOT SOLVED THE RIDDLE OF CAD GODDEU.
THE EYES OF THE DRAGON. DID YOU SEE ALL YOU WISHED?
ENOUGH FOR A VERY INTERESTING REPORT TO THE CALIPH. AND MORE IMPORTANTLY, ENOUGH TO LEND SOME AID HERE.
DID YOU KNOW HOW THE CAULDRON WORKED?
DO YOU?
POWER FLOWS THROUGH THE BARROW LEY LINES, BUT THE CAULDRON TRANSFERS IT. THE WATER IN THE CAULDRON CONNECTED MARGUL TO THE LAND, AND WHEN I DISRUPTED THAT CONNECTION--
HOW PROSAIC. I PREFER TO SEE IT AS THE LAND PROVIDING ITS OWN REMEDY TO THOSE WHO WOULD STEAL FROM IT.
YOU WILL HAVE TO FORGIVE SHAHIDAH. SHE HAS NEVER SHARED MY OWN SPIRITUAL BENT.
IT SEEMS EVENTS HERE HAVE RUN THEIR COURSE.
I THINK NOT.
LORD EDNYFED HAS RELEASED YOU, BUT WHAT MAKES YOU THINK WE SHALL BE SO MERCIFUL?

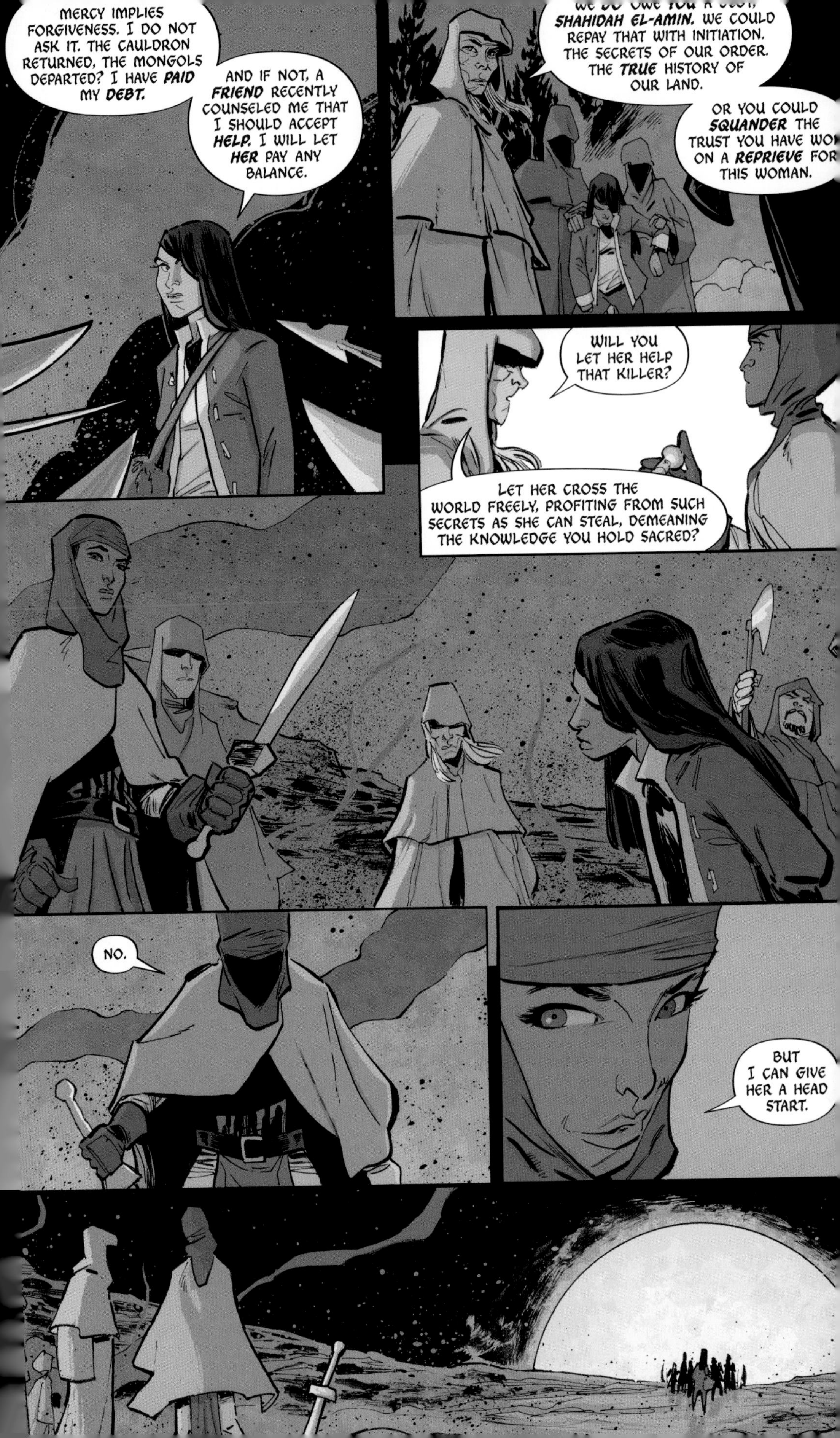
MERCY IMPLIES FORGIVENESS. I DO NOT ASK IT. THE CAULDRON RETURNED, THE MONGOLS DEPARTED? I HAVE PAID MY DEBT.
AND IF NOT, A FRIEND RECENTLY COUNSELED ME THAT I SHOULD ACCEPT HELP. I WILL LET HER PAY ANY BALANCE.
SHAHIDAH EL-AMIN. WE COULD REPAY THAT WITH INITIATION. THE SECRETS OF OUR ORDER. THE TRUE HISTORY OF OUR LAND.
OR YOU COULD SQUANDER THE TRUST YOU HAVE WO ON A REPRIEVE FOR THIS WOMAN.
WILL YOU LET HER HELP THAT KILLER?
LET HER CROSS THE WORLD FREELY, PROFITING FROM SUCH SECRETS AS SHE CAN STEAL, DEMEANING THE KNOWLEDGE YOU HOLD SACRED?
NO.
BUT I CAN GIVE HER A HEAD START.

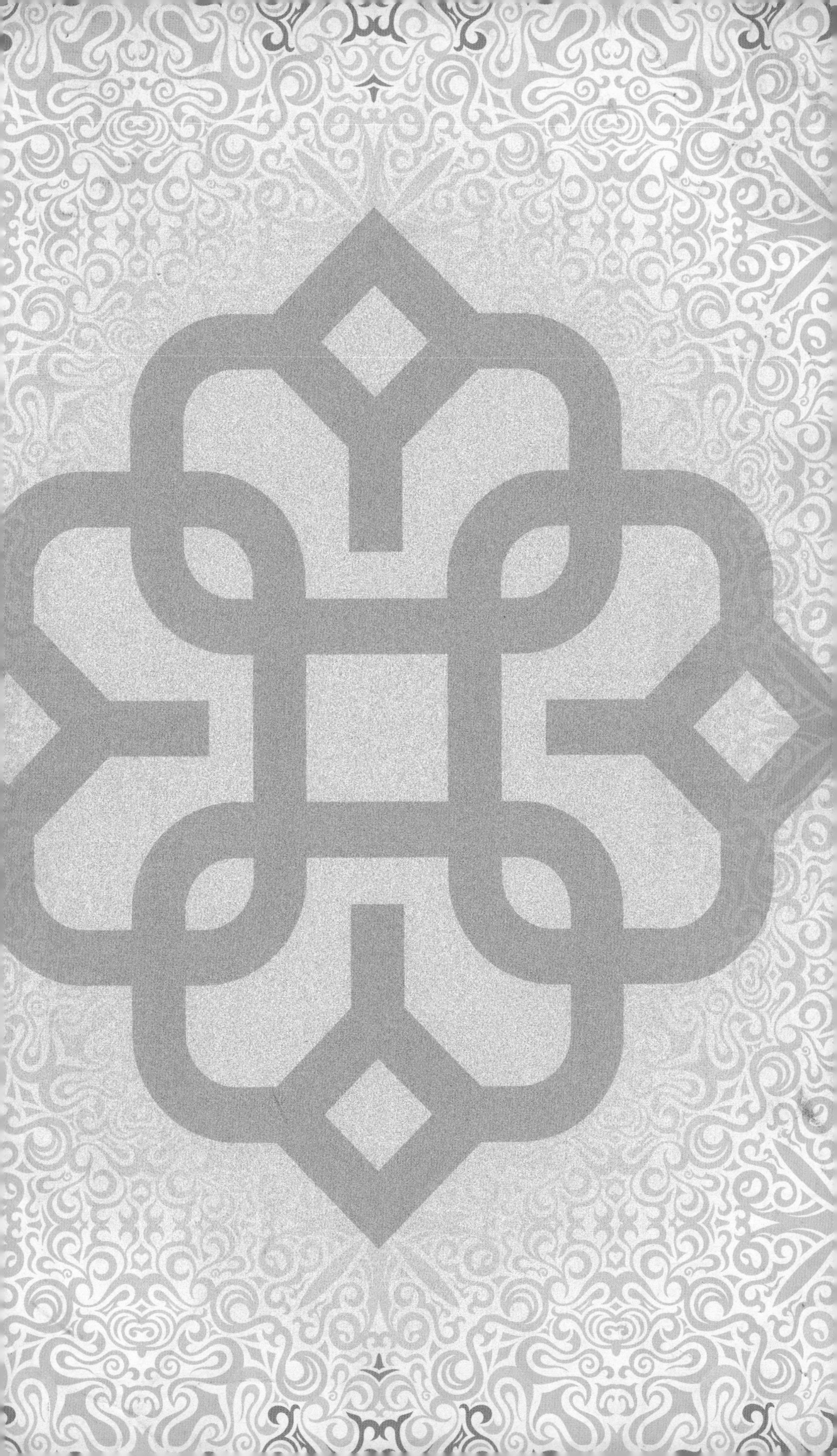

Qasim — please add the usual "O Caliph, whose mercy touches" etc. Low on ink. My report on the Cauldron to follow in detail. Neither tragedy nor farce, profitable or futile, I am left with observations, reservations, and a profound relief to be alive. Following is my contribution to the Endless Map, with the usual annotations.

You heard about the Tisza River, I suppose? Well, Al-Bakri's old writings are a little out of date by more than just the Mongol conquests. My big worry is that this big a slaughter is going to attract more of the local ghouls. Look up 'wieszczyca' in the archives if you've forgotten. They're not burying all these dead soldiers with stones on their heads and stakes through their chests.

I should say that whilst the Emperor suns himself in the Sicilian sands, the Styrian voivode have managed to get their hands on the 'Entführerpfeife.' I hear that they sent an agent into Saxony and lured an entire town's youth over to the Carpathians. If that's not recovered shortly, I expect we'll see all kinds of trouble.

went this way

Our House has a sister institution in Sienna. The curriculum is limited to the three L's—Latin, logic, and law—and no permanent facilities, but like Bologna before it, it is a spark in the darkness, well worth the tending.

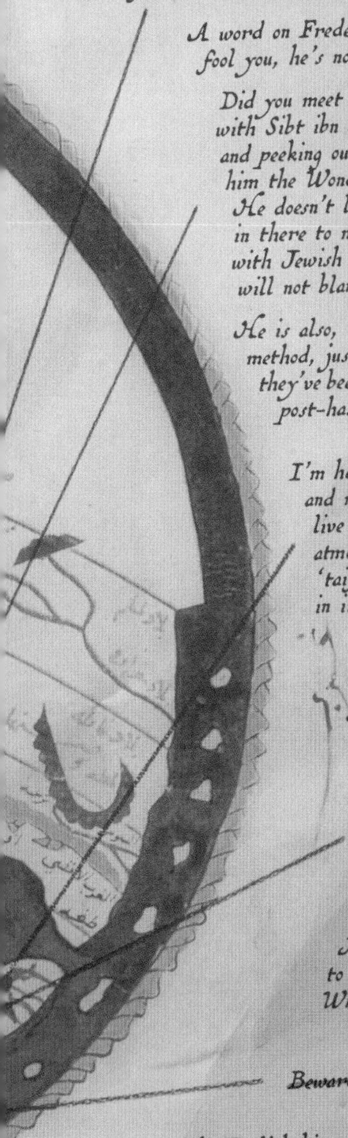

A word on Frederick II. Don't let the seat of the Holy Roman Empire fool you, he's no German—he's Sicilian through and through.

Did you meet him when they crowned him in Jerusalem? I was there with Sibt ibn al-Jawzi and Abdullah, as a girl, hiding behind his robes and peeking out at the foreign delegations. Some of the barbarians call him the Wonder of the World. Others, the Herald of the Antichrist. He doesn't look like much, red-haired, short-sighted, but there's a mind in there to make even the Mongols worry. He surrounds himself with Jewish translators and men of our faith, on the assumption they will not blanch at killing the Pope for him.

He is also, in his own fashion, a scientist. Remarkable as it is, he understands the method, just with no morals at all. I interviewed some of his sages, and what they've been asked to do—ghastly! Abdullah should dispatch a Compass, post-haste, or I fear Tall Sanqur and his swords will be dispatched next.

I'm headed out through the 'taifas' of Al-Andalus. Christians, Muslims, Jews, and magi, all bound under the greatest faith of all: commerce. Pay the 'jizya,' live as you like. It's certainly different, even compared to the cosmopolitan atmosphere of home. I'll try to bring back something of interest, but the 'taifas' will need to stop squabbling sooner or later; Cordoba is now firmly back in infidel hands, and they're not going to stop. Seville will be next, I suspect.

If Frederick is Christendom's most dangerous mind, their most dangerous fist remains very French. Fortunately, it seems, they're happy being dangerous to themselves right now. They are taking all the energy they usually use to sack our cities and menace our borders and turning it on themselves. They call it the Albigensian Crusade, where they hunt down their Cathars: Christians who believe the world is the province of the Devil, and they are damned into it. The Black Friars, the Dominicans, are preaching everywhere, but more critically, some of them form something darker that they call the Inquisition. It's a local madness for now, but the French powers rule the Outremer, the stolen lands—Athens, Nicaea, Constantinople—are going to hear from them sooner or later, waiting to shake out the remains of Eastern Orthodox faith for their Catholics. Who knows what comes next?

~~Beware, haunted by the screaming~~ woman never mind

The English king, Henry III, is a far greater threat to poor Gwynedd than Margul was. With his nose still bloody from a century of wars and uprisings (and every sign they will continue), he has somehow become obsessed with buying the conquest of the throne of Sicily. His support from Pope Innocent IV was unlimited so long as he vexed the ambitious Holy Roman Emperor, but Innocent is dead, and the Papacy now belongs to Alexander IV, who is demanding the incredible sum of £125,000! And they say they don't lend money. Henry, suffice it to say, is in trouble.

Cold, wet, dull

ric the Lisp and Lame has been deposed and restored since our last visit. Publicly, he has nciled with the revanchist Folkungs, but nobody can truly be comfortable unless the crown is ly under one heel or another again. Is that a mixed metaphor? The Bjelbos play at being ilist—one man, one vote—but everyone, the Bjelbos, Knutsson, even Magnusson—have agents for the regalia of Eric the Lawgiver.

ill have that under lock and key, right?

BIBLIOGRAPHY

The individual issues of *COMPASS* contained essays on the historical and mythic basis "behind" the story herein. Sadly, we don't have space to reproduce those here, but the tale you've just read would be incomplete without some form of a summary of the historical basis of the story. To that end, we have included the reading list from the monthly issues. Happy reading!

- *The Crusades Through Arab Eyes* by Amin Maalouf
- *The House of Wisdom: How Arabic Science Saved Ancient Knowledge and Gave Us the Renaissance* by Jim Al-Khalili
- *Pathfinders: The Golden Age of Arabic Science* by Jim Al-Khalili
- *In the Wake of the Mongols: The Making of a New Social Order in North China, 1200-1600* by Jinping Wang
- *Genghis Khan: Life, Death and Resurrection* by John Man
- *The Devil's Horsemen: The Mongol Invasion of Europe* by James Chambers
- *Genghis Khan and the Making of the Modern World* by Jack Weatherford
- *Leprosy in Medieval England* by Carole Rawcliffe
- *The Mabinogion* translated by Sioned Davies

Amin Maalouf
The Crusades through Arab Eyes

THE HOUSE OF WISDOM
How Arabic Science Saved Ancient Knowledge and Gave Us the Renaissance
JIM AL-KHALILI

Jim Al-Khalili
Pathfinders
The Golden Age of Arabic Science

Jinping Wang
IN THE WAKE OF THE MONGOLS
The Making of a New Social Order in North China, 1200–1600

REVISED AND UPDATED
GENGHIS KHAN
LIFE, DEATH AND RESURRECTION
JOHN MAN

THE DEVIL'S HORSEMEN
The Mongol Invasion of Europe
James Chambers

GENGHIS KHAN
and the Making of the
MODERN WORLD
JACK WEATHERFORD

CAROLE RAWCLIFFE
LEPROSY IN MEDIEVAL ENGLAND

The Mabinogion
A new translation by Sioned Davies
OXFORD WORLD'S CLASSICS

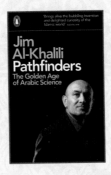

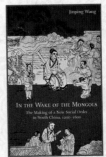

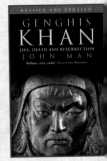

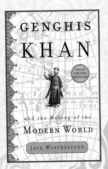